Totally Bound Publishing books by SJD Peterson:

Fractured Hearts

I0526286

FRACTURED HEARTS

SJD PETERSON

Fractured Hearts
ISBN # 978-1-78651-864-4
©Copyright SJD Peterson 2016
Cover Art by Posh Gosh ©Copyright January 2016
Interior text design by Claire Siemaszkiewicz
Totally Bound Publishing

Published in 2016 by Totally Bound Publishing, Newland House, The Point, Weaver Road, Lincoln, LN6 3QN, United Kingdom.

Totally Bound Publishing is a subsidiary of Totally Entwined Group Limited.

FRACTURED HEARTS

Dedication

To Becca, who blessed my life the moment she entered
it. Thank you for opening my eyes to the gift of
romance stories. Without you, I would never have
written this book

Prologue

Charlie looked up at the clear blue sky and scowled. It should be raining.

In the movies and on TV, it was always gloomy and raining at a funeral and the characters would cry. At the age of ten, when her parents had died, it had been raining and she had sobbed uncontrollably. Maybe that was why she couldn't seem to shed a tear today—it wasn't raining at Gram's funeral.

Truth be told, she hadn't cried since walking into Gram's room two days ago and finding her in bed not breathing, having passed away in the night. Charlie had walked quietly out of the room into the kitchen and had called the number a hospice nurse had left to inform them that Gram had died. She'd then walked out onto the front porch, wrapped her arms around herself and sat to wait for the ambulance to arrive.

I'm a smart woman. I understand the 'normal' grieving process. First shock, then denial, followed by sadness and anger, before acceptance. Charlie had bypassed the first, had gone straight to downright pissed off, and screw acceptance.

Looking around at the phony sniffling faces of the few townsfolk who had come to pay their last respects to Ms. Eudora McCarty had Charlie desperate to scream in rage.

Where the hell had these people been when Gram had been alive? When Gram had first been diagnosed with metastatic cancer a little over a year prior, not one of them had ever offered a single hand of help to her or Gram.

Not that Charlie would ever regret having to care for Gram, it was the least she could do since Gram had taken her in when her parents had died. Still, she thought at least one of these people could have offered to sit with Gram while Charlie had gone to her senior prom, homecoming dance, or hell, just to hang out one night at the local malt shop and be a kid.

She had spent every day of her senior year with Gram and been homeschooled for the last semester of the year when Gram had gotten too weak to get out of bed. Gram had urged her to go out and have fun, to be a kid, but Charlie just hadn't felt right about leaving her alone.

Over the year, Charlie had learned to control her emotions. She could hide her disappointment, fears and anger. She'd learned to put on an airy, confident attitude around people and had kept it in place right up until Gram died.

Today, however, she was just tired of staying in control. She wanted to scream, to hit something or someone. She refused to think about which someone she'd hit first.

Nope, not today. This is about Gram, not you!

Agony as well as longing bubbled at the surface, trying to take hold of her heart and shred it again. With a strength that only years of heartache had taught her, she forced it back down, deep into the dark recesses of her brain, so she could slam the door on it and lock it tightly. Only in weak moments like today did it try to sneak past her carefully laid defenses.

She'd celebrated her birthday nearly a year ago, and although she could hold on to hope for a few more months before her eighteenth year was behind her, it would be in vain. She knew. Knew it in her heart, in her soul, even in her bones, she was now completely and utterly alone. Charlie brought the tissue to her mouth and muffled the sob that worked its way up past her throat. He was to have come for her over two hundred and thirty-four days ago, but he hadn't, and he never would.

Best not to think about all that right now, Charlie.

The pain of that hurt even worse than the pain of watching Gram being slowly lowered into the cold ground. Gram hadn't wanted to leave her, to take away her hugs, smiles and warmth. She had fought so hard to stay with Charlie, tried to hide the pain in her eyes as the cancer had ravaged her body. She would wrap her arms around Charlie, rock her slowly and comfort her with kisses to her head as she shushed her with soothing words. All the while, she had fought for breath and against the pain. Gram had desperately battled to stay with her.

He had chosen to leave her, to walk away with a promise to come back for her. He'd sworn he would always be there for her no matter what and that she would never be alone. She didn't need to sit and wait for the inevitable to prove that he had lied to her. He had taken her heart, then snuck away with it, never to return.

It was gone, just as cold and dead as Gram was now. Charlie laid her head back against the folding chair, the sound of the coffin lowering still audible over the preacher's last prayer for the dead. She opened her mouth in a silent scream and felt the first drops of cool rain land on the bridge of her nose.

Tears finally escaped her eyes, ran down her face and mingled with the cold rain.

It always rained at funerals.

Chapter One

Seven years later

"I can't believe I let you talk me into coming here."

Charlie knew she was pouting, but she didn't really care at the moment. She hated honky-tonks.

She looked around Jack's Place. It was like all the other cowboy bars she had allowed Rae to force her to. The standard chicken wire stretching across solid wooden beams closed off the small stage in an attempt to protect the local cover bands from rowdy patrons and wayward longnecks. Sawdust covered a wood-plank dance floor that sported couples whirling and twirling in two-step fashion while twangy music blasted from a jukebox in the far corner. The decor did nothing to cover up or distract from the thick, harsh aroma of stale beer and cigarette smoke—it assaulted the nose and eyes just the same.

Rolling her eyes at Rae, Charlie continued to pout. "Dammit, Rae, this was supposed to be a celebration for my seven years of hard work. Not just another excuse for you to hogtie some poor, unsuspecting cowboy." She stuck her tongue out at her best friend.

"C'mon, Charlie, this is about you. What better way to celebrate your success and burn off a little stress than surround yourself by tight asses? If I happen to get a chance to hogtie one, it's just an added bonus. You know what you need?"

"Oh, do tell."

"You, my friend, need to get laid."

Charlie snorted a laugh, nearly choking on her beer. "Ha! If I needed to get laid — which I don't — the last place on earth I'd look for a date would be somewhere like this."

Rae lifted an eyebrow at her. *How the hell does she do that?* Charlie had spent hours in the mirror trying to perfect that look and just couldn't get it right. It was a look that made the recipients instantly start questioning themselves.

"See, that's your problem right there. I never said you needed a date, just that you should get laid. What's it been, like a year? Is that even possible? Honey, what you need is one of these big, strong, hot and horny cowboys to work all that tension right out of your system."

Actually, it had been one year, eleven months and four days — not that she was counting or anything. The image of rope-callused hands as they stroked up and down her body made Charlie squirm in her chair. She would certainly never admit it to Rae, though.

The self-induced celibacy was sometimes even a bit much for her. She had her reasons and knew she had made the right choice not to get involved with anyone, physically or otherwise. But dammit, some days were harder than others.

"Besides," Rae continued, "it would do the locals good to see their new town vet with her hair down and having some fun."

"First of all, I'm just an overworked, underpaid resident. I won't officially be able to call myself a vet for another year. Secondly, I don't really think the 'locals' will give a damn whether my hair is up or down when I have my arm shoved up their cows' asses."

"Eww." Rae grimaced. "TMI, Charlie, TMI!"

A roar of laughter escaped Rae and Charlie joined her. They laughed until tears rolled down their cheeks and Charlie's sides ached. They wiped the tears from their eyes as their waitress approached then set down two longneck bottles of beer and two shot glasses that smelled strongly like tequila.

Charlie stared at the waitress through watery eyes. The woman was short, but what she lacked in height, she obviously tried to make up for with the size of her surgically enhanced breasts. They strained against a size too small T-shirt that advertised she got 'off' at Jack's Place. Calling the material she wore across her ass shorts would be adding length to the barely there garment.

Charlie couldn't help but wonder how uncomfortable it must be to have to wear such an outfit at home, let alone in public. Maybe that was why the woman had a look of disgust in her eyes and a snarl on her bright-red lips, though she highly doubted it.

"Compliments of the cowboy at the end of the bar," the waitress drawled, jerking her head in the direction indicated. She met Charlie's eyes with a look of pure hatred before she stalked off.

"Jesus, what the hell is her problem?"

"Who cares? Holy shit, Charlie! Turn around and look at the wet dream that just bought us drinks," Rae murmured. "I think I just came in my panties."

Charlie picked up her beer and turned toward the bar with every intention of saluting the cowboy with the beer in a gesture of thank you. When her eyes locked on the man standing at the bar, she was too stunned to move.

"Holy shit is right," Charlie panted.

At the end of the bar stood a curly, dark-haired mountain of a man, a black Stetson pulled down low over his eyes. Olive skin accentuated a strong masculine face with full lips turned up into a sly smile above a strong, square jaw with just a hint of dark stubble.

The man was a god, pure and simple, and the look on his face showed he knew exactly what effect he had on the opposite sex. Hell, he was gorgeous enough that he probably had the same effect on most of the same sex as well.

Charlie let her eyes travel downward from his handsome face to his broad shoulders and thick chest, which tapered beneath a tight white T-shirt to lean, narrow hips. His jeans were loose, hung low on his hips, and covered tree-trunk-sized thighs.

Charlie took in the sight of him with a deep appreciation as she moved back up the man's smoking hot body and locked on those piercing eyes. Her quickened heart rate increased to hummingbird speed and her lungs forgot the need for oxygen as the sexy cowboy's smile moved from sly to dazzling, then winked in her direction.

Heat rushed through her body like a freight train and heated up every cell of her body, only to merge into one lava-hot charge between her thighs.

Turning back to face her friend, Charlie knew the awed, dazed look on Rae's face was a mirror image of her own. She worked hard to slow down her breathing and squirmed in her seat, attempting to relieve the ache in her sex.

"Rae?" she whispered.

Silence.

"Earth to Rae."

Rae continued to stare in the direction of the bar, never once blinking until Charlie kicked her shin under the table. "Please tell me I'm not imagining that the sexiest man on the planet is standing against a bar behind me and just bought us a drink."

Rae jumped with a start, nearly knocking her beer over, and they both burst out laughing.

"So, what were you saying about not needing to get laid?"

"Well, I do believe that Mr. Yum-Yum might be able to convince me otherwise given the right motivation."

"Uh-huh, might? Riiiight! On that note, I think I'll head to the little girls' room to wring out my panties."

Charlie watched Rae's exaggerated hip swings as she swished and swayed her way across to the back of the bar and had to giggle. She was actually having a good time. She had met Rachel 'Rae' Lang during her first semester in college, and the woman always seemed to know exactly how Charlie was feeling and just what she needed.

She so needed this tonight. She just wanted to spend one evening without thinking about school or anything else. During the semester, she was able to immerse herself completely in her studies with little time to let the loneliness she felt take up residence in her thoughts.

In between semesters, void of the schedule and the endless hours of researching and studying, were the hardest times for her. Rae was the only person on the planet who seemed to give a damn if Charlie existed or not. At twenty-five years old, she had no family and only one friend. Just how pathetic was that? A twinge of pain hit Charlie as she wondered what the hell she was going to do when Rae finally found the cowboy of her dreams and settled down. What then?

You go back to being lonely and miserable like you are whenever Rae's with her family.

Not really a comforting thought. Charlie sighed, realizing the truth of it as she took a sip of beer.

Feeling a heavy hand land on her shoulder, she nearly jumped out of her skin when a deep, sultry voice whispered in her ear.

"Dance with me."

The soft command sent a hot thrill through her.

Charlie turned and looked up into the most captivating chocolate-brown eyes she had ever seen. Before her brain had a chance to react to the command, her body took over and followed him across the room to the dance floor.

Once engulfed in the sea of dancers, the cowboy pulled her against his rock-hard body. He cupped his right hand behind her neck and settled the other at the small of her back, his touch searing her skin.

Though the music that blared from the jukebox inspired a two-step hoedown, the mysterious man seemed oblivious to the upbeat tempo and pulled her against him, adjusting her slightly until his powerfully built thigh was nestled between her legs. His muscles flexed and rippled against her heated skin as he began to sway in a slow, sensual movement that had Charlie fighting to control her breathing.

The urge to pant was overwhelming. Rough fingertips stroked the exposed skin at the small of her back. The nerve endings seemed hardwired directly to her core. She shivered as moisture heated between her thighs.

Those wonderful fingers at her back began to slide under the waistband of her skirt, the heat singeing her flesh and making it difficult to concentrate on anything but the sensual touch that kept rhythm with the sway of his hips against hers.

Charlie was losing her ever-loving mind and fought to keep from grinding against the thick thigh wedged between hers. The hard bulge pushing against her hip was doing little to help her with that battle.

A warm breath ghosted against the sensitive skin below her ear. "Tell me your name."

He expected her to speak? She couldn't think past the sensations consuming her body. How the hell was she supposed to form a coherent thought when his whisper turned into open-mouthed kisses down her neck? She forgot all about words and questions, or hell, breathing for that matter. Instead, she did the only thing she could think of under the onslaught of that warm, wonderful tongue. She eased her head back and gave him plenty of room to work.

A low, deep chuckle rumbled next to her ear and again he whispered, "Tell me."

"Huh?"

"Your name."

"It...it's Charlie," she said breathlessly as his tongue continued to assault her skin and keep her off balance.

The hand at her back skimmed slowly up her spine, and she felt the hair clip at the base of her neck pull away. Both hands moved to her neck to untangle the knot and smooth her waist-length hair down from the base of her neck to the top of her ass. He pulled her in closer.

His powerful arms surrounded her and she responded to his strength and nearness as if her body was his to command. She couldn't catch her breath and her pulse soared out of control. With the insistent pressure, her knees trembled and she was afraid to release the grip she had on his shoulders for fear her weak legs wouldn't be unable to hold her up. She was at his mercy.

"I'm Trevor," he whispered. He continued his exploration of her backside as he ducked his head back down to meet hers. His strong masculine scent enveloped her and a jolt of need traveled through her. Warm, soft lips feathered against hers, and he slid his tongue lightly across her lower lip, encouraging her to respond.

"Let me in, Charlie."

Charlie parted her lips on a gasp and he dove in to devour her mouth. She responded to his persistent tongue without a conscious thought. It shocked her how quickly he had taken control of her body and long-buried needs.

No one had been able to make her lose control like this. It was unsettling. She'd had a few lovers during college, but none had been able to make her truly respond. After a couple of years, she'd finally given up dating altogether. It wasn't fair to compare every man to the one who had captured her heart at thirteen, and she grew tired of the guilt of seeing his face behind her closed lids every time another man touched her.

Yet this dark cowboy coaxed her body back to life in a hot rush that left her weak and breathless.

Charlie sighed. *Finally, I can forget.*

As the kiss deepened, she closed her eyes and behind her lids was a familiar sexy face. The image of a light-haired dimpled cowboy flashed through her mind, but to her relief it was quickly replaced by the stranger holding her.

She didn't dwell on beautiful sapphire eyes or a gorgeous dimpled smile from a time long past. Instead, through the haze of lust, she remained in the moment with the man in her arms. She reveled in the way his hands felt against her skin instead of the ghost touches of a phantom lover who had never really been hers at all. He'd only been the ideas and dreams of fantasy that she had molded and shaped.

For the first time, she wanted exactly what was in front of her, a real thing she could lose herself in, but she remembered where she was and took notice of her surroundings.

Charlie reluctantly broke the kiss and pulled away a little. They both panted for breath. The cowboy rested his forehead against hers, stared at her with heated dark eyes and whispered, "God, you're beautiful."

Charlie's face flushed and her toes curled at the compliment from such a godlike creature, but she had no clue how to respond. Instead, she laid her cheek against his chest to hide her embarrassment. Trevor leaned over and snuggled her tighter against him, seeming content to explore her body without words.

Through song after song, his slow, sensual sway never changed tempo. God knew Charlie was more than happy to let this man guide and caress her as if no one but the two of them existed.

"I don't think I've ever wanted anyone like I want you."

Charlie pulled back, startled, and looked up at his face. The black of his pupils had eaten up the iris, leaving him looking feral and wild. Only one thing made a man look like that, and the pure unbidden lust in his eyes made it difficult to tell if he was sincere or not.

"Does that line usually work?"

He had the good sense to look embarrassed as he shrugged. "Usually, but in this case I'm telling the truth."

Charlie couldn't stop the giggle that passed her lips. It wasn't so much that she was laughing at him, but it was just ridiculous that a man like him would want someone like her after only a few dances.

He cocked his head to the side. "You don't believe me, do you?"

"I'd probably believe you more if you told me you sprouted fur with the full moon."

He paused for just a heartbeat and his lips turned up in a slight smile. "Can I ask you something, Charlie?"

"Hmm?"

"I was here waiting for a friend…"

Charlie blinked, her heart sinking. That he'd wanted her had been hard to believe. That he had someone lined up, ready and willing to fall all over him, she didn't doubt in the slightest. She could just imagine the beautiful woman who would be meeting a man like this.

She tried to hide her disappointment. "Oh…sure, I understand. I should be getting back to my friend as well."

Strong fingers cupped her chin, forced her to meet his gaze. "I was saying I'm here to meet a friend and would love it if you would join us for a drink? He should be here soon." He added with a wink.

Before thinking better of it, she blurted, "Well if he looks anything like you, I'm sure I could twist Rae's arm to join us." Charlie felt the flush creep up her neck in embarrassment. Damn, what was it about this man that made her feel like a stupid schoolgirl?

Studying her eyes, the cowboy gave her a devilish grin and ducked his head to nuzzle her neck. "No, I was hoping you would join us both." He nipped her ear, causing sensations to tingle through her body.

"Mmm... Your body is saying yes," he whispered.

Charlie's breath caught, her body trembling uncontrollably at the thought of being sandwiched between the hard bodies of two hot cowboys. She had to stifle a groan as the wetness in her panties spread.

"I fucking love the way you tremble for me." He grabbed her ass in both of his hands and pulled her hard against his bulging erection.

Charlie's head was spinning. His naughty, dominant words affected her as nothing ever had. Oh God, he was taking control of her entire mind and body.

"I...I don't think..."

He laid a finger across her lips to silence her and whispered into the crook of her neck, "Don't think. Your body knows what it wants. Listen to it. Just feel, Charlie."

With his face gently pressed to her neck, his voice vibrated against her throat. "Let us make you fly. Imagine us as we explore and stimulate every inch of this gorgeous body, our sole purpose to please you. My hard cock buried deep in you while..."

"Stop! God, no more, you're driving me crazy," Charlie begged, pulling herself away from the heat of his body, insistent lips and hands. She needed to breathe, to think.

Lord, how could she possibly want what he offered? The better question was, how could she not?

She glanced over in the direction of her table and spied Rae snuggled up to the cowboy she had set her sights on earlier. Well, there went that excuse. She ran through excuses in her head, but couldn't think of a good enough one not to join this sexy man and his mysterious friend. Did she even want to come up with an excuse?

Her body screamed at her to stop thinking and give in to this erotic fantasy, yet her brain ordered her to walk away. This wasn't who she was. She always had complete control over her emotions and body. The thought of this man taking all that away scared the hell out of her.

The cocky, confident look in his eyes made the decision for her. She started to turn from him without a word, afraid to open her mouth. She'd only made it a couple of steps when he grabbed her wrist and spun her around to face him.

"Just join us for a drink, talk to us, and then decide. Just one drink, Charlie, nothing more." He kissed the tender flesh on the inside of her wrist, his intense gaze locked on hers. "Unless you decide otherwise."

"Okay," Charlie agreed before she could stop herself. "You'll join us?"

Charlie nodded and he took her mouth in another bruising kiss. When he pulled away, he placed one last kiss on the tip of her nose. "Go make your excuses and come meet me at the bar. From the looks of your friend, I don't think she wants the three of us intruding."

Charlie walked away, dumbfounded that she was actually considering giving control of her body to not one but two men when a loud smack and a spark of pain radiating across her ass made her yelp. "Ow!"

"Don't keep me waiting long, Charlie." Trevor's animalistic growl rumbled from his chest. "Don't make me come and get you."

Charlie couldn't control the shiver that raced through her.

Chapter Two

Charlie stood in front of the large mirror in the well-lit ladies' room, shocked at her reflection.

Charlie McCarty, who had mastered the art of self-control, had been reduced to a raging sea of lust and need. Her dark chestnut hair was tousled, her green eyes glazed, and her lips red and kiss swollen.

"Holy fuck!" she exclaimed, earning curious stares from the other women crowded around the mirror. What the hell was she doing?

Two men?

Seriously?

Her treacherous body hummed and screamed for the release it craved. Her nipples were painfully hard against the fabric of her blouse, and her clit throbbed. The past three years of vet school had been difficult, yet she knew the next year working at the Redfield Animal Clinic with Dr. Stone would be even harder. This might be her only chance to live out her darkest fantasy, to experience forbidden pleasures.

She wanted to give up control, to allow someone else — or in this case two others — to take over. Could she actually surrender to complete strangers? She remembered the way Trevor had commandeered her body, how he tasted and felt against her. Hell yes, she would willingly give up control for just another taste of his mouth!

She ran a brush through her hair and smoothed it back to a silky shine, straightened her clothes, then touched up her makeup. Satisfied with her reflection, she headed back out into the bar, eager to get back into the arms of her dark fantasy man.

Charlie glanced in the direction of the bar. Her heart stopped and the breath rushed from her lungs. Standing next to Trevor was a light-haired cowboy with his back to her. He was as thick and immense as Trevor was. His pale-blue cotton shirt stretched tightly across his shoulders, looking as if the threads barely kept the pieces of fabric together. His thick blond waves hung down a few inches past his collar and the color was so unique, it seemed oddly familiar.

He leaned forward slightly at the waist and rested his elbows on the bar. It was the perfect stance to accentuate just how sexy his ass was in his skintight blue jeans.

Charlie couldn't help but think that if this man looked as good from the front as he did from the back, giving up control was going to be a very small price to pay. A very small price indeed.

Just as she prepared to take her first step in their direction, the blond cowboy turned his head toward Trevor, laughing at something he must have said.

Charlie froze. The memory of where she'd seen that hair color before came back in a painful rush. Standing there in front of her was the last man she ever thought she'd see again—the cause of her tormented heart and mind for years.

Kegan.

Spinning on her heel, Charlie fled back to the safety of the ladies' room.

No. No. No! It couldn't be him. No way could Kegan be in the same bar, could he? It felt as if her lungs were going to explode from not enough air.

She grasped the counter to steady herself as she fought to get air into her lungs. It couldn't be him, had to be her overactive imagination. She'd recently thought about him and that had to be why she was seeing things.

No way could her sexy cowboy have been waiting for her tormentor. Though this cowboy appeared to be the same height that she remembered Kegan being, he was broader in the arms and shoulders. Kegan had been thin and lanky.

Shit! Who was she kidding? That thick, sandy blond hair and dimpled smile left little doubt. Years she had tried to forget him. Years of heartbreak, and on the first night she could finally let go, here he was.

"Damn him!" She had to get the hell out of here!

Charlie pulled her cell phone from her pocket and sent Rae a text.

Mind if I call it a night?

No way was she going to face Kegan after she had wantonly thrown herself at his friend. *Oh God, is Kegan the man Trevor wants to share me with?*

Her stomach lurched as realization dawned on her. What if she hadn't spotted him first? What if she'd been standing at the bar when he arrived? Her muscles were weak, and her body shook. She gave a silent thank you to whoever had spared her the embarrassment of seeing Kegan again for the first time under the pretense of being entertainment for him and his friend.

No wonder he didn't come back for me. Why would he want some stupid country girl with silly dreams of being swept off her feet and settling down in a cute little house with a white picket fence? He obviously had other things besides monogamy in mind.

What did she have to offer when he obviously enjoyed being with Mr. Tall, Dark and Gorgeous? Her simple country charms, the dream of having two-point-five children and a future as a soccer mom attending PTA meetings wouldn't hold his interest. God, she was truly pathetic to have thought she could have that with someone like Kegan.

Her cell phone vibrated in her hand.

No problem, as long as you won't mind if I stay awhile. :) Call me tomorrow.

Be safe and I expect all the gory details tomorrow, Charlie replied, then shoved her phone in her pocket and headed out into the bar.

Keeping close to the wall and praying no one would notice her, she headed toward the back entrance. As she reached out to push the door open, she snuck one last look over her shoulder to make sure she hadn't been followed and looked right into Trevor's confused eyes.

"Ah crap!" Charlie muttered as she stepped out into the parking lot, letting the door bang shut behind her.

She didn't think he really meant his threat, '*Don't make me come and get you,*' but wasn't taking any chances and hurried across the lot to her car.

Once seated behind the wheel, Charlie finally took her first deep breath since seeing Kegan again. No one had followed her and she hadn't heard the heavy door bang shut again.

She felt a slight twinge of regret that she hadn't apologized to Trevor for standing him up, but hell, what could she have said? *'Sorry I can't join you and your friend in a cowboy sandwich because your friend happens to be the man I was hoping you would fuck right out of my head.'* Not likely.

Charlie had just inserted her key in the ignition when the door flew open and she was pulled from her car. Charlie gasped as Trevor pushed her up against the car, pressed his body tight against hers and pinned her hands at her side.

"Going somewhere?"

Panic assailed her, not so much from a stranger hauling her roughly from the car, which should have scared the hell out of her, but because she was frantically looking around in the hope that Kegan hadn't followed him out.

Satisfied that they were alone, Charlie focused her eyes on the ground. "I'm so sorry, please just let me go." Crazy, commanding cowboys she could deal with, just as long as she didn't have to face Kegan.

He released her wrists and lifted her chin with his fingers so she was forced to look at him. "Ah, hells, baby, what's got you so spooked? I would never have forced you to do anything you didn't want to do." He brushed his thumb softly across her trembling bottom lip, then bent to touch his lips to hers. "Talk to me, tell me what you need."

Charlie looked deep into his eyes and saw such sincerity, she felt ashamed that she had run without an explanation. Though the shame still wasn't enough to make her walk back into that bar.

"I'm really sorry. I shouldn't have run out without at least saying goodbye, but trust me, it's better this way."

"Why is it better? I just wanted a chance for you to get to know us."

"Us? I'm really sorry, I can't go back in." Charlie tried her best to keep the emotions from showing on her face and bit down on the inside of her cheek to keep the hurt and anger at her own stupidity from bubbling to the surface. She took a deep breath. "I already know your friend, and trust me when I say he won't be happy to see me."

Trevor tensed and Charlie took advantage of his disbelief to free herself from his grip and move back toward the open door of her car.

"You know Kegan?" he whispered.

Charlie just gave a slight nod then slid into the front seat, pulled the door shut and made sure she hit the lock this time. She didn't want to deal with these feelings and certainly didn't want to embarrass herself by admitting to this stranger that she wasn't the kind of woman that Kegan wanted. Nor was she going to give him an opportunity to try to coerce her back into the bar.

She stole a glance back at Trevor, confused by his reaction to the news that she knew his friend. He stood rigid, repeatedly clenching his hands into fists. She couldn't tell what emotions were most dominant in his dark eyes as he seemed to go from shock, to sadness, to anger and what could possibly be jealousy.

Charlie knew there wasn't anything left to be said and turned the key in the ignition. She just wanted to escape before Kegan came out looking for his friend. The sound of the car roaring to life brought Trevor out of his trance and he whipped his head around in her direction. In one long stride, he leaned down to meet her face to face through the glass.

"Wait! I don't want you to go! I'm not sure how you know Kegan, but please just come back inside. I want a chance to know you too."

Charlie could see he was dealing with some kind of emotional turmoil and felt like she should say something to explain her history with Kegan. But since she had never really dealt with her feelings for Kegan, and each year that he hadn't contacted her had made her more bitter, she knew she couldn't explain it to Trevor.

Charlie rolled her window down and reached out to place a hand against his cheek. He leaned into her touch. Her throat was so dry she could barely swallow, and she had to clear it a couple of times before speaking. "I have to go. Your friend would not thank you for inviting me, and I can't walk in there knowing what you proposed, what I was actually... Never mind, it doesn't matter, just trust me on this. If I follow you back into that bar, your friend will be very disappointed." Charlie leaned in closer and placed a soft, chaste kiss on Trevor's cheek. "I'm sorry."

She drew her hand away, put the car in gear then pulled out of the parking lot as the first tear rolled down her cheek.

Trevor stood and watched, helpless, as Charlie drove away.

He was torn between the need to chase after her and walk back in the bar to beat the shit out of Kegan. He couldn't explain it, but he wanted Charlie more than any other woman before.

She was beautiful with an amazingly sexy body, but there was more to it than that. It was something in the way she had seemed surprised by his attraction to her, as if she had no idea just how desirable she was. There was an innocence to her that turned him on almost as much as the feel of her body against his.

He closed his eyes. His skin still tingled in all the places she had touched him while they'd danced, and his body still sought her soft touch. Trevor brought his hands to his face and inhaled deeply, breathed in Charlie's sweet scent, and a need so strong racked his body it nearly knocked him to his knees. Behind his closed eyes, he saw her brilliant green eyes that had spoken so loudly to him the first time he'd spotted her, had drawn him to her. He suspected that she didn't even realize her eyes revealed so much, but to him it was as if a beacon had called to him. Her loneliness screamed at him. He recognized it where most others might not and it called to the same loneliness deep in his own soul.

"I have to find her," he mumbled.

Pain filled his chest and his heart squeezed as if in a vise as it dawned on him that Kegan would know where to find her. What the hell was their relationship and what had she meant that Kegan wouldn't want her? Irrational jealousy overwhelmed him, and he couldn't decide which hurt worse—knowing that Charlie and Kegan had once been acquainted or that Kegan had kept her a secret.

Kegan had been his best friend and business partner for the past five years. Trevor had never been closer to or cared more about another human being than he did for Kegan. They shared everything, and over the last few years that included women. It was never spoken aloud, but they had developed a committed relationship between the two of them. Trevor no longer took any woman without Kegan there, and until tonight, he would have sworn Kegan hadn't either.

He felt betrayed.

Trevor stomped back toward the bar as jealousy goaded his anger. "Son of a bitch has some explaining to do."

Trevor walked into Jack's Place, his blood boiling to nuclear.

Kegan leaned against the bar, completely casual and comfortable, laughing while two blonde bimbos rubbed their hands up and down his body. His thick blond hair was tousled like someone, or someones, had been running their fingers through it, making his soft waves spike and stand out in disarray. Though his hands dangled casually on the side of the bar, his demeanor and the heated look in his eyes clearly encouraged the women's exploration. He seemed right at home with the blatant sexual performance the three of them were performing for the bar crowd.

Instantly, Trevor was consumed by such raging anger, he literally saw red. He crossed the room, grabbed Kegan by the shirt, and slammed him back against the bar. "You no good rotten prick!" He shoved Kegan against the bar a second time before the man could react.

Kegan's eyes grew wide with shock, and the two little blonde bunnies yelped and jumped back.

"What the hell is wrong with you?" Kegan tried to remove the fists from his shirt, but Trevor had no intention of letting go and he slammed Kegan against the bar again.

"I can't believe you." He jerked his head in the women's direction. "Were you planning on fucking these two behind my back too?"

"What the hell are you talking about? What the hell has gotten into you?"

"Don't! Don't even try your innocent bullshit on me. I just had the most amazing woman run from me like a scared colt because of something you did to her, and then I find you in here looking for your next conquest." Trevor pulled at Kegan's shirt again, intending to slam him into the bar once more, but Kegan reached out, ripped the hands from his shirt, and grabbed onto Trevor's wrists.

The two little bar flies looked from Trevor to Kegan and back again, then scurried away.

Trevor heard one of them say, "Told you all the good ones were either married or gay."

Any other time he would have snatched them back and proceeded to show them just what his preferences were, but right now, he gave no fucks what they thought.

"Trevor, I don't know what the hell has gotten into you, but I suggest we take this outside. I don't think Jack is gonna appreciate us upsetting his customers when we start bitch slapping each other."

"Fuck you! You know what, it doesn't matter what you do. I'm outta here. You're on your own. Maybe one can watch over you while you fuck the other." Trevor spun around, wrenched his wrists from Kegan's grip, then stormed to the exit.

He punched open the door then kicked it closed behind him. He was so furious, his body trembled. He knew he was being unfair and should have let Kegan explain, especially after he'd seen the true confusion on his face. But he was still too pissed off about losing Charlie and how it felt to have Kegan rub it in his face by letting someone else stroke their hands all over him.

He leaned back against the brick wall, took long, deep breaths, and tried to get himself under control. He really felt like banging his fool head against the brick and knocking all the confusing images and thoughts out. As soon as he closed his eyes, images of Kegan's powerful body wrapped around Charlie tormented him and he forced them open again.

Shit, shit, shit!

He couldn't stand the thought of them together without him and his chest tightened further.

The bar door slammed open. Before Trevor could even blink, Kegan was standing directly in front of him, their noses nearly touching,

"Trev, you've got some explaining to do. What the hell's gotten into you tonight?"

Trevor looked toward the night sky and refused to meet Kegan's gaze. "Go away. I told you I've got nothing else to say to you."

"Oh hell no you don't! You don't get to grab onto me, knock me around, insult me and accuse me of all kinds of shit, then tell me to go away."

Trevor jerked his head to the side, and he pinned Kegan with a hard glare. "Fine! What did you do to Charlie?"

Kegan blinked slowly. "Who the fuck is Charlie?"

"Don't play stupid with me, Kegan. I met the most incredible woman I've ever seen and got her to agree to meet with us, but the instant she laid eyes on you, she ran like she'd seen a ghost." Trevor ran his hand over the back of his neck to ease some of the tension. "Ah hell, Kegan, what the fuck did you do?"

Kegan stepped away from Trevor to lean against the wall. "I'm telling you, I have no idea what the hell you're talking about. I can promise you, though, I have not fucked anyone without you. You know I can't. I have only met one girl named…"

Kegan went rigid and took in a harsh breath. Every ounce of color had drained from Kegan's face, and his fists clenched so tight, his knuckles were white.

"Hey, you okay?"

"Trev, describe Charlie," he whispered so quietly Trevor nearly didn't hear him.

"Hell, Kegan, you should have seen her." Some of the anger drained from his body, only to be replaced by pure need as Trevor closed his eyes and started to describe Charlie.

"She has straight dark chestnut hair all the way down to the top of her ass. It's like silk in my hands and smelled of honeysuckle." Trevor's body stirred and his arousal renewed as he remembered the feel and smell of Charlie.

"She was taller than most girls I've known, probably around five nine, hell, maybe even five ten. She had the tiniest waist. I swear I could have spanned it with one hand. Her breasts were perfect. Not too big and not too small, ya know what I mean? I'm telling you, she had the most sensual body I've ever seen or been lucky enough to touch."

His cock pulsed, hardening at a painful angle, and he adjusted himself to get a little more room in his jeans. An image of Charlie as she rubbed her tight body against him flashed in his mind, and he had to stifle a moan.

A low raspy growl brought him back from his thoughts. "Trev, goddammit, describe her face."

"Well… I don't know how to describe her other than perfect. I mean she had this perfectly fuckable body and this sweet, innocent-looking face. The thing that blew me away most, though, was her eyes! Such a brilliant shade of green, they fucking took my breath away." He reached up to touch the spot right below his right eye. "And she has a tiny little birthmark right here that looks almost like a tear."

Kegan slumped against the wall and slid down, assplanting on the ground. His breath left him in a rush, and he began to shake so hard, it scared the hell out of Trevor.

"What the hell?" Trevor knelt down next to Kegan. "Damn, you look like shit! You okay?"

Kegan slowly looked up at Trevor, his eyes wild, and took a couple of deep breaths before he responded. "Trev, remember when I told you about the one thing I've been missing from my life before I met you?"

Kegan dropped his forearms onto his bent knees and leaned his forehead on them. "You just met her."

Chapter Three

A tongue slid along her neck, leaving a warm, wet trail against her tingling skin. Large hands palmed her breasts roughly, calluses scraping across her hard nipples sparking a slight edge of pain. She writhed against the damp cotton sheets, unsure if she was trying to pull away or move closer to the agonizing pleasure. The low commanding voice at her neck made it difficult to concentrate on anything except the sensations racking her body and the insistent voice.

Rough fingers pulled hard at her nipples until she wanted to scream from the pain, only to have the sting soothed away with the lightest of touch, causing her to shudder.

"That's it, baby. Shake for us. Show us how good we make you feel."

The deep voice stirred memories, familiar, yet Charlie was awash in so many different sensations, she was having a difficult time placing it. Somewhere in the back of her mind, she had the sneaking suspicion she shouldn't be here. Something big was happening, something she needed to control or perhaps stop, but with the overload of pleasurable stimulation, her brain was in a fog.

"Don't think, just feel, Charlie. Shut off your mind and just let us make you fly."

She wanted to obey the commanding voice, but the pain in her chest and the pesky voice in the back of her mind told her she should break away and run. Something bad was going to happen if she couldn't escape. Her flight or fight responses were working overtime, her pulse racing, but as bad as she wanted to run, she was unable to pull her body away from the touch.

It was consuming her.

She was drowning in the sensations and simply didn't have the strength, or perhaps the desire, to swim upward.

Warm, roughened fingertips ran up and down her inner thighs, the tingling touch wired directly to her swollen clit. She trembled, writhing, muscles tightening as her orgasm built.

"That's it! I can feel how close you are. We're going to bring you right to the peak, then keep you on the edge of that pleasure and not let you fall either way. We want to hear you beg to feel us sheathed to the hilt inside you! Hear you scream our names and then beg for more."

That damn insistent voice kept pushing and commanded her body to obey while her mind fought to break free.

Electric jolts swirled around her. They were connected to the voice, and the hot breath and tongue at her neck, traveled down to those strong hands on her breasts, and down even farther to the fingertips as they inched their way closer to her sex, then looped back to that demanding voice and begin the circuit all over again.

Charlie raised her head and peered down at the shadowed figure that hovered over her lower body. His face was obscured by the larger silhouette that nuzzled her ear. As one man licked from one side of her collarbone to the other, she met the bright blue eyes of the figure seducing her lower half. As their gazes met, he pulled back as if he'd been burned and glared at her with disgust in his eyes.

Beep. Beep…

Charlie bolted upright in bed, unable to catch her breath, her heart racing. She scanned the area around her, unsure of where she was. Relief washed through her as her mind focused and she realized she was alone in her bed, the sheets wrapped around her midsection. *Shit! It was only a dream.*

Her body still hummed from the effects of the dream. She could still hear that deep, commanding voice buzzing in her ear, while her body was covered in a light sheen of perspiration. Her swollen sex throbbed painfully. Shame assaulted her as she remembered the look in Kegan's eyes. She covered her face, as heated tears flowed.

For the last two weeks since she had run from Jack's Place, erotic dreams of Trevor and Kegan had hijacked her sleep. Each night the dreams worked her body into a frenzy, then she awoke unfulfilled with the look of disgust in Kegan's eyes seared into her brain.

For the most part, she'd kept busy during the day and was able to push the men out of her mind. She had gotten good at controlling her body and emotions, and refused to let painful memories take form in her mind. Yet in her dreams, she was at their mercy, defenses stripped and unable to protect her heart from the pain.

God, what I wouldn't give for just one night of peaceful sleep.

She swung her legs over the side of the bed, noted the time of six a.m. on the clock on the bedside table, and placed her feet on the floor. The last few nights she had fought sleep, afraid to close her eyes, fearing the dream. Obviously she'd lost the battle with exhaustion sometime early this morning. The dream had found her just as she'd feared.

Charlie padded across the cold bare floor to the bathroom and splashed water on her face. Looking at her reflection in the mirror, she winced at the clear signs of the effects the sleepless nights were having on her. Her eyes were red and swollen, and dark circles stood out in deep contrast against her pale skin.

"Damn them," Charlie cursed as she spun away from the mirror to turn on the shower.

After stripping out of her nightshirt and panties, she pulled back the shower curtain then walked beneath the hot spray.

What a great impression I'm going to make on my first day at work. The animals will probably run in terror the way I look.

With a sigh, she lathered shampoo into her long hair and washed quickly, all the while trying to avoid lingering too long on her more sensitive areas. She refused to give in to the needs her dreams produced.

She was looking forward to getting out of the apartment and back to work. Hopefully by the end of the day she'd be too exhausted and the dreams would leave her in peace.

Though thoughts of Kegan had slipped past her best defenses from time to time over the years, since spotting him at the bar, they seemed to be doing it with increased frequency. Years ago, she'd accepted the bitterness she felt toward him and his broken promises and betrayal of her trust.

In fact, the bitterness had been what had helped heal her heart, or at least lessen the effects on it. After she'd realized he was never coming back, she had refused to feel anything for him except intense indignation. Yet since seeing that dimpled grin across the room, she couldn't help but think of the Kegan she'd once known. That Kegan had been her hero and the one true friend she'd thought she could always depend on. The man she'd thought to spend the rest of her life with. She couldn't help but mourn his loss.

Stop it! She cursed herself for doing it again. No need dwelling on things she couldn't change.

Pushing thoughts of Kegan to the back of her mind, she dried off and quickly dressed in jeans, a long-sleeve teal T-shirt and boots. She still had an hour before she had to meet Dr. Stone, so she took her coffee to the small kitchen table and started up her laptop to do some research on the side effects of vaccinations, a perfect subject to keep her focused while she dried her hair.

She and Dr. Stone had a nine a.m. appointment at the Trev-Ke Ranch to give West Nile virus boosters. A cattle ranch in a neighboring county had reported a possible outbreak of the virus and the owners of the large horse-breeding ranch were taking no chances.

Trev-Ke Ranch boasted some of the rarest breeding horses in South Dakota as well as a number of more common equine breeds. From what Dr. Stone had told her, the ranch currently had approximately two hundred horses, and she looked forward to the long day of work ahead.

At eight o'clock, Charlie shut down her laptop and felt confident that she could answer any questions that Dr. Stone or the owners may have. She placed it in her bag, tied her hair into a loose ponytail, slung her messenger bag over her shoulder, then headed out, relieved that the effects of her early-morning dreams had nearly worn off.

* * * *

As Charlie walked up to the small café at eight-twenty, she noticed Dr. Stone sitting at an outside bistro table, and he waved her over.

"Good morning, Dr. McCarty, please join me." He motioned to the opposite chair with a wave of his hand. "I took the liberty of ordering us coffee, but if you'd like something else…?"

"Good morning, Dr. Stone. Black coffee is exactly what I need this morning. Thank you, and please, call me Charlie."

"If you insist, but while we're working in any professional manner, you understand that I will refer to you as Dr. McCarty. The owners of the ranch we're working with today won't question your abilities, they're down-to-earth good people. In fact, you'll stay at Trev-Ke Ranch during the birthing season.

"On the other hand, I have to warn you that there are a few people in this town that don't really take too kindly to trusting their animals — their way of making a living — to a woman, and as such need to be reminded that you are in fact a doctor. Some men around here tend to live in the Dark Ages and feel women should know their place." He winked and tried to reassure her with a kind smile that reached his eyes. "I happen not to be one of those fools and look forward to working with you."

"Thank you, sir, that means a lot to me. I look forward to working with you as well. I truly appreciate the opportunity you've given me to do my residency with you. I have heard some —" Charlie took a sip of her coffee and peered over the edge of her cup. "Some great things about you."

"You have, have you? Would that little glint of fear I see in your eyes have anything to do with my reputation?" He brought his cup to his lips and took a sip. "It's all true, you know, the rumors about me."

"Oh God!" Charlie whispered, slumped in her seat, then tightened her grip on her mug. She had heard he was hard to work with and sometimes got physical with his students, but she had hoped they had just been silly rumors to scare her.

Dr. Stone reached out, grabbed one of her hands and patted it. "Don't worry, Charlie, I have heard great things about your abilities and your professors have highly recommended you. They also have much praise for your compassion, so I'm sure you and I will work great together. I don't tolerate students who don't put the feelings of their patients before their own. They may be animals, but they deserve your best and to be treated with respect and care." His smile turned just this side of devilish as he continued to pat her hand. "I've only had to use that cattle prod on a colleague once and I'm sure you won't require that kind of reminder."

Charlie's eyes widened and she gasped. *Jesus, the rumors really are true.*

She must have had a shocked look on her face because he laughed and his eyes sparkled with humor. He rose to his feet and reached out a hand to her. "C'mon, Dr. McCarty, we have patients to attend to."

Charlie took a last sip of her coffee, then allowed Dr. Stone to help her to her feet.

Shit! He looks like a sweet old grandpa. Cattle prod? Charlie groaned to herself and followed him to the van with Redfield Animal Clinic painted on the side.

Ten minutes later, Dr. Stone pulled into a long, tree-lined drive, a welcoming arch informing visitors they were entering the Trev-Ke Ranch. The drive turned and twisted through large oaks and maples that created a canopy over the road. Small streams of light escaped through the trees and formed a crosshatch pattern across the road. In full summer, it would be deep in shadows, but in early spring, the light had a dazzling effect.

When they emerged from the trees into a clearing, Charlie smiled in appreciation at the impressive colonial-style home with massive white pillars, which stood out from the bright-red brick façade and black shutters. The lawn was masculine in appearance with stark box-shaped hedges running the length of it on either side of the front entrance, but still seemed welcoming. A white fence was set back from the house and appeared to go on for miles, enclosing the numerous barns and outbuildings.

Charlie stepped out of the van, awed at the site of a large herd of horses running in the enclosure to her right. In the distance, the sun was high above the mountains and cast streaks of gold across the fields. It was truly breathtaking.

"Beautiful, isn't it?" Dr. Stone commented as he joined Charlie at the front of the van. "It's one of my favorite places to visit and work. The views are as extraordinary as the animals. They complement one another, don't you think?"

Charlie was speechless and could only nod in agreement.

"Why don't you wander on back to the barn there on your right? The stable hands should be bringing the horses in for us. I'll just grab my bag and let Mr. Kingsington know we're here."

"Are you sure you don't need help with anything?"

"No, I've got it. Go on back and get yourself acquainted with your patients. I'll join you in a moment." He strode off in the direction of the house and Charlie navigated her way to the barn alone.

Entering the large barn, she was impressed with its size and grandeur. Large airy stalls ran the length of the barn on both sides. Each stall had its own large open window. She was impressed at the design, that someone would go through the extra cost and labor to ensure each animal had a comfortable stall with fresh air.

Men were leading in horses through the back entrance and filling the stalls rapidly. She was excited to get to work, even though the sheer number of animals they had to treat in one day was overwhelming.

"Charlie."

She turned to see Dr. Stone enter the barn and walked toward him.

"Mr. Kingsington had some errand to do this morning so he left instructions for us to go ahead and get started. He'll meet us here later."

"Okay, sure, where would you like me to start?"

"I was thinking you could do the right half of the barn and I can work down the left. Am I correct to assume that you have done assessments on large animals and are familiar with immunizations?"

"Yes, sir. USD has a great veterinary program with a full working farm. Though if you prefer, I would be more than willing to assist you until you're sure of my skills?"

"No, no, you'll do just fine. Your willingness to assist shows me much of your personality and your confidence. Thank you. On each stall, you'll find a clipboard with each animal's pertinent information. Please chart your vaccinations and any abnormalities you may note during your assessment. If you come across anything you're unsure of, just holler." He handed her a large tray of supplies and walked off to do his own work.

Charlie worked through the morning, happily humming to herself. She was impressed with the health and care of each animal. They were well-fed and their coats and manes were brushed to a shine. Hooves were trimmed and meticulously tended to with no evidence of any disease in any of the animals she inspected. This Mr. Kingsington seemed to care a great deal about the well-being of his horses. She was thoroughly impressed with him already and looked forward to meeting him.

"Hey, Charlie, you about ready for lunch?"

Charlie looked up to see Dr. Stone peering down at her from over the stall, wiping the sweat from his brow with the back of his hand.

"Oh… Wow! I didn't even realize it was noon already." Charlie removed her rubber gloves and patted the horse's flank she had just finished injecting. "I'm ready for lunch whenever you are."

"I have some calls I have to return before I can eat, but go ahead up to the back porch. Mrs. Miller has set out quite a spread."

"If you don't mind, I think I'll just take a walk and explore a little. I need to stretch my legs and I brought my own lunch. I think I'd like to eat while enjoying the amazing scenery around here."

"Okay, meet you back here in an hour or so. Enjoy."

Charlie headed out toward the back. She'd been so wrapped up in the sheer volume of work that she hadn't had a chance to appreciate the sights around her.

She walked toward a corral, drawn to a large chestnut stallion. She reached out and allowed him to smell her hand, his muscles rippling as he shifted and lowered his head to take in her scent.

She placed her palms against his muscular neck and massaged the thick-corded muscles. He nodded his massive head as if appreciating her soft touch. His coat shone in the afternoon sun, his mane and tail reminding her of deep hues of silk.

Charlie ran her hands through his mane and down his neck, marveling at the luxurious feel. She allowed him to nuzzle her and take in her scent further. Taking his face in her hands, she placed a soft kiss to his nose. "You are a magnificent creature."

"I thought the same thing the first time I saw you."

Charlie's breath caught and her heart skipped a beat at the sound of the familiar deep, sultry voice. Her body trembled and her throat went tight, prohibiting her from responding. She felt him move closer to her, and his heat radiated at her back. A fleeting touch at the base of her neck sent a shudder down her spine. He leaned in closer, his breath hot against the sensitive spot beneath her ear.

"Hello, Charlie." His lips brushed lightly against her skin.

She spun away from his touch and faced him. Trevor stood an arm's length away. Too close. She took a step back and grabbed onto the wooden fence to steady herself. He was even more handsome here in the bright sun than she remembered from the night in the bar. He wore the same dark Stetson, pulled low to protect his eyes from the glare of the sun. A tight, dusty blue T-shirt stretched across his broad shoulders, and threadbare loose-fitting jeans hung low on his lean hips. Charlie refused to let her gaze drop any farther down his gorgeous body and raised her eyes to meet his.

"Oh God, what are you doing here?"

Charlie hated how shaky her voice sounded. What the hell is he doing here? She had hoped to never see him again and, after the last two weeks of being constantly assaulted by dreams of him, was completely unprepared to deal with him, especially on the job. She turned her back on him, focused her attention on the stallion.

"I could ask you the same thing, but I wouldn't really care. I'm just glad you are." He moved closer, placing his large palm at the small of her back, and heat streaked along her spine. "Are you here for me, Charlie?"

Charlie shrugged away from him again, hating how her body instantly responded to his voice, and gaped at his nerve and arrogance.

"I believe I made it clear it would be a bad idea—a very bad idea—for me to see you. Why in the hell would I come looking for you?" She couldn't believe how cocky he was and it just pissed her off that she couldn't seem to control her body around him. "I was invited here by the owner, so if you'll excuse me." She turned and started to head back toward the barn.

Before she could take a second step, he reached out and grabbed her around the waist. The instant her back made contact with his broad chest, a wave of pure lust shot through her, and she had to force herself not to push against his heat.

"Whoa there, little wildcat." He nipped at her ear and damned if her whole body didn't beg to respond. "I don't remember inviting you here."

Okay, this had to stop. Two minutes in this man's presence and she was reduced to a mindless and boneless mess.

Sheesh, Charlie, have some control.

She pulled from his grasp, refused to look at him, and strode off back toward the barn. "I didn't ask for your invite," she tossed over her shoulder.

Charlie entered the barn, driven by an urgent need to get away from him before she did something stupid, but damned if the arrogant cowboy didn't follow her. She spotted her mentor helping coax a spooked colt into one of the stalls. Before she could reach him, Trevor strode past her, winking as he went. *Bastard.*

"Hey, John, good to see you." He reached out and slapped Dr. Stone on the back. "Thanks for coming on such short notice."

Charlie stopped dead in her tracks.

Oh God, this isn't happening.

The one time in her life when she had actually considered doing something wild and crazy and enjoy a moment, consequences be damned, was coming back to bite her in the ass. Hard.

Oh hell no, she couldn't have just picked up an anonymous stranger in a bar for hot, meaningless sex. She'd had to get all greedy and go for two. Her one night of indiscretion had not only had her throwing herself at someone who had basically told her he didn't want her, but now that choice could jeopardize her career before it even began.

Way to go, Charlie. You can kiss your career goodbye. Not only did you pick a man who is friends with Kegan, but with your boss as well. Shit!

She didn't really think Dr. Stone would kick her out of the program, but she was sure he would no longer respect her or take her seriously if he found out what she had nearly agreed to do at Jack's Place.

"Trevor." Dr. Stone slapped him on the back in return. "Don't mention it. It was a perfect opportunity for my assistant." He spotted her and waved her over.

Charlie sighed, resigned herself to what was coming and forced her feet to start moving.

"Charlie, this is Trevor Kingsington, one of the owners of Trev-Ke Ranch. Trevor, meet my new assistant, Dr. Charlie McCarty."

Trevor reached out and took her hand in his. "Pleasure to see you again, Dr. McCarty." He ducked his head, kept his eyes locked on hers, and placed a soft kiss on the top of her hand.

"I didn't realize you two knew each other." Dr. Stone flicked his gaze back and forth between them, confusion evident on his face.

With her eyes, Charlie pleaded for Trevor not to say where they'd met. She could only pray he would be able to read her expression. He lifted his head slowly and winked before he addressed Dr. Stone.

"I found her out back admiring one of my stallions."

"Ah I see. Well if you have a minute, Trevor, I'd like to go over some of the things that Dr. McCarty and I have found."

"Sure, no problem. Let me just grab my books and I'll meet you in my office."

"Great. Charlie, will you be okay finishing up here?"

Yes, if you'll both leave right now, I'll care for a thousand horses alone.

"Yes. I'll be just fine, sir." She turned to Trevor. "Nice to meet you, Mr. Kingsington."

"I look forward to seeing you again, Dr. McCarty. I'm sure you'll be an" — he raked his gaze up and down her body — "amazing asset around here." His voice was thick with sexual innuendo. Obviously the man just couldn't let it go without the last word.

Charlie gritted her teeth, turned quickly then walked off in the opposite direction.

Asset? What the hell was that supposed to mean? She was relieved that it had gone as well as it had and that Trevor hadn't mentioned meeting her in a cowboy bar. But the way his silky voice had suggested she would be a great asset had her a little unnerved.

Okay, she could do this. She just needed to finish up here as quickly as she could, pack up, then hide in the van until Dr. Stone helped her escape. She hated being a coward, but in this instance, she had no other alternative. She had made more than one mistake that night two weeks ago. Hopefully she could evade said mistakes for the next couple years. How hard could that be?

She made quick but thorough assessments and packed up their gear as Dr. Stone gave their final reports to the ranch foreman. Once they were pulling away from the house, Charlie let out a deep breath, one that she hadn't even realized she'd been holding.

"You did a great job today. I see now why you were so highly recommended."

"Thank you, sir." Charlie felt a little uncomfortable with the compliment and her cheeks heated. She was glad he didn't know the truth about where she had really met Trevor and hoped he never would.

As they drove slowly down the canopy drive, they were forced to pull off to the shoulder as a large silver dually pickup approached them. Dr. Stone raised his hand to wave, obviously recognizing the vehicle. The truck pulled up alongside them and stopped. Their reflection was cast back at them in the dark tint of the windows. The window remained up and as the long uncomfortable moment stretched out, Charlie felt the hairs on the nape of her neck rise and a chill run down her spine. The whirl of the window sounded, and she stared, transfixed, as it made its descent in slow motion.

When it reached halfway, Charlie's heart stopped and a fresh wave of dread washed through her system as piercing sapphire eyes stared back at her.

Kegan.

Dr. Stone raised his hand to wave again. "Hey, Kegan. Thought I was gonna miss ya today. Good to see ya, son."

Kegan continued to stare at Charlie with those intense blue eyes as if he hadn't been spoken to. She was afraid to look at him, fear of seeing the disgust she knew would be there. She dropped her gaze and stared at her tightly clasped hands as her pulse raced. She should have realized that Kegan would work with Trevor. Hadn't Trevor suggested they shared everything? Her stomach lurched as realization dawned. Trevor had surely told Kegan that she'd basically agreed to hook up with two strangers from a bar.

Please, God, let the earth open up and swallow me now.

Dr. Stone must have noticed Kegan staring at her and spoke up, "Oh, sorry, Kegan, this is my assistant, Dr. Charlie McCarty. Charlie, this is Kegan Colburn, the other owner of Trev-Ke Ranch."

An uncomfortable silence hung like heavy fog in the air. Charlie could feel Kegan's gaze boring into her, but couldn't find the courage to lift her head and look at him.

"I always knew you would become something special, Charlie."

Charlie heard such sincerity in his deep baritone, even though he seemed to choke on her name. His words sounded so heartfelt, Charlie dared to raise her eyes to his, and what she saw stole her heart.

His eyes were full of such pain and longing, the twenty-year-old man she remembered. She was instantly transported back to the day she'd found him at the creek bed.

She came up on Kegan sitting with his back against a tree, his head resting on his big forearms and across his bent knees. She thought he was asleep and crept closer on silent feet, hearing soft sobs coming from his shaking body.

"Kegan, are you okay?"

He snapped his head up, startled by her presence. His beautiful blue eyes were red-rimmed. His tears had left wet streaks down his face. Obviously uncomfortable having been found crying, he lowered his head back to his arms. "Go home, Charlie."

She reached out, wanting to hug him and take away the horrible pain in his eyes, but as her fingers reached him, he jumped up and spun away from her.

"I'm going away, Charlie."

Charlie ran to him, wrapping her arms around his waist and pressing her cheek to his broad back. "Where are you going and when will you be back?"

"I won't be coming back, Charlie. I can't stay here anymore. I've got to get away from that bastard before I do something really stupid."

He tried to pry her arms from around his body, but she refused to release him. She held him with everything she had, knowing if she could just hold him tight enough, he wouldn't be able to leave her.

"Please, Kegan, you can't! Please tell me you won't leave me. You're my best friend and I – "

He turned and hugged her, placing soft yet fierce kisses on the top of her head.

"I'll watch over you, I promise, and I'll come back for you, bichito. I swear when you're eighteen, I'll come back and take you with me." He ripped himself from her grasp and took off at a dead run in the direction of his house.

She wanted to follow him, convince him that he could stay and she would help him with whatever had happened, sure

Gram would let him stay with them until he found a place of his own.

Everyone in the county knew what his father was capable of and what he had inflicted upon Kegan over the years. She just knew if he asked, people would help however they could. They had to, he couldn't just leave.

As much as she wanted to follow him, tell him they would work it out together, she couldn't. Her heart was breaking into a thousand shattering pieces. The only thing she was capable of at that moment was to hug herself tight as she lay down in the grass and wept.

"Charlie?"

A hand on her arm brought her back into the present, and she lifted her head and met Dr. Stone's concerned eyes. "Are you okay?"

"Huh? Oh, I'm sorry. Yes, I'm fine. What were you saying?"

"I was saying I didn't realize you and Kegan knew each other."

Charlie lowered her eyes. "Yes, sir. We grew up together." She refused to meet either man's gaze.

Remembering that broken promise shattered her heart all over again, the pain so raw and just as powerful now as it had been when she'd been eighteen and had first realized that Kegan wasn't coming back for her.

"I'm sorry, Dr. Stone, I'm not feeling very well. I think the day is finally catching up with me. Would you mind taking me home?"

Charlie vaguely acknowledged Dr. Stone and Kegan saying their goodbyes. The ride from the ranch was a blur as Charlie struggled to get her emotions under control.

Dazed, she walked into her apartment, dropped her bag at the door and let her tears fall.

Chapter Four

Although a cool stream of air blew from the vents in the dash of the truck, it felt hot and oppressive, too thick to take a deep breath. The muscles of his hands began to cramp and twitch as he clutched the steering wheel tight, trying to get himself under control. Kegan had never doubted that it was Charlie who Trevor had seen in Jack's. Hell, his entire being ached to see her, but not like this, not yet.

He'd done some asking around, found out where she was living, but hadn't worked up the nerve to contact her. Luck was on his side that he hadn't been arrested as a Peeping Tom, considering the number of evenings he'd spent lately parked outside her house just hoping for a glimpse of her.

Seeing her dark outline through the curtains had made him ache to go to her, but his cowardice kept him rooted in his seat. He was astonished that Trevor hadn't found out where she was staying, but Kegan hadn't volunteered the information. Given Trevor's reaction to her and his damn pushy attitude, he'd be beating down her front door the first night, demanding entrance.

It wasn't that he didn't want to see Charlie or he was trying to keep her away from Trevor. Kegan still didn't have a clue what to say to her, couldn't find the right words that didn't make him sound like a dolt. He also didn't want to reveal just how obsessed he was with her, certain she'd run screaming from him, thinking him some crazy, lovesick stalker.

The moment Kegan had laid eyes on her again, all coherent thought had left him and he'd been unable to breathe, let alone say anything remotely intelligent. She was even more beautiful than he remembered. He'd always thought Charlie pretty, and even when she'd been more of a snot-nosed pest, she'd been easy on the eyes. As a teen, when he'd first realized she was no longer just a cute pest but someone who starred in his late-night fantasies, for him, no other woman was as beautiful.

The Charlie of today was exquisite.

Trevor's lust-filled description was far from how desirable she truly was. Breathtaking was the only description that came to mind when Kegan thought of her.

Kegan took a few more moments to calm himself, not an easy task given the emotional and physical toll Charlie was having on him. Anger, regret, guilt, longing and desire all battled for supremacy. By the time he was able to pry his fingers from the wheel and head into the house in search of his best friend, anger had won out.

"What the fuck was Charlie doing here?" Kegan slammed his hands down on Trevor's desk, his heart pounding.

"Shit, is she gone?" Trevor looked up at the clock, stunned.

"Yeah, she's gone. Now, you wanna tell me why the fuck she was here in the first place?" Kegan slumped in the chair opposite Trevor and ran his hand through his hair. "Dammit, Trev, I wasn't ready to see her yet. You knew that."

"I didn't invite her. I was shocked as hell when I went out back and found her standing at the corral. She's John's new assistant." Trevor shook his head. "She was here half the fucking day, and I didn't even know it."

"Yeah, well, you could have at least called and warned me." Not that it would have done any good, but maybe he would have been able to avoid her for a little bit longer until he could figure out what the hell to say to her.

Trevor sat back in his chair and stared at him, concerned. "Ah shit, Kegan, I'm sorry, the phone kept ringing with one disaster after another and I lost track of time."

"Well now I have a disaster, don't I?" Unconsciously, Kegan rubbed at an ache in his chest.

"And just what is that supposed to mean? I apologized. I feel just as bad that I missed Charlie and didn't get a chance to call you, but we do still have a business to run. What the hell do you want me to say?"

Kegan could tell he was pissing Trevor off, but at the moment he just didn't give a damn. He was pissed off as well. Running into Charlie with no warning was a disaster in his book and one that could have been avoided with a simple phone call.

Kegan got to his feet and paced. He needed to burn off some of the tension raging through his body. "Doesn't matter, she's gone."

Trevor jumped to his feet. "The hell it doesn't!" He moved into Kegan's path. "You've moped and been miserable for the last two weeks because you've wanted to see her."

"Get out of my face, Trev. I'm in no mood for your shit."

"Yeah, well, you're gonna get it anyway. How long do you plan to wait before you figure out what to say to her? Eight years wasn't enough?"

Kegan clenched and unclenched his fists. "That was a fucking low blow, and I'm warning you, Trev, back the fuck up."

Trevor threw his hands up and started toward the door. "Fine, Kegan, if you're too much of a spineless pussy to go after her, then you deserve to be miserable. I'm done waiting on you to figure it out. I'm going after Charlie."

Panic zipped through him, ignited him to near detonation. He grabbed Trevor's arm before he even realized what he was doing and spun him, pinned him against the closed door with his body and drew his fist back. Jealousy roared through him like a raging forest fire at the thought of Trevor going after Charlie without him.

Charlie's mine!

"What the fuck?" Trevor stared at him in disbelief. Anger and confusion flashed across his face, and he glanced at Kegan's fist. "Well?"

Kegan's heart was pounding out of his chest and his stomach rolled as the realization of what he'd just done hit him. So overcome with such a powerful possessiveness for Charlie, he hadn't thought, had only acted.

Kegan stumbled back and dropped his hands to his sides. His head spun, his brain unwilling to accept what his soul was telling him. He wasn't willing to give meaning to his thoughts.

"Christ! I'm sorry, Trev. I shouldn't have... Jesus." Kegan's throat tightened, he couldn't speak. He didn't understand what the hell had just happened, so how was he going to explain it to Trevor? He cleared his throat a couple of times and stared at his friend, who looked as confused as he felt. "Dammit, I'm sorry... I gotta go."

Trevor grabbed Kegan's wrist. "Wait! Talk to me, man. What the hell is going on with you?"

Kegan lowered his gaze, unable to meet Trevor's eyes. "I can't," he whispered.

"What do you mean you can't? Don't you mean you won't? You've been shutting me out for the last two weeks and it's really starting to piss me off." Trevor let go of his wrist and ran both his hands through his hair, clasped his fingers together behind his neck. Something Trevor always did when he was irritated or stressed. "C'mon, Kegan, this isn't like you. You've always told me everything. We've never kept secrets from one another. Just talk to me."

Kegan stepped back, needed more distance between them. His emotions were so raw, he didn't trust himself. He needed to get the hell out of this room, away from Trevor and figure out what the hell was wrong with him. He needed to find the answer to what he was feeling, why he was so out of control. It terrified him to feel this way.

"Trev, I'm gonna just go walk it off. I need to get my head on right. I have no fuckin' idea why I just did that."

Trevor reached out for Kegan again, placing his hand on his shoulder. "Kegan, come on, you're killin' me here. Don't shut me out like this. We're closer than brothers, when you're hurting, so am I."

Well that was the problem right there. It wasn't only Charlie who brought out Kegan's possessiveness. His feelings for Trevor had recently been changing, feelings which went beyond brotherly love. He couldn't tell Trev, he wouldn't understand. Christ, he didn't understand it himself. Nothing made sense anymore.

"Look, Trev, I'm sorry I lashed out at you. I think it was just the adrenaline from the shock of seeing Charlie. Just let me go take a shower and get my shit together and we'll talk about it over dinner, okay?" It wasn't a lie. He really did need to get his head together. Still, not being able to be completely honest with Trevor made him feel like an even bigger shit, but he couldn't deal with it right now.

"Yeah, go on, take your shower. I'll go see about dinner." Trevor wrapped his arms around him in a bear hug and slapped him on the back. *Just like a brother.*

Kegan headed for the bathroom, trying to figure out what he was going to tell Trevor.

You are one messed-up man, Kegan. Better figure out what the hell you're feeling or you'll lose him just like you lost Charlie.

Trevor headed to the kitchen to see what Mrs. M had left for dinner, still shocked by Kegan's outburst in his office. Hell, the man always had such a tight leash on his anger he rarely raised his voice. Trevor was usually the one to use anger as a way of handling shit that upset him. Lash out and apologize later was always his modus operandi. It was why they worked well together—he was the hothead, Kegan was the laid-back logic.

He knew Kegan had had a rough childhood. The no-good son of a bitch he called Dad had really fucked with his head, and Trevor knew Kegan's greatest fear was turning out just like him.

Kegan never lashed out or raised a hand to anyone. Trevor seriously doubted it was just running into Charlie that had set him off. Yeah, it sucked that it had to happen the way it did, but still, it wouldn't have caused Kegan to behave the way he had.

Something had rocked Kegan...hard.

Trevor had been dealing with his own demons lately, and couldn't really be pissed at Kegan for holding things back from him. He'd been keeping a big problem he was having with Kegan a secret from him. He couldn't understand why he had felt so possessive and jealous at the thought of Kegan being with a woman on his own. He felt betrayed and damned if he knew why.

It wasn't like they were a couple or anything, but that night he remembered a voice in the back of his mind screaming *mine* when he'd imagined Kegan with a woman. He was a bit freaked out by the realization that he wanted a committed relationship with Kegan. Trevor was uncertain about what it meant, but it went beyond being business partners, the sexual exploits they shared or even being best friends.

Trevor was placing the plates at the table when he heard heavy footsteps on the stairs and the back door open then slam shut. Kegan obviously wasn't ready to talk yet. No longer hungry, he left the plates on the table, then went out to the back porch.

It was a nice evening, spring having finally pushed the last bit of winter away along with the remaining snow. He sat in one of the old rockers and listened to the crickets and frogs, watched the stars come out. The sky was lit up as if a thousand fireflies had taken over the heavens. The effect calmed the intense emotions from earlier. He figured Kegan would be back when he was ready. Trevor didn't see the sense in going after him. It was driving him batty, but it was probably best to let Kegan work it out on his own. It would do no good to push him until he was ready.

Trevor wasn't sure how long he sat there, lost in his own thoughts, when Kegan joined him on the porch and sat down next to him.

"You done thinking?" Trevor asked.

"Yeah, didn't do any good. Can't seem to get my head right, ya know?"

"Yep. Sometimes it's better to talk it out with someone."

Kegan stared at him with a somber expression. "It was rough seeing Charlie today. You know how I feel about her. I mean her being a doctor and all now... I must have done the right thing by leaving her alone when we were younger, right? But...but seeing her today makes me question that. You should have seen the pain in her eyes." Kegan ran his hand over the stubble on his chin. "Shit, Trev, I know I'm the one who put that look in her eyes and I don't know if I can forgive myself for that."

"You were young when you left home, I'm sure if you just talked to her—"

Kegan shook his head. "Not gonna happen. The thing is, remember me telling you about the day I left home?"

"Yeah."

"Well, Charlie found me right after the fight I had with my old man. I told her I was leaving and she begged me not to go." Kegan laid his head back against the rocker and took a few deep breaths.

Trevor knew there was more, had already heard this part of the story but didn't want to push him too hard, so he continued to watch the night sky. After a bit, Kegan still hadn't said anything, and Trevor began to wonder if he had fallen asleep. He turned his head to find Kegan staring at him as if waiting for permission to continue.

"That last day I saw her, I promised I would always watch over her and come back for her when she turned eighteen."

"Shit, Kegan."

"Yeah I know. I had every intention of keeping that promise, but I had no money, nowhere to live. Hell, I didn't have anything to offer her. I loved her, still do, I reckon, but figured the best I could do by her was to leave her alone."

Silently, Trevor watched the stars as he thought about what Kegan had admitted to, but it still didn't explain why he was so angry. He understood his hurt and the boatload of guilt, but it didn't explain the violence in Kegan that he'd seen.

"What else happened?"

"Damn, you don't think that's enough?"

"Doesn't explain why you were so pissed off earlier. There has to be more from the way you were about to beat the shit out of me when I mentioned going to look for her. Unless you don't plan on sharing Charlie with me, intend to keep her for yourself."

Kegan turned his head away and closed his eyes. "It's not that, I don't plan on…" His mouth opened a couple of more times, but then he clamped it so tight his lips went white.

"Don't plan on what? You don't reckon I deserve the truth?" Trevor ran his hands through his hair and clasped his hands behind his neck, never taking his eyes off Kegan.

After a few minutes, Kegan finally looked at him again. "Yeah, I suppose you do, I just haven't figured it out in my head yet."

"Not good enough, Kegan. We don't keep shit from each other." Well, they didn't used to—now it seemed they were both hiding things.

Kegan got to his feet and walked to the edge of the porch, leaned against the support beam. He kept his head low while he stared at the ground, then tromped down the stairs.

"Kegan?"

Kegan bent down and picked up something off the ground. "Ah fuck!"

Trevor jumped to his feet and went down the stairs to see what he had found. Looking over Kegan's shoulder, he saw a small silver locket in his palm. It took Kegan a couple of tries to open it since his hands shook. He finally opened the delicate clasp then closed his hand around it quickly.

Kegan stood ramrod straight, turned toward Trevor, and handed him the locket. "It's Charlie's."

Trevor looked down at the locket and saw a younger Kegan's smiling face. He looked up and met Kegan's pain-filled eyes. "Ah hell, Kegan, I know what you're thinking."

"No, no, I don't think you do." He shook his head a little too fast, his blond waves shading his eyes. "She used to wear this all the time. When she was little, she showed me the pictures of her parents inside. She said she liked to have the people she missed the most close to her heart."

Kegan shook so badly, Trevor worried he was going to fall over. He reached out and wrapped his arms around his waist to steady him. Kegan lowered his head and rested it on Trevor's shoulder, allowed him to hold his weight. "You have to return it to her for me, Trev. I don't think I could do it."

"You sure? This might be a good opportunity for you to talk this out with her."

Kegan shook his head. "Can't do it, man. Please, I need you to do this for me."

Trevor hugged his friend tight. "Yeah, I got it."

Chapter Five

Sitting at her kitchen table, Charlie sipped her second cup of coffee, hoping the jolt of caffeine would help throw off the fog of sleep. The emotional rollercoaster ride from the day before and the damn dream that had kept her up most of the night had left her on edge.

She couldn't deal with the overload of emotions that Kegan and Trevor had brought to the surface. Since Gram's death, she had been able to avoid emotional attachments. She'd learned throughout her life that having any connections to anyone always ended in pain. She needed to get out of this town.

Charlie drummed the fingers of her free hand against the table, staring out of the window as the early-morning sun began to rise. Maybe she could have her residency changed to another city. She took another sip as she considered it, deciding another country would work for her.

She forced the thoughts that raged to the back of her mind, knew they'd have to be dealt with later, but right now, she just didn't have the energy. She needed to take a hot bath and force her brain to concentrate on the workday ahead.

She downed the rest of her coffee then headed toward the bathroom but was stopped by the sound of her cell phone ringing. Charlie picked it up off the counter and read the display. She didn't recognize the number but answered it anyway.

"Hello?"

"Hello, Charlie."

How the hell had Trevor gotten her number?

"Charlie?"

She couldn't answer him, her ability to speak forgotten.

"Charlie, answer me or I'm coming over there."

Crap. "No… I'm here."

Trevor chuckled. "Aw, you don't want me to come over? I'm hurt, Charlie."

"Yes… I mean no…" Charlie huffed out an exasperated breath. "I'm sorry, Trevor, I can't talk right now, I'm getting ready for work."

Not to mention that just the sound of your voice drives me insane.

"I have something that belongs to you. Meet me for lunch today."

"What is it?"

"Meet me at the Redfield Café at noon." The line went dead.

Charlie stared at the silent phone, shocked by his arrogance. "Well, Mr. Cocky Cowboy, looks like you'll be dining alone today." She put the phone back on the counter then went to take a bath.

Staring at the clothes in her closet, she tried to figure out what to wear. Didn't matter what she wore, she was not meeting that arrogant bastard for lunch.

She shimmied into a pair of new tight black jeans and a form fitting green T-shirt. Her choices had nothing to do with how the jeans accentuated her ass and hips or how the T-shirt showed off her ample breasts and brought out the color of her eyes. She didn't spend an extra half hour on her hair nor did she meticulously apply just the right amount of makeup to highlight her eyes and make her lips look a little more pouty because she had plans to meet anyone for lunch.

Charlie worked in the clinic throughout the morning, busy with the large amount of patients coming through the door. She had received a text from Rae earlier, wanting to meet for lunch.

When she declined the invite, it had nothing to do with Trevor and his damned command, *'Meet me at the Redfield Café at noon.'*

With the high volume of patients today, she might not get a lunch break and didn't want to stand up Rae. It had nothing to do with a cocky cowboy.

However, precisely at noon, Charlie found herself standing outside Redfield Café, cursing herself for the damn fool she was. She took a deep breath and smoothed out her hair, still trying to convince herself she was only here because he had something that belonged to her. With her shoulders pulled back in a confident posture that she didn't really feel, she walked into the café.

Trevor sat at a small table in the back of the room with a cocky smirk on his face and motioned her over to join him.

Bastard.

As she approached the table, Trevor stood and pulled out a chair for her. Just being near him had her heart pounding. Charlie was sure he could see it beating through the thin material of her shirt.

Unable to resist, she raked her eyes down his body, appreciating the way his jeans accentuated his lean hips and the way his tight T-shirt showed off his thick chest and broad shoulders. For the first time he wasn't wearing a cowboy hat, and his dark curls hung down over one eye, framing and emphasizing his strong, handsome face. She hadn't thought it possible, but he was even more gorgeous.

Charlie hated the way her heart rate sped up and her body thrummed when in his presence, but instead of running like she should, she sat in the chair he held out for her. As he pushed her chair in toward the table, he leaned down and lightly brushed his lips against her neck.

"I'm glad you came, Charlie." His musky smell sent heat rushing through her.

Damn him.

Trevor took the chair next to her, moved it closer so their legs rested against each other.

She refused to respond to the tingling sensation his nearness caused. "On the phone you said you had something that belonged to me?"

He leaned over, placed his arm along the back of her chair. "Let's order lunch first."

Charlie needed to get some control over her rising libido, which scattered her brain. She scooted her chair away from his and stared at him. "I'm not hungry, so if you don't mind..."

Trevor smiled and waved the waitress over. "I'm hungry, join me while I eat. We need to talk."

"No, I really don't think we do." She turned her gaze away from his. "I made a mistake that night at Jack's Place and I would really prefer not to relive it."

"Good afternoon," the waitress said by way of greeting and held out two menus.

"Actually, we're ready to order. I'll have a cheeseburger, fries and a Coke. The lady will have the same."

"Yes, sir. I'll be right back with your drinks."

Of all the nerve.

Once the waitress was out of earshot, Charlie glared at him. "I told you I wasn't hungry. What is it with you and your need to command people to do what you want?"

"Why do you think you made a mistake?" he asked, ignoring her protest and question.

"I shouldn't have been there and certainly shouldn't have been thinking about jumping into bed with you and your friend."

Trevor chuckled, a deep, rich sound she felt deep down to her toes. "So you were thinking of going home with us, were you?"

Charlie realized her mistake and her cheeks heated. "Uh, no... Well, actually..." She put her head in her hands. "Oh God!" She wanted to crawl under the table and hide.

Trevor pressed his hand against the small of her back, rubbing in what should have been a soothing manner, but instead those damn pesky sparks raced up her spine.

The waitress brought their drinks and set them at the table. Trevor thanked her while Charlie was too mortified to lift her head.

"Look at me, Charlie."

She shook her head. *No thanks. I'm still trying to figure out how to dig a hole right now.*

He gently pushed her hands from her face and tilted her head up in his direction. "I want you so bad. I feel like I'll lose my damn mind if I don't have you, and I'm not embarrassed to admit it." He ran his thumb over her lower lip. "Don't be afraid of what you want, what your body wants."

"I don't let my body command my mind. Besides, it's a lot more complicated than that and you know it."

"Because of Kegan?"

Charlie wasn't sure she was comfortable talking about Kegan with Trevor, knowing their relationship was deeper than just friends who worked together. If they shared women, how much else did they share?

The waitress brought their food and set it down in front of them. "Is there anything else I can get you?" The way she looked up and down Trevor's body, the offer went beyond what was on the menu, and Charlie felt a stab of jealousy. *And just what the hell is that about?*

"No thank you, darling. We've got everything we need right now," he said with a wink and sent her away with a pout on her face.

Charlie pushed her plate aside. The way her stomach churned, she was afraid she wouldn't be able to hold anything down. Trevor, on the other hand, had no problem digging right in.

"How much has Kegan told you about me?" Charlie asked.

"He's told me everything about you. Why?"

Charlie's face fell and she had a hard time maintaining eye contact with him. "If you and Kegan share everything, including women, why are you here? You have to know that isn't possible with me."

He raised a dark eyebrow at her while he continued to devour his food. He waited until he swallowed, then asked, "Why not?"

"It just isn't." She wasn't about to go into details and dredge up those painful truths.

Trevor took her hand, his gaze locked with hers. "I know about the promise Kegan made to you."

Charlie couldn't have been more stunned or humiliated.

"He didn't break his promise because he didn't want you."

Charlie's anger rose. The bitterness she had learned to live with instead of the hurt crept up again. She hated to relive the pain of losing Kegan—the one thing in her life that had the power to hurt her most.

That Trevor knew about everything—Kegan's promise, her not being what he wanted or worth keeping a promise to—made her humiliation and hurt that much sharper.

"This is none of your damn business. I refuse to talk about this with you." She welcomed the rage, anything was better than the heartbreak. She was not going to cry in front of this man. She was already mortified enough, no way was she going to add to it with her stupid weak tears.

Trevor stood, threw some bills on the table, and held his hand out to her. "Come with me."

"What? I can't, I have to get back to work."

"Get up, Charlie. I'll give you a ride."

Relieved Trevor wasn't going to push her any further about Kegan, Charlie gratefully took his hand and let him lead her out to his truck. Trevor helped her into the passenger side and reached across to buckle her in. He placed a chaste kiss on her cheek before he hurried around the front of the truck and slid into the driver's seat, then pulled out of the parking lot and turned left.

"Trevor, the clinic is to the right."

He didn't turn to her or say anything, just increased the speed, driving in the opposite direction. Panic began to rise inside her. "Trevor, turn the damn truck around and take me to the clinic."

He locked the doors.

She reached for her seat belt. The thought that maybe she could jump from the truck when he stopped at a light or slowed down flashed through her mind before she quickly dismissed it. Trevor reached over and grabbed the buckle, refusing to let her undo it.

"Dammit, Trevor! What the hell are you doing? You're starting to scare me." Her breathing went into overtime and she began to tremble.

Still he refused to look at or talk to her. He wasn't only cocky, he was crazy.

When they turned onto Old Country Road 10, Trevor slowed the truck slightly and released his grip on the buckle and finally spoke.

"It's time you talk to Kegan."

Her rapidly beating heart skipped a beat. "Oh no, I can't, I have to go back to work. Please, Trevor, just take me back."

She couldn't do it. Wasn't ready.

Her panic grew, stealing her breath, and her heart was pounding so wildly it felt as if it would leap out of her chest. She reached for the handle and fumbled with the locked door. The only thing she knew, the only thoughts her mind could grasp was that she needed to get out of the truck.

Trevor reached over, grabbed her hand, and held it tight. "Look, Charlie, he's hurting, and I can't stand it. I see the same hurt in both your eyes and it tears me up inside." He traced circles on the back of her hand with his thumb. "You two need to talk this out so we can all move forward."

"I don't want to see him. Why are you doing this to me?" A single angry, frustrated tear slid down her cheek. "Why are you forcing me to do something I don't want to do?"

Trevor glanced over at her and released her hand. He turned it over, palm up, and placed her locket in it. "I know you do, Charlie."

Charlie blinked at the locket. She had no idea how he'd gotten it, but what she did know was that she still wasn't ready to talk to Kegan. Didn't know if she ever would be. "Please, Trevor," she whispered. "I have to go back to work. Don't make me do this."

"Charlie, I would never do anything to hurt you. I called John before lunch and asked him if I could take you to the farm to look at one of the colts."

As he turned into the drive for Trev-Ke Ranch, Trevor reached over and undid her buckle. Wrapping an arm around her, he pulled her tight against his side. He placed a kiss on the top of her head. "Please, just trust me?"

As the house came into view, Charlie sat rigidly, too stunned to respond.

Trevor's nerves were prickling as he parked the truck in front of the house. When he'd left earlier, his intentions had been to meet with Charlie for lunch, return her locket, then maybe coax her into coming back to the ranch with him to talk to Kegan or, at the very least, spending the afternoon with him. He certainly hadn't set out to kidnap the woman. But after seeing the same pain in Charlie's eyes that he had in Kegan's the night before, he knew he had to do something.

He only hoped he'd live through the afternoon because Kegan would no doubt want to skin him alive. He paled slightly at the thought as he stepped out of the truck and pulled Charlie across the seat and into his arms.

She didn't say anything, just allowed him to hold her. She was trembling so bad he doubted whether he was doing the right thing by forcing her to come here. He could tell she was skittish as hell and knew she would run if he let go of her for long enough.

Of course she would, you dumbass. You kidnapped her, for Christ's sakes!

There wasn't much he could do about that now. What was done was done and they were all just going to have to figure out together what to do about it. If he had to take an ass-whooping in order to get the two of them to talk, then so be it, though he didn't rightly relish the thought.

Charlie clung to Trevor. She wanted to run, but the tremors coursing through her made it impossible for her to let go of the broad shoulders she currently had in a death grip. Trevor cupped one of his big hands around her head and pulled her cheek against his chest.

"Shh, baby, it's okay."

No, it wasn't okay, it was so totally far from okay. What the hell was wrong with her? She should be fighting, kicking and screaming — anything besides just standing there holding onto her captor. The man had basically forced her to come here against her will and here she was melting against him.

Charlie took a few deep, calming breaths. As the adrenaline surging through her veins began to dissipate, her brain came back online. She pulled her head away from his chest and met his gaze with a confident one of her own. "Take me home," she said, her voice firm.

He shook his head, never breaking eye contact. "I can't, Charlie." He brushed his lips against hers, punctuating each phrase with a kiss. "You need this. He needs this. God, I need this." He kissed her deeper.

Confused, Charlie found herself responding.

She wasn't sure if it was defeat that made her give in or just pure need, but she opened for him, allowed his tongue and taste to fill her mouth. Charlie fisted her hands in his thick curls and drew him in even deeper. Her action was rewarded with a groan deep from within his chest.

He pulled her even harder into his tight embrace, tangling his free hand in her hair at the base of her neck. God, she wanted to forget everything and just give in to this commanding man so badly. She was so tired of the loneliness and guarded control. She just wanted to stop overthinking everything and let someone else manage things, even for just one night. Hell, one hour.

A momentary lapse.

Charlie sighed into his mouth and reluctantly broke their kiss. It didn't matter how much her body craved this man, he wasn't the one she could allow to take away her control. He refused to let go of her neck, and they stood breathing each other in.

Someone cleared their throat and startled Charlie. She tried to spin away from Trevor, but he held her close, refused to let her even move an inch.

"S'cuse me, boss, I have a message for ya."

"What is it, Cade?" He spoke to the man standing behind them, his gaze never leaving hers.

"Mr. Colburn told me to let you know he was out fixing a break in the back forty and asked that you wait for him to come back."

"Thanks, Cade. If you see him, let him know I'll be in the house, will ya? And, Cade?"

"Yes, sir."

"Stop calling me sir. And if you keep calling him Mr. Colburn and it goes to his head, I'm gonna kick your ass."

Cade just chuckled as she heard him walk away.

Trevor rested his forehead on hers. "Well, you just got a reprieve, little lady."

Her relief was so profound she couldn't help but smile. "Oh darn, just my luck. Guess we'll have to do this another time, huh?"

Have your people call my people. We'll set up a lunch date in say…never!

He threw his head back and laughed, a deep full-belly laugh, then grabbed her hand and pulled her toward the house. "I said you got a reprieve, not a pardon."

He led her up the front steps. Charlie followed him easily now that she wouldn't run into Kegan in the next few moments. Perhaps she still had time to talk Trevor out of this nonsense and convince him to take her home. If that didn't work, she was lean, she could easily fit through a bathroom window. It wasn't that far back into town. It would totally be worth the walk.

He held the door open and she entered a wide, high-ceilinged foyer—an impressive entrance to complement the equally impressive exterior of the house. Deep hues of burgundy and green dominated the walls that stood in sharp contrast with the light oak hardwood floors. It had a very distinctive yet comforting masculine feel. Charlie started to pull her hand from Trevor's in order to remove her boots, but he held tight.

"Uh, hello. Kind of hard to take my boots off with one hand."

He glanced down at her feet, yanked her over to a bench near the door, and sat her in his lap. He wrapped one hand around her waist and removed her boots one at a time with the other. "No problem, that wasn't so hard one-handed." He chuckled.

Charlie started to wriggle and squirm on his lap to force him to release her, but it had the opposite effect. As her ass brushed against his growing erection, he hissed and tightened his grip on her waist, immobilizing her.

"You keep squirming like that and we're gonna have a big problem that is hard, very hard, to deal with."

Charlie gasped but held perfectly still. The thought of how his body reacted to her gave her courage. She wasn't the only one losing control. "Mind letting me up, then?"

"Hungry?" He nuzzled her neck.

"What the hell does that have to do with letting me up?" His arrogance was starting to annoy her, but then her stomach rumbled loud enough for him to hear.

Trevor chuckled, slid his hand to her belly, and rubbed. "Your body is saying yes. Listen to it, Charlie, it knows what it needs."

Charlie felt the walls of her sex contract and moisten as she remembered the night in Jack's Place when he'd told her what he wanted to do to her body with his friend.

The pain in her heart and an image of Kegan overshadowed the lust that nearly consumed her. She bolted up off Trevor's lap, unable to look at him. For some reason he could read her like a book and she didn't want him discover all the secrets between the covers.

He stood and grabbed her hand. "C'mon. My kidnapping escapade made you miss lunch. The least you can do is let me make up for that."

She followed him into a massive room with nine-foot ceilings. Plush carpets accented the leather furniture grouping in hues of burgundy and green, as in the foyer, giving the same masculine feel to the room.

"Wow, your rooms are beautiful."

"You say that as if you're surprised."

"No, that's not what I meant. It fits you." Charlie's cheeks flushed and Trevor chuckled.

He walked into a well-lit modern kitchen, which seemed out of place against the old-world country feel that she'd seen already. He motioned for her to take a stool at a large granite center island, then proceeded to pull plates of cut meats, cheeses and fresh fruits from the fridge before placing them on the counter in front of her.

"Help yourself. Mrs. M always makes too much food. She's worried Kegan and I will starve."

"Mrs. M?"

"Mrs. Miller is our cook and full-time housemother. She's been with us a couple years now. I swear that woman thinks were still growing boys."

"So how did you meet Kegan?" Charlie blurted before she thought better of it. Deep down, what she really wanted to know was why Kegan had chosen Trevor over her.

"You eat and I'll tell ya."

She popped a piece of fruit in her mouth and looked at him expectantly.

"Well, Kegan showed up to my family's ranch one day looking for work. The old man never was one to turn down cheap labor and hired him on the spot. The man had a way of recognizing people who were desperate and then used it to his advantage. He hired Kegan for little more than room and board." Trevor looked down with an almost-embarrassed gesture. "Old man did that a lot."

"Doesn't sound like you think much of your dad?"

"Grew up hating the bastard, truth be told. Reckon I still do. He was rich and powerful and mean as shit." He turned his gaze back to hers. "But that's not important. The day he hired Kegan was the best thing that ever happened to me, so I guess I've forgiven him for some of his shortcomings."

Charlie felt a stab of envy as she thought of Trevor sharing his life with Kegan while she fought to heal her heart and forget. She didn't blame Trevor, just envied him.

"Sounds like you both got lucky." She cringed at how sad her voice sounded.

Trevor took her hand and squeezed. "He's a good man, Charlie. That's why you still love him and the reason I…" He looked down and coughed into his hand.

Charlie couldn't help but wonder exactly how deep the relationship was between them. She heard the respect and affection in Trevor's voice when he spoke of Kegan and the look of longing in his eyes.

"Does Kegan know you love him?" It wasn't really any of her business, but she couldn't take it back.

Trevor looked up at her with narrowed eyes. "It's not like that, Charlie. See, the thing with Kegan and me is that he's the first person in my life my old man didn't have to pay to hang out with me. I can't exactly explain what I feel for him, been trying to for quite some time now." He smiled a lopsided grin that made her toes curl. "It's a work in progress."

He caught the rung of her stool with his boot. He pulled her closer to him and wrapped his arms around her waist. "What about you, Charlie? What do you love about him?"

Charlie wasn't sure what it was she felt for Kegan anymore and wasn't convinced Trevor was the right person to be discussing it with. She had never even told Rae the whole truth about Kegan.

Over the years, she'd learned not to talk about him. Blocking him from her thoughts worked better for her sanity than remembering.

She took a deep breath and worked to show no emotion. "I don't, Trevor. I may have thought I did at one time. But it was just a silly teenage crush and a long time ago. I rarely thought of him until two weeks ago."

She raised her chin and forced herself to maintain eye contact. She hoped the show of confidence would convince him.

Trevor ducked his head, kissed just below her ear, and whispered, "You're such a terrible liar, Charlie."

She started to pull away in protest when a low, flat baritone voice filled the quiet and sent a chill racing along her spine. "Trev, we need to talk."

Charlie jerked away from Trevor's embrace, but he refused to let her flee. Dammit, he was always grabbing her. He held her against his body tighter. If she wasn't so scared to face Kegan right then, she would tell him just what kind of pushy bastard he was.

Trevor turned his head in Kegan's direction. "S'pose we do, as soon as you stop being a bastard and greet our guest properly." He leaned in closer and kissed her forehead before he let her go.

Charlie couldn't believe what was happening. What the hell was she supposed to say to Kegan right now? To make matters worse, he had just walked in on his best friend nuzzling her neck.

She turned in Kegan's direction and shielded most of her face from behind Trevor's body.

Kegan leaned against the door frame of the back door, his broad body taking up most of the space, his large arms crossed over his chest. His Stetson partially covered his eyes, but the hard set of his clenched jaw told her that he was less than happy about what he had just witnessed.

As she tried to get a read on Kegan's reaction to her, he tilted his hat back and his sparkling sapphire eyes met hers, the lines around them softening. But had they really softened or was she merely seeing something she wanted to see?

"Hello, Charlie."

God, just the sound of his voice was enough to bring her to her knees. Charlie lifted her head and faced him head-on, watched as a smile tugged at the corner of his handsome face.

"Hello, Kegan." To her surprise, her voice sounded calm and didn't betray the battle that raged inside. Perhaps it had been possible to keep her emotions in check, because he didn't show any signs of disgust that she usually saw in the dreams that haunted her night after night.

Chapter Six

Kegan sat on the back porch steps waiting for Trevor to join him after he showed Charlie to the restroom, puzzled about what had just happened in the kitchen.

He hadn't meant to be the bastard Trevor had accused him of. He'd just been beyond shocked to find them nuzzled together. It was the jealousy that had reared its ugly head when he'd seen them locked together that had come out as a gruff voice and curt statement. The thing was, he wasn't so much upset at seeing them together as he was with the realization that whatever was beginning to grow between Trevor and Charlie, he could never be a part of it.

He'd had time to think on why he'd been so upset at the thought of the two of them together and had realized that as possessive as he felt about Trevor, he knew he had no right to be. He certainly had no right to consider those feelings about Charlie.

He and Trevor had been recently talking about how old the one-night stands were getting, not that they didn't enjoy them. There wasn't much they hadn't done to a woman sexually.

They'd always picked up women who knew the score, one night with the two wild bachelors—they would fulfill her wildest, darkest fantasies, but that's where it ended. No snuggling all night, breakfast in the morning, or promises that they would call.

Fuck 'em hard and leave 'em fast but sated. Now things were changing. They wanted more and had talked about wanting to find one woman who would want to settle down with both of them. Not that there was a real good chance of ever finding a woman who could not only handle the social stigmas of a committed ménage à trois, but to also put up with the challenges of two very stubborn, demanding men.

Then, as now, he knew it was a fantasy. The chances of finding that one woman they could share in a lifelong relationship was slim to none. It only made sense that he should back away from both Trevor and Charlie, stop being a selfish bastard with dreams of something that would never happen and let the two of them see where their relationship could go.

The back door slammed and pulled Kegan from his thoughts. He looked up as Trevor sat down on the steps next to him.

"You pissed at me?" He didn't meet Kegan's gaze, only stared into the glass of wine in his hand.

"Nah, nothing to be pissed off about. Well, other than the fact that you keep giving me heart failure."

"Look, I'm sorry about that. I didn't plan to bring her here, it's just... I saw the way she looked and acted when she talked about you and I cracked. Next thing I knew, I was bringing her here. Figured you two needed to talk this out. Didn't really give much thought beyond that. Then after talking to her, I realized that I may have gone about it the wrong way, but I did the right thing. She loves you, Kegan, and you two have to talk."

"Trevor…"

"No, you shut up and listen to me. I'm sick of seeing you mope around here like a wounded puppy. Then I see her and she's acting the same way when I mention your name."

"Look…"

"Dammit, I said shut up. I'm talking now and you're damn well gonna listen."

Kegan ground his teeth. "Fine, but when you're through I get to have my say, so careful what you call me." Kegan figured it best to just let Trevor get whatever was bothering him off his chest or he wouldn't give him a moment's peace.

Trevor took a long, deep breath then blew it out in a huff. "I care a lot about you, and I can't stand to see you hurting. I'm not sure what it is about Charlie that has me so tied up in knots, but I can't stand to see her like this either. I want her, Kegan. Not for just one night, but for so much more."

Kegan nodded. "I saw the two of you together in the kitchen. You're beautiful together. You don't need Charlie and I to kiss and make up before you go after what you want. It's not your job to fix my problems. With what I did to Charlie, I don't think it can be fixed."

He rubbed his hand on the stubble starting to sprout on his chin. "I didn't do right by her, Trev, and just because I screwed up doesn't mean you have to pay for that. You two are both damn good people, you could have something special."

"Christ, you're a goddamn idiot, you know that? Didn't you listen to a fucking word I just said? The woman loves you!" Trevor flung his wineglass on the ground, shattering it.

"Just what do you think you would do if I ran off with Charlie anyway, become a fucking hermit? I know you think you need me when you're with a woman, maybe you do, but to be perfectly honest, I think I've grown to need it too. All I'm asking is that you just talk to her. If you can't work it out, I'll drop it and we can go back to being the most talked-about bachelors in the county."

Trevor stood and slapped him on the back. "Just think about it, that's all I ask." He left and went back into the house without a backward glance.

* * * *

Charlie was ready to go when Trevor came back inside. She didn't feel comfortable sitting in their house and had seriously thought about sneaking out of the front door and hitching a ride home. Curiosity had kept her planted in her seat.

"So did he talk some sense into you and you're going to stop holding me here against my will?"

"Nope. Wouldn't matter anyway since I'm too hardheaded to listen to reason most of the time." He sat on the stool next to her and took her hand. "What is it you really want, Charlie? If you want me to take you home right now I will, but I'm hoping you'll stick around for a while."

Charlie snatched her hand away and glared at him as she stood. "I told you he wouldn't want to talk to me. I'm not a fool, Trevor. I know what is going on. You told me that you and a friend liked to share women and were hoping to get lucky that night at Jack's Place. It didn't happen and it's not going to. Why can't you just accept that and find someone else to play with?"

Charlie heard the anger rise in her voice and didn't even try to suppress it. She was pissed off that he had forced her to come here and to talk to Kegan. She hadn't even realized until Trevor had walked back inside without Kegan that somewhere in the back of her mind she had hoped Kegan would want to talk to her.

Instead, she'd gotten a big helping of disappointment with a side order of humiliation. *Oh whoopee!*

Trevor stood so fast, his stool crashed to the floor behind him. Without even missing a beat, he stood over her, a dangerous glint in his dark eyes. "Is that what you think? That I brought you here today only with hopes to fuck you?"

Charlie didn't back down. "You know what? That's exactly what I think. You don't know a damn thing about me other than the fact that you danced with me in a bar and you wanted me to be the meat in your sexual sandwich." She waved her hands around in a dismissive manner. "Forget it. You've done enough to humiliate me for one day. I can find my own way back to town."

She stormed out of the kitchen and into the massive living room, Trevor right on her heels. She sat on the bench in the foyer and started to put on her boots. "Would you just go away and leave me alone? God, what is wrong with you? I'm sure you can find a filly or two around here that won't mind you sniffing after them. I happen not to be one of them." She pulled her boot back in her clenched fist and planned to throw it at his too-damn-sexy face if he took one more step toward her. "Go away!"

Kegan's deep laugh boomed behind Trevor.

Charlie jumped and dropped the boot.

Kegan then slapped Trevor on the back. "She always was a feisty little hellcat." He gave Trevor an unapologetic smile. "Guess I should have warned ya, huh?"

That right there was enough! Charlie snatched her boot from the floor and stomped her foot into it. She seethed with anger that consumed her body like a match to dry brush. She was furious at Kegan for his broken promises and refusal to talk to her. She was even more enraged at Trevor for having such control over her body and for humiliating her by forcing her to come here.

Above all, she was mad at herself for hoping. Hope was like frogs praying for wings so they didn't bump their asses when they hopped. But there weren't any flying fucking frogs! *Screw hope and these two cowboys with their little smirking faces.*

She reached for the door and yanked it open. "To hell with you both! I can find my own way home."

Trevor reached out for her. "It's fifteen miles. Let us take you home at least."

Before he could pull her in, she spun out of his grip. "Fifteen miles isn't that bad. Besides, I have a thumb." She held it up for emphasis.

"C'mon, Charlie! I'll forgive you for insulting me if you'll forgive me for kidnapping you."

Charlie stopped dead in her tracks and turned on him. "Forgive you? Are you fucking kidding me?"

Two weeks of sexual frustration plus years of hurt and loneliness boiled to the surface, and the careful shield she had hidden it all behind broke wide open. Charlie jabbed her finger into his chest.

"Look here, you arrogant bastard! I'm tired of your damn roaming hands enticing my body into something that I shouldn't be coaxed into. Keep your big paws off me or I swear I'll press charges against you for kidnapping."

"Now, now, bichito, he didn't mean anything by it," Kegan chuckled.

She turned that raw pain and anger on him. "And you! How dare you call me that! Don't you ever call me that again!" she screamed. "I am not your little bug. I haven't bugged you for eight fucking years. Eight years, Kegan. Eight goddamn years of me trying to figure out what the hell I did to make you leave." She slammed her hands against his chest over and over.

"You promised me you'd come back and you lied. You left me, and Gram died and I was completely alone and you still didn't come back!" The tears streamed down her face and she couldn't catch her breath or stop the flow of words coming from her broken heart.

"I never stopped wondering where you were and what you were doing. Wondering if you were okay, if you were happy and praying you were just as miserable as I was. Then I find you here and your life is wonderful. You have a great home, a great job, someone who loves you, and a string of women in your bed." She clawed at his chest, tried to rip his heart to shreds the way he had shredded hers. "You left me alone, scared and broken while you were off living the high life. Stupid me, I never stopped waiting for you, hoping that you'd come back, praying that you'd want me. Damn you, I tried to hate you but I never stopped loving you."

Her hands flew over her mouth. *Oh God, what have I done?*

Charlie felt lightheaded and her body shook so hard she couldn't stand. She was unable to catch her breath, the pressure on her chest a pain that was too hard to endure. Black dots swirled around her vision. Just before everything went black, she felt strong arms wrap around her.

Chapter Seven

Blinking her eyes open slowly, Charlie let her gaze adjust to the bright light. Dazed and unsure of where she was, she could tell she was lying on a bed, just not sure in whose bedroom. She glanced around until her eyes focused on Kegan sitting in a chair next to the bed.

His shoulders were slumped as he rested his forearms on his knees and stared at the floor.

Everything came back to her in a rush. *I never stopped waiting for you or loving you!*

How could she have lost such control? Charlie blinked rapidly, tried to hold back the tears that burned the backs of her eyes.

Christ, you're pathetic. No wonder Kegan left your stupid country ass. A small, desperate groan escaped her lips before she could stop it.

"You're awake."

Charlie closed her eyes like the coward she was, unable to meet his gaze. "I'm so sorry, Kegan. I shouldn't have… I didn't mean… Oh God, I shouldn't have hit you. I'm so sorry."

"Yeah, you should have. I deserved it, Charlie, and so much more."

She wasn't sure what to say. On one hand, she had wanted to cause him pain, for him to feel at least a fragment of the pain he caused her, but it still wasn't right. She had attacked him and he'd never lifted a hand to defend himself.

"No, it's not okay. No matter what I was feeling, I had no right. I'm sorry. I know saying sorry doesn't make it better, but please know I am. It was unfair to lash out at you just for living your life the way you choose. From everything I've seen and heard, you're a good man, Kegan. How can I be so selfish as to blame you for moving on and doing what was right for you?"

Kegan scooted his chair closer to the bed. "Please, Charlie, look at me."

She didn't want to face him knowing what she had done to him, but the tenderness in his voice compelled her to turn her head and open her eyes. His eyes were red-rimmed and swollen. His brows were drawn down, pain evident on his face.

"It's me who has no right to say I'm sorry. Saying it won't ever make up for what I did to you. I didn't realize—"

"Kegan, it's okay. You don't have to say anything."

"Yeah—yeah I do, Charlie." He ran his hands over his face before looking back at her. "I know you probably don't want to hear any excuses from me, and I won't blame you for telling me to get the hell out right now, but I'm hoping you'll give me a chance to try and explain."

She wasn't sure she was ready to hear why he'd stayed away. She'd been able to block out most of the pain from that part of her life into a little bubble, and she wasn't sure she wanted to open that up any further than she already had. It was one thing to let out what she was feeling, but she was scared of hearing what he would say.

The old saying 'ignorance is bliss' was so very true sometimes. But the sadness in his eyes won out over her fear and she nodded in encouragement for him to continue.

"See, I was pretty messed up the last day you found me by the river. My old man and I had gotten into one hell of a fight and I knew I couldn't stay. I didn't want to leave you, Charlie, I swear I didn't, but I couldn't stay anywhere near my old man. I wandered for a bit with no particular destination in mind, no money and nowhere to stay. I was getting pretty hungry and desperate when I walked up on the ranch Trevor's dad owns. He hired me, gave me a place to stay and three square meals, but that's all I had, Charlie. I didn't have any way of taking care of you and I figured you'd be a hell of a lot better off without someone like me.

"I swear, Charlie, I didn't know about your grandma. I knew in my heart that she would always take care of you since I couldn't. I'm so sorry she's gone." He paused to clear his throat, as if his confession was taking a toll on him.

Charlie wished she could reach out and soothe the pain on his face but wasn't sure she could. She stayed still and waited for him to continue.

"It took two years or so to get on my feet. I got there mostly due to Trevor's help. By then I figured I'd messed up everything with you and you wouldn't appreciate me showing back up in your life after that long. The longer time passed, the more I realized I had given up any right to have you." Kegan was wringing his big hands together so hard his knuckles were turning white. He lowered his head. "You are the only thing I missed after I left. I never stopped missing you, but I fought it. I didn't want to ruin your life."

Charlie felt her heart open up to Kegan's confession, but she was still wary. How could he have thought she cared about whether he had money or not? Had he really thought her so shallow that she wouldn't want him if he were poor? Hell, he'd been poor all his life and it hadn't mattered to her.

Her suspicious mind prevailed over the desire to comfort him as she thought of how lonely she had been after Gram had died. The only thing that had seemed to matter to her, that had helped her get through those hardest days of her life, was that Kegan would come back for her. She hadn't let anyone other than Rae get close to her in years because of his broken promise.

Did he have a clue what loneliness really felt like? She sat up in the bed, crossed her arms and hugged herself. She pushed farther away from Kegan, let her bitterness wash over her like an old friend to chase away the need to comfort. "You broke your promise because you were poor?" Charlie shook her head. "I have to wonder if you ever knew me, Kegan."

He looked up at her. "No! That's not what I meant. I knew I couldn't take care of you, Charlie. You had dreams and goals. I knew if I stuck around or you followed me, you wouldn't be able to reach them. It was hard for me to stay away, but I had to. You deserved so much more than what I could offer you." He lowered his arms onto the bed and held his head in his hands. "I'm so sorry, Charlie. I know I have no right to touch you, but God I wish I could just hold you once. I'm not so good with words, but if I could just hold you, I could show you what you mean to me."

Charlie had wanted that, had spent years dreaming and praying for Kegan to wrap her in his arms. Had missed him every day, even when she'd told herself she didn't. The need to feel his hands against her skin, even when the bitterness had consumed her.

Now as she stared at him, she didn't know how to reach out and touch him. She wasn't even sure she wanted to.

"You're right, Kegan, you don't have a right to ask. You made your choices and had no respect for me to allow me to make my own."

Kegan opened his mouth to speak when the door behind him opened.

"Everything okay?" Trevor asked as he entered the room.

Charlie felt some relief at his presence. She hadn't known how to respond to Kegan and was glad for Trevor's distraction.

"I'm fine. I'm not sure what came over me."

Trevor, clearly not feeling any of the awkwardness that she and Kegan felt, jumped onto the bed behind her and pulled her tight against his chest. "No apologies needed. I'm glad you finally got all that off your chest. Must have been a bitch carrying it around all these years." He stroked her hair as he spoke to Kegan. "See, you could learn a lot from this little wildcat. You don't always have to keep such a tight rein on your emotions all the damn time."

With his free hand, he stroked Charlie's leg, up and down, from her knee to the top of her thigh. Little sparks of electricity surged through her.

She had to be going insane. How could his touch arouse her while she was sitting there across from Kegan? Why in the hell didn't she push him away?

Kegan's eyes followed the movement of Trevor's hand as if the motion hypnotized him.

After a few more caresses, Charlie started to feel uncomfortable with the game. How far would Trevor go before provoking Kegan to respond? How long could she allow it to continue? Would her bitterness allow her to punish Kegan, allow someone else to touch her and throw it in his face that Trevor was able to touch her and that he had given up that right a long time ago? Or was she hoping that Kegan would finally respond in the way she had waited for nearly a lifetime to experience? Whatever the reason, she couldn't move. She didn't encourage Trevor or pray for one or the other, she just sat and waited.

His hands roamed over her belly, thumbs teasing the underside of her breasts. Trevor leaned down and brushed his lips against the side of her neck. "You feel so good, Charlie."

His voice was deep and husky. She knew Kegan had heard when his blue eyes dilated and darkened and his nostrils flared as he breathed in.

Trevor continued to explore, running his hands up her sides, across her collarbone, then sliding them lightly back down her body. The combination of his warm hands and Kegan's lust-filled gaze caused her heart to race and her breath to quicken. Her body seemed hyperaware of the presence of both men.

"He's aching to touch you. Let him, Charlie."

Her head swam, and arousal poured off both men in waves that were almost palpable they were so strong. It wrapped around her, caressed her skin like a lover's touch.

Kegan stood, his big body seeming to vibrate, yet he didn't reach for her. He stared down at her, his eyes roaming all over her body as if he were trying to decide where to touch first if invited.

"Reach out to him, Charlie," Trevor whispered, coaxing her, his breath hot against her ear.

She stopped thinking, shutting her brain off and giving in to the feeling. Before she'd even realized it, she responded to his command and held her hand out to Kegan.

After a slight hesitation, Kegan took it in his and moved to sit next to them on the bed. He leaned in as if to inhale her scent as his grip tightened on her hand. His free hand trembled as he placed it to her cheek. Her body instantly responded and she pushed into his hand. His eyes bored into hers as he breathed in shallow pants.

"Ah God, Charlie." He brushed his lips against hers.

As he breathed out, Charlie inhaled and his warm and familiar scent filled her. Trevor placed soft, delicate kisses to her neck as Kegan's mouth pressed against hers again.

Kegan swiped his tongue across her bottom lip and she opened to him. As his tongue found hers, they both moaned and deepened the kiss. Charlie wrapped her arms around his neck to pull him closer. The kiss was hard and passionate and she lost herself in the sensations. She had dreamed of this kiss for so many years, but none of her fantasies could prepare her for the reality of it. The dual sensation of both men's mouths at once took away her ability to form rational thought. Trevor lowered her onto the bed, sliding out from behind her. They rearranged themselves till he was on one side and Kegan on the other.

She was amazed at how they worked in tandem and controlled her body without saying a word to each other. This is what they did, they shared women, and how smoothly they worked together could only be a result of experience. The notion they had done this same thing many times before didn't sit well with her. Was she just another of their sexual conquests? What exactly was it they wanted from her? If it was just sex, she knew she couldn't deal with the loneliness that would surely destroy her in the aftermath.

She pulled her mouth away long enough for her to find her voice. "Wait."

Trevor nuzzled into her neck. "What is it, Charlie? Tell us what you need."

"I need to stop, to breathe. God, I need to think." Everything was happening too fast. She needed to get her thoughts straight. Kegan had told her he had missed her, thought about her, but he'd never said he loved her. Did she really want to open up those old hurts? How could she trust his words? She didn't even know him anymore.

"I'm sorry. I just need time to sort this all out. I'm not sure I can trust..." She shook her head. "I'm not sure of what I'm feeling right now."

Kegan stood, took a step back and gave her room to rise. She looked up into his beautiful sapphire-blue eyes. She tried to find any signs of deceit, wanted to hate him, but found tenderness, which only made it worse.

She wanted to stay mad at him, blame him for all the years of loneliness, but she knew that was unfair. She hoped that she was more than just another one of their women, but false hope always hurt in the end and she knew it.

"I'd like to freshen up." Her voice was barely above a whisper.

Kegan tried to smile, but it didn't reach his eyes. "Of course. We'll be on the back porch if you need anything." He turned and walked away, his shoulders hunched.

"It's going to be okay, Charlie," Trevor said behind her. "Kegan has a hard time talking about his feelings, but I know he cares about you. Just be patient with him. Please."

The anger flooded back. Anger she could deal with. It had become a familiar friend. It was much better than the hurt and confusion. It allowed her to regain some control of herself.

"No, Trevor, it's not okay. I don't owe him patience. If he's hurt, embarrassed, or whatever it is he's feeling, it's your fault. You had no right to bring me here and force Kegan to have to deal with his past. It should have been his choice, not yours." She tightened her arms around herself to keep from trembling. "You made him lust after me with your little game, and it was unfair. To all of us." She headed for the door.

"Charlie?"

She stopped at the door but didn't turn around. "What?"

"I'm not sorry I brought you here. I'm only sorry that I've given you the impression that the only reason I brought you here was about sex. I hope you'll give us a chance to show you it's more than that."

Unsure of how to respond, Charlie walked away.

* * * *

Trevor joined Kegan on the back porch, handed him a cold beer before opening his own, then sat in the chair next to him. "We seem to be spending a lot of time out here lately."

"S'pose we are."

Trevor took a long pull from his beer. "What are we going to do about her?"

That was the million-dollar question, wasn't it? Kegan knew what he wanted to do with her. He wanted to keep her close and replace all the bad memories with good ones to take away some of the pain he had caused. He'd give just about anything to have the chance.

"I'm not sure what we can do. I don't even know if I have a right to ask her for a chance."

"It has to start somewhere. Hiding is a lot easier than facing the hard stuff, but it won't get you what you want. She's mad as hell at me right now, but it won't stop me from going after her. So you have to ask yourself — are you going to be a coward and hide, or are we going to figure out how we get Charlie?"

"And then what? What exactly would we be offering her if we are able to win her over?"

Kegan didn't want a single night with Charlie, he wanted a lifetime. He'd compared every woman he had ever been with to her. Not a single one of them could bring out the feelings within him that Charlie did. She'd owned a big chunk of his heart and soul since he was eighteen years old, and he knew that would never change. "What exactly do you want from Charlie, Trev?"

"I'm not sure," Trevor admitted then took another long pull on his beer before continuing. "The only thing I do know is there is something about her that calls to me. I want to know everything about her, all her secrets and desires. I don't want to just have sex with her, if that's what you're asking me. But in all honesty, Kegan, I have never been affected by anyone like I have been by her." He ran his hand through his hair as he stared at Kegan. "What about you? Are you willing to share Charlie with me or do you hope to claim her as solely yours?"

Kegan had thought about that same question since first learning that Trevor had met Charlie. When he was younger, he had always dreamed of sweeping Charlie off her feet, marrying her and spending the rest of his life loving her.

Things had changed. His dreams were different and his idea of a perfect life wasn't just him and Charlie anymore. It was the three of them together.

I think I have grown to need it too.

Trevor's words kept playing in his head. It was one thing to talk about the two of them settling down with one woman, but totally another to actually do it. Was it fair to chase Charlie when he was so unsure of where he and Trevor were headed and what they wanted?

Kegan could admit to himself that he could in fact share Charlie's heart if he could ever win it back. What he wasn't so sure of was whether he should try to or not. He wasn't willing to give up Trevor for Charlie, but what if she asked him to? As much as he wanted a life with Charlie, as much as he wanted to make up for all the pain he had caused her, he didn't think he could do it at a price as high as losing Trevor.

Kegan finished the rest of his beer, then answered. "I could share Charlie with you, body and heart. I hope that she could grow to love us both, but I don't want us going after her if you're not committed to having more than just sex with her. She never has been nor would she ever be just a one-night stand for me."

Kegan cleared his throat. This last part was the hardest. "You'd have to be committed to both of us." He kept his gaze locked on the empty beer bottle, afraid to meet Trevor's gaze.

"I'm already committed to you, Kegan, have been for a long time. The only thing missing from our lives is the one woman we can both care for. I would like the chance to find out if Charlie is that person, but if she isn't—"

The sound of the back door opening had them on their feet and staring at Charlie as she came outside. She looked tired and a little dazed. "Would you mind taking me home, Trevor?"

Trevor walked over and put an arm around her waist. Kegan was relieved when she didn't flinch or pull away.

"We both will."

She looked up at Trevor, then met Kegan's eyes and nodded. "Thank you."

* * * *

The ride back into town was quiet. Charlie sat rigid between them and stared straight ahead.

Kegan should say something, tell her how much he wanted her to stay with him and Trevor. Hell, he was ready to move her in tonight, but she was far from ready to hear that. Thankfully, Trevor seemed to be deep in thought as well and wasn't pushing.

Trevor could be a bloodhound on a scent when he wanted something. He didn't take no for an answer and pursued what he wanted until he got it. Trevor kept his hand on her thigh, though, his thumb stroked absently as if he needed the contact with her. Kegan fought his own urge to touch her. He didn't want to scare her any more than they already had and she seemed to draw comfort from Trevor's touch.

If only she could feel the same way about his.

He had seen how wary she was of him and knew it would take time for her to accept him. He had seen the distrust and he deserved it, he just had to figure out how in the hell he was going to convince her that he was someone she could count on.

As they drove into town, Kegan realized he couldn't let Charlie know that he already knew where she lived. It would probably freak her that he had spent many of his evenings staring up at her windows. "Which way now, Charlie?"

She turned and blinked at him a couple of times. "Oh…um…turn left there on Main Street. It's the fourth house on the right."

He pulled up in front of the large Victorian home. "Wow, this is your place?"

She looked at the house and nodded. "I have one of the upstairs apartments."

He stepped out of the truck and offered her his hand. She stared at it, seemed to consider it for a moment, then finally decided to accept his help. He hated the way she hesitated to touch him.

Charlie slid out of the truck, her hand rested in his for a moment longer before she pulled away. To Kegan, it was a small victory.

Trevor jumped out from his side of the truck and came to stand next to them, then slipped his arm around Charlie's waist. "C'mon, we'll walk you to the door, and then you can invite us inside." He winked at Kegan.

So much for not pushing her. Kegan fell in step behind them as Charlie allowed Trevor to lead her to the side entrance and up the stairs to her apartment. Once at the top, she stopped and drew out of his hold.

"I'm sorry. I really do need some time alone if you don't mind." She looked back and forth between him and Trevor and sighed. "You two are a little overwhelming, and it's hard for me to think when I'm around you."

Trevor brushed a loose strand of hair behind her ear and stroked her cheek. "Then don't think, Charlie. Sometimes it's better to just feel."

She looked up at Kegan as if pleading with him to understand her need to be alone. He leaned toward her and gently brushed his lips against her temple. "It's okay, Charlie. You don't have to invite us in tonight, but will you think about seeing us again?"

Her brilliant green eyes locked on his, and he could see the battle swirling in them — confusion and wariness, but also need and desire. He took that as a small hope that she would see them again. He kissed her cheek and stepped back.

Trevor placed a chaste kiss to her lips. "That's the second time today you've gotten a reprieve."

He kissed her again, turned, then made his way down the stairs, Kegan close behind. "Remember, Charlie, it's only a reprieve, not a pardon."

Chapter Eight

"Oh. My. God. You mean to tell me that two hot, sexy as hell cowboys want to make you the third in their sandwich and you had them bring you home?" Rae shook her head in obvious disappointment. "Please tell me you are at least thinking about taking them up on their offer?"

"Dammit, Rae, do you ever think with anything above your waist? I swear if I didn't know better, I'd think you had a dick between those legs of yours."

Of course, Charlie had thought the same thing when both Trevor and Kegan had been kissing and touching her. They had heated her body to burning and stolen her ability to think past the need for their touch. Her entire being had craved them. The only thing that had stopped her from giving in to what her body begged for was the stronger need to protect her heart.

"Charlie, why can't you, just once, enjoy something without having to overthink it? You act as if men are the only ones allowed to enjoy the pleasures of the flesh. I swear the stress you put on your brain is gonna cause you to stroke one of these days." She flopped down on Charlie's couch, beer in hand, and patted the seat next to her. "And I won't be the one to push you around in a wheelchair or wipe the drool from your chin."

Charlie sat down and snuggled into her friend. Rae always tried to make light of most situations, but she knew that she could always count on her to listen. "It's not as simple as just enjoying the moment. You know how I felt about Kegan and it's hard to just forget all those years of uncertainty and anger." She looked at Rae. "I wish I knew how but I don't."

"I know it's hard, babe, but maybe this is what you need. Perhaps you need to take control over them and that will take away the power you think they have over you."

Could it be that easy? Would she be able to handle both of them? If she could figure out how to leave her heart at home — oh, and her traitorous body — she might have a chance.

"I don't know, Rae. In theory it sounds simple, but when I'm around the two of them, it's like my brain is on vacation and I can't seem to think."

"Yeah, but from what you've told me, both times you've seen Kegan, it was more of a surprise you weren't prepared for. Certainly all the times you've seen Trevor he's been in control. So next time, you set the scene — control the place, time and amount of contact you will allow. I know you care about Kegan and you have some obstacles to overcome where he is concerned, but you won't ever know if it can be defeated if you don't at least take a chance." Rae pulled at her hair playfully. "And if you can't control them and it gets to be too much, call me and I'll take them off your hands. It would be the least I could do for a friend."

They both cracked up laughing. "Oh God, you're just too much." Charlie was glad she had called Rae instead of sitting alone to worry and fret. She was still uncertain but at least she no longer felt miserable. "So tell me, Dr. Rae, in your professional opinion, how does one go about controlling two very overwhelming and smokin' hot cowboys?"

"It's really quite simple, actually. As you so eloquently put it, men think with their dicks first, their smaller brains second. The challenge for you is to keep them off balance. Keep them so full of lust and need that they will do anything just to catch a whiff of your scent." Rae clinked her beer against Charlie's. "Then you blow their minds and make them beg for more."

Charlie was just about to ask what to do if it was her mind that got blown, but the ringing of her cell phone interrupted. She checked the caller ID to see Dr. Stone's number. "Hello."

"Good evening, Charlie. I hope all went well at the ranch today."

Shit! She had been such a mess after Kegan and Trevor had dropped her off she had forgotten to check in with him. What was it that Trevor had said? Something about a sick colt? "Uh, yes, sir, everything went fine, false alarm."

"Good, glad to hear that. Listen, the reason I am calling is, why don't you take the next couple of days off to get your stuff packed? I can pick you up on Friday to take you out to the ranch."

"Pack my stuff, sir?"

"You do remember I told you that you will be required to work as an on-site doctor during the birthing season?"

"Oh right. Yes, sir, I remember. I thought I would be going out next Monday, but this weekend is fine."

"Good. I know it's a little early, but this will give you time to get settled. Mr. Kingsington is worried that one of his mares is likely to go early, so he requested that you come this weekend."

Charlie's pulse quickened as panic started to overwhelm her. "Mr. Kingsington?"

"Yes. I send a resident out to their ranch every year. I do believe we talked about it. You'll get more experience there than anywhere else in this area. You've already been out to the Trev-Ke, so you shouldn't have any problem settling in. Look, Charlie, I have another call. I'll see you at nine on Friday."

"Wait! Dr. Stone... Hello?"

Charlie gasped for breath as she turned to Rae. "I hope you have a Plan B because Trevor just took control again."

"Breathe, Charlie. It's okay. Just breathe and tell me what happened."

"No, it's not okay. You told me to take control of the time and place and that bastard took it away." She took a few deep breaths, tried to ease the panic coursing through her. "Take one guess where I'll be living come Friday night?"

* * * *

The first streaks of gray streamed through the small kitchen window as Charlie sipped her first cup of coffee. Sleep had been a rare commodity the last couple of days, with last night being the worst. Her first plan after learning she would be staying at Trev-Ke Ranch was to run. Hell, even running away to join the carnival or a convent had both been briefly entertained. Yet here she sat, waiting for Dr. Stone to arrive.

She really couldn't say she was still mad at Trevor so much. Hadn't she sat in this very room making plans to control him and Kegan? What pissed her off was that he had beaten her to it.

Damn cocky cowboy.

She liked being in control, had spent most of her life learning to rule her emotions. Control meant order and without it chaos, which she couldn't tolerate. After the panic had subsided, Charlie had begun to plan. The last two days had been spent trying to figure out how to regain some of the power those two cowboys had over her. Since leaving her body at home wasn't an option, she had decided to take a little of Rae's advice.

Now she sat with a suitcase full of the sexiest clothes she owned and an entire collection of new undergarments that made her blush.

They might have won the battle, but they certainly wouldn't win the war for control.

Since Trevor seemed to have such command over her body, she was going to use it against him. She had known since puberty the effect her body had on men, that she had been blessed with a long lean body and curves in all the right places.

A smile curled her lips as she brought the coffee to her mouth. When she was done with him, Trevor would have to redefine the meaning of cocktease.

She downed the rest of her coffee, her mood turning sober when her musings settled on Kegan. He owned her heart and he wasn't really anything she should play with. Though he told her he had missed her, it wasn't an admission of love.

The thought of allowing him back into her life only for him to leave her again scared the hell out of her. If she could just keep her heart off her sleeve and hidden away from him, then maybe...

Maybe nothing! It will kill you and you know it.

Charlie sighed as she took her cup to the sink and, resting her hands on the counter and staring out of the window, watched the sun finally rise. Well if she couldn't keep her heart out of it, then maybe she could at least show Kegan just what a fool he had been for walking away from her.

* * * *

"Wakey, wakey."

How in the hell does anyone sound that fucking cheery in the morning? He was so not a morning person, but Kegan obviously was today if his happy voice was any indication. "Sleep," Trevor grumbled and snuggled deeper into the bed, hoping to get a little more shut-eye.

"Get up. Do you know what today is?"

"Yeah, the day I kick your ass if you don't go away and let me sleep."

"C'mon, Trev, don't make me pull your sorry ass out of that bed. We got shit to do before she gets here."

Trevor pulled the covers over his head and groaned. "I *am* getting shit ready. I'm making sure I have my strength for when that little hellcat gets here. You know she's going to be major pissed that I pulled strings with John to get her out here early."

"I've already done the morning chores, freshened up her room with flowers, showered and shaved. So if you want Charlie to see just how damn ugly you are in the mornings on her first day here, then it's no skin off my ass."

Damn, the man was like a gnat you just couldn't swat away no matter how many swipes you took. "What time is it?"

"Eight-forty-five."

"Fuck! Why in the hell didn't you say that in the first place?" Trevor jumped out of bed and nearly hit the floor as he tried to get the covers unwrapped from around himself. "Dammit, Kegan, why did you let me sleep so late?"

"Hmm, let me think about that. Could it be because you're such a sweetheart early in the morning? I'll meet you downstairs. Coffee's ready."

Trevor stumbled into the bathroom. He used the facilities then adjusted the shower, and stepped in. He lathered the shampoo into his hair and ran the soap over his humming body, eager to have Charlie close.

She'd finally be at the ranch where she belonged and he could stop taking so many damn cold showers. He'd been worked up since she'd been with him the last time, and he was getting damn tired of trying to control his lust.

He ran his soapy hands down his body and cupped his balls in one hand while he ran the other up and down his growing erection. He should be hurrying to meet Kegan in the kitchen, but he was as hard as granite and doubted he could make it through the day with Charlie around and not relieve a little pressure first.

God, she makes me like a fucking green lad.

Trevor could still imagine her scent and the way her body trembled when he touched her. He stroked harder, the vision of Kegan watching as he caressed up and down her luscious body filled his mind. His hand tightened. He imagined it was her delicious mouth wrapped around him, sucking him hard.

Trevor's knees began to buckle and he reached out and placed one hand against the tile wall as he felt heat race along his spine. He thrust hard into his hand as his balls drew up tight. He threw his head back, swallowing a silent scream as the first burst of his release shot from his body. He had to bite down on the inside of his cheek to keep from yelling out as his body jerked with each pulse of his orgasm.

"Get your ass moving!" Kegan banged on the door as the last drops of cum dripped from Trevor's still-throbbing cock.

Trevor chuckled to himself as he rinsed off. "Fuck off."

Kegan had his preparations to take care of and Trevor had his.

Chapter Nine

Trevor and Kegan said their goodbyes to Dr. Stone as Charlie stood in the front foyer of the Trev-Ke home, suitcase in hand, and tried to calm her raging emotions.

This was such a bad idea on so many different levels. Why in the hell had she even thought that she would be able to control anything about these two?

The moment they'd pulled up in front of the house, Charlie's gaze had settled on Kegan and Trevor as they'd stood on the front porch waiting for her, and her body battled her brain for supremacy.

Kegan was dressed in tight-fitting jeans and a white button-up shirt stretched across his massive chest. The first two buttons left undone showed off his smooth, sun-darkened skin, and his light hair brushed the tips of his shoulders, framing the amazing dimpled smile that stretched wide across his face.

Trevor was the dark contrast to Kegan's blond boyish good looks. He was dressed in those damn loose jeans that hung low—did the man not realize how sexy and inviting they were? He had to know that they begged a hand to slip down the front of them. A tight plaid shirt accentuated his equally impressive chest. The stark difference in their appearance was even more pronounced by the looks on their faces.

While Kegan had a happy, almost childlike look to his smile, Trevor had his Stetson pulled low over his dark eyes, and a devilish smirk pulled at the corners of his full lips.

Charlie had to give herself a mental shake as the image of them naked and wrapped around her filled her vision and she felt her insides spasm.

Shit! So not good! You can't even look at them without losing control. Good luck!

After telling that pesky little voice inside her head to shut the hell up, she had stepped out of the truck with a confident set to her head and shoulders and greeted them professionally. She'd refused to let her hand tremble even slightly as she'd shaken their hands.

She'd looked up into each one of those way-too-sexy gazes with her best detached look and thanked them for the opportunity to work with their amazing animals, blah blah blah…

Kegan's hand had lingered just a moment on hers, his thumb caressing her skin. The sensation had rippled straight along her arm and back down her chest to explode between her legs.

Well, at least her control had lasted for five minutes. Not good enough. She definitely needed to work on that if she was going to survive the next thirty days and come out of it in one piece. Charlie groaned at the enormity of the battle she faced.

Kegan stepped into the foyer and reached for her suitcase. "I'll show you where you'll be staying."

She snatched back on the handle and refused to let him take the case. "I can carry my own belongings, thank you very much."

Kegan shook his head, chuckling. "I'm sorry. I forgot how independent you are. It won't happen again." He held out his arm, allowing her to precede him up the stairs.

Her head jerked up as she heard Trevor bound through the front door and make his way up the stairs behind them.

"Kegan, you damn country bumpkin, why the hell is she carrying her own bag?"

"Piss off," Kegan grumbled. "Why don't you come up here and try to take it from her? I could use a good show."

Trevor pushed past Kegan as they reached the top of the stairs, elbowed him out of the way, then grabbed her suitcase from her before she could protest or tighten her hand around the handle.

He ducked his head close to her face, placed a soft kiss to her gaping mouth, and with his gaze locked with hers, said, "Sometimes you have to show a woman what she needs."

His eyes roamed over her body slowly, and his tongue darted out to lick across his bottom lip as he returned his gaze to hers. He had the look of a man starved preparing to devour a feast. She shuddered.

"You have to listen to what she's saying, not just the words she's using." He winked as he brushed past her, then went down the hall, opened a door and waited.

Charlie's face heated with a combination of outrage at his pushy attitude and a powerful kick of arousal.

Bastard.

Charlie stormed toward him and refused to acknowledge his cocky smirk or Kegan's belt of laughter behind her.

She stepped into a large suite. Unlike the rest of the house, this room had a distinctly feminine feel. It was pretty obvious what they used it for.

A large four-poster bed sat as a focal point, covered with luxurious fabrics in hues of royal purple and shimmering silver. Large vases of flowers filled the space with the pleasing scent of jasmine and heather.

Trevor set her suitcase on the bed and opened a door to a large walk-in closet. "You can put your things in here."

Kegan walked to a set of ornately carved double doors and pulled one open. "This is your private bath."

Charlie stepped closer and couldn't help but whistle. A large Jacuzzi tub sat directly in the center of the room surrounded by candles and fresh-cut flowers. The tub was clearly large enough for more than just a private bath. Ornate mirrors decorated three of the walls, while a fourth had an enclosed shower that encompassed the entire length. Like the bath, it looked like it could accommodate a small sports team, rather than just one.

Oh yeah! This just proves what they use this room for.

Charlie ignored the twinge of jealousy as well as the two heated looks she was getting from Kegan and Trevor. She needed to stay focused for the battle.

"It's beautiful and far more than I'll need as I plan to spend most of my time in the stables." She shot Trevor a look that dared him to object. "If you and Kegan would excuse me, I'd like to unpack and get a look at the mare requiring my immediate attention."

* * * *

The temperature for early April was in the mid-seventies, a rarity for this part of the country this time of year, and Charlie took full advantage of it.

Not only was she enjoying the gorgeous sunny day, but it also allowed her to set one of her plots into action. She dressed in light khaki pants made of a stretch material that hugged her ass and hips. The black thong she had chosen was barely visible beneath the thin fabric, but hinted just enough to roaming eyes at the lack of material.

A tight red tank top completed her ensemble. She rarely wore it in public as it had an irritating way of riding up to expose her stomach and back, but today it was perfect. She left her long hair down, allowing it to gently tickle the exposed flesh of her lower back as she walked. Her hair appeared to be a weakness for Trevor, since he couldn't seem to stop himself from reaching out and touching it whenever he got the chance.

On the way to the barn, she had to tighten her lips and restrain her smile, as more than one stable hand's head turned in her direction as she walked by. She nearly laughed outright when she entered the barn and Kegan looked up with a dumbfounded expression on his face.

She could just picture his tongue rolling out the side of his mouth and him drooling like a big hound dog. He strode quickly to her side and scanned the area around him to see if anyone had noticed her. He stopped inches away from her in a male dominant stance of possession.

First shot, direct hit. Yay me.

She giggled to herself and glanced at him, her expression neutral and her voice professional when she said, "I would like to examine my patient if you would be so kind as to point me in her direction."

Kegan stared at her, a confused and befuddled look on his face. This was exactly what she wanted, to see both men off balance. Over the last couple of days, since she had become their live-in vet, they had used every excuse they could think of to spend as much time with her as possible.

She had kept them both at bay for the most part, refusing to talk about anything personal with them and keeping their conversations to a strictly professional level. She was proud that she was able to keep enough control over herself to hide the fact that they had driven her mind-numbingly insane with lust most days. She was grateful to hide behind the locked door of her room and relieve herself. Her only consolation was that she had driven them just as insane.

Kegan placed his hand at the small of her back and led her toward a large foaling stall. It was empty. "Well?" she asked.

Kegan shrugged his shoulders. "Cade has her out back to groom her." His voice was deep and husky, which could only be described as being barely controlled sexual frustration.

How do you like it?

"You can wait here, and I'll bring her in to you."

"No, I'll head out there since she's the reason I'm here." She flashed him a brilliant smile then turned away in the direction of the back door. It didn't surprise her in the least when he fell in step directly behind her. She could feel his eyes boring into her backside and fought the urge to wiggle her ass just a little more wantonly. In the end, logic won out. It was one thing to bait a bear but another entirely to poke a stick at it.

Stepping out behind the barn, she spotted Trevor speaking to a devilishly handsome man with sun-darkened skin and wide eyes that reminded her of the dark blue of twilight. He was much smaller than Kegan and Trevor, standing about five foot eight. Then again, most men were small compared to them.

As they approached, he waved in their direction and drawled, "Afternoon, boss."

She recognized the voice as Cade's, though she hadn't actually seen the man's face the first time she had been here. She snuck a peek in Trevor's direction and ignored his dark, brooding expression. Charlie reached out to shake Cade's hand.

"Hello, I'm Dr. McCarty, but you can call me Charlie. We seem to keep missing each other. I'm very glad I finally got the chance to meet you in the flesh. I look forward to working with you."

Flirting? Who her? Nah.

As he took her hand, she could practically feel the simultaneous snorts that came from the two men now flanking her. Cade didn't seem intimidated at all by the scowling cowboys behind her.

"Welcome to the ranch, Charlie." His smile was bright and there was a hint of amusement to his tone. He bent and placed a kiss to the top of her knuckles as he bowed. "I think you and I will get on right nicely."

She was impressed as hell and instantly liked the man. He hadn't even flinched when Trevor had let out a low growl as his lips had touched her skin.

Trevor leaned in closer to her. "Charlie, can I have a word with you?"

"Sure. Right after I'm done with my patient, I'll be sure to give you a full report." She gave Cade a wink and could swear he was holding back his laughter.

"Now, Charlie." Trevor's voice was nearly a grunt as he tried to control his frustration.

She was done taking orders from him or allowing him to command her to his will. She spun around and glared up at him, hands on her hips. "And I said when I am done with my patient." She turned her back on him before he could respond and, in a syrupy sweet voice, asked Cade, "Do you have her chart? I'd like to review it before examining her."

Cade's broad smile grew even bigger, if that was possible, and he motioned her toward the barn. "Right this way, ma'am."

She didn't even glance back, but she could feel their stares and let her own smile broaden.

Kegan stood beside Trevor, stunned as Charlie moved toward the barn with Cade.

"I am going to paddle that stubborn little ass but good."

Kegan huffed at Trevor's barely controlled anger. "I do believe we have been challenged."

"Duh! We're going to have to rethink this. She's stubborn as hell. Has she always been like this?"

Kegan remembered the time when she was sixteen and had shown up at the drive-in with Johnnie Carroll. It hadn't mattered that he knew she was doing it simply because he had told her to stay away from Johnnie. The boy was just bad news and Kegan had been pissed to see her in the same car as that loser, not to mention that she'd seemed to find perverse pleasure in defying him. He had snatched the door open, pulled her from the car and warned her, "Time to go home, bichito."

She had glared at him, anger burning in her brilliant green eyes. "Kegan Colburn. You take your hands off me this instant. You have no right to manhandle me."

When he had tried to pull her away from the car, she had dug her heels in and slapped at him, growling, "You take your hands off me right this instant or I swear you'll pay for this."

Kegan had done the only thing he'd been able to think of at the time. He'd picked her up, tossed her over his shoulder, put her in his car and taken her home. She'd screamed the entire drive. After he'd deposited her on her front porch, she'd stomped off madder than a drenched cat and had refused to speak to him for over a month. Instead, she'd kept showing up at the lake whenever he was there and had pranced around in her damn string-thing of a bikini, giggling and laughing at the fool boys chasing after her. She'd stopped every so often to send a nasty glare in his direction.

Kegan shook his head and brought his thoughts back to the present. "You have no idea, Trev."

He watched as Trevor's eyes darkened, a dangerous glint shining in them. He recognized that look and knew things were going to get very interesting around here. Trevor never backed down from a challenge, and this time the stakes were higher than they ever had been.

Kegan had always known that Charlie could affect him like no one else. One touch of her fingertips against his skin made him damn near forget his own name. He had watched his only friend grow up, and as she'd matured, he had looked at her with different eyes and had ached for her.

She'd been fifteen the first time he'd realized that Charlie had moved beyond a friend. Since he'd been nineteen and considered an adult at the time and she had still been a kid, it had just proven to him that he was a sick bastard. Though he'd never acted on those feelings, even when she would teasingly run her fingers through his hair, blow pouty kisses at him with her full lush lips or bat her long thick lashes with a 'you know you want me' look in her eyes, he'd just watched and ached.

She was now twenty-five and Trevor was just learning the power that was Charlie.

The same power that she had always wielded over Kegan now captured his best friend.

* * * *

By the end of the first week, both men had been reduced to randy lads, ready to shoot in their jeans if the wind blew just right.

The little vixen had kept just out of their reach for days, swishing and swaying her hips at them as they followed behind her like a couple of horny tomcats chasing a scent.

She giggled and flirted with the ranch hands until Kegan and Trevor were ready to kill every damn man on the ranch that dared to look at her.

Kegan felt the reins he kept tightly bound around his control begin to fray. His possessive instincts screamed at him to claim her now. They needed to stake their territory, so that every man knew to whom she belonged.

"Trev, I can't hold back much longer. She's killing me," he growled as he watched Charlie lean over the rail of the corral and laugh with one of the stable hands. Her pert little ass, raised high, just begged for a good spank. Trevor stood next to him, seething as he clearly tried to get hold of his own control. His body was wound so tight, the man was on the verge of exploding.

"It's time Charlie learns just who in the hell she belongs to," Kegan announced.

He knew Trevor was done waiting too. It had been nearly four weeks since either of them had first touched her, and Kegan had waited even longer to claim her. They needed to be inside her and hear her scream their name as they possessed her body and soul.

Kegan's hunger darkened and burned through him. God help him, he knew he could wait no longer.

"C'mon, Trev, I'm done waiting." He stalked off, not caring if his best friend followed or not.

He headed in Charlie's direction, eager to claim their woman.

* * * *

Charlie knew the exact moment she had pushed Kegan and Trevor too far. She had felt their desire grow all week until they were ready to burst. She'd stoked that fire, let it wane slightly before pouring more gasoline on it, only to let it simmer down to embers before stirring it up again.

Instead of just baiting them, she'd poked at them with that damn stick over and over. Charlie felt the heat radiating off them as they moved up behind her.

"Are you finished for the day?" Trevor's voice was dangerously smooth.

"Oh, I'm far from finished." She tossed her hair over her shoulder.

Poke, poke.

The stable hand with her was not as brave as Cade. His eyes had gone wide with the approach of the two men and sweat appeared on his brow. He swallowed hard a couple of times and his eyes dilated further. A real look of terror distorted his face as Kegan and Trevor scowled at him.

"S'cuse me, Miss Charlie, I—I gotta get back to work," he stuttered as he backed away.

Coward! She prepared to make a quick exit herself when a large arm wrapped around her waist, pulled her from the fence and she was carried in the direction of the house.

"What the hell are you doing?" she huffed. "Kegan Colburn, I'm not some stupid sixteen year old you can manhandle. Put me down this instant!"

"Oh, Charlie, I am very, very aware that you are no longer sixteen," he growled into her ear as he tightened his grip.

She glanced over at Trevor. He wore the same expression of pure male arrogance as Kegan. "Dammit, Trevor, can't you control him?" The hunger burning in his dark eyes told her he had lost his ability to control himself, let alone anyone else.

"You pushed us to this, sweetheart. Now we're going to give you exactly what you've begged for all week."

Had she intentionally pushed them too far? She had watched them slowly unravel all week, yet she had kept pushing. Had she actually begged them to take control away from her?

Charlie had only set out to put them off balance, yet she had to admit that as the week had gone on and she'd been able to see the fires of longing raging through them, it had begun to spark her own need. Their lust and desire bore into her through heated eyes and ignited her deep in her core. The power of unhinging these two powerful men had become like a drug. She had known she was pushing them to their breaking point and still couldn't stop. She hadn't realized until it was too late that in her greed, she had handed them the power on a silver platter. Was she ready to pay for that self-indulgence?

She had pushed them to this and now she'd have to surrender. The idea caused Charlie to grit her teeth. The hell she did. She squashed the little voice in her head that doubted her resolve. She could still control this. Couldn't she?

Trevor held the door open as Kegan entered the massive living area with her still held tightly in his arms.

"Kegan, I mean it, put me down. This is ridiculous."

He ignored her demand but let her slide down his body until he held her in his arms, her feet suspended off the floor. His heated gaze locked on hers as he lowered his head and took her mouth in a possessive kiss.

He slid his tongue into her mouth and mingled with hers. She opened up further, his taste making her lightheaded. He slid his tongue along hers, and she moaned softly as he pulled his lips from hers to kiss and lick his way across her jaw. He left a wet trail from his open-mouthed kisses and scraped his teeth across her sensitive skin.

"God, Charlie, I want you so bad. You don't know how long I've wanted you," Kegan murmured against the sensitive flesh beneath her ear.

Everything was happening in a rush. She needed to ask him what exactly he wanted from her, but before she could form any words, Trevor's mouth covered hers. His lips weren't as hard and fast as Kegan's, but sweet and tender. With a slow, gentle caress, he explored her tongue with his own. The combination of his taste mingled with Kegan's was an erotic double-punch of musk, spice and pure male.

As Trevor pulled his mouth away, Kegan's was there to take his place. Trevor moved up behind her, caressing her, and he encouraged her to lean her head on his shoulder as he placed hungry kisses along her neck.

Kegan's large hands touched and roused her muscles to respond, and he shifted and adjusted her position until she had her legs wrapped around his waist. He hissed as her groin connected with the rock-hard bulge in his jeans.

They overwhelmed her, didn't give her time think, and barely let her breathe. Her body hummed in anticipation and fear. She didn't fear them hurting her in the physical sense, but that they would completely consume her, strip her emotions bare and leave her broken. She tried again to pull away, but Kegan clasped her cheeks, refused to let her break the kiss.

Trevor must have sensed her hesitation and whispered, "Stop thinking, Charlie, just feel." His voice rough with arousal

"Wait," she mumbled into Kegan's mouth. He broke the kiss but kept his lips against hers, their breathing and passion mingling while their eyes locked. There was a fire blazing in his eyes. Hunger, need, as well as soul-deep pain shone in his beautiful blue eyes.

She felt her heart open up to him, her need to comfort him automatic. She blinked away the tears that tried to escape. The ache to have him nearly suffocated her.

She wanted what they were both offering her, wanted to feel without thinking just this once. To let someone else have control and simply feel pleasure, but this was Kegan. She couldn't detach her emotions. She loved him and didn't think she'd survive if she gave in and he left her again.

"Don't say no, Charlie. Please let me show you how much I want you," Kegan murmured.

Trevor's touches along her back soothed her and Kegan's gentle kisses made her melt.

Take a chance. Dammit, for once, let go.

She never could deny Kegan anything. His vulnerability tore at her control.

Charlie grabbed the back of his neck and pulled him to her.

Chapter Ten

Kegan's gaze met Trevor's as Charlie pulled him toward her.

The relief in his best friend's eyes had to match his own. They had decided they weren't going to let anything stand in their way of possessing Charlie. They wouldn't stop until they convinced her. She belonged to them.

Kegan was just damned glad he didn't have to wait to prove it to her. She didn't trust him, he could see that much in her eyes, but she wanted to. She still held part of herself back from him and he couldn't really blame her after the way he hadn't come back for her. He would gratefully take whatever she gave him now. It would take time, but he'd prove to her that he was never going to walk away from her again. He never made the same mistake twice. He would demand everything from her and they would give her just the same.

Kegan let Charlie's body slide down his until her feet touched the floor, but kept her tight against him. He needed the contact of her body. He claimed her mouth and deepened the kiss. Her flavor was so sweet and warm, a powerful aphrodisiac.

Trevor grasped the hem of her shirt and pushed it slowly up her body. Kegan reluctantly broke the kiss when she raised her arms to allow the shirt to be pulled free. He caressed the length of her arms, encouraged her to clasp them around his neck.

Before Kegan could reclaim her mouth, Trevor tilted her head in his direction. "My turn," he growled and pressed his lips against hers.

It was hot as hell watching Trevor devour and claim Charlie's mouth. The position he held her head at exposed her long, elegant neck and it was too much of a temptation to resist.

Kegan licked and nibbled along the pulse throbbing just under the skin. She moaned into Trevor's mouth and Kegan felt the vibration on his tongue. He continued his assault across her collarbone and lightly bit and nipped her flesh, just enough to cause her body to jerk when he marked her. He sucked at her warm skin until the blood rose to the surface, then soothed the dark spot with his tongue and soft kisses. The sight of his mark on her pale skin made something primal deep inside him rejoice in triumph.

Trevor unclasped her black lace bra and shoved it down to cup her perky breasts. He pushed them up and together in an offering to Kegan's watering mouth. He sucked one of her swollen pink nipples, his teeth scraping across the sensitive bud, then teased it gently with the tip of his tongue. Kegan watched as Trevor pinched and rolled her other nipple between his fingers.

"Christ, that's hot, Trev." He let his tongue flick across the nipple Trevor pinched. The taste of Charlie and Trevor against his tongue sent a jolt straight to his cock and engorged it even further to a near painful ache.

"Open your eyes, Charlie," Trevor murmured against her neck. "Watch Kegan loving you, it's beautiful."

Her heavy-lidded eyes fluttered open and she looked down her body to Kegan. She gasped as he bit down lightly on her nipple again. The passion and need in her eyes spurred him further. He pulled her hips forward and forced Trevor to support her weight as he kissed and licked down her flat belly. She whimpered as he darted his tongue in her navel.

Kegan dropped to his knees, never taking his eyes from her heated gaze, unclasped the button of her jeans and slid the zipper down. She barely suppressed a moan as he pushed the jeans over her slender hips and exposed the thin lace covering the hint of dark curls. He positioned her feet back on the floor to straddle his thighs. He feathered his hands back up her body.

"You're so beautiful," Kegan whispered.

She held his gaze as her body trembled with need. Kegan couldn't stand it any longer. He could feel the heat of her arousal and needed to taste her, take something of her into him. He reached up, slid a finger under the lace of her thong and teased her swollen lips. "I'm going to taste you here."

Charlie gasped as his finger spirited across her tight clit.

"And here."

"Oh God," she whimpered and her eyes started to close.

"No. Keep your eyes open, Charlie. I want to see what you're feeling and the pleasure in those stunning eyes of yours."

Her eyes popped open at his command, the hunger and anticipation there like a lightning bolt to his dick.

In one quick movement, he ripped the material of her thong, and the tattered scraps of lace fell to the floor.

"Mmm." She was beautiful all over. "You're perfect." He ran his finger from her opening up to her swollen clit before he ducked his head and let the flat of his tongue follow the same path. She tasted incredible, like a sweet musky honey. A deep moan of approval rumbled up from deep in his chest.

"How does she taste?" Trevor growled, sounding barely in control.

Kegan didn't answer with words, but action. He tightened his grip on her hips and hummed his satisfaction against her flesh as he lapped at her sweetness.

Trevor let out a low curse, grabbed Kegan's hand, lifted it to his mouth, then sucked the finger Kegan had run across her sex.

Kegan couldn't take his eyes off Trevor as he moaned and sucked at his finger, cleaning every drop of Charlie's flavor with his tongue. His cock twitched and Kegan fought the urge to palm his dick, knowing one hard pull would make him come in his pants. With Trevor and Charlie in front of him, he wasn't going to come anywhere but inside or on Charlie. He tightened his hold on her hip, and forced himself not to give in to the need.

Trevor pulled Kegan's finger from his mouth with a pop. "Holy fuck, you taste sweet." He licked her lips and shared her own taste with her.

One look at Charlie's wide, heat-filled eyes told Kegan she found the act as hot as he did.

Kegan slid his hand across her hip until he met naked and wet swollen lips.

"You're wet for me, Charlie."

Trevor stroked a hand down her body and joined Kegan's. They each slowly ran a finger up and down the heated flesh of her sex. Kegan penetrated her sheath with one finger, followed by Trevor's.

"Feel good?" Kegan crooned as he teased his tongue across her neck.

"Yes," she moaned pushing into their touch. Her head fell back on Trevor's shoulder.

Charlie's breath caught as their fingers plunged and twisted inside her. Her head spun and her knees threatened to buckle. Only the tight hold Trevor had on her kept her on her feet. Over and over they penetrated her at an excruciatingly slow pace until she was on the verge of orgasm.

Kegan dipped his head and sucked at the flesh of her inner thigh while Trevor brushed his lips along her neck. "That's it, baby, just let go."

Trevor swept his thumb back and forth across her clit as Kegan licked and nipped at her. Their fingers slid in and out of her slit, moving faster and faster.

The orgasm that exploded caught her off guard. It wasn't the slow building pleasure she was used to whenever she was alone. This orgasm ripped through her so suddenly she screamed as her body pulsed and wetness seeped between her legs.

Trevor and Kegan continued the same rhythm and forced every last drop of satisfaction from her body, until she slumped against Trevor and gasped for air.

Trevor scooped her spent and pliable body up into his arms. "Let's move this to the bedroom." His voice sounded husky and strained against her ear.

Charlie rested her cheek against his chest and snuggled into his strong body, working to slow her panting. His scent surrounded her as he took the stairs two at a time. When they neared her room, Kegan brushed past them and opened the door. He moved across the room to the bed and drew back the comforter.

Trevor set her on her feet next to it. She felt a little self-conscious being naked while both men were fully clothed. She looked up at Trevor and grinned sheepishly. "I think you two are way overdressed."

Trevor chuckled as Kegan moved behind her. The hungry look in Trevor's eyes made her hesitate a little. Kegan stood against her back and placed her hands on Trevor's chest. His muscles flexed and rippled under her palms. She fumbled with the buttons of his shirt and only Kegan's hands on hers kept her from ripping the buttons off in frustration. Kegan pressed his mouth to her neck and rubbed it across the beating pulse. He made it even more difficult to manage the task.

She finally pulled Trevor's shirt from his jeans and Kegan guided her hands to push back the material of the shirt, exposing the strong tanned chest beneath. They let his shirt fall from his body as they explored the ripped muscles. She brushed her palm over Trevor's erect nipple, which pulled a moan from him.

Charlie loved the way his chest hair felt against her skin, as they roamed their hands downward across the tight muscles of his abdomen, the dark line of hair tickled her flesh and mesmerized her. Anticipation built. She wanted to follow the path to his cock.

As if he could read her mind, understand her desire to follow that treasure line of hair, Kegan encouraged her hands to move to the top of Trevor's jeans and she popped the button before sliding down the zipper. Charlie took confidence in his sure hands against hers and pushed the jeans down past Trevor's lean hips. He tilted his head back and moaned deep as Charlie freed his bulging erection.

She swallowed her gasp of surprise at the sight. She knew he was well endowed, had felt it pressed against her ass when he'd held her, but hadn't realized just how big he was. He was huge, bigger than any man she had ever been with, and a twinge of uncertainty shot through her while at the same time her pulse quickened. Charlie had never gone down on a man before, never had the desire to. She wanted to now, but her insecurities gave her pause.

What if she couldn't take him, couldn't satisfy him? Would they find her inexperience undesirable and a waste of time?

She rested her hands on the soft skin of Trevor's hips as Kegan pulled his hands from hers. She suddenly felt lost without the confidence of his hands on hers and was unsure of what to do next.

"Kegan?"

"Touch him," he whispered in her ear.

"How?"

"Wrap your fingers around him gently and stroke him from base to tip."

Charlie looked up at Trevor. His gaze burned into hers with such hunger it stole her breath. His eyes were dilated and his nose flared as he breathed in short pants. She was encouraged by the arousal she saw and tentatively reached out and let her fingers trail lightly down his erection. Trevor hissed at the contact, his big body tightened. She wrapped her slender fingers around him. She loved the feel of the silky smooth skin as she stroked up and down his entire length.

"That's it, baby. He likes it hard. Squeeze your hand tighter." Kegan's big hands pressed on her shoulders, encouraging her down as he spoke into her neck, going to his knees with her.

"I can't."

"Use both hands," Kegan murmured. His breath came out in gusts of air, and she could feel his erection pressed hard against her ass every time he thrust.

Charlie moved her other hand to join the first and squeezed Trevor's cock.

"Fuck," Trevor bit out, his voice deep and gravelly as his hips thrust into the tunnel of her hands. "Harder!"

Charlie looked up at him, a sly grin on her face. She loved the power she had over him at this moment. The pleasure she gave Trevor and the encouraging wicked words from Kegan spurred her confidence. She brushed her thumb across the head on each stroke, the pre-cum that seeped from the tip slicking his flesh as she continued to tighten her hands around him.

Kegan pushed his hands into her hair, massaged her scalp with his powerful fingers, encouraging her head forward. "Now part those sweet lips of yours and take him in your mouth."

Charlie slanted her head in his direction, panic making her breath hitch. "I've... I haven't done this before." She couldn't stop the feeling of inadequacy, yet her desire to please was stronger than her apprehension.

"It's okay, baby. I'm right here." He nuzzled her throat. He slid the hand in her hair down her arm as he cupped her full breast in the other. "Listen to his body, let it guide you." His voice went lower, deeper. "I'll be right here, wishing it was my cock your pretty lips were wrapped around."

Kegan's naughty words and the feel of Trevor's erection in her hands made her body tingle and her sex ache. She leaned forward, then licked her dry lips before pressing them to the head of Trevor's shaft. She darted her tongue out to gently swipe across his slit, tasting his musky flavor. They all groaned in unison.

"That's it, now open wide and take him in. Let your tongue swirl around the head," Kegan encouraged as he pulled and pinched at her swollen nipples.

Charlie followed his command, loving the way Trevor's cock slid across her tongue. She took him farther into her mouth as she pulled up from the base and squeezed.

She bobbed her head up and down, quickly finding a rhythm with her hands and mouth, pulling a sharp curse from Trevor.

"Ah, shit," he groaned. He clenched her hair in his fists to pull her closer.

She looked up, feeling wanton and powerful seeing Trevor lose control. With a wicked grin, she let the head slip from her mouth and swirled her tongue around the sensitive underside. She continued to tease him with soft flicks of her tongue until his hands tightened even further and sharp sparks of pain radiated across her skull.

Kegan obviously picked up on Trevor's growing tension. "That's it, Charlie. Now take him back into your mouth and suck hard."

She did as he'd ordered, her cheeks hollowing with each stroke. She wrapped her fingers tightly around the base and pulled him toward her as she worked him harder and faster with her mouth.

Kegan pulled away from her and she heard the ping of buttons hitting the floor as he ripped off his shirt. He pressed his naked chest against her back and his hands found her breasts, squeezing and caressing them briefly. He ran his hand down her stomach, further still until his fingers teased the light curls of her mound.

"Suck him harder," he growled as his finger penetrated her wet sheath.

Charlie moaned around Trevor's cock, her pleasure multiplying and consuming her with a raging need.

"Good girl. Now suck just the head, let your teeth scrape lightly against it," Kegan demanded, his breath tickling her ear, his fingers moving faster and deeper inside her.

Charlie did as she'd been instructed.

"Fuck!" Trevor pulled from her mouth with a pop and grasped his pulsing shaft as he tried to hold back his orgasm, his entire body shaking from the effort. After a few seconds, he blew out a heavy breath. "Holy shit, that was close."

Charlie didn't have time to feel the loss of him as Kegan thrust his fingers hard inside her one more time. She screamed as he brought her to orgasm again. His fingers stayed deep inside her until the last of her shudders eased.

Kegan's laughter vibrated along her neck. "What's the matter, Trev? That was only her second orgasm and you're ready to blow already? Tsk. Tsk."

"Fuck off." He shot Kegan a hard glare. "C'mon." He held his hand out to her, and she grasped it without hesitation. He led her over to the bed and pulled her down beside him. He took her mouth in a hard kiss, his tongue pushing in deep as he claimed her mouth.

She stole a glance toward Kegan when he joined them on the bed. He had shucked his jeans, his erection standing proud. He wasn't as thick as Trevor, but longer, the head swollen, his arousal seeping from the small slit.

Trevor broke the kiss and spoke against her lips, "Show Kegan how good you feel." He nibbled at her lower lip before he pulled away and urged her to roll in Kegan's direction.

She turned and met Kegan's gaze. He looked at her with such passion and need, her chest tightened. She wanted him with an all-consuming hunger, had wanted him nearly her whole life. The reality of actually being in his arms had her blinking back tears.

Dammit, don't you dare cry.

Charlie refused to think about Kegan leaving her again — she'd deal with those feelings later. Right now, she wanted his body wrapped around and deep inside her.

Kegan palmed the back of her neck and pulled her mouth to his in a blistering kiss. Trevor pushed up to her back. He lifted her leg up over Kegan's hip, murmuring encouragements. He caressed and rubbed, pushing her harder toward the erection pressed against her belly as he rocked his hips.

Trevor set a slow, steady rhythm, forcing her clit to rub along the soft skin of Kegan's erection. At the slow, sensual pace, the heat of their bodies enveloped her, and all thoughts fled from her mind until it was only the sensations of their joined bodies, in a leisurely seductive dance, that she focused on.

The feel of Charlie's warm skin against his was the most amazing thing Kegan had ever experienced. He fought the urge to thrust hard, to roll her onto her back and bury himself to the hilt in her heat. The image of her sexy mouth wrapped around Trevor's shaft, sucking him long and deep, was more than he could stand.

"Let me love you," he whispered into her mouth. "I need to be inside you before I lose my mind. Let me show you what you mean to me."

Trevor pushed his hand between them. He separated the lips of her sex and dipped a finger into the slick folds. Kegan snatched a condom and quickly covered his erection. His hips jerked in response to the slide of Trevor's finger slowly easing in and out of Charlie.

"That's it, open up for him, Charlie," Trevor urged

He rubbed a finger in a tight circle around her clit. Trevor's knuckles rubbing against Kegan's cock with each movement only escalated his desire. He stilled, closed his eyes for a moment and let the pleasant sensation wash over him. He wanted this moment to last, to spend forever right here with the two people he cared most about in this world.

Kegan opened his eyes when Charlie moaned to see her trembling with need. Unable to deny her any longer, he pressed the head of his erection at the entrance of her core. The wet heat against his sensitive flesh pulled an unstoppable groan from deep in his chest. She was so hot she burned him alive. Kegan pushed the head into her and froze, giving her body a chance to adjust to the invasion. "Ah Christ, you're tight, bichito."

Her slick walls clamped around him, and she gasped and wriggled beneath him, making it all the harder to keep from slamming home. He gritted his teeth, pushed in painstakingly slowly, and watched Charlie's eyes glaze over as pleasure swept through her body. Her cheeks flushed, and a long, continuous moan escaped her lips. Kegan pushed until sheathed to the hilt. Her insides contracted around him, and the heat and friction was so goddamn sweet he wasn't going to last long. She was so tight and hot.

"Harder," Charlie groaned as her hips thrust toward him and her head fell back onto Trevor.

"Give me a minute—"

Charlie pinned him with a hard stare, fire blazing in her eyes. "No. Now!"

She was like a tight fist clamped down on him with every pulse in her body. The pressure combined with her feverish demands, and he couldn't help but pull back then thrust again, hard. He wanted this to last, to be so good for her, but he couldn't seem to control his body.

He yanked her hips and rolled her to straddle him. He placed his feet flat on the bed and pushed up hard into her giving flesh, groaning long and deep. Charlie's head rolled back against Trevor as he knelt between Kegan's spread thighs and grabbed her nipple, rolling and pinching in time with each thrust of Kegan's body.

"Ah fuck, that's it. Take me. Take all of me." A knot formed at the base of his spine and his balls drew up. There was no way he'd be able to hold back, his orgasm already racing down his spine. "Not gonna last, baby, you feel too good," he gritted out. He slammed into her once, twice, then white light swirled behind his closed eyes as the heat shot up his cock and burst in a blinding flash of pleasure.

He forced his eyes open and they settled on Charlie's gorgeous body as he cried out her name while he came buried deep inside her.

Before the aftershocks had even slowed, Trevor put a hand between her shoulder blades and pushed her down to Kegan's chest.

"On your knees!" He groaned, barely able to get the words out before he pulled her hips up and off Kegan's sated erection and buried himself deep inside her with one hard thrust.

Charlie threw her head back and screamed as she was overcome with the pleasure that rocketed through her. Kegan reached down and rubbed his thumb across her clit as Trevor pumped into her at a brutal pace. His muscles were tight and rippled as he grasped Charlie's hips and pulled her hard against him.

"Feels good, doesn't she?"

"Fuck, I've never felt anything so damn sweet. I can feel her gripping me, milking me."

Kegan pulled Charlie's mouth to his, captured her screams.

"That's it, baby. Come for us," Trevor encouraged as he continued to piston in and out of her.

Her body went rigid as her orgasm overwhelmed her. She pulled away from the kiss and cried out as Trevor pumped his own release deep in her body. Charlie slumped onto Kegan's chest, breathing in short pants. He could feel her heart pound as Trevor's weight on her back pushed her deeper into his.

"Are you okay, baby?" He brushed the damp hair from her beautiful face. She lifted her head and looked at him, a happy sated smile twitching at the corners of her mouth as she nodded.

Trevor rolled to the side and disposed of the condom before he pulled her to him and sandwiched her warm, pliant body between them. "Nap," he groaned. "Then round two."

Charlie looked back toward Trevor as he spooned against her back. Kegan chuckled at the surprised look on her face. He rose from the bed, disposed of his own condom, then fetched a warm, damp cloth.

Returning to join his lovers in bed, he placed a soft kiss to Charlie's forehead and gently cleaned the wetness from between her thighs. "It's okay, baby." He threw the cloth onto the floor beside the bed and snuggled closer to her. "Just rest."

He stroked her hair as she settled back and relaxed between them. Her breathing slowed as she drifted off to sleep.

Kegan didn't think he could ever be happier than he was at that moment. The scent of the three of them filled the air as his eyes closed.

Chapter Eleven

Charlie woke to warm arms wrapped around her in a cocoon of heat and instinctively snuggled closer to it.

"You're awake," Trevor whispered in her ear.

"No. I think I'm still dreaming."

Last night had been the most amazing night of her life. The way they'd made her feel loved and cherished was something she had never experienced before and she still had a hard time believing it had actually happened. It had a dreamlike quality to it because there was no way reality could ever be that good.

Trevor, true to his word, had been more than ready for round two. He and Kegan had taken her over and over with their voracious, insatiable sexual needs that had left her completely and utterly sated.

Warm hands caressed her from stomach to breasts and lightly stroked her hard nipples. "Does this feel like a dream?"

"It's feels like heaven so it must be a dream," she murmured.

Trevor turned her in his arms and placed a soft kiss to her forehead. "Open your eyes, Charlie."

She squeezed her eyes tighter and shook her head. "Nope, can't make me. I'm enjoying my dream."

Trevor peppered her face with soft kisses. "You're not dreaming, baby, and I'll prove it."

"Ow! What the hell was that for?" Charlie's eyes flew open when pain shot through her backside as he pinched the fleshy meat of her ass cheek.

"Proving you weren't dreaming." He chuckled and dipped his head, then caught her mouth in a soft kiss. Before she could pull away, he soothed the abused flesh of her ass.

Breaking the kiss with a pout, she rested her cheek against his broad chest, playfully swatting at him. "Brute."

She stretched and snuggled deeper into his chest, loving the little aches and pains in her muscles as she moved. As her eyes adjusted to the bright morning light that filtered in through the large open windows, she scanned the room. It became quickly obvious that she was alone in bed with Trevor.

Kegan was gone. The painful realization assaulted her and she struggled to keep her breathing steady, but the weight that squeezed her heart like a vise didn't allow it. Her stomach lurched and she fought to keep down the bile that threatened to rise in her throat.

She should have known she wouldn't have been able to keep the past or her heart out of the equation. This was supposed to be about letting go and enjoying the moment. Instead, deep down, she had allowed herself to hope and had ruined everything. Hope was something she did not believe in. Hope was disappointment, and Kegan's absence just reminded her of that fact.

Everyone always leaves you.

"Charlie? You okay?"

No. "Yeah. I'm fine."

"Baby, you're shaking. Are you having regrets?"

He tried to lift her chin to meet his gaze, but she refused and shook her head.

Hell yes she was having regrets. She had just spent the most intense night of her life with Kegan and Trevor and she had allowed hope to destroy it. "No... I'm... I need a shower." She pulled away from his embrace, refused to meet his gaze, and fled to the bathroom.

She slammed the door shut and locked it behind her before she slumped back against it and fought the urge to bang her head.

Stupid! Stupid! God, she had to get control of herself. It was just sex, the most mind-blowing sex of her life, but just sex. She wasn't the first woman they'd shared and she wouldn't be the last. She was such an idiot.

A soft rap at the door startled her. She moved toward the tub and wiped frantically at the hot tears that rolled down her cheeks.

"Charlie, babe, are you okay?"

She reached in and turned the water on. "I'm just gonna take a shower, Trevor. I'm fine." The sadness in her voice made her cringe.

"You don't sound okay. C'mon, babe, open the door and talk to me."

Please just go away.

She couldn't handle the thought of him seeing her weak tears, which just gave more credence to the stupid-country-girl image she had no doubt already given Kegan. She stepped into the stream of hot water before calling out, "Just let me take a shower and I'll be right out."

Trevor pounded on the door. "Open the door."

She ignored him.

"Charlie, I swear I'll break this goddamn door down."

The last thing she was going to do was open that door. She'd be damned if she'd obey his commands this time. That was how she'd found herself in this mess in the first place.

She'd ignore him and eventually he'd get tired of this stupid game and go away. She grabbed the shampoo bottle. The sound of wood splintering and the door slamming open made her jump and she dropped the bottle.

Before she had the chance to recover from her surprise, Trevor entered the shower and pulled her body tight against his.

"What the hell is wrong with you? I told you—"

His mouth smashed down on hers and cut off her words. She refused to give in to him and shoved at his chest, but he was a rock-hard wall of muscle that didn't budge a fraction of an inch and he refused to let go of her mouth.

His arms tightened around her as he kissed along her mouth, down across her jaw then up her neck. "Now, are you gonna tell me what has you so upset?"

"Besides the fact you just broke down the bathroom door while I'm trying to take a shower? Nothing." She sniffed.

Trevor cupped her chin in his large palm and forced her to meet his gaze. "Don't lie to me, Charlie, it pisses me off. You can regret what we've done, can tell me that you don't want me around, but do not lie to me." His dark eyes narrowed, the intensity startling her.

"Fine," she said breezily and slapped at his hand. "I have regrets, okay?"

He released her, then bent to pick up the shampoo bottle. "Turn around."

She readily obeyed the command, not because he had ordered her to, but because she didn't want him to see the pain that was surely evident in her eyes. He massaged shampoo into her hair, kneaded at her scalp, and she relaxed a little from his gentle caresses.

"Why do you regret what we did? It certainly didn't feel like a mistake to me." With his body, he eased her forward into the spray of water, stroking through her hair as he rinsed away the suds.

"That wasn't me last night, it's not who I am."

Trevor grabbed a bar of soap and lathered it in his hands before he ran them along her back and across her hips. "What the hell is that supposed to mean?"

Dammit, she didn't want to get into this with him. She just wanted to take her shower and escape.

He moved down her legs then trailed back up around her stomach. He made it hard for her to think. Her body awakened in response to his touch and she fought to keep her thoughts away from the way his hands made her body tingle.

"I've never had a fling. It's just not me. I'm not trying to judge you and Kegan if that's what you're into, I just mean…"

He spun her around so fast that she felt dizzy and reached out to him to steady herself. He grasped her arms hard, his body practically vibrating as anger flared in his black eyes. "Is that what you think?" He shook her. "You still think we just wanted to fuck you?"

Words were one thing, actions spoke much louder. Like the fact that Kegan hadn't even wanted to wake up next to her. Charlie averted her eyes and forced nonchalance into her tone. "It's no big deal." She looked down at his hands still holding her. "Want to stop manhandling me?"

He ignored her. "You want to answer the question?"

Charlie ducked her head and spun away from his slick grip, exited the shower, then grabbed a towel to wrap around herself. "No."

Trevor followed her and grabbed his own towel to secure it to his waist. "No, you don't think we wanted to just fuck you or no, you don't want to answer the question?"

God he's persistent. Charlie left the bathroom, heading for the closet in her room to get dressed. Not so surprisingly, the cocky cowboy followed, leaned against the doorframe with his arms crossed over his chest and blocked the exit.

"Answer the goddamn question, Charlie."

She grabbed her jeans, shimmied into them and pulled a sweater over her head before she faced him. "Yeah, I do think you just wanted to fuck me."

Anger started to boil within her. She wasn't angry at him but at her own stupidity. However, she still took it out on him full force. "You made it clear the first night I met you what you wanted, and you got it. At least you were gentleman enough to wake up next to me. Obviously Kegan couldn't be bothered." She blinked rapidly, refusing to shed one more damn tear.

In one quick movement, Trevor grabbed and pulled her against him, forcing her head against his chest. "Ah, hell! Is that what this is about? Kegan not waking up with us?"

He kissed the top of her head, cupped her chin and pushed her to look at him again. "I convinced Kegan to go out and get the crew started. He couldn't keep his damn hands off you and I was afraid he was going to wake you." He kissed her nose. "You looked so damn sweet all snuggled up."

She stared at him, searching for signs of deceit, but only found tenderness and sincerity in his eyes. Still, even if he had sent Kegan out, that didn't mean it wasn't just about sex. She couldn't really be upset about that fact since she had decided to take Rae's advice and just enjoy the moment, which she certainly had done. It wasn't their fault she had hoped for more. Unsure what to say, she just stared at him.

Trevor placed a soft kiss to her lips then led her from the closet. "C'mon." He stopped only long enough to grab his jeans and slide into them before he pulled her along behind him again.

"Where are we going?"

"You don't look convinced, so I'm going to prove it to you."

She tried to pull away, but he held her hand tight in his grip. "Prove what?"

He continued to pull her along behind him, down the stairs and into the kitchen, where an elderly lady poured juice at a set table.

Trevor dropped Charlie's hand and strode over to the lady. "Good morning, Mrs. M," he greeted then kissed her cheek. "Kegan make it back yet?"

She swatted his hand as he tried to steal a slice of bacon off one of the plates.

"Oh no you don't, you wash them hands before you touch food in my kitchen, young man." She pushed him toward the sink before she turned to Charlie and thrust her hand out, a warm smile on her face. "You must be Charlie. Wow, Kegan was right, you are a stunner."

Charlie's cheeks heated at the compliment as she shook the offered hand. "Nice to meet you, ma'am."

"I'm Mrs. Miller, but most folks call me Mrs. M." She patted the back of Charlie's hand. "Have a seat, breakfast is just about ready." She pushed her toward a chair.

"Oh, I'm really not very hungry."

"Nonsense, you're nothing but skin and bones. Don't worry, I'll get some meat on you in no time."

Trevor chuckled as he took the seat next to her. "Doesn't do any good to argue with the woman, she can be relentless. She's been at her son's place all week pestering him and undoubtedly fattening him and the grandbabies up."

Mrs. Miller filled their coffee cups before setting the pot on the table. "Don't pay him any mind. I haven't met a man yet that doesn't need a woman telling him what to do."

Charlie stiffened as the back door slammed and Kegan strode into the kitchen. He walked straight for her, pulled her out of her chair and into a tight embrace.

"Damn, Charlie, you're even more beautiful in the morning." He placed a soft kiss to her lips. "I hoped to find you still snuggled up in bed when I got back."

Charlie felt her cheeks flame with embarrassment as she heard Trevor chuckle. *Oh God, this woman must think I'm a total floozy.* She had just come downstairs with one half-naked man and now another had just admitted to having her in bed. Charlie wished she could climb into a hole.

"Put her down," Mrs. Miller chastised. "Go wash them hands, your breakfast is getting cold."

Kegan laughed, set her back in the chair and placed a kiss on her temple before strolling to the kitchen sink. Charlie grabbed her coffee cup, eyes down. *Way to make a great first impression, Charlie.*

Mrs. Miller placed a basket of biscuits on the table in front of her. If she was appalled by Charlie's behavior, she hid it well.

"It was nice meetin' you, Charlie. I'll be in the other room if you need anything else." She winked as Charlie peeked up at her over the coffee cup. "I know how to handle these boys. You need any advice, you come find me."

"Thank you, ma'am, I may just take you up on that." Too bad she hadn't met her the night before. She might have avoided all this embarrassment.

Kegan joined them at the table, taking the seat on the other side of Charlie as Mrs. Miller left the room. He scooted his chair closer to hers and placed his hand on her thigh. "Aw, don't be embarrassed. We've told Mrs. M all about you."

Charlie groaned into her coffee, refusing to look up. This day just got better and better. The tramp tattoo stamped on her forehead was becoming inevitable.

A long, uncomfortable silence filled the room as they ate. Charlie wasn't sure what to say. She was more embarrassed than she could ever remember being. It didn't help that she was going to have to face this woman every day until her job was done. Shit, what if she said something to Dr. Stone? Charlie was going to kick Rae's ass for talking her into this.

Kegan looked back and forth from her to Trevor. "You two okay? Is something wrong?"

"Why don't you tell him what you told me?"

Charlie glared at Trevor, who leaned back in his chair, a dazzling smile on his too-smug face.

Bastard.

Kegan squeezed her thigh, staring at her expectantly.

Charlie refused to play Trevor's little game of let's embarrass Charlie further. She started to stand, eager to hide.

Trevor placed his hand on her shoulder and pushed her back down into the chair. "Not so fast, missy. It's just the three of us and we're gonna hash this out right here and now."

"Okay, Trev, what the hell is going on? I leave for a bit and you piss her off? Way to go, dumbass."

"I didn't do anything to her. If anyone should be pissed, it should be me. She insulted me."

Charlie stared at Trevor, mouth agape. "How the hell did I insult you?"

Trevor popped a slice of bacon in his mouth, chewed furiously, and pointed at her, his eyes on Kegan. "Little Miss Charlie here is under the impression that we're just a couple of dogs. That we brought her here just to fuck her and add a notch to our bedpost or something."

Kegan squeezed her thigh again and glared at Trevor. "How the hell did you give her that impression?"

Charlie couldn't help but giggle at the stunned look on Trevor's face.

"Me?" Trevor pointed a finger at Charlie. "She freaked when she woke and found you gone."

"And you're the one who told me to leave her alone." In a very impressive imitation of Trevor's drawl, Kegan said, "'Leave her alone, Kegan, and let her sleep. She's gonna need her strength for what I have planned.'"

Charlie laughed outright at the embarrassment on Trevor's face as he grumbled something unrecognizable.

Kegan reached up and ran the back of his knuckles gently along her cheek. His expression was serious as he spoke. "I know what you must think, but it's not like that. We never get involved with a woman who doesn't know the score up front, never lied to anyone. I know it's gonna take time for you to trust that we want you for so much more than sex. I'll do whatever I can to prove to you how much I want you, how much I've always wanted you. Just give me a chance." He leaned in and brushed his lips against hers, making her melt a bit inside. "Please, Charlie. Give us a chance to show you."

Charlie stared into his gorgeous blue eyes, her heart soaring. Was it possible that he really wanted her in his life? That they both did? It just didn't seem possible. How could she trust what they were saying when she really didn't know Kegan anymore and barely knew anything about Trevor? Did she know or even understand what the score was? She had to still be dreaming. On the flipside, what if she did trust him? Could she survive another broken promise? Yes... No... Maybe.

"I can't promise you, either of you, anything long-term. But I won't leave today. I will stay for the full thirty days, that's all I can promise."

Kegan wrapped his arms around her. "Thank you. I promise..."

"Shh, no promises, Kegan. Let's just take it one day at a time."

Trevor snuggled in on her other side. "How about we start the day by finding a way for you to apologize to me for calling me a dog?"

Charlie couldn't stop the smile that curled her lips. "And just how would one go about making that up to someone?"

He stood and extended his hand toward her. "You can trust me to think of something."

"Isn't that what the spider said to the fly?"

Trevor just laughed and led her up the stairs.

Chapter Twelve

The new foal rose up on shaky legs as it tried to stand for the first time before tumbling back into the soft bed of hay.

Charlie watched, bursting with pride at the life she had helped bring into the world. She couldn't ever remember being as happy as she was at this moment. She had spent most of the day and night before in the arms of the most loving, tender and mind-blowingly talented men. Her body bore the delicious aches in all the right places, as well as a few dark marks left behind when Kegan and Trevor had tried to prove who could mark her best. She still had many questions for them both, but none had to be asked right away. She just wanted to enjoy every precious moment she had with them and worry about tomorrow later.

Warm hands wrapped around her waist and heat radiated at her back as the scent of dark musk and spice enveloped her. *Trevor.* It amazed her that after only a couple of days she could tell them apart just from their scent alone.

"You about ready for lunch?"

Charlie turned in his arms, pressed a kiss to his lips. "Depends on what we're having."

He spun around, clasped her arms around his neck and pulled her into a piggyback hold. "You." He chuckled and headed back to the house.

She was still laughing when they walked into the kitchen and nearly ran into Kegan.

Kegan had watched the two of them walk across the yard to the house tickling each other, both full with laughter. It amazed him how quickly Trevor had fallen completely head over heels for Charlie.

It really shouldn't be that big of a surprise, since Charlie had affected him like that since she'd first entered his life, but Trevor was more of the ladies' man than he was. Though they had talked about settling down, he hadn't really thought Trevor ever would. He'd loved their life as the most talked-about bachelors around, loved the chase and the conquest. Then again, he hadn't come across anyone like Charlie until now.

Neither noticed Kegan standing in the door until they nearly knocked him over. He leaned past Trevor and placed a kiss to Charlie's lips.

"I have to say, the sound of you two laughing has got to be the most beautiful thing I've ever heard." He licked at her lips, coaxing her to open to him.

As soon as her lips parted, he dove in and devoured her mouth. The taste of her on his tongue was a powerful punch to his growing arousal. The sensation of Trevor's warm breath against his throat, hearing him inhale deeply, made his own breath catch and his heart race. He moaned into Charlie's mouth, nearly staggering back from the intensity building in him. Trevor's hand snaked out and caught him around the waist as he swayed slightly.

"Shit, don't fall over," Trevor drawled, pulling Kegan closer to his body. Their erections touched and they both jerked at the contact.

Just as Kegan tried to pull back from the contact, Charlie grabbed him around the neck, pulled him deeper into the kiss and his body tighter against Trevor's. It was as if a freight train had slammed into him. The sensation of Charlie's warm, sweet tongue battling his coupled with the rock-hard bulge pressed against his own sent waves of lust rolling off him with such a force it was difficult to breathe.

"Bed. Now." The low, guttural voice blowing heat against his neck pushed Kegan's excitement even higher.

He ripped his mouth from Charlie's and stepped to one side as Trevor tightened his grip on Charlie's thighs and headed for the stairs. Kegan stayed right on his heels and fought to get his body to slow the fuck down or he'd lose it in his jeans before he even made it to Charlie's room.

Trevor couldn't believe the heat that surged through his body. He had never experienced anything so powerful in his life. His body's reaction to Kegan being pressed up against him was shocking.

Whenever they had shared a woman in the past, they'd avoided contact with each other. The few times that it had happened, they had both jerked away reflexively. Yet when they were with Charlie, the feel of her body combined with Kegan's felt like the most natural thing in the world. It just felt right.

He let Charlie ease down his back until she sat on the edge of the bed, then turned to her and placed a deep, possessive kiss to her parted lips. Her response was gentle, yet demanding.

This was intimacy, the beginning of a possible lifetime of kisses. Warmth spread through his chest as he felt Kegan's presence next to him. He broke the kiss, let his lips brush across her cheek and up to the soft spot below her ear, giving Kegan room to place his own kisses to her lips.

Trevor spoke into the warmth of her neck, placing soft, open-mouthed kisses between words. "You smell like sunshine. Sweet grass. And unfortunately, horses."

Charlie giggled. "I thought you liked the smell of horses?"

"I do, but I don't want to lick one." He nipped at her ear. "But I do plan on licking you. All of you."

She shuddered as he pulled back, grasped the hem of her shirt and pulled it up over her head in one swift movement. "Kegan, want to go get that shower started?"

"One step ahead of ya, Trev." Kegan was already strolling to the bathroom, his clothes leaving a trail behind him.

Trevor reached for Charlie's hands and encouraged her to stand. He watched her bright green eyes as he helped her out of the rest of her clothes.

She was so amazing, so giving.

He fought the urge to throw her back on the bed and bury himself deep in her sweet, sexy body. He pushed her toward the bathroom, nearly drooling as her tight, perfect ass swayed before his eyes and mesmerized him. He shucked his own shirt quickly and practically ripped his jeans off as he followed behind her.

Kegan helped Charlie into the shower while Trevor slipped in behind her and joined them under the warm spray coming from the wall of showerheads. His eyes were riveted to the water droplets sliding down her creamy skin. He reached out to unravel her tightly bound braid as Kegan washed the front of her body.

Trevor skimmed his hands down her skin, and her silky hair brushed his fingertips, the length of it reaching the top of her ass. As he washed her long locks, he encouraged her to lie her head back against his shoulder, her chest pushed out in open invitation to Kegan, who jumped at the opportunity.

Kegan lowered his head, caressing the swollen nubs with the tip of his tongue. Charlie's lips parted on a moan, and Trevor covered her mouth with his in a deep, devouring kiss. His urgency matched hers. A bite or suck counteracted each stroke of his tongue as the kiss deepened.

On and on it went until the pulse pounded in his ears and the need for air forced Trevor to break the kiss. His lips swept over hers as they breathed each other in. He loved the sweet taste of her.

Charlie's eyes nearly rolled back in her head as she panted. Her body trembled and arched into the greedy friction of Kegan's mouth against her sensitive breasts. Her slim fingers fisted in Kegan's hair, held him close as if he were her lifeline.

Trevor watched, enthralled by Charlie's parted mouth, as her tongue darted out to lick at her bottom lip. The urge to have that kiss-swollen mouth wrapped around his shaft made him mindless with lust. Trevor moved his hand down her body until it brushed the thin curls of her sex.

As he grazed the tip of her clit with one finger, Trevor felt Kegan's hand move down to meet his. His big hand covered Trevor's and together they let their fingers slide down to part her sweet, wet lips. Their groans mingled as they felt how wet and needy she was.

Each plunged a finger in her tight sheath, and Charlie cried out at the penetration, her hips jerking to meet their touch. As he and Kegan increased their thrusts, Trevor drew the pad of his thumb in tight circles around her swollen clit. Tremors wracked through her body.

"That's it, baby. Let go. Come for us."

As if his command was what she was waiting for, she tightened around them and cried out as her orgasm ripped through her.

Kegan raised his head from her neck. "Damn, girl, I'll never get enough of you. I love it when you come for us. Knowing we make you fly makes me so damn hard."

Trevor's cock twitched wildly. Charlie did things to his body that no one had ever done and he marveled at it. Her innocence mixed in with a healthy dose of eagerness had him in a perpetual state of need—the necessity to not only to claim her body but also her heart as thoroughly as she had claimed his. He brushed his mouth against the pulse throbbing at her neck and pushed his hardness against the water-slick skin of her backside.

"Do you feel what you do to me, Charlie, how badly I want you?" He turned her head toward his and touched his lips to hers. "I want to feel this full, sweet mouth wrapped around me."

Charlie's eyes lifted a little to look at him seductively under thick lashes in wanton invitation.

They turned her in their arms. Kegan placed one hand between her shoulders and encouraged her downward while he grasped her hip with the other and forced her to bend at the waist.

Trevor fisted his shaft, stroking it in long, easy pulls as he moved his engorged head toward her and allowed his arousal to paint across her bottom lip. As he teased her mouth, Kegan gripped his own shaft and rolled a condom down its length, then teased it along the crease of her ass in a slow, gentle caress before he entered her.

As Charlie's clever little tongue hit the bundle of sensitive nerves at the underside of the head, Trevor's eyes locked onto Kegan's and the bliss he saw on his best friend's face surely mirrored his own. They stared at each other in awe as they both thrust into Charlie slowly, an unspoken acknowledgment of the perfection of this moment in their synchronized dance.

As their pace increased, Charlie began to squirm and thrash between them. Constant moans vibrated against his thickness and caused his balls to tighten up against him.

Never taking his eyes off Kegan, he grunted. "Ah Christ, I'm not gonna be able to hold back much longer." He groaned as Charlie swallowed him deeper and hummed while electrical shocks raced through his body.

Kegan pushed deeper into her, then froze as his mouth went slack and eyes dilated. Trevor was pushed to the edge of ecstasy by the unadulterated pleasure on his best friend's face.

White heat flashed through his body like molten lava as his orgasm ripped through his body and shattered him into a million little pieces. He roared his release, felt and heard Charlie join him.

As he floated back to his body, Trevor stared at Kegan and Charlie. He knew that at a deep emotional level, they'd affected him as nothing else in his life had ever accomplished.

He belonged to them. Body, mind and soul.

* * * *

Charlie sat on the bed between Trevor's spread thighs, Kegan's head lying in her lap. She loved the feel of Trevor's fingers running through her hair as he brushed her damp locks. She ran her fingers through the silky strands of Kegan's pale hair. He looked so peaceful and sated as he stared at her. His sapphire-blue eyes made her melt with a look of reverence, made her feel cherished.

She traced her fingers down his long elegant nose, across his full lips and down to his strong jaw, then ghosted across his cheekbones. Her emotions swirled and a feeling of giddiness came over her as she stared down at this delicious sun-darkened god of a man who looked back at her as if she were the most precious thing he'd ever seen. Not to mention the other godlike creature snuggled up against her.

"Why do you do it?" Charlie asked as she continued to trace Kegan's face with her fingers.

"Hmm? Do what?"

"Share."

Kegan closed his eyes. "It just sort of happened one night."

Charlie could see the pain on Kegan's face, the lines around his eyes tight and drawing his brows into a frown. He stayed quiet, breathed deeply for a long moment. Charlie began to wonder if he was going to continue or if he was simply going to leave it at that. Just as she decided on the latter, Kegan opened his eyes to look at her with so much pain rolling off him, so palpable, that it was nauseating.

"I'm sorry. It's none of my business. I shouldn't have asked." She wished she hadn't. The beauty of the moment they'd shared had been shattered by some ugly past memory.

Kegan sat up in front of her, petting her thighs with light touches. "No, it's okay. You have a right to ask." He seemed to struggle with his thoughts for a moment, then continued. "One night Trevor met this feisty little thing that wanted us both and it just sort of happened. We realized we could give so much more pleasure to a woman together than we could alone."

The blasé comment didn't explain the pain and anguish she had seen. Charlie's insides tightened and her heart broke at the bleak sorrow, the agony she had seen in his eyes.

How did he bear that kind of pain without it consuming him? Her hands itched to touch him, pull him into her arms and take away whatever hurt him. The way he held his body tight and aloof told her he wouldn't welcome her touch right now. He was fighting hard to bury some deep memory, desperate to portray a calm, uncaring façade, but failed miserably.

She looked back at Trevor, who stared at Kegan with such understanding of his pain, as if he knew exactly what had put it there. She realized in that moment that Kegan did indeed share everything with Trevor. Not just work, a home or women, but the secrets in his soul.

Charlie waited, hopeful he'd continue to explain why he looked so pained. She wanted to know the secret that he obviously shared with Trevor. After a long silence, she concluded he didn't feel he could trust her enough to share those same memories with her, and the pain of that knowledge was so violent, it nearly crushed her. The control she kept over her emotions that she had allowed to loosen at the commands of these two overwhelming men began to rebuild anew. She was the queen of denial.

Hurt Charlie and she smiled. Break her heart and she turned that smile to brilliant.

She patted Trevor's thighs. "Well, sounds like it must have been one hell of a night." She leaned over and gave Kegan a chaste kiss on the cheek. "I'm gonna go out and check on the new foal. I'll see you boys at dinner." She didn't look at either of them as she scooted off the bed, grabbed her clothes, then headed for the bathroom.

"Want some company?" Trevor asked.

"Nah, I think I'd like the alone time, if you don't mind." She was proud of the way her voice sounded so calm and didn't give away any of the turmoil that raged through her.

Charlie managed to hold onto her control until she made it out to the barn. She really didn't have any reason to be upset with Kegan. He and Trevor had spent years together and shared everything. Nothing like the stupid school crushes like the one she'd had on Kegan. He hadn't shared his secrets with her back then, why would he share them with her now?

Envy ate at her. She had been living in a fantasy world to think that it would work between all of them. Charlie had never been able to maintain a relationship with one man — she had been a fool to think she could with two.

Did she really need thirty days to prove the inevitable?

If she stayed that long, it would probably just make it that much harder to walk away and would hurt a hell of a lot more. She had spent the last eight years of her life learning to live without Kegan. She knew she could do it again. She hated the idea of going back to the unemotional coldness she had wrapped around her heart in order to do it, though.

But what choice did she have? If Kegan couldn't share the love and the pain in his heart, then there would always be a barrier between them. She couldn't accept half a heart. She wouldn't be an outsider to the closeness that Kegan and Trevor shared.

"Hey, Charlie."

Charlie turned to see Cade headed her way and smiled, happy for the distraction to her thoughts. "Hi, Cade."

He leaned on the stall door next to her. "She's a beauty. You did a great job helping that mare. I didn't think she was gonna make it through the birth."

"Thanks. To be honest, I didn't think she was going to either. I think we have to thank a higher power than me, though."

Cade shook his head, a smile tugging at the corners of his mouth. "You're too modest. You did a damn fine job. The ranch is real lucky to have you during this foal season."

Charlie turned her head away and stared at the foal. She had to stay. Not only had she promised the boys she'd stay the full thirty days, but she would also ruin her program if she left. It would be hard as hell trying to start another one next year, especially if word got out that she'd walked away from a ranch after sleeping with the owners. Her career would be over. But staying with Kegan and Trevor was a very bad idea.

"Cade, is anyone staying in the guest house?"

"No, ma'am, not that I'm aware of. Why?"

She ignored his puzzled look. "Would you show it to me?"

"Something wrong with the room the bosses set up for you?"

Yeah, it's right next to the bosses.

"No, it's great. I just think I'd like to be closer to the stables, is all. I hear it's set up with monitors and alarms wired directly to the foal stalls."

"Yes, ma'am, it is. Sure, I'll show ya and help move you in if you need a hand. Ain't been fireworks at the ranch in a mighty long time." He gestured toward the door, a devilish look in his eyes. "Right this way, Miss Charlie."

Chapter Thirteen

Kegan pulled the wire tight and wrapped it around a transformer before he snipped the end off with wire cutters. He'd spent the afternoon fixing fences, a job he thoroughly hated. He usually had one of the hands tend to them, but he had needed to keep busy and away from the house and Charlie.

He should have told her the whole truth about why he and Trevor had started sharing women. He hadn't lied to her, at least not completely. The sharing had started the way he'd told her. He just hadn't told her why it had started, why it continued, or why he needed it.

Deep down, he knew Charlie wouldn't judge him for what his old man had done. Hell, she had seen the bruises, split lips and missing teeth that were part of his life growing up. But she hadn't known the full extent of the abuse and he didn't want to hurt her with those kinds of memories. Truth be told, he didn't want to think about what had happened in that fucking hellhole, let alone have to relive it.

He damn sure didn't want her to ever find out his reaction to it.

He angrily threw the snips in the back of the truck and moved down to the next break.

He was on the last of the fences when he heard hooves coming up hard and fast. He leaned back against the post and wiped the sweat from his brow with his bandana as he watched Trevor approach. Kegan could tell by the hard set of Trevor's jaw and the tense way he sat on his mount that something had pissed him off.

Trevor swung down from the saddle then stalked toward him and stabbed a finger at him. "You have to tell Charlie the truth. All of it."

"Tell her what, Trev? That my old man was an even sicker bastard than she ever thought? That not only did he beat the shit out of me weekly, he also got his fucking jollies off on beating women?" He ran a shaky hand across his face and tried to steady his pounding heart. "I don't want her to have to imagine that kind of sick depravity. It will hurt her and I can't stand the thought of that."

Trevor leaned beside him, their shoulders resting side by side where they stood next to the post. "She's already hurting and doesn't think you trust her enough to tell her everything."

"This isn't about trust and you know it. It would hurt her a lot more if I told her everything." He shook his head. "I can't do that."

"Then we're going to lose her."

"No, we won't. I'll talk to her. My past doesn't have anything to do with what we have now."

"That's where you're wrong. As soon as Charlie asked you about the sharing, the pain radiating off you was so thick in the room, we all nearly choked on it."

Kegan moved to put his tools in the truck. Dammit, why in the hell couldn't the ugly part of his past stay buried where it belonged? He was happier than he had ever been in his life. Charlie had been the one thing missing and now he felt complete. He was fated to be with her, just as he was Trevor. The three of them had something good, something pure. He refused to let his past tarnish it.

"She moved out of the house."

Kegan whirled around to see a bleak expression on Trevor's face. "She left the ranch?"

"No, she had Cade help her move her belongings to the guest house. Guess she can't do this either."

"What the fuck does that mean?" Kegan could barely control the anger that steadily built inside him. He had struggled to put his past behind him, fought against the power his old man had over him, yet somehow the bastard still wielded it.

Trevor reached out, placed his hands on Kegan's shoulders and ignored his anger—or at least didn't acknowledge it.

"Look, we're asking her to trust us without question. To live in our home, share her heart and body with us and trust us not to hurt her. Yet you're not willing to trust her with the truth. I hate that you have to rehash this shit. I would love nothing more than to kill that sick fuck for what he did to you. Hell, I wish I could talk to Charlie about this for you, but I can't. She needs to hear it from you, needs to know you trust her."

Kegan didn't want to admit Trevor was right. He wanted Charlie to give him everything, to both of them, yet he wasn't sure he could give her the same. What if he sickened her when she learned the truth, the whole truth? He could lose her. That prick of a man he was cursed with as a father had already made him miss far too many years of Charlie's life, he couldn't stand the thought of losing one more day.

Trevor squeezed his shoulders. "Hey, we'll do this however you want. I'll stand by whatever decision you make and we'll deal with whatever happens together. Right?"

Kegan slapped Trevor on the back and pulled him into a tight embrace. "We might lose her if I tell her."

"Yeah, we might. But we've already lost her if you don't. Your call, man."

Shit! Losing Charlie was not an option. He'd tell her what he could—she didn't have to know everything. Hell, he'd make up something if he had to. No sense hurting her with all the fucked-up facts.

He patted Trevor's back one last time. "Let's go. I'm not losing her again." He spun away and headed for the truck. "I'll meet you back at the barn."

Kegan didn't need to look back to know Trevor followed. Regardless of what Trevor said, he wouldn't have let Kegan walk away without saying something to Charlie. No doubt he'd have convinced him and wouldn't have been above using any and all means necessary. The man didn't take no for an answer and when he wanted something, he was ruthless.

What he wanted right now was Charlie.

* * * *

Belongings unpacked, shower taken and glass of wine in hand, it was no surprise to Charlie when there was a knock on the door just as she sat down. She knew Kegan and Trevor wouldn't let her move out of the main house without some kind of explanation, but she'd hoped to at least have a few minutes alone, maybe finish her glass of wine or the whole damn bottle first. It would have been a waste of a good wish to hope for one night alone.

She knew when she'd considered the guest house, she was going to try to force Kegan's hand. She sucked at poker but had bluffed in hopes that Kegan would fold and open up to her. On some level she knew it was her own insecurities that had brought her to this point—her scars ran wide and they ran deep—but what choice did she have? Some things were easier to overcome than others, and learning to trust again wasn't one of them. Sighing, she thought about ignoring them, but after the incident with the locked bathroom door, she knew it wouldn't hinder Trevor. She tightened the belt of her robe and headed to let them in.

"And to what do I owe this little visit?"

They stood outside her door, both of them looking as incredible as ever, hats in their hands.

Kegan wore a tight pale-blue shirt with mother of pearl snaps. The blue intensified his eyes so they were the first thing she noticed about him, though the hard body was a close second. Trevor had chosen a tight black T-shirt to go with his oh-so-loose jeans, and the color of the fabric had the same effect on his eyes as Kegan's had. But it still wasn't the first thing she noticed about him since he hid his eyes behind a thick wave of his dark curls. The first notable thing was how tight the shirt was where it tucked into his low-hanging jeans and how it accentuated the triangle of muscles that pointed straight down to his groin.

She hesitated at opening the door up farther, knowing the moment she did, they would barge in and overwhelm her. Looking the way they did and the effect they had on her body, how could they not? "I was just getting ready for bed."

Without an invitation, Trevor pushed past her and headed for the living room. Kegan shrugged as his gaze followed Trevor. "Sorry to bother you. We were hoping to talk."

She stepped out of the way and held the door open wide. "By all means, just make yourselves at home. No need to wait for an invite." Sarcasm made her words sound harsher than she'd intended. Another of those damn defense mechanisms ingrained in her.

Charlie took a seat at the farthest end of the couch, pulled her feet up under herself and sipped her wine. She couldn't find it within her to start this conversation, unsure of which emotion would take the forefront, afraid it would be the grief that won out. She chose to stay silent. She had jumped into this with the two of them without fully thinking about the ramifications beforehand. She wasn't about to make that mistake a second time.

Kegan sat in the chair directly across from her while Trevor stretched out at the opposite end of the couch. "Why did you leave the main house without saying anything?" Trevor barely kept his ire hidden, which was just fine with her. Ire she could battle against.

"Oh sorry, didn't realize that I had to ask for your permission." She swirled the wine around in her glass and took a sip before she continued. "I made it clear from the beginning that I had the option to decide how much contact I had with the two of you as long as I stayed for the full thirty days. Don't tell me you're going to go back on our agreement?"

Kegan shot a warning glance at Trevor before he answered, "We're not here to force you to come back.

We just want to talk to you and find out why you felt you had to leave."

Well if he wanted to tiptoe around the issue, then so could she. "I'm just beginning to realize that the agreement was made before I really had a chance to think it through. I let my body make the decisions for me instead of logic."

"Bullshit," Trevor growled. "Everything was going just fine until you asked about why we shared. I've told you, Charlie, don't lie to me. It pisses me off."

"And just what do I have to fear from you when you get all pissy? Neither of you have been totally honest with me — or each other, for that matter." She wouldn't allow Trevor to take over the conversation and spin it in his favor. She had already made up her mind and the only question now was what she was going to do next. "I don't need thirty days to know that the sex between us is amazing, you've already proven that. It's all the other things that I'm not so convinced would work out."

"It's only been a few days, Charlie. Please let's just give it a little more time." Kegan shifted in his chair uncomfortably. She could tell he was holding back and that wasn't something she could ever accept.

"No, Kegan, I don't have to give it a little more time. I've been waiting for you for eight years, living half a life." She could feel the tears build and refused to allow them to fall.

Charlie didn't cry, and dammit she had cried more over the last few weeks than she had in years. Just one more thing she was tired of. She stood then turned her back on both of them as she went to the small bar and poured another glass of wine. She drank half of it down before readdressing them. "You're asking me to accept both of you at face value and to trust you, yet you don't seem to trust me."

Kegan stood and started toward her, only to stop, as he seemed to think better of it and stood a few feet away. "It's not about not trusting you, Charlie, I swear. When you asked me about why I shared women with Trevor, I didn't lie about how it started."

Charlie held Kegan's gaze, the look of pain in his eyes nearly her undoing. She wanted to take away his pain, but if he wasn't able to share the reason for it with her, then there was nothing she could do.

"This isn't about the first night that you shared a woman with Trevor. You looked at me with so much anguish I couldn't help but wonder what caused it. Was it sharing women—me—that hurt? You're not saying anything, so I'm left to draw my own conclusions."

"Shit… I mean…" He fidgeted with the leather gloves in his hands. "I'm sorry I made you feel that way. Having you here has been the best thing that has happened to me. I wasn't upset about sharing you with Trevor, it feels so right. Your question just stunned me for a minute and I remembered some painful shit that I fought a long time to bury."

Charlie forced herself to stay where she stood while her arms ached to wrap around him in comfort. Another part of her needed to understand everything. Kegan leaving her had been one of the most painful things she had ever experienced in her life and she needed to understand why it had happened before she could ever truly let the pain go.

Trevor came up beside her and reached for a bottle of whiskey and two glasses. "Let's have a seat, huh? We're not going to let you go, so we might as well get comfortable while we talk this out. I know I have all night."

The man just exuded confidence—Charlie envied him that. He seemed so sure that there wasn't anything they couldn't work out. She wished she felt the same. She looked at Kegan, his eyes pleading, and she found herself walking over to take a seat at the end of the couch. Before she got comfortable, Trevor pulled her to the middle between the two of them.

"Don't make us fight over who gets to sit next to you."

She rolled her eyes at the silly grin he had on his face, but didn't try to move away. "Do you ever take anything seriously?"

He poured two drinks and handed one to Kegan. "Of course, I take a lot of things seriously. I just happen to know that the problem we're facing right this moment can be overcome. You claimed that we don't trust you, we plan to prove that we do. Problem solved," he announced, raised his glass in toast, then drank a good measure.

The absolute confidence in Trevor's voice shook her resolve to keep the two of them at arm's length.

"Don't ever be afraid to ask us anything or to tell us what's on your mind. If we don't know how you feel about something that's bothering you, how can we fix it?" Trevor continued. He made it seem as easy as deciding to take a stroll in the gardens. She wished like hell she could feel half of his ease.

"I—It's not so much trust... Well, it is, but that's just part of it." She took a deep breath and swallowed hard around the lump that had formed in her throat. "It's... I look at you and Kegan and see what you have together and how much you trust each other and I can't help but feel like an outsider. I've been an outcast my whole life and I don't want the rest of my life to be the same way."

Kegan wrapped an arm around her, caressing her shoulders as Trevor stroked her thigh. "Charlie, you could never be an outsider with us. We want you to be our equal. Like three parts of a whole," Kegan said with complete conviction.

She looked up at him, needed to see his eyes as she dug deeper. "Then why couldn't you tell me why you were so sad when I asked about the sharing? I know that you've told Trevor. I could see it in the way he looked at you and understood your pain. I waited to see if you would trust me enough to share it, but you didn't. I want someone in my life who can give me their whole heart. I refuse to accept half."

"It wasn't that I didn't trust you. I just don't want to burden you with that kind of pain. You already know too much about my father and I don't want you to live with that kind of hurt in your heart. At times I felt that the weight of it would crush me, destroy me, and I would never want you to feel that because of me."

She touched Kegan's face, gently caressing the stubble along his jaw. "I need to know all of it, Kegan. I need to understand what you feel. If I can't handle the bad, then what right do I have to accept the good? I've wanted you since I can remember ever wanting anything. Now you've come back into my life and asked me to be with you, but that in order to be with you I have to accept Trevor too. I have to understand that need, to know that this isn't just some phase you two are going through. How do I know that you won't tire of it—tire of me? Will either of you force me to make a choice between the two of you later?"

Kegan threw back the rest of his whiskey and winced as it burned down his throat, then handed his glass to Trevor to refill. He took the full glass and stared into it, perhaps trying to find the answers.

He finally looked back up at her, his eyes brooding. "You know my old man was a mean bastard. Beat me most every day of my life as far as I can remember. But I wasn't the only one he seemed to enjoy whipping on. More than once I saw his handiwork on the women he'd share his bed with."

Kegan's whole body was tense, the muscles in his shoulders twitching with the effort. Charlie rubbed along his arm with a soft stroke of her hand, silently letting him know she was there for him.

He took a deep breath then let it out slowly. "I was thirteen the first time I walked in on him. He had a woman tied to his bed and was lying on top of her, grunting and groaning. I couldn't help but stare. I was too scared to move, too riveted by the sight. Suddenly, he roared up to a kneeling position, still thrusting, and started to hit her. He screamed nasty curses, his blows in rhythm with each slam of his hips. When he finally got off, he slumped forward on top of her. She looked right into my eyes, her face a swollen and bloody mess, crying and begging someone to help her, but I just stood there. I couldn't move."

His hand shook as he drained the last of his whiskey then set the glass on the table. He didn't raise his eyes again. "I snuck out and hid in my room. I didn't help her."

Charlie took his hand. "Kegan, you were just a kid. You can't blame yourself."

He shook his head but allowed her to hold his hand. "That was the first time it happened. I didn't see the other women, but I heard the screams. I knew what he was doing to them and didn't stop him or tell anyone. That last day I was home, I walked in the house and heard a woman's screams. When I went to his room, sure as shit, there he was beating and fucking her. Something in me just burst and I let every bit of rage in me explode and beat the shit out of him.

"The son of a bitch just smiled, almost as if he was proud of me for finally using my fists. As he lay on the floor, his face a battered mess, he grinned at me with blood running out of his mouth like some fucking madman. Then he asked me how it felt. *'Feels good, don't it, boy? The power is a fucking rush, huh?'* That was the last time I ever saw him. It happened the same day you found me by the riverbed."

Trevor stood and went around the back of the couch, knelt behind Kegan and placed a hand on his shoulder while stroking his hair with the other. Kegan looked up at him. When Trevor nodded his head, Kegan let out a long breath and continued.

"After I got a job with Trevor's old man, I would go out on the weekends with the rest of the ranch hands. They bugged me because I would never mess with any of the girls. Then one night, this girl came onto me pretty hot and heavy. I was drunk and figured what the hell. I took her home that night and couldn't get it up. At first it didn't worry me much, figured I was too damn drunk, but it happened again. Every time I would think about having sex, these sick images filled my head and I would worry about losing control. I worried that I was just like him."

Charlie could see the toll these painful memories were having on him. His big body tensed and jerked under Trevor's touch. His eyes were red, as if he was holding back tears. She was sickened knowing she had forced him to relive these horrors and wished she could take away the painful memories.

"Kegan, you don't have to tell me any more, I think I understand."

His head shot up and he looked at her with such anger and pain, she gasped at the intensity. "No, you don't understand, Charlie. That first time I walked in on my old man, I got fucking hard. Stood there watching him beat the hell out of someone and I got a goddamn erection. How sick is that?"

Tears rolled down his face. He brushed them away roughly. Charlie felt hot tears stream down her own face. She tried to be strong for him, but seeing his pain was overwhelming.

"I couldn't trust myself to be with a woman knowing that the only time I'd ever truly been aroused was when I heard or saw a woman screaming in pain. The night Trevor asked me to join him with a girl he'd picked up, I explained why I couldn't, but he wouldn't let me say no. I agreed to just watch but found that with Trevor there, I didn't have to worry about hurting anyone. When the sharing first started, I believed that was the only way I could have sex — with someone there to keep me under control. I could finally let go and enjoy what was happening because I knew Trevor would never let me hurt anyone. It started out as a necessity, but over the years, with Trevor's help, I realized that I'm not my old man. I am a good man and wouldn't hurt anyone."

Kegan ran a hand over his face, wiped away the last of the tears and looked at Trevor before he turned his gaze back to Charlie. Tenderness replaced the pain that had been in his eyes just moments before and he let a small smile touch his mouth. "I can't imagine my life without Trevor any more than I can imagine not having you. It's not a phase, I could never choose between the two of you, nor would I ever ask you to choose between us. I want you both—for a lifetime."

Charlie allowed him to pull her onto his lap. She needed the contact with him as much as he seemed to need it from her. Trevor wrapped his arms around both of them, somehow completing them.

Kegan kissed the top of her head. "I love you," he whispered, his breath warm against her scalp. "I know I'm asking a lot from you, to accept us both, but I can promise you that we will love you more than anyone ever could. We'll make this work. We will spend every day trying to make you happy if you'll just give us a chance."

Trevor brushed his lips against the side of her neck as he murmured, "Give us a chance, Charlie. Listen to your heart."

Charlie's heart soared with Kegan's declaration of love, words she had prayed to hear but had never thought she would. She was so overcome with emotion she couldn't respond. The whisper of their breaths, the promise of their hearts and scents wrapped around her like their arms—a warm quilt on a chilled night. It felt right.

Charlie melted into their embrace, knew Kegan had given up a lot of himself and trusted her with his secrets. She still wasn't sure how everything was going to work out but knew she wanted them both, wanted to try.

Her biggest obstacle would be to learn to return their trust.

Chapter Fourteen

The first rays of sunshine were streaming through the open windows of her bedroom when Charlie opened her eyes and found Kegan smiling down at her, his hard erection pushed against her hip.

How the hell could someone be so eager this early in the morning?

In the two weeks since she'd moved back into their house she had learned that Kegan was very much a morning person. Always up before dawn with a happy smile and hard for her.

"Good, you're awake. I thought I was gonna have to start without you."

"Go back to sleep," she chastised, but was unable to keep the smile from curling at her lips.

"Ah, c'mon, Charlie, I've been waiting over an hour for you to wake up. Do you know how hard that was?"

Charlie reached out and curled her fingers around his erection, then slid her hand up and down. "Poor baby, feels like it was very, very hard for you to wait."

He groaned and pushed into her fist. "It's your fault. If you weren't so damn sexy lying between us all naked and luscious, I wouldn't have this problem."

"You're the one who made the no clothes in bed rule. So tell me, this is my fault how?"

"Well, you don't see me popping a boner for Trevor and he's naked."

Charlie laughed at the silly lopsided grin on Kegan's face.

"Would you two pipe down? Trying to sleep here," Trevor growled his usual morning greeting. Trevor was definitely not a morning person. He liked his sleep even more than Charlie did. But she knew that as soon as Kegan started his morning wake-up waltz, Trevor would roll over, a brilliant smile stretched across his gorgeous face and he itched to join in.

Charlie had to admit that she was fast becoming a morning person. She loved how the three of them started each day wrapped in each other's arms, and welcomed the day making love. Charlie pushed her bottom into the small of Trevor's back playfully.

"Sheesh, you sound like a bear with a sore paw this morning."

Trevor rolled over, threw a big heavy arm over her and snuggled close. "I got something that's sore this morning, but it certainly ain't my paw."

Trevor's hardness pushed against the crease of her ass. "You two damn virile men are gonna kill me."

Trevor nuzzled her neck and sucked up a mark just below her ear before she could push him away.

"Dammit, why do you two always do that? At this rate I'm gonna need a blood transfusion."

Kegan sucked the skin at the base of her neck, left his own mark before she was able to stop him. He chuckled and pulled her back against him. "We like people knowing you're taken and belong to us."

"Well, could you come up with another way? It's starting to get too warm out for the turtleneck shirts you force me to wear because of these marks. I'd die if I had to wear shorts and someone saw the insides of my thighs."

"I'd like to see the inside of your thighs." Trevor's voice was deep and husky as he kissed his way down her body.

Kegan pulled her head to the side and took her mouth in a deep kiss.

The stall alarm buzzed and had them all groaning. Trevor muttered dark curses and placed one last kiss to her belly before he flopped back on the bed.

"Guess you boys are gonna have to finish this up without me," Charlie teased as she scooted off the bed. They both aimed glares her way and made her laugh as she dressed.

"I know it's gonna be a shitty day when I have to start it with a cold shower," Trevor grumbled and headed for the bathroom, holding his swollen shaft against his body. Kegan winced as he tucked his own rock-hard erection into his sweats and kissed her cheek before he headed out of the room, full of complaints about it being a long time until lunch.

Hearing the dual showers running, Charlie giggled and headed downstairs. Her body shuddered and tingled when she thought of the mood they'd be in by lunch.

* * * *

Charlie was exhausted by the time she headed back to the house. She and Dr. Stone had spent most of the day trying to save a mare from hemorrhaging, but in the end, even with their best efforts, they had lost the battle.

Charlie took some comfort in the fact that they were able to save the foal, but it still hurt like hell to lose a patient. All she wanted to do now was take a hot shower, eat and snuggle up to the men she loved. She hadn't told them that she loved them yet. She felt it might be too soon, though they had both let her know with words and actions that they loved her. She wasn't sure why she hesitated.

'Cause you're a fool who can't believe how damn lucky you are.

Ignoring her irritating thoughts, she walked onto the porch and found Trevor waiting for her at the back door.

"I was just coming out to find you. You okay?"

Charlie wrapped her arms around his waist and leaned into his warm, hard body. "Yeah, I am. It just sucks, ya know?"

"I know, babe. I'm sorry you had to go through that, but I know you and John did everything you could."

"Thank you." She let him hold her for a moment longer, savoring the feel of him, before she looked up. "I need a shower. I'm pooped." She moved back and started to pull off her boots.

"I need to warn you. We're having company tonight."

"I'm not sure if I like the sound of that. Sounds ominous."

"Yeah, I just found out that my parents are in town and they want to stop by tonight."

Charlie nearly fell over and reached out to grab Trevor's leg to steady herself as her boot came off. She stood and faced him. "Do they know about me?"

Trevor shook his head. "No. I haven't spoken to them in a long time. They left a message on voicemail to say they're on their way."

Charlie's panic rose within her. Trevor never talked about his parents, but she knew he didn't think too highly of his father and never mentioned his mother.

What would they think of the living arrangements their son had with her and Kegan? The ranch hands, Mrs. M and Rae were the only people who knew about their relationship. They hadn't really spent much time off the ranch and she hadn't had to contemplate what others would think about seeing them as a threesome.

"Maybe I should go see Rae tonight and let you have some time alone with your parents. I'm sure you have a lot to catch up on."

"I would like you to be here. I want them to meet the woman I love."

And I would just as soon hide out at Rae's like the coward I am. "I just thought…"

"This is my home, baby. Hopefully you will think of it as yours one day as well and I don't want you to feel like you have to leave when people visit."

Charlie wasn't sure what she should say, so she nodded and headed for the stairs.

The day was turning out to be just a grand ole day from hell. Whoopee!

* * * *

The living room felt stuffy, the tension in the air thick as Trevor sat in silence with his parents and a brooding

Kegan nursing a beer while they waited for Charlie to join them. He hadn't seen his parents in nearly four years and had as much in common with them now as he had back then. Nothing.

"So, Dad, what brought you to my neck of the woods?"

"We had business in the area and wanted to see how our son was doing, make sure you're okay. It's been a long time since we've seen you."

"It's been two years since I've even heard from you so excuse me if I seem a little curious." He heard the irritation that poured out with his words but didn't care.

"I know it's been a while. It is regrettable, but I don't get much time off. In my line of work I can't just drop everything and make social calls."

"I heard they have a new invention, it's called the telephone. Maybe you should Google it."

"Trevor, please!" his mother begged. "Your father has come all this way to see you, could you please just try to be civil?"

Civil my ass!

He gritted his teeth to keep from saying it out loud. "Fine. I'm doing great. Kegan and I have been very fortunate our ranch has grown and is doing so well. Can't imagine how my life could get any better. I'm happier now than I have ever been."

Let them suck on that little tidbit. He was happier than he'd ever been while growing up with the two of them, and he didn't give a damn if it hurt their feelings or not. Though, knowing the Kingsingtons were more worried about appearances to the outside world, Trevor doubted they would feel anything or even act like it had upset them, since none of their high-society friends were present.

"I've heard great things about this place. I've been informed that you're now the largest rare-horse breeding ranch in the country. Very proud, son. Well done." He took a small sip of his Scotch then set it back down. "Martha, make sure Michael sends Trevor a case of Cutty Sark. This stuff he's serving guests is atrocious."

Trevor should have known his father would find something to criticize. Instead of acknowledging his father's praise, he started to tell his dad were he could shove his Scotch but then Charlie walked in the room.

She was dressed in a simple black dress that hugged her body like a glove. Her long dark hair flowed down her back to that perfectly sweet ass that made him want to cry mercy. His ire at his father drained away as he looked at her. She and Kegan were all that mattered, not his snobby, self-righteous parents. He stood and went to her side, placed an arm around her waist and led her into the room.

"Mom, Dad, this is Charlie McCarty. Charlie, these are my parents, Martha and Spencer Kingsington."

Charlie reached out and shook his parents' hands, smiling. "It's very nice to meet both of you."

They both gave a generic greeting as Charlie took a seat between him and Kegan and the interrogation began.

"So, young lady, what do you do here at the ranch?" his father asked.

"I'm the resident veterinarian here during the foal season."

"You're quite lovely for a doctor. I take it you met my son here?" his mother inquired.

"No, I actually met your son when I was out with a girlfriend of mine, and thank you for the compliment."

"Did you know at the time you hooked up with my son that he was the owner of a successful ranch?" His father scrutinized her with wary eyes, and Trevor's blood started a slow simmer. He didn't want to start a battle with Charlie sitting next to him and would allow the interrogation for now, but only to a certain line. The look Kegan was throwing at him told him he didn't share his sentiment.

"Actually, no, I didn't realize he was the owner until I was out here immunizing his horses with my mentor, Dr. Stone."

"And where is it your family is from? Would I have heard of any of them? I know a heart surgeon from Cambridge by the name of McCory, any relation?"

Trevor knew exactly where his father's line of questioning was going, but Charlie seemed to be up for the challenge so he didn't interfere, only glared at them with cold, angry eyes.

"It's McCarty, so no, I am not related to him. I'm from a small town south of here called Prudenville. I'm sure you wouldn't know any of my relatives."

"Ah, I see. Judging from the way my son is glaring at me, I'm guessing he doesn't like me asking you these questions." Dad turned to look at him. "Trevor, I'm simply curious about the woman you have allowed into your home. Take it from me, when you come from wealth such as you do, you can never be too sure."

Trevor tensed and felt Kegan do the same. "Who I allow in our home is none of your damn business. I don't have to remind you that you're a guest here and your invitation can be terminated at any time I see fit."

"Now, now, son, I only have your interest in mind. Your mother and I want the best for you is all."

The old anger and resentment he'd thought he'd put behind him bubbled to the surface.

Best interest, my ass. Was it in my best interest to make fucking appointments to see my own father? Was it in my best interest to spend the first eighteen years of my life being the responsibility of the nanny, butler or cook because you two were too damn busy climbing your social ladder?

Trevor bit his tongue, refusing to give his parents the satisfaction to know they could affect him in any way, good or bad.

"So, Charlie," his father continued and brushed a piece of lint from his tailored suit. "I take it from the greeting my son gave you that you're more than just the resident vet. What exactly is your relationship with our son?"

Charlie seemed to tense for a moment before brushing a stray piece of hair behind her ear and lifting her chin in a defiant manner. "Mr. Kingsington, I am sure you'll understand if I decline to answer the question, since our personal relationship is simply that, personal, and something I don't feel I have to explain."

Trevor felt his chest swell with pride. God, he loved her.

His father's eyes narrowed and he looked at Charlie as if she were beneath his standing. "That's where you are wrong, young lady. I have every right to know what kind of woman is involved with my son, my sole heir. Though I must admit, I am pleased to see that he has chosen such a beauty to drape on his arm. I was beginning to wonder if he was going to spend the rest of his life with Kegan as his trophy wife." His deep chuckle held no amusement.

Trevor wanted to scream at him to get the fuck out of their house and tell him where to shove his damn money, but Mrs. Miller entered the room before he could form the words.

"Dinner's on the table."

No one stood. Trevor just glared at his father, wishing like hell he could blink them gone, then take Charlie upstairs and spend a quiet evening with her and Kegan.

"Trevor, Kegan, Charlie, y'all bring your guests to the table. I won't have you ruining my supper by allowing it to get cold." Mrs. M stood with her hands on her hips. The way she had emphasized *guests* made Trevor want to kiss her. She knew who they were, and although he hadn't told her what he truly thought of them, she had obviously guessed. She was a very observant woman.

He turned to her and gave her a genuine smile. "Yes, ma'am." He took Charlie's hand and headed for the dining room.

Dinner was a quiet affair. His parents seemed to recognize the barely controlled anger in Trevor and Kegan, and for once were smart enough not to ask too many personal questions. Though his father seemed to enjoy the meal, he just couldn't help but make a comment on the inferiority of the wine. His mother, on the other hand, picked at the food, taking dainty bites occasionally, but thoroughly enjoyed the wine, glass after glass after glass.

He totally understood her need for alcohol. He'd need to drink if he lived with the bastard too. Though honestly, she deserved him. The truth was that it no longer affected him, which in and of itself was sad.

"Charlie, my dear." His mother spoke between sips of wine. "You seem awful young for a doctor."

"As I've already mentioned, I'm actually a resident working under Dr. Stone right now."

"I see. You seem like such a sweet girl. Are you not worried about the scandal it will cause, you living here with two men like this? Surely in your profession you must worry about your social status?"

Charlie tensed and took a sip of her own wine before she responded. "I would hope that in this day and age one is judged on their performance and ability and not by living arrangements."

"Well, young lady," his father barged in, "you're quite young and naïve if you don't think that social status is important. It will determine if you have a successful practice or a common one. I'm sure given my son's status, you would not want to hurt his reputation by acting in such a manner."

"Dad, that's enough." Trevor hissed through clenched teeth. He could see Charlie considering his father's words and the last thing he wanted was for her to have further reservations about their relationship. She turned and looked at him, doubts crowded in her eyes.

Shit!

"It's okay. Your parents just have your best interest in mind." She rose, wiped the corners of her mouth, then placed her napkin on the table before whispering, "If you'll excuse me, I have had a very long day and I'm not feeling well."

He jumped to his feet. "Charlie, wait."

She looked at him with such hurt in her eyes he wanted to howl in rage at the way his parents looked down their noses at her. "Baby, don't pay them any mind. Their opinions don't matter."

She ignored him and turned to his parents. "Mr. and Mrs. Kingsington, it was a pleasure meeting you. Now if you'll excuse me." She turned and fled from the dining room before he could stop her.

He looked over at Kegan. He'd hardly said two words all night, but now rose from his chair, vibrating with anger, and pointed a finger in the direction of Trevor's parents. "Trevor, do something with them." He stormed out, following in the same direction Charlie had.

Trevor turned his rage on his parents. "Who the fuck do you two think you are?" he roared. "You come into my home after two years of not a single word from either of you and think you can look down your snobby noses at us?"

"Trevor, that's about enough," his father demanded.

He glared at him then let the years of frustration wash out of him. "No, it's far from enough. When the two of you made the choice to let your hired help raise me, you gave up any rights to have an opinion in how I live my life. I don't want your goddamn money and I don't give a fuck about your reputation. I've made a damn fine job of making my own way in life, a good life, and couldn't care less what the Joneses think."

His father stiffened his spine ramrod straight and jutted out his arrogant chin. "You never did take anything seriously. How you live your life does affect me, and I'll be damned if you'll tarnish our good name when I've worked so hard to achieve the status that I have for this family. You have to realize that a girl like Charlie will only bring shame to you."

"This family? What family?" He made a wide sweeping motion with his arms. "Look around you, do you see any family? I don't know where you were when I was growing up, but I certainly wasn't any more a part of your family than I am now. How dare you judge Charlie? She is the most loving, giving and unselfish person I have ever met, unlike either of you."

"Trevor, pl—" His mom tried to speak, but he cut her off.

He pointed a finger in her direction. "You… Please, Mother, don't even open your mouth. I might be able to understand why he did what he did when I was young. He lives by some sick macho bullshit ideals of the way a man provides for his family. But you, dammit, you were supposed to be my mother. You should have been the one that taped my skinned knees or read to me at night, but you couldn't be bothered. You're just as bad as he is. At least in his warped mind he thought he was providing for me." He ignored the tears running down her cheeks. They weren't tears for him, they were as fake as her teased and dyed hair and her high-polished French manicure. Looking at his mother, Trevor realized that it didn't matter what they thought. They were strangers to him and they could no longer affect him.

"I've got a newsflash for the both of you that is sure to rock you out of your snooty, overpriced loafers. Charlie's not the only one I'm in love with. I'm just as committed to my relationship with Kegan as I am to her and she wants us both. None of us gives a damn about your money or social standings. You can both choke on your fake fucking class. Share that with your country club friends."

Trevor turned to leave, no longer concerned about the people sitting at his dinner table. His family waited for him upstairs.

As he walked out on their shocked looks, he tossed over his shoulder, "I'm sure even you two can find the door without butlers to give you directions."

* * * *

Charlie rested her head against Kegan's broad chest, let the comfort of his steady heartbeat and the caress of his fingers soothe her. She wasn't sure why the comments made by Trevor's parents bothered her so much. It wasn't like they were going to be a big part of their lives. But if Trevor ever wanted to re-establish a relationship with his parents, their bond would certainly hamper that. They already thought her common and nowhere near good enough for their son. She could only imagine what they would think of her if they knew she shared her bed with both men. Would their relationship really hurt her chances to become successful in her own right?

"Hey! Don't let what they said bother you, they're pompous asses on a good day."

"I'm sorry for being a coward," she whispered into Kegan's chest. "I can't help but think that if they see me that way, what will other people think?"

Kegan rolled, kept her close to him with one hand. He propped his head up with the other and looked down at her. "Why do you care what other people think? Are you happy?"

"Yes, but what if my being here ruins any chance for Trevor and his parents to rebuild their relationship?"

"I never had a relationship with those people, and I don't plan on wanting one in the future." Trevor's voice was tight, his anger barely under control.

She looked over her shoulder as he stretched out on the bed next to her and wrapped his body against her back.

"Yours and Kegan's opinions are the only ones I care about."

"But they're your parents. I don't want to be the cause of something bad between you and them. I saw how upset you got and I'm so sorry."

"Babe, don't you dare apologize. You didn't do anything wrong. The only thing I'm upset about is the way they made you feel. There hasn't been anything between us my whole life. I grew up with nannies, maids and butlers taking me to my T-ball games, helping me with homework.

"Hell, I remember once they took me to Disney World when I was about eight. I was so excited, thought my parents were finally going to spend some time with me, except when we got there, they bunked me in a room with my nanny and they entertained guests all week while I rode the rides and explored the parks with the staff." He shook his head. "I was like another pawn in their power game. Look how cute and well-behaved our son is, look how well he knows his place. The thing is, Charlie, I didn't really have a place with them. I was a commodity like the rest of their stock. If I did well, they put money into me, if I didn't, it was time to bail. How could you think that I would worry more about their feelings than yours or Kegan's?"

She couldn't help but feel sorry for Trevor. Even though her parents had died when she was young, she'd had Gram, who had done everything with her. She couldn't imagine what it would be like to live in the same house as your parents and not even know them.

"I don't care what they think of me," she admitted. "But they did get me thinking. I can't help but worry about what our relationship will look like to others, how it will affect our careers and ultimately us if it's not accepted. We can't always live in a bubble hiding out on this ranch."

Trevor and Kegan nuzzled her neck on either side, making it difficult to think past the warm lips and tongues against her flesh. Trevor spoke against her skin, his warm breath making her tingle.

"Fuck what other people think. As long as we're happy, who cares?" He slid his tongue up to her earlobe, teeth teasing. "Please tell me you're happy, Charlie," he said as he began kissing his way down her body.

Kegan whispered in her other ear, "Mmm, I wanna make you happy right now." His free hand ghosted across her breasts, her nipples hardening at the touch.

Trevor ran his hand up her inner thigh and groaned when he reached her moist sex. "Your body is happy, baby."

How could she question this? They didn't seem to worry about what others would think, why should she? They were happy, and oh God, the way they caused her body to tremble made her very happy at this moment. She still had a week to decide, she'd worry about it then.

Charlie reached up and ran her fingers through Kegan's hair while she pushed into Trevor's touch. She let them know with her body just how happy they made her.

She gasped as Trevor pulled aside her thong and tickled her clit with his tongue. When his tongue pushed into her, she nearly came up off the bed at the sensation rocking through her.

Kegan leaned up and, in one swift movement, removed her dress. His nimble fingers made quick work of her bra before he bent down and took a taut nub into his mouth, sucking hard. His teeth scraped against her flesh and caused tiny sparks of pain that he quickly soothed away with his tongue and lips. It was so good and yet nowhere near enough.

"Please."

"Tell us what you need." Kegan responded as he licked his way down her stomach, teased her navel.

"More."

Their mouths and hands made it difficult to speak more than simple words. Her mind shut down as her body took over.

Trevor worked her thong down her legs, his mouth never leaving her. She felt them shift on the bed and looked down her body, watched as they both pulled her legs apart, their heads bent over her. Trevor licked from along her entrance while Kegan began a soft caress on her clit with the tip of his tongue.

Charlie sucked in a harsh breath. With their heads close together between her thighs and the feel of their mouths against her, she was losing control rapidly. Her orgasm had already begun to roll through her body.

"Oh, don't stop." Her eyes rolled back in her head. Not wanting to miss a moment, she gave herself an internal shake and looked down her body once more, captivated by the scene before her.

"Didn't plan on it," Kegan reassured her as he sucked her clit into his mouth at the same time as Trevor speared her hard with his tongue.

She was lost in the pleasure that ripped through her body. On and on her orgasm pulsed through her until she flopped back on the bed, panting, and tried to catch her breath.

"Again."

She wasn't sure who spoke in that moment, but they couldn't be serious. "Are you —" A groan replaced her words as Kegan and Trevor both pushed a thick finger deep inside her still-convulsing sheath.

"Christ, you're hot when you come. I can feel you grip my finger hard and pull me deeper into you," Trevor murmured in a husky tone. He continued to work his finger in and out, exploring as Kegan's moans vibrated against her swollen clit.

Charlie tensed when Trevor replaced his finger with his thumb and let his slick finger brush against her back entrance. She lifted her head and her breath left her in a rush at the sight of Trevor running his fingers through Kegan's hair, pushing him harder against her as he looked down at him.

It was sexy as hell the way they touched each other to bring her more pleasure. Trevor's eyes lifted to meet her gaze as he pushed his finger past the tight ring of muscles at her back entrance. The pleasure-pain and the needy look in Trevor's dark eyes nearly sent her over the edge again. Slowly, he moved his finger in and out of her in tandem with his thumb, his gaze never wavering from hers. She felt her body relax, open up to him, and the slight pain interchanged with pure pleasure, the friction so perfect.

"Does it feel good, Charlie?"

"Mmm hmm."

"You feel like silk around my finger."

"Uh-huh," she panted, reduced to moans and grunts by their tandem efforts.

Trevor pushed a second finger in and she welcomed another bite of pain, which the sweet friction quickly replaced.

Kegan pulled back to watch Trevor pushing into her ass, while he added a second finger of his own between her folds. He circled her throbbing clit with his thumb and caused her to cry out. Her heart seemed to thump a mile a minute. Excitement, fear and pleasure swirled through her all at once.

"Trev, you're gonna make me blow if you keep doing that. Fuck, that's hot." Kegan sat back on his haunches, popped the button on his jeans, and his cock practically leaped into his hand as he unzipped. He stroked himself while he pushed his fingers harder and harder into her.

Trevor reached down with his free hand, undid his own jeans, then wrapped his fist around his cock as he scissored his fingers inside her, stretched her further. "Don't you dare, I've got plans for Charlie and it doesn't include you blowing your load like a damn teenager. Lie across the bed."

Charlie whimpered as Kegan eased his fingers from her. She instantly missed the fullness as she watched him remove his jeans, roll on a condom then lie next to her as Trevor had instructed him.

"Now, baby, I want you to straddle Kegan."

Trevor had naturally become the most dominant of the three of them. He was only truly in control of her and Kegan during sex. It was in that role that he could push both of them past their normal, comfortable limits. He pushed them to experience more pleasure than they'd ever be able to reach without him. She didn't even think, her body simply bowed to his commands without question. His fingers never left her backside as she rolled over and spread her legs wide across Kegan's waist.

Trevor bent and kissed the small of her back. "Do you trust us?"

"Mmm hmm." She did trust them, at least here anyway. The verdict was still out on whether she could trust them with more than her body, but for now, it was enough. She was beyond words or rational thought. Her only focus was the way they looked and touched her. It was all that mattered.

Kegan wrapped a tight fist around his shaft. "Wrap your hand around mine, Charlie."

Charlie entwined her fingers with his and he grabbed her ass, lifting her up and forward.

"Guide me in. Charlie. I wanna feel you tight and hot around me."

The feel of her hand entwined with his and the wicked words made her sex clench as she positioned herself over him and started to push down, accepting his thickness into her body.

"Oh… Oh damn." She couldn't help but grind her hips against his hand as the head of his erection stretched her wide. Her muscles quaked with what felt like mini orgasms. She watched his face as he stared down at their bodies, enthralled as he eased ever so slowly into her. Kegan lifted his gaze until he met hers, and something flashed in his eyes.

Charlie didn't have time to try and decipher the look as he pulled their hands away from his shaft in one quick motion and arched his hips up at the same time. She screamed as she took every inch of him. The only thing she knew in that moment was the wicked burn and sensation of having every glorious inch of Kegan within her body. She had to fight to keep from floating away on the pleasure.

"Lean forward." Trevor encouraged, his fingers still stretching and filling her from behind.

Trevor's voice brought her back from the edge of the abyss, and for a moment, she had something other than the pleasure of Kegan's body to focus on. Charlie followed his command, and Kegan captured her mouth in a deep kiss. She tensed when she heard the snap top of a bottle of lube.

"Shh, we're gonna make you fly, baby."

Charlie knew they would never hurt her. They always seemed to know exactly what her body needed. They pushed her pleasure higher and higher each time they touched her. She relaxed into Kegan's kiss as she felt the blunt head of Trevor's cock nudge at her ass. They had used fingers and toys on her ass but nothing as big as one of their cocks. She instinctively tensed as Trevor nudged forward. Kegan went still beneath her, except for his thumb stroking across the sensitive nerves around her clit. "Relax, baby, just let us love you."

Charlie felt her body give into Trevor's insistent pressure until the head of his shaft pushed past the ring of tight muscles. She felt full, so full. "Oh... Trevor... It...it's too much," she stammered. She fought to relax, tried to give her body time to adjust to Trevor's thickness. She panted harshly, her mind whirling as to whether she could handle the pain in the face of the exquisite feeling of fullness. Full of them, her men, her lovers, becoming one with them.

Trevor didn't move—how, she had no idea. His fingers dug into the flesh of her hips and his body shook in an obvious attempt to keep himself from thrusting into her. He leaned forward a bit and licked her spine from base to nape. "Relax, baby. Your body knows what it wants. You're wrapped tight around me. Your body is begging for me." Trevor pushed in another inch.

Charlie held her breath as the burn scorched through her, then she whimpered into Kegan's insistent mouth. He whispered soothing lover's words into her mouth, kept her focus on him.

As the pain receded, she relaxed, and her hips began to move on Kegan. She pushed back farther against Trevor, took him in slowly — inch by agonizing inch — until he was buried to the hilt in her ass.

"Fuck! She's burning me alive, I gotta move." Trevor groaned, low and harsh.

Trevor pulled out slowly as Kegan pushed in. They worked in perfect sync, in and out, over and over. Charlie could no longer tell where she ended and they began. They were one entity, complete.

As they picked up speed, their bodies moved in harmony until Charlie began to unravel, back arching. Her stomach tightened as a tingle raced down her spine. The first burst of liquid heat of Kegan's release coated her walls and she was blindsided by the most mind-blowing, all-consuming orgasm she'd ever experienced.

She was barely aware of Kegan and Trevor both screaming her name as they came deep inside her. Black spots formed behind her eyes and she floated out of her body as her muscles contracted, demanding every drop from her lovers.

Charlie slumped forward, heavy lids closing, only slightly aware when Trevor and Kegan withdrew from her body and a warm cloth bathed her now very sore, but very deliciously sated body.

She drifted on a cloud of overpowering bliss as they wrapped their bodies around hers and sleep pulled her under.

Chapter Fifteen

For the first time in nearly a month, Kegan woke up alone. Well not totally, but he didn't really count Trevor. He was fully aware that he was in bed with him since the man snored loud enough to wake the dead. But he had gotten so used to waking and coaxing Charlie awake that he felt out of sorts this morning.

He looked over at the nightstand, the red digital numbers flashing 5:00 a.m. Where the hell is she? He strained to listen for sounds coming from the bathroom or anywhere else in the room, but only heard Trevor.

"Hey, wake up." He shoved at Trevor.

"What? Huh?" Trevor sat straight up in bed, eyes wild, before he looked at Kegan, then flopped back on the bed. "It's still dark, leave me alone."

"Duh, we own a ranch, remember? Morning feedings, all around fun shit."

"Yeah, well I think Charlie is trying to kill me. I thought my goddamn head was going to pop off the last time I came."

Kegan chuckled. Last night had been the most intense, wildest night the three of them had shared yet. He had to agree that if it kept getting better, he'd have a damn hard time walking. "Well, did you notice the bed is a little colder this morning? You didn't happen to hear the foal alarm go off, did you?"

"Shit, I slept so hard I don't think I would have heard a stampede of horses if they ran right through the room."

Kegan rolled to his side and stared at Trevor. "The thirty days we asked for is just about up. Do you think she's gonna stay with us?"

"I dunno. If she listens to her body, then I'd say hell yeah, but Charlie's a complicated little thing. We're asking a lot from her."

"She's happy, that's gotta count for something, right?" Kegan couldn't keep from asking the question. He needed some kind of reassurance, some hope.

"Women are strange creatures. They want that fairytale life, you know, Prince Charming sweeping them off their feet. Charlie will have to settle for two demanding and possessive bastards, something she never considered before." Trevor rolled to face Kegan. "You ever think that maybe this would be easier for her if it was just you trying to sweep her off her feet?"

Kegan couldn't stop the incredulous look that crossed his face. Did his friend really think that he would want to spend the rest of his life without him? What the hell kind of fairytale ending would that be?

"Maybe, but it's not gonna happen." He couldn't choose between Trevor and Charlie.

There was no way he would ever be one hundred percent happy without both of them. He couldn't lose Charlie, but dammit, he wouldn't give up Trevor to keep her. He didn't completely understand what he felt for Trevor, but as time passed he was beginning to. He could easily say he was in love with Charlie, but still had a hard time wrapping his mind around the fact that what he felt for Trevor was just as strong. Different, yet the same, and hence where his confusion lay.

Charlie brought out a side of him that was soft—the side that liked cuddling in front of the fire, taking slow rides around their land, and taking care of someone and being taken care of.

Trevor was the one that appealed to his more macho side. He liked to hang out with him, work the ranch, wrench on equipment and share their love of raunchy jokes and the ability to tease the shit out of each other. He could let his rougher side out around him. And if he were being completely honest with himself, Trevor stirred a fire within him, a yearning that soft, smooth hands couldn't ignite.

"I'm not saying she won't want us both, but..."

"Stop! I'm not gonna choose." Kegan needed to explain to Trevor how he felt about him. He knew there might be a chance that he would think he was pussy-whipped, but if the three of them were going to make this work, he had to be completely honest. And, well, if Trevor decided to walk, then there wasn't really much he could do about that.

"Look, Trev, you know you're my best friend, right? But... Well, I think I might have crossed a line somewhere along the way and now you're more than just a best friend."

Trevor's dark eyes narrowed. "Explain."

Kegan took a long steadying breath, hesitated. *Chickenshit, just tell him.* It was now or never, so he pulled up his big-boy pants and decided to lay his emotions out on the table.

"Remember that night I found out that Charlie had been here and I freaked? Wanted to beat the shit out of you?" He fidgeted with the quilt. *Damn, this is hard.* Trevor's warm hand against his stilled his nervous fingers, he then gave Kegan an encouraging look.

"Keep going."

"Well, see, I wasn't just pissed off that you didn't call me to tell me she was here. It was like something inside me just went off and I thought of you with Charlie and... I was so fucking jealous I wanted to hit something." He stared at the wall behind Trevor, afraid to meet his eyes. "And here's the thing. I wasn't just jealous of you being with Charlie, but also of her being with you. Everything in me screamed that you belonged to me, that you're mine, at the same time it also roared that she was mine too. One was just as strong as the other and it freaked me the fuck out."

Kegan held his breath, waited for some reaction from his best friend. Finally, after a long, tension-filled moment, he finally worked up the courage to meet Trevor's gaze.

Trevor stared back at him, blinking, his reaction unreadable. Kegan waited for Trevor to walk out, call him a queer, to say anything. He did none of that, just stared at him.

Shit, that didn't come out right at all. He needed to come up with some better way of explaining this. He envied Trevor and his ease with people and the ability to say exactly what was on his mind. "Look, man, I don't know what exactly it is, but—"

Trevor reached out and pulled him closer. "Shut up, idiot. I love you too."

Kegan's heart swelled till he thought it would burst. He leaned in closer, the urge to brush his lips against Trevor's making his head spin and his heart race.

"It's about damn time you two admitted that to each other."

Kegan jerked away from Trevor. Charlie strolled in the room with a large tray and a brilliant smile on her face. She set the tray on the dresser and leaped into bed, worming her way in between them.

"Charlie, it's not like that... I mean... Well it is...but not like I like, I mean love..." Kegan blew out a frustrated breath.

Charlie rolled her eyes at him. "Trevor's right, you are an idiot. I swear, I don't know how men run this country without blowing it up from all the macho testosterone bullshit. I know exactly what is between the two of you. I see how you look at one another and how you always have each other's back. You think if you love another man that isn't family, then there is something wrong with it. I mean look at you two, what's not to love about these gorgeous bodies?" she purred. She raked her eyes appreciatively over each of the bodies in question and licked her lips.

Kegan followed her gaze as it roamed over Trevor's body. Kegan's body heated and he had to fight the urge to do the same thing and lick his lips.

When both he and Trevor remained silent, Charlie glanced back and forth between them, not with disgust as he'd feared, but as if hearing them admit their love to the other was the most natural thing in the world. "I like it that you two don't have an issue and can share displays of affection with one another. It's kinda sexy."

"Well, don't expect any more than that. I like touching you inside and out too much."

"Why not? I mean, watching Trevor run his hands through your hair or the way your body reacted to his that time I pulled you up against him... Hell, that just flat-out does it for me."

Kegan ignored her comment. It was one thing to fantasize about but to actually act on those desires wasn't a step he was willing to take at the moment. He nuzzled her ear, inhaling Charlie's scent, and loved the taste of her on the tip of his tongue. Now this was the way he was meant to start his mornings.

Trevor nuzzled the other side of Charlie's neck. "I think we should show her just how much we like touching her, what do ya think?"

"See, that's why I love ya, Trev. You're a smart man." Kegan ran his fingers slowly down between Charlie's breasts. "A very smart man."

Trevor's hand joined Kegan's as they caressed down her stomach and stopped just before reaching her light curls. They moved their hands back up her body to each cup one of her breasts. They bent forward simultaneously to each take a nipple in their mouth. Charlie shuddered as the dual sensation made her gasp and arch her chest up to their greedy mouths.

She slid her fingers into their hair, marveling at the contrast of Trevor's dark silky curls and Kegan's coarser, thicker waves. Their hands explored her lower body, fingers pinching and caressing every inch of her. She could drown in the incredible sensation of it.

Kegan lapped at her nipple, his tongue leaving a wet trail from her chest to her neck until his mouth found hers. He licked at her lips, brushed his against hers in slow, unhurried kisses. Trevor followed the same path.

They all groaned deeply as both men pushed their tongues into her mouth at the same time. The three of them battled for control of the kiss. The fact that Kegan was kissing Trevor as much as he was her pushed her from wet to drenched. The combined taste was a powerful aphrodisiac, sending her soaring. She pulled them tighter to her, loved the way their bodies felt against hers. She trembled as she thrust and bucked to rub their bodies against hers, needing more friction, more something.

"That's it, baby, tremble for us. I fucking love it when we make you shake," Trevor breathed into her mouth as he continued to battle with the kiss.

"We're going to touch every inch of you, Charlie, inside and out. Prove to you how much we love you."

Kegan reached down with his free hand, pulled her leg up and over his hip as Trevor did the same, draping her other leg over his body. Christ, it was amazing how they knew exactly what the other was doing. Like a well-rehearsed dance, they moved across her, touched and positioned her in perfect sync without so much as a word spoken between them. Their focus was completely on her. As fingers invaded her pussy, she nearly came at the first touch, her body quaking with need for release.

"Oh God!"

Trevor met Kegan's gaze. "We have her reduced to Oh God already and we've barely started."

Charlie wanted to scream at him to shut up and take her, but couldn't get her throat to work past the moans and the occasional plea for more. Within minutes, they had her hovering on the edge of orgasm.

"Come for us now," Trevor demanded as they both thrust fingers deep into her body.

She obeyed him before any thoughts formed and she screamed out as her first orgasm ripped through her with such force that only the strong hands on her body kept her grounded to the bed.

Charlie lay back, eyes closed, and gasped for breath as she floated. How the hell did he have such command that she would come when he ordered her to? Was he just so in tune with her body that he knew how close she was? It really didn't matter — though it unsettled her a little, she wouldn't complain either way.

"Keep your eyes closed," Trevor whispered.

Her arms were lifted over her head and something soft bound around her wrists. She started to open her eyes, but Trevor's insistent words halted her. "Keep them closed, Charlie, or there will be consequences."

A tremor shot through her body at his threat. Did Trevor mean it? Would he really punish her? The thought frightened and excited her at the same time.

"Consequences?" For a split second, she thought about disobeying him just to find out what kind of punishment the man would dish out, but thought better of it in the next second and kept her eyes closed.

"Do not talk, move, or open your eyes. Just clear your mind of everything but what Kegan and I are doing to you."

Her arms were pulled away from her body and within minutes she was bound to the bed. This was a test, giving them complete control of her body, the ultimate trust. Could she do it?

Light touches flicked down her body and she wanted to squirm, but she clamped down on the urge. She would at least try to trust them. Her heart sped as strong hands drew her legs apart and her ankles were bound. She was now at their mercy. Panic started to overwhelm her and it was a struggle, but after several deep breaths, she was able to keep it from overwhelming her. It didn't help much against the adrenaline that rushed through her veins, but at least the excitement and anticipation fought a good battle against the panic. Something cold touched her belly and she jumped.

"No moving," Trevor reminded her.

"Shit, that's cold."

Teeth clamped down on her bottom lip, and the sparks of pain caused her to yelp.

"What the—?"

"I told you, no talking," Trevor said against her mouth before he licked at her abused bottom lip.

Charlie forced herself to clamp her mouth shut. She gritted her teeth as the cold moved up each side of her body to her nipples. Heat... Melting... Cold droplets of water ran down her breasts. *Ice.*

She stifled a moan as the ice circled her nipples. They swelled painfully hard and she was unable to hold back the sounds as warm mouths heated her skin, followed by a stream of cool air blown across her nipples. When ice-filled mouths sucked hard on each of her nipples, the sensation of warm tongues, hot breaths and cold ice caused her to tremble uncontrollably. She squeezed her eyes shut as she tried to obey their commands, but it was difficult.

Kegan's scent surrounded her as warm lips brushed gently against hers. "Good girl."

She pulled at the bindings, felt the bite of leather into her wrists as she tried to follow his lips as he pulled away. She eased back, forced herself to lie still, but the anticipation and arousal had her fighting against her desire to obey.

A moment of unease struck her when the bed dipped then bounced as she felt them both leave the bed. She wanted to open her eyes and demand to know where they were going. They wouldn't actually leave her here tied to the bed, would they? She strained to understand the whispered conversation between them but couldn't make out what they were saying.

She heard drawers open and close, heard the shoveling of fabric and their murmured voices. Knowing they were still in the room burned off the unease, anticipation building as rapidly as the arousal. Just the slightest touch would send her over the edge. A grin spread across her face when the bed dipped again as they rejoined her. She jerked when something cool and wet landed on the skin between her breasts, then moaned when warm hands spread it in to her flesh. Thick thighs straddled her chest as knees pushed up against her armpits and large hands pushed her breasts together.

"I've dreamed of fucking these gorgeous tits," Trevor groaned at the same time he pushed his hard shaft through the valley between her breasts.

He thrust slowly. His male scent teased her senses as heat radiated from his cock and pushed between her breasts, coming close to her parted lips. She had the overwhelming urge to open her mouth wide and lick at him with each thrust. Thankfully, Trevor seemed to sense what she needed.

"Lean up and open your mouth. I want to watch those pretty lips of yours wrapped around me."

Charlie did as he'd commanded and groaned as the head passed her lips and moved onto her tongue, his flavor filling her mouth with the hint of berry from the gel. Her hips began to move involuntarily with the slow steady thrusts of his hips to match his rhythm. She gasped and her eyes snapped open when Trevor rose up onto his knees and pushed farther into her mouth at the same time as two thick fingers penetrated her pussy.

Trevor loomed over her with a knowing smirk on his face, as if he had known she wouldn't have been able to keep her eyes shut or her body still at the onslaught of pleasure they were assaulting her body with.

Trevor softly ran his finger across her cheek as he moved in and out of her mouth. "I should spank that sweet little ass of yours for disobeying me, but" — he slid in and out of her mouth a couple times — "this feels too fucking good to stop."

Charlie hummed her agreement around Trevor's shaft, her arousal growing, partly from the image of him actually spanking her and a whole lot more from Kegan's engorged head as it rubbed against her swollen clit. It felt so incredible but not nearly enough — far, far from enough.

She arched her hips, begging for more with her body as the tingling and heat in her groin intensified. Kegan seemed only too happy to comply and she heard a long groan escape his lips as he pushed deep, filling her to the hilt in one long, slow stroke. Trevor's cock pulsed on her tongue and he lost his rhythm. His movements became jerky and clumsy.

"Shit! You're ruining me… I'm gonna…"

His words died away and turned into a nearly animalistic howl as the first hot burst filled her mouth. Charlie lapped at him, sucked harder until his entire body shuddered. She eased her mouth, gently licked at the sensitive head and savored every drop until he softened against her tongue.

Trevor slipped from her mouth and she instantly missed his warmth when he rolled off her, but then he was taking her mouth in a hard, devouring kiss, fanning the flames deep within her. Charlie gave back as good as she got, shared his taste with him. She moaned into Trevor's mouth as Kegan picked up the pace, thrusting into her harder and faster.

Trevor ended the kiss, leaning his cheek against hers as they both stared up at Kegan, the muscles of his arms and chest quaking with the effort it took to keep up the brutal pace.

He was so powerful, so gorgeous, and the way he moved inside her, stretched her, caused Charlie's entire body to tremble. Close, she was so fucking close, but she held back, not wanting the moment to end. Yet Trevor had other plans—he surged up and licked a path from Kegan's stomach to his neck, and when he took Kegan's mouth in a hard kiss, she exploded. The walls of her sex contracted around Kegan as she cried out her release, and he froze, his muscles tense. Trevor ended the kiss, sitting back on his heels with a satisfied look on his face, and Kegan's head fell back seconds before he filled her with blistering heat.

Spent, Kegan collapsed on top of her, his big head nuzzling into her sweat and lube-covered chest. Trevor eased down next to her and draped his arm over Kegan, holding him and Charlie. The three of them lay there, each trying to catch their breaths.

Charlie couldn't ever remember feeling more satisfied in her entire life, nor had she ever seen anything as hot as Trevor kissing Kegan. It was something she couldn't wait to witness again, but for now, she wanted to simply lie there in her lovers' warm embrace. Unfortunately, there was a ranch to run and horses to tend to, not to mention the stacks of paperwork she had fallen behind on.

Damn insatiable men were going to kill her. Well, at least make it a tad bit uncomfortable to walk or ride. A smile curved her lips at the thought of how a few sore muscles or a hitch in her giddy-up was so worth it. She'd gladly endure it all for another go at them or to watch them go at each other.

Mmm, the things those boys did to her body. What they could do to each other's powerful body...

Charlie shuddered.

Chapter Sixteen

"Ow! Ow." Charlie groaned as the muscles in her fingers knotted into one hell of a cramp. She rubbed at the soreness, wincing until the muscle finally eased. She glared at the stacks of paperwork sitting in front of her and swore they laughed and mocked her.

Kegan and Trevor didn't give her much time to do a lot of studying—or working, for that matter. At the rate she was going, she would have to work another four years before she could get everything completed. Her work at the ranch, rotating between Equine Medicine, Equine Surgery, and her elective blocks was more than she thought she could handle.

Add in the fact that she now had two very demanding and persuasive men vying for her time, and she didn't know whether she was coming or going half of the time. Not that she complained much. Hell, not at all. The pace might be exhausting, some days painfully so, but giving up her career or either of the men in her life wasn't an option. She wanted it all and was willing to work for it. The rewards were oh so wonderful. A pleasing tickle ran down her spine at the thought.

A door slammed, rattling the walls and causing her to jump. She nearly knocked her coffee on her laptop but thankfully grabbed it at the last second. She looked up to see Kegan stomp through the kitchen, a scowl on his face. He didn't see her or at least didn't acknowledge her sitting there.

"Kegan?"

He continued on as if he hadn't heard her, which was followed by the slam of the office door then an eerie silence. Something was terribly wrong. Kegan never ignored her. He usually went out of his way to seek her out during the day, as if he couldn't stand to be away from her for even the briefest moment.

Trevor walked in, looking solemn. "Hey, babe, how goes the studying?" He kissed her head before he sat next to her.

"Studying is fine, but what's the matter with Kegan? He just came storming through here as if he didn't even know I was in the room and shut himself up in the office."

"His old man called."

"What?" Charlie stared at him, mouth agape. She'd heard the words, just couldn't comprehend them. They seemed totally foreign.

"Seems his old man just got out of prison and he needs a place to stay and some cash."

"I didn't know he was in prison. I mean, it doesn't surprise me, but still. Did Kegan know?"

"Yeah, he knew he was in prison but not that he would be getting out anytime soon. He was sentenced twenty-five years to life, but got a get-out-of-jail-free card"—he made air quotes—"on some bullshit technicality."

"Seriously? What was he sent to prison for?"

"That's Kegan's story to tell. But the bastard sure as hell shouldn't be out on the streets."

"What's he gonna do?" She couldn't imagine Kegan would allow his father to come here. The man was the meanest soul she had ever met, and after what Kegan had told her, Mr. Colburn plain scared the hell out of her.

"Kegan told him to go to fuck himself, of course, but I guess he threatened to show up on our doorstep. Spouted off some bullshit about Kegan owing him for all the years he had to take care of his sorry ass."

"So what now?" Charlie reached over and entwined her fingers with Trevor's, needing to feel his skin against hers to help her combat the dread that grew inside her.

Trevor stared at her, his eyes intense and nearly black. "For starters, you're not to go anywhere without one of us with you, not even the barns. You're not to leave this house alone, do you understand?"

"Don't you think that's a little dramatic? I mean, even if he showed up here, I doubt he would do anything. He wants a place to stay and money is all. Besides, I have work at the clinic and my work here. I have to be free to come and go to do my job."

Trevor pried his fingers from hers and grabbed her wrist in a bruising grip. "I mean it, Charlie. You're not to leave this house alone. Say it! Say you won't leave this house without one of us."

"Trevor, you're hurting me."

He looked down at their hands as if he hadn't realized he was squeezing, but loosened his grip only slightly, the intensity in his gaze only hardening further. "Say it, Charlie, so I know you understand. This man is dangerous and we're not taking any chances of him coming anywhere near you. Say it."

"Okay! I won't leave the house alone."

He pulled her onto his lap and held her tight against him. "I couldn't stand it if he hurt you or took you away from us."

Trevor's body was taut with tension, and Charlie knew he needed reassurances. She kneaded the tight muscles of his shoulders. "He's not gonna hurt me or take me away. He told Kegan he wanted money and a place to stay, why would he jeopardize that by hurting me? I don't think he will, but I promise I'll be careful." She let Trevor keep a firm hold on her, even though she could hardly breathe, but she knew he needed this.

"I don't want you to do this just to make us feel better. I want you to do this because it's the smart thing to do. You understand how dangerous he is. You shouldn't take any chances."

Charlie thought about the numerous times she'd seen Kegan with bruises, split lips and other various injuries when they'd been younger. Some of them had been severe enough that he'd needed medical treatment, but his dad had never allowed him to see a doctor or to talk to anyone about how he had been hurt. She could only imagine the horrendous threats he'd made to his young son to ensure his silence. The idea made her stomach roil.

Charlie had known the truth of the injuries even without Kegan saying a word, but she'd been too young to understand how to get him the help he needed. She would bet her life that the rest of the community had known as well, but no one had offered to help. They'd all turned their heads when Kegan had come to town with a new bruise. No one had wanted to get involved, and the majority of them — if not all of them — had just been flat-out afraid of Drake Colburn.

For Charlie it wasn't just the violence she knew Drake was capable of that frightened her. She had only been to the Colburn house a few times, but the way Drake had stared at her was more of how a predator studied his prey. It made her skin crawl but he had never done anything beyond stare.

By the time she was sixteen, Kegan had asked her not to come anywhere near his house for any reason. When he had told her, there had been such a haunted look in his eyes, she hadn't argued or questioned it. Now thinking back about the way Drake had watched her, knowing what he had done to so many women, she knew exactly where Kegan's haunted look came from and what had put the disgusting look on Drake's.

"I know how dangerous he is," she whispered as a sick dread washed through her. "I won't take any chances." She burrowed deeper into the heat of Trevor's body, allowing his strong arms around her to help push away the ugly thoughts that threatened to engulf her.

"What about Kegan? Do you think we should go talk to him?" Charlie asked after she'd gotten herself back under control.

Trevor shook his head. "No, not yet. He needs to work this out in his own head first. Plus he's gonna call the sheriff and have him keep an eye out for Drake, just in case he does make good on his threat."

Charlie hated that Kegan had locked himself alone in the office. She wanted to run in and wrap her arms around him, take away some of the anger and pain she knew he had to be feeling. "I can't stand the thought of him in there having to deal with this alone."

"I know, babe, but he'll come find us when he's ready. Just give him a bit, okay?"

Charlie nodded. Trevor was probably right. Kegan would need some time on his own, but the wait until he finally did come seek them out was going to be pure torture.

The dread that seeped into her upon hearing about Drake spread through her and took up residence in every cell of her body. Something horrible was about to happen. She wasn't sure exactly what it was but knew deep down in her soul that Drake Colburn was going to affect their lives in a terrible and horrifying way.

Lord, please let me be wrong.

Charlie sighed and snuggled deeper into Trevor's chest, knowing on some level she wasn't wrong.

* * * *

It was three agonizing hours before Kegan joined her and Trevor on the back porch. His shoulders were slumped and concern showed in the sharp lines around his eyes and mouth. He didn't look at either of them as he dropped into one of the old rockers next to them.

Charlie leaped to her feet and threw herself onto Kegan's lap. He instantly pulled her into a tight embrace. He didn't say anything, just rubbed his cheek against the top of her head and rocked them. She wasn't sure how long the three of them sat there in silence, lost in their own thoughts.

When Charlie couldn't stand the quiet any longer, she raised her head and looked up at Kegan. "Are you okay?"

Kegan shook his head. "No, not really. I just don't understand how a man can be convicted of five brutal rapes and attempted murder and be back on the streets in only three years. I'm so goddamned outraged I just can't seem to grasp how this could happen."

Charlie wasn't shocked to hear what Drake had been convicted of, only had a sickening feeling in the pit of her stomach that the man was walking free. Her heart also hurt for his victims — knowing he was once again on the streets had to be pure hell. "You don't really think he will come here, do you? I mean, they will be keeping a close eye on him, won't they?"

Kegan laid his head back against the chair, looked up at the night sky and held her tighter. "Yes, Charlie, I do think he will come here. The thought of him anywhere near you drives me so insane I can't fucking breathe."

Trevor stood and walked behind their chair and placed a firm hand on Kegan's shoulder. "We won't let him get anywhere near her. I've already made Charlie promise she won't leave the house without one of us."

Kegan jerked up and he pinned her with fiery blue eyes. "I want to hear it. I want to hear you promise me that you won't go anywhere without one of us. You have no idea what this man is capable of."

Charlie laid a hand on each side of his face and returned his gaze with a fierce one of her own, her voice firm. "I promise, Kegan. I won't leave the house without one of you with me."

He grabbed her and covered her mouth with a desperate kiss. When he finally pulled back, his eyes were tear-filled. "Thank you. I can't lose you again, Charlie. I won't lose you again because of that spineless son of a bitch."

He was breaking her heart. "You're not going to lose me because of him." The instant Charlie had said the words, she realized her mistake as pain flashed briefly in Kegan's eyes.

Neither Kegan nor Trevor knew about the decision she had made when it came to a future for them. The sheer sadness in his beautiful eyes almost had her confessing to them on the spot, but she stopped herself. She didn't want the beginning of their lives together to be overshadowed by Drake Colburn, nor did she want the happiest moment of her life to be any part of a memory that included his evil.

She would tell these two protective, loving and amazing men how she truly felt about them as she had planned. But only when it was all about them and could only be remembered as a happy memory.

She leaned in and kissed Kegan's brow gently, then feathered her fingers against the lines until he relaxed a little. "You're not going to lose me," she whispered against his lips then nuzzled into his chest.

She hoped her body conveyed exactly how much she truly loved him without giving away her secrets.

Chapter Seventeen

Charlie found herself astride a bareback Taz, Kegan's favorite stallion. Taz, short for Taz-Mania, was the same stallion she had been drawn to the first day she'd been at the ranch.

It was easy to see why Kegan was so fond of the animal. They were identical in the fact that both were magnificent to look at with large, well-defined muscles under a handsome exterior. There was such power just below the surface that was controlled with an iron-clad will. The other similarity was that deep beneath it, they both possessed the sweetest disposition. Their need to be touched, snuggled and physically close to someone seemed more important to them than the show of power, thus making control a little easier to manage.

The twin in question to Taz was currently against her back, his hands lightly caressing the inside of her thighs.

Charlie tried to concentrate on her surroundings. The mid-spring blooming frenzy was in full swing and gave the fields and bordering woods a fresh feeling. Scents of new growth and rebirth moving with the wind made everything seem so alive. The mountains set as a backdrop to an already spectacular view should have been enough to keep her attention. But the only thing that she could concentrate on was Kegan's heat and the play of his hands as they swayed together in sync with Taz's graceful stride. She had a hard time controlling her body when she was around Kegan. She seemed to have the same effect on him, as was evident with how happy his body seemed pressed against hers. Some parts lower seemed to be very, very happy.

"I thought you said you wanted to show me your land?"

"I thought that was what we were doing." His voice was deeper than it should have been just from enjoying the sights.

"You know exactly what you're doing and it's not sightseeing."

He pushed up a little closer against her, and his lips played along her neck. His warm breath made her skin tingle as he spoke, "I've already had the tour, and I'm enjoying the beautiful sights right here in my arms much more."

Charlie still had a very difficult time with the compliments Trevor and Kegan gave her, as if they just couldn't help themselves. She wasn't sure if the compliments made her feel uneasy because of their past with women or her own insecurities. It was easier to believe the first since she had a hard time believing that they found her as beautiful as they claimed. She did what she did most of the time with their compliments, blushed and ignored it.

They dismounted near a creek that ran through a grove of trees. After securing Taz and feeding him apples, Kegan spread out a blanket where they would get the full effect of the warm spring sun.

Charlie watched as he removed his boots and stretched out on his back. His movements were amazingly graceful, which shouldn't have been possible with a body so taut with thick muscle. Charlie's pulse quickened and her body responded with warmth as Kegan gave her a come-hither look and motioned her over.

She sat on the edge of the blanket and removed her boots without looking at him. She wasn't sure why she suddenly felt so unsure, but for some reason she was nervous. She fiddled with arranging her boots, delayed going to Kegan, but why? Was it because Trevor wasn't here to push them along as he usually did? He always seemed to set the pace, never let Kegan or her think about anything too long. He pushed them along with a flow of sensations and encouraged them to feel instead of think.

"Charlie, is there something wrong?"

"No, I'm fine. I think I'm just still feeling a little jittery after last night." She moved back and lay down next to Kegan, unable to look at him, and stared up at the white marshmallow clouds set against the bright-blue backdrop.

She wasn't being totally untruthful. They had all been a little nervous after finding out what Drake had threatened and none of them had slept very soundly. She didn't want to have to think about Drake this morning or the dread deep inside her. She wanted this morning to be just about her and Kegan.

She looked over at him. He was as tense as the night before, with the same haunted look in his eyes. "Hey, stop that. No ugly thoughts this morning. I'm sorry I brought it up." She took his hand and laid it on her stomach, covered it with her own. "So how did you get out of the heavy negotiations with the Kentucky breeders?"

Kegan looked at her and blinked slowly a couple of times as if to clear his head. A slight smile played at the edge of his mouth. "Trevor pulled the short straw."

"You mean you gambled to see who would get babysitting duty?"

"No, we gambled to see who would get the privilege of spending the day with you. I have a feeling Trevor may have drawn the short straw on purpose."

Charlie couldn't control her body as it tensed at the thought that Trevor didn't want to spend the day with her. She knew he probably had his reasons but old insecurities were hard to overcome.

Kegan must have felt her tense because he quickly added, "It's not that he didn't want to spend the day with you, I think he just knew I needed it more than he did today." He traced small circles on her stomach with his fingertips. "I know everyone thinks Trevor is just a playboy, and up until recently I probably would have agreed with them. But I've never seen him react to anyone the way he does you. Hell, I don't think he has ever gone on a second date with a woman, and now it's like he can't get enough time with you to satisfy himself."

"Are you trying to make me feel better?"

"No. I mean yes, I do want you to feel better but it's still true. You have the same effect on him that you've always had on me."

"What effect would that be, Kegan? Make me love him and he leaves—" Charlie knew she sometimes spoke before fully thinking. She regretted it even more when she saw the effect it had on him. Kegan looked stunned and hurting. "I'm sorry... I don't know why I said that, I didn't mean that." It had been a mean thing to say but it was like a freight train without brakes.

Kegan's face crumbled and his sapphire blue eyes lost most of the shine that had been there only a moment before. God, how could she have been so cruel to him? Was she trying to push him away as she had with everyone else in her life since she was young?

"It's okay, Charlie, I know you didn't intend to say that, but you did mean it."

"Kegan..."

He held up his hand. "I deserved it. You couldn't have known how I felt about you back then and you did what anyone would have done... Hate the person who hurt you."

Charlie turned fully on her side, met his gaze, let the love she felt for him shine through. "I don't hate you. I tried, and at times I thought I had succeeded, but I never could truly hate you. Sometimes I wanted to hurt you so badly, wanted you to feel some of the pain I was living with. That's still no excuse for what I just said to you. It's my stupid insecurities coming through. I can be such an ass sometimes. I'm sorry," she said sincerely, then pressed a kiss to his cheek.

Kegan snuggled in a little closer, his fingers playing along her back. "You don't have to apologize, Charlie. You still don't trust me yet. I get that, hell, I understand, I'm just glad you're at least giving me a chance to try and make up for leaving. I do know about pain and hate."

He laid his head down on his arm, his gaze locked with hers. "I hated my father every day for what he did to those women and to me, but I hated him even more for causing me to lose you. I know what it's like to miss someone so much the pain in your heart feels like it's going to crush you. I know what it feels like because that is how I felt when I left you. I know it was my choice and that almost made it worse. Knowing that I was the one who walked away, who wasn't man enough or stronger to keep a promise. I will regret that for the rest of my life—"

Charlie stopped him by pressing her lips against his. She hadn't really wanted to hurt him or bring up the past, but now that she had, she wanted to make it up to him. Even more than that, she wanted to show him how much she loved him. How much she wanted him here and now.

Kegan responded to the kiss with an urgency that was almost frightening. He took command of it and deepened it like his whole life depended on it. He explored her mouth as if he were trying to memorize every inch of it with his tongue. He pulled her to him at the same time he pushed toward her, their bodies melding together.

Clothes flew off in a blur as they searched frantically for the skin underneath. His body was an oasis in the middle of a desert and without it, she would die from the heat that consumed her.

The frenzy ended with Kegan on top of her, their naked bodies pressed together, each trying to touch as much skin as they could. Kegan looked down at her and she was lost. In this one perfect moment, everything seemed crystal clear and neither the past nor the future mattered. There was only them and nothing else existed.

Kegan took her mouth again in a slow, sweet kiss, as soft and as gentle as the last had been hard and hungry.

His body rocked against hers, encouraging her to respond to the gentleness of his movements.

Her heart rate and breathing slowed from the fevered pace and the rush of blood in her ears cleared. Charlie was acutely aware of every touch, every bead of sweat that formed on her body and either rolled across her skin or mingled and melted into his. The taste of his mouth was more intense, the slide of his tongue even more intimate.

His lower body pulled away from hers as he broke the kiss. He stared down into her eyes and held her gaze as he entered her agonizingly slowly. She felt every ridge and inch of him push past her opening. The delicate look on his face, the tenderness in his eyes increased the effects his body had on hers and she experienced the strangest desire to scream her pleasure and weep at the same time as she looked at him.

As much as she had grown to love Trevor, this was what she had dreamed of. This moment between just her and Kegan had been what she had prayed for. The reality of it was better than any fantasy she could have ever conjured up in her limited imaginings.

Kegan pushed the last of himself into her and lowered his body against hers, grasped her hands in his and stretched their arms up over her head so that even the skin of their arms were in an intimate embrace.

He rocked inside and out, surrounding her. Charlie gave herself over to him completely. The slow dance of their bodies caressed places deep inside that no one had ever touched. It was not only an entwining of skin and flesh but of heart and soul. She wanted to stay in this moment forever, but at the same time, she wanted more, needed him deeper inside, and pressed harder against him.

Charlie wrapped her legs around his waist, and the new angle made them both gasp. He began to pull out of her body farther with each stroke and push back inside her with more strength each time. The walls of her sex began to contract and clutch at him, desperate to keep him buried deep within her.

Heat washed over her and ran from the base of her neck down her spine, and she knew she was unable to stop or contain it. Her core grasped him tight as the world around her exploded in brilliant flashes of light.

Her breathing hitched and even her heart stopped for an instant as pleasure consumed every inch of her flesh, then pushed beyond it as she heard her name like a sigh from Kegan's lips. His heat filled her with a warm rush that bathed her.

Kegan collapsed next to her while they fought to catch their breaths and basked in the afterglow of sensations.

Sensations so big and amazing that even while she was experiencing them, there were no words to describe them.

Kegan rolled to his side, pulling Charlie along with him, unable to let go of her even for a second. Jesus, the way she made him feel, as if he was the luckiest fucking man in the world… He supposed he rightly was.

With her and Trevor in his life, his own piece of land and a job he loved, he couldn't imagine there was anyone happier than he was at this moment. Charlie completed him. No, she completed both him and Trevor. It was as if a part of him had been missing and he hadn't even realized it until he'd found her again.

He looked down at a Charlie all snuggled up close, a content look — like the cat that had just got the cream —

her skin all flushed and glowing, beads of perspiration glistening in the sun. He gave in to the temptation and licked the sweat from her neck, savored the taste of her sweet skin.

She opened her eyes slowly and looked up at him with a sated smile. "Hey."

"Hey yourself." He kissed her lightly on the lips and spoke against them. "That was amazing."

"Mmm hmm. You can say that again."

"Not bad for my first time, huh?"

Charlie looked at him, puzzled, and he chuckled. "First time what?"

"Making love with a woman."

Charlie pulled back, looked him square in the eye, and started to laugh. "Okay, and the punchline is what?"

"No punchline, I'm dead serious. I have never made love to anyone alone. Hell, I've never even had sex with anyone alone. I think I was pretty amazing at it and totally feeling studly here." He leaned in and licked her pouty lips.

Charlie slapped his arm. "Yeah, you were totally a stud but you don't need to try and make it more than what it was—spine-tingling, mind-blowing and amazing. You don't need to feed me a line of bull to make it even more perfect. Besides, did you forget that I've known you most of your life, including your teenage years, so I know about Emily Thornton." She frowned and muttered, "The bitch!"

Emily Thornton? Oh shit! He hadn't thought about her in years. Christ, she had been as bad as Charlie had when she was younger, always following him around. However, Emily had been a grown woman, one who had a damn hard time taking no for an answer. He hadn't minded Charlie following him around, had come to look forward to it even when she was still in those silly little ponytails, but he had minded the way Emily had sniffed after him.

"Emily Thornton? If I didn't know you any better, bichito, I'd swear you sound jealous."

Charlie pushed him away, sat up, then reached for her clothes. "I'm not jealous," she huffed but the tone of her voice and the frown that creased her brow told otherwise.

Kegan snatched her clothes from her, threw them over his shoulder out of her reach and pushed her back down. "Aww, Charlie, you are. That's so cute. I knew you always hated Emily, but I thought it was just because she was a spoiled rotten brat who didn't use any of the sense God gave her, not because of me. Hell, I only went out with her the one time and it was enough."

Charlie's frown deepened. She looked up at him as if she could find the truth somewhere hidden in the lines of his face or the flecks of color in his eyes. "You really didn't sleep with Emily Thornton?"

Kegan shook his head from side to side. "Nope."

"Jesus, Kegan, you knew the whole school was talking about the two of you! If I remember right, I didn't talk to you for nearly a month after I heard the rumors. You let everyone believe that you did... Dammit, you let *me* believe it and... Oh my God! The mess I made of her pretty little sports car."

He laughed his fool head off. He remembered Emily's car after someone had scratched the paint. Hell, he'd been standing against Matt Crosby's pickup just two cars down when she had come out of the school and seen it for the first time. She'd been so mad she'd jumped up and down and screamed shit that would make a sailor blush. And the look on her face... He had thought for sure that when her skin went from red to purple, her head was gonna explode right then and there.

He'd known Charlie had been the one to do it and as good as he could figure, Emily had deserved it, maybe not because of the rumors, but just because of the way she had treated Charlie. Emily had always looked down her nose at Charlie and called her a pathetic little wannabe. Charlie had only done what half the girls in that school had wanted to do.

He couldn't help but laugh harder when he looked at the little hellcat in his arms who had been spirited enough to do it.

Tears of laughter rolled down his face as Charlie slapped him again good and hard. "Ow."

"Kegan Colburn, you stop laughing right this second. It is so not funny." Charlie could barely contain her own laughter, her shoulders shaking with the effort. "Why would you let everyone think you and Emily did the nasty? God, I destroyed her car because... Why the hell didn't you say something?"

"What was I was going to say to you? You were fifteen and I was just figuring out for the first time that you weren't just some little bug but someone who stirred all kinds of feelings in me. I couldn't tell you. Jesus, Charlie, I was eighteen and still a virgin. I wasn't about to admit to any of the guys that I wasn't the greatest lover she'd ever had when half of them had already said they'd been in her bed. Instead of saying they were either a bunch of damn lying fools who hadn't ever touched her or they sucked so bad at it that a virgin was better than anything they'd done with her, I kept my mouth shut and let them think what they wanted."

Kegan claimed another kiss and the laughter melted away into something much more serious but just as wonderful. "Only you, Charlie, I swear it. Yeah, I played my share with the women Trevor picked up, but it never meant a damn thing but a good time. I never looked at a single one of them as something serious. I guess I always hoped we'd find one another again. Not until you did I ever put my heart and soul into it." He locked his gaze with hers, let her know he was telling the truth and hoped like hell that he had earned at least that bit of trust.

Charlie hesitated briefly, then pulled him into a kiss and wrapped herself around him, just as content as could be. Yeah, she believed him and he thanked God that he had earned that much. He knew he still had a ways to go to win her full trust but he was okay with that.

He had the rest of his life to prove it to her.

Chapter Eighteen

Flowers in hand, Trevor rushed through the back door. He pulled a pink carnation from the bouquet and handed it to Mrs. M, who was standing near the stove. "A pretty for a pretty," he said and pecked her on the cheek.

"Boy, butter wouldn't melt in that mouth of yours," she chastised lightly.

Trevor grinned slyly and went to Charlie, who was sitting at the kitchen table snapping peas. "And for you," he announced, handing the rest of the flowers to her.

"They're beautiful. Thank you."

"Just like you." He kissed her on the temple. "Kegan in the office?" he asked, already heading in that direction.

"I believe so."

Kegan looked up from the desk when Trevor entered. "I take it the meeting went well?"

"Yeah, yeah, fine," he said dismissively and propped his ass on the corner of the desk next to Kegan. "Well?"

Kegan sat back in his chair and cocked his head. "Well what?"

Trevor narrowed his eyes at him. "Don't make me beat it out of you."

"You want to do what?" Kegan asked in mock horror and grabbed his crotch like he was protecting it.

The image of his hands wrapped around Kegan's cock, stroking him to orgasm, popped in Trevor's head so quickly and vividly, heat rushed to his groin. He'd always had a very active imagination. Now, Charlie took the lead role, but lately Kegan had gone from a supporting participant to a very active costar of Trevor's naughty musings. He shifted as his arousal grew and laid his forearm over his lap to hide the evidence.

"Would you knock it off? You know exactly what I'm talking about. How'd it go with Charlie this morning?"

"It was nice," Kegan drawled and ran his hand over his jaw, no doubt trying to cover his smile, but he couldn't hide the glint of mischief in his eyes.

"That good, huh?" Trevor asked and waggled his brows.

"You have no idea." Kegan leaned back farther in his chair and propped his feet up on the desk. "I'm a total fucking stud."

"I already knew that." *That's why I want to jump your bones.* "But I want details."

Kegan let out a long, dramatic breath. "I never kiss and tell."

Trevor's hand shot out, and the instant his fingers tightened around Kegan's dick, the man fell forward with a loud oomph.

"What was that?" Trevor encouraged wryly and tightened his hold on Kegan's shaft.

"Ow! Jesus. Uncle."

"I thought so." Trevor chuckled and eased his grip, allowing his fingertips to caress across the thick bulge as he pulled his hand back. He crossed his arms, tucking his hands beneath his armpits to keep from touching Kegan again.

Kegan ran a hand over his crotch, scowling at Trevor as he rubbed his abused flesh, but then his features softened and he relaxed back into his chair. "We went for a ride, Charlie enjoying the sights of our land while I was enjoying the way her body felt against mine as Taz moved. We stopped by that grove of trees out by the pond and…" A content smile crossed Kegan's face as if he were remembering it, then he met Trevor's gaze. "It was better than I could have ever imagined it would be."

"Dude, that's awesome. You've been devirginized." He held out his fist.

"I was very, very far from virginal." Kegan laughed as he bumped his knuckles against Trevor's.

Oh, didn't he know it. He'd been a witness to Kegan's prowess. However, to have overcome such a huge obstacle in his mental psyche was a milestone to be celebrated whether Kegan realized it or not. "Still, it's a huge deal." Trevor pushed off the desk and went to the liquor cabinet. "This calls for a toast."

"I am so not toasting to that," Kegan scoffed.

Trevor set two glasses on the desk and poured a good measure of bourbon in each. "Fine, then we'll toast the fact I procured a Blue Roan Gypsy stallion without it costing me a nut."

"Now that I'll drink to." Kegan raised his glass, and Trevor clinked his against it. "Way to turn on the charm."

Trevor threw back the alcohol in one gulp, wiped his mouth on the back of his sleeve, then took the chair on the other side of the desk with a satisfied grin on his face. "Went up against some tough negotiators, but come next week, we'll be the proud owners of the new stallion. So back to you…"

"What about me?" Kegan asked, trying to sound shy and innocent. He didn't pull it off.

Trevor arched an eyebrow. "Kegan," he warned.

"It really was amazing. We talked a little about our childhood, shared some laughs. Even talked about my old man briefly, but then she kissed me and…" Kegan swirled the rest of his bourbon as he stared down into the glass for a second longer, before a wide smile stretched across his face when he looked up. "I'm nothing like him."

"Well, duh."

"No, seriously, Trev. It was slow and sweet and the moment her lips touched mine, the only thing that ran through my mind was how much I loved her and how badly I wanted to please her. Not one ugly thought. Not even a single naughty one." He laughed happily.

Trevor stared at him incredulously for a few ticks of the clock then shook his head. "No, no, this won't do at all." He went to the door and hollered, "Hey, Mrs. M, how long before dinner?"

"Half hour."

Perfect. He looked back at Kegan and motioned him over with a wave of his hand. "C'mon."

"Where we going?" Kegan asked, following him out of the office.

"I've been having naughty thoughts all day about the two of you. I'll share some."

Charlie looked up to see her men walking into the kitchen with predatory glints in their eyes seconds before Trevor scooped her up. "Trevor," she protested as the bowl of snap peas toppled over. "I was helping Mrs. M. Now put me down."

Trevor paused briefly. "Mrs. M, you need Charlie to help with dinner?"

"Nope, those there are for canning. Would it have mattered?"

"Nope."

"Good man. I'll set the stew to simmer."

Kegan snorted as he righted the bowl and cleaned up the spilt peas.

"Leave 'em. You go enjoy yourselves."

"Yes, ma'am."

"Mrs. M, don't you go encouraging them." Charlie squirmed, trying to free herself from Trevor's embrace. Instead of letting her go, he threw her over his shoulder and patted her ass as he headed for the door.

"Oh, honey, those boys don't need no encouragement from me. Lucky for you," Mrs. M said with a sly grin then turned back to the stove.

At the top of the stairs, Kegan rushed past them and held open the door to their room. Charlie was hit with a feeling of déjà vu, only this time she knew exactly what to expect and didn't have even the slightest hesitation, nor did she doubt what was about to happen. Her pulse raced in anticipation and with the rush of blood came a sweet tingling sensation along her clit. Oh yeah, she so knew exactly what was about to happen. She grabbed two handfuls of tight ass and smiled.

"Let me shuck these jeans and you can grab it all you want, baby," Trevor declared and set Charlie on her feet next to the bed.

"How'd it go with the breeder?" she asked, curious as to if it had anything to do with his sudden excitement.

Trevor shot a look at Kegan and she swore she saw him roll his eyes right before he pulled his T-shirt over his head. "Fine," he said and tossed the shirt behind him before he unbuckled his belt. "Now get them clothes off." He looked over at Kegan again. "You too."

Neither she nor Kegan were ones to argue about getting naked, so clothes went flying in record time. Once she'd shimmied out of her panties, the predatory looks were back in Kegan's and Trevor's eyes as they stood staring at her, large erections hard and straining upward. Charlie's mouth watered in anticipation of getting her hands and mouth on them both.

"You ever seen anything so beautiful, Kegan?" Trevor asked as he raked his eyes up and down Charlie's body.

"Nope. At least not since the last time she was nekkid," Kegan responded, his voice low and husky. "How you want to do this?"

Trevor put his hands on his hips, continuing to stare. "I might need to give this some thought."

"How about you two move a little closer and let me play while you're thinking on it," Charlie suggested wantonly. She was itching to get her hands on their gorgeous bodies.

"You're a greedy girl, ain't ya?" Trevor chuckled. "You just behave for a moment. The way I see it, you and Kegan done got off today so I think this should be all about me."

Kegan bumped his shoulder against Trevor. "Seeing as it's all about you, how about you rub one out and get caught up. I'll keep Miss Charlie company until you're done. You know, get her nice and ready for ya."

"Not fucking likely," Trevor growled.

"Didn't think so," Kegan laughed. "So what ya got in mind?"

Trevor stepped up closer to Charlie, cupping her breasts in his hands, and kneaded them with his callus-roughened finger. He ducked his head and dragged his lips over one taut nipple. His warm breath against her heated flesh caused goosebumps to bloom across her skin.

He looked up at her with a sly grin. "I'm trying to decide whether to suck these or fuck 'em."

"Well since your mouth is right there," Kegan drawled. His hand suddenly shot out and he grabbed her other nipple, pinching it nice and hard just as she liked it.

Charlie went up on tippy toes and gasped at the harsh treatment. When she released her breath, it came out as a deep moan when Trevor sucked the other one, swirling his tongue around the hard nub. The sounds intensified when Kegan licked his way up her neck, nipped her earlobe before he took her mouth in a heated kiss.

Charlie gave herself over to the kiss while Kegan and Trevor worked in perfect, quiet harmony, moving her onto the bed without ever taking their mouths from her lips and body until she was lying in the center of the mattress. Only then did Trevor move up and join them in the kiss. Once again the idea of Trevor kissing not only her but Kegan as well caused her internal walls to contract and weep with arousal. She fisted her fingers through their hair, turning their heads slightly toward each other. It was all the encouragement they needed.

Suddenly the two men were devouring each other's mouths inches from hers. Charlie's body thrummed and she squirmed as an ache settled between her thighs as she watched.

"Fuck that's hot."

Kegan jerked back from the kiss, panting harshly as he stared at Trevor. It was still a little strange kissing Trevor, but the funny thing was, Kegan didn't feel the least bit shocked or embarrassed having given in to the temptation. He didn't quite understand it. It wasn't like he was attracted to men, had never once looked at any other guy and wondered what he looked like naked or wanted to bang him. But Trevor... Well, Kegan didn't rightly know. Perhaps it was because he was in love with the man or it was simply the fact that it was Trevor. Didn't matter.

What he did know was Charlie was right. It was fucking hot and he wanted more of the sharp, biting kisses. He grabbed the back of Trevor's head, curled his fingers in the dark strands and smashed their mouths together again.

Trevor moaned and opened up to him. Kegan dove in, shoving his tongue deep, a full-out assault. Kegan wasn't gentle, didn't have to be, and for the first time in his life — another first — let go and put his full strength into the kiss, into his grip on Trevor's hair, knowing Trevor could take it. Not only could he take it, he gave it right back. Trevor's rough hand grabbed the back of his neck, pulled him harder still, their tongues twirling in a battle for dominance. The kiss ended in a draw when Charlie whimpered and shifted beneath them.

"You liked that, didn't you, baby?" Trevor asked Charlie, but he never took his gaze from Kegan's nor did his smirk fade.

"God, yes. I think I could come just by watching you two go at it."

Kegan's dick twitched at the suggestion. He had no doubt he'd detonate like a fucking bomb if Trevor was to actually go at it.

Trevor wiped his kiss-swollen mouth with the back of his hand. "Whatcha think, Kegan? Want to try and make our girl come?"

Kegan cut a glance to Charlie. Her body was flushed and pure lust and want showed in her darkened, heavy-lidded eyes. It wasn't only Charlie's desire that had Kegan nodding but his own as well.

Kegan leaned down and pressed a soft kiss to Charlie's lips then sat back on his calves. "Okay, but you ain't fucking me."

"I don't know," Trevor said, arching an eyebrow. "Your body is liking the idea." And to prove his point, he reached over and wrapped his fist around Kegan's shaft and pumped it hard a few times.

Kegan groaned and snapped his hips. The rough treatment, the calluses, the power in Trevor's touch made his head swim and his pulse race. Fuck, it felt good, better than he'd imagined it would, and he couldn't help but thrust again.

Trevor laughed at Kegan's heady reaction to his touch. "Lay down on your back next to Charlie."

Kegan eyed him suspiciously but did as he'd been told. He looked down his body, his cock standing tall and proud, weeping his arousal from the darkened flared head. He was turned on beyond belief, his balls aching something fierce. "As bad as I want your hands and mouth on me, you still ain't fucking me, Trev," Kegan grit out.

Trevor crawled up between Kegan's legs, the soft hairs on his thighs tickling the insides of Kegan's, and Kegan tensed.

"Scared," Trevor murmured as he ran both his hands over Kegan's chest.

Trevor's impressive cock was straining upward, bobbing with each movement. His cockhead was wide, intimidatingly so, and the thought of it ramming into his ass had Kegan involuntarily clenching. "Ass clenching in fear," Kegan responded then groaned when Trevor pinched his right nipple between his fingers, rolling it, sending sparks of pain radiating through Kegan. And holy fuck he wanted more, harder. "Just remember, I get my chance at you next."

"I can't wait." Trevor smirked then deftly leaned down and bit Kegan's other nipple.

"Ow. Dammit," Kegan cried out, but it quickly turned to a deep rumbling groan when Trevor eased the sting with his hot, wet tongue and soft lips.

"Fuck, you don't know how bad I've wanted to do this," Trevor murmured against Kegan's flesh. "Dreamed about it."

Kegan was a little stunned by Trevor's admission, but from the brilliant smile stretching across Charlie's face and the small moaning sounds, she was liking what she was hearing and seeing.

Trevor turned his head toward Charlie, still lapping at Kegan's nipple. "You wet, baby?"

"Soaked," Charlie admitted, sounding breathless. "But I thought this was supposed to be about you?"

Trevor shifted and leered down at Kegan. "Oh right, I gotta catch up. Hold on." He planted a hand on either side of Kegan's head and thrust his cock against Kegan's equally hard one. "Don't come."

Was he out of his ever-lovin' mind? The friction of cock against cock, Trevor's rapid breath, the way his thick muscles flexed and rolled. How the hell was he supposed to not come? Kegan gritted his teeth, scarcely breathing, as Trevor rutted against him hard and fast. No fucking way was he going to be able to hold back, balls already drawing up, aching.

Kegan wrapped his arms around Trevor's back, digging his fingers into the warm flesh of his back, holding on as his body coiled tighter and tighter like an overwound clock until he was trembling with the effort of keeping from giving in to what it demanded.

"I'm going to come," Trevor barked, arching as he threw his head back and thrust hard and fast, coating Kegan's cock, stomach and chest with hot seed.

The only thing that kept Kegan from tumbling over into orgasm from the onslaught of unadulterated pleasure was the tight fist Trevor wrapped around Kegan's shaft, squeezing to just this side of painful as he continued to shoot his spunk until he'd emptied every last drop and slumped forward, spent.

Kegan held him, still digging his fingers into Trevor's sweat-dampened back, allowing him to catch his breath. It was painful, his dick pulsing and throbbing, begging for attention, but still, Kegan reveled in the feel of Trevor. In his heat, his scent, in him. Kegan's head lolled to the side and he met Charlie's gaze. "Well?" he whispered.

Charlie responded by leaning closer and placing soft open-mouthed kisses to Kegan's lips. "So goddamn hot," she murmured in between flicks of her tongue. Her kisses both eased him and inflamed him further.

"You can say that again," Trevor huffed and pushed up enough to place a kiss to Charlie's temple before sitting back on his calves. He ran a hand down his cum-covered belly, a sly smile curling his lip. "Messy, but hot."

Charlie propped herself up on her elbow and traced a random pattern through the cum on Kegan's stomach. "I can take care of that," she murmured and dipped her head down.

Kegan sucked in a harsh breath the instant her tongue swiped across his flesh. Her moan vibrating against his skin sent a jolt straight to his dick, causing it to twitch wildly. "Jesus."

"Here, let me help you with that," Trevor offered.

Kegan watched mesmerized by the way his two lovers lapped at him, sharing Trevor's flavor with each other, smiling and laughing as they did so. Moments before, Kegan would have sworn watching Trevor come all over him was one of the hottest things he'd ever witnessed. However, witnessing the two of them as they cleaned up the mess was right up there at the top, and when Trevor ran the flat of his tongue along the entire length of Kegan's cock, that just fucking did it.

Trevor's rough hands and eager mouth mixed with Charlie's soft caresses and sweet mouth were a one-two punch directly to his balls and it only took two hard thrusts and Kegan's eyes rolled back in his head as a powerful orgasm ripped through him. Before he could open his mouth to warn them, Kegan exploded. Pulse after pulse, he came, the pleasure so consuming he was barely aware of Charlie's cry and the wet heat against his thigh as she found her own release. Whether it was from the friction of her humping against him or something Trevor had done, Kegan didn't know. Hell, he scarcely knew his own fucking name. What Kegan did know as he came down from his orgasmic high with two warm bodies surrounding him, the intoxicating scent of sex in the air, was that he was the happiest and luckiest son of a bitch on the planet.

Chapter Nineteen

The scent of jasmine was strong as it mingled with the warm steam rising from the large tub. Charlie breathed in the sensual aroma, absorbed it and let it calm her.

As much as she loved her big, overbearing cowboys, there was something to be said for a hot bath, scented candles, soft music and alone time. For two days, they had followed her from house to barn and room to room. They even stood outside the bathroom when she put her foot down and refused to let them follow her in. It had taken some convincing, but both Kegan and Trevor had agreed to give her some space while they went into town. They'd reluctantly given in but only after she'd promised she wouldn't step a foot out of the house, not that she could anyway with Cade standing guard outside. Their protectiveness was both comforting and a bit overwhelming.

The dread she felt knowing Kegan's father could show up on the ranch hadn't disappeared, but it had calmed some. They made her feel safe. She had learned more about them in the last couple of days than she had in all the previous time she had spent with them. They were fiercely loyal to her and made her feel cherished above all other things in their eyes. Precious.

Knowing that Kegan was in love with Trevor, and vice versa, hadn't shocked her. Trevor had basically admitted to her that he loved Kegan, they just had a hard time accepting and understanding their feelings. Fear of each other's reactions had kept them silent.

It made her smile to think that their relationship had a damn good chance of working out. It wasn't just that they both loved her, but that the three of them loved each other without bounds. She had never given much thought of what it would be like to watch a man touch another, but the visual was something that had turned her on so much, it had pushed her to heights she had never imagined she could reach. And that kiss they'd shared… She definitely wanted to see more of those, and so much more. She couldn't wait to explore new things with them as all of them settled into their relationship. A tingling sensation settled between her legs and she shuddered.

"Stop it." She laughed at herself. She'd have plenty of time to enjoy such things later. Right now she needed to focus on her plans for the evening.

She forced her wandering mind away from the naughty thoughts and concentrated on the preparations for the night before her. Mrs. Miller had made all of Kegan's and Trevor's favorites and they were waiting in the oven.

Make sure to turn the oven on three-fifty at five. Check.
Gifts wrapped and ready? Check.

The special gifts she'd bought for each of them that would mark the beginning of their new lives together brought a smile to her face. Now she just needed to relax and rest up for what was sure to be the most important night of her life.

If she correctly anticipated how Kegan and Trevor would react to the news that she wanted to stay with them and work on building a lasting relationship, she doubted she'd be walking without a few well-earned aches and pains come morning.

Kegan still had trouble expressing to her and Trevor how he felt about them, but damn could the man show it over and over again. Charlie sighed and snuggled down deeper into the tub. A broad grin spread on her face as the water rushed over her and soothed her into a dreamlike state, her thoughts wandering to another place, another time.

"I think we should show her just how much we like touching her, whatcha think?"

"See that's why I love ya, Trev. You're a smart man." *Kegan ran his fingers down between Charlie's breasts, slowly. "A very smart man."*

* * * *

Charlie woke with a jolt, unsure how long she had dozed, but the water had started to turn cold and she was shivering. "Shit! How long was I out?"

She looked over at the clock—four-thirty. Dammit, she only had an hour before her cowboys were due back. She climbed out of the tub and grabbed a towel as she hurried to dress.

Halfway to her closet, she froze. Dread washed over her so powerfully she had to lock her knees to prevent herself from falling. *What the hell?*

She looked around her room. Nothing seemed to be out of place, there was no noise other than the soft rustling of the wind against the window.

The hair at the nape of her neck stood on end and a chill ran down her spine. Something was wrong, but as she scanned the room, she couldn't find anything amiss.

Slowly, she continued to the closet. The door was ajar and light came from within. She stared into the open door, looking for anything that would give her a hint of why her heart raced, but again nothing was out of order.

Charlie hurriedly donned the new dress she had bought for her special night—black silk of the finest blends hugged her body like a glove. The halter-style top plunged dangerously low, her ample breasts threatening to spill over the deep V. The back was nearly nonexistent as it exposed her entire back to the swells at the top of her ass and flared at the hips. The soft material teased her skin as she walked.

Three-inch stiletto heels completed the view. Underneath she wore a black silk thong with matching garter belt and stockings. Her men were lovers of soft, sexy things and she had bought the lingerie with the intent of driving the two of them completely out of their minds with lust.

Fully dressed, Charlie moved back into the bathroom, brushed her hair and left it to flow down her back. Trevor loved the feel of her hair beneath his palms when he stroked her back and Kegan loved to wrap it tightly around his fist when he kissed her.

The hint of skin exposed at her back beneath her hair was sure to get a powerful reaction. She couldn't help but smile at the image in the mirror as she applied light makeup and daubed jasmine-scented oil behind her ears and in the cleft of her breasts. She pushed the strange feeling of dread from her thoughts.

She had to be more nervous than she'd thought. Convincing herself she was simply being a worrywart, she blew off the unease as her own anxiety. Nothing would go wrong tonight. Tonight was the start of their lives together. It was going to be perfect.

Okay, so maybe not perfect, she still had a few lingering doubts on how the three of them would make their relationship work, yet she didn't doubt their love.

The small fear that she wouldn't be enough for them still gnawed at her, old insecurities died hard. That had to be why she was feeling cold claws at the base of her neck. Doing her best to push those thoughts from her head, she turned out the light and headed out of the door.

As Charlie left the bathroom, she gasped as a vise grip wrapped around her waist and a rag was placed over her mouth before the scream that pushed up in her throat was given wings.

Fear and confusion clouded her mind as a thick, noxious scent filled her nose, burning the delicate tissues and making her throat ache painfully. Gray fog clouded her eyes as she turned her head and stared into Kegan's eyes.

As the blackness began to take her under, her last thought was that Kegan's eyes seemed so tired...so old.

* * * *

"I swear, Kegan, I'm not taking you back into town. We'll have to sell off half our stock if you keep up your spending habits."

"I can't help it. I'm making up for years of missed gifts." Kegan didn't feel the least bit remorseful that he had spent so much on Charlie. Hell, she deserved everything and much, much more.

"Well I just don't see the point in buying her so many nighties. Between the two of us, she doesn't get to wear them."

"Yeah, but you have to admit, there is something about tearing them off that hot bod of hers that makes the cavemen in us roar." Kegan felt his erection stir and rise at the thought of ripping off the sexy lingerie he'd just bought for Charlie, especially the red corset-styled one. The image of it lifting Charlie's perfect breasts made his mouth water.

"Damn fine point, my man." Trevor's laugh sounded just shy of evil.

Kegan's smile faded as they pulled into the drive and doubt assailed him. "What if she doesn't stay?"

"She's gonna stay. She loves you, and I know she cares about me. Not sure if it's love yet, but I know she will come to love me as much as I love her. If she just gives it time, I know it'll happen."

"But what if she doesn't?" Kegan had felt something twist in his gut all afternoon. Something like dread kept taking over his thoughts and he wasn't sure if it was his old man he was fearful of or Charlie leaving.

He kept going back over every minute of the last thirty days, trying to find something that might make Charlie want to leave them, but couldn't think of a thing. Well, other than the fact that she had to deal with two very possessive and demanding men. The trust between them all was growing, each settling into their new role of committed partners with ease. He was happier now than he'd ever been, knew Trevor was as well, and he believed Charlie was truly happy with them.

So why the hell did he feel like something bad was waiting in the wings?

"I swear you're gonna grow old before your time if you keep this worrying shit up. I can see the hairs turning gray on your head before my eyes." Trevor pulled up to the house, turned off the truck, then looked at Kegan, his face serious. "Look, I know you're worried, but there's really nothing we can do if she decides to leave, right? If she does, we won't give up. Charlie belongs to us, whether she'll admit it now or later, I know she'll figure it out eventually. Besides, you know how persistent I can be when properly motivated. And I am so very, very motivated, so stop worrying, will ya?"

"Yeah, I guess you're right." Kegan rubbed the aching spot across his chest as he stepped out of the truck and followed Trevor toward the house.

They rounded the corner to the back porch and the pain in Kegan's chest exploded. "What the fuck!"

They both bolted up the steps at a dead run to the body lying in a heap on the porch.

"It's Cade. Call the sheriff," Trevor barked, but Kegan had already pulled out his cell and had begun dialing before the words were out of Trevor's mouth.

"Nine-one-one emergency."

"This is Kegan Colburn out at Trev-Ke Ranch. I need an ambulance and a cruiser now!"

"Sir, what is your emergency?"

Kegan trembled. He had to find Charlie. "Just get the fuck out here," he roared then disconnected the call.

Trevor bent down over Cade and placed his fingers to his neck. "He's breathing. Looks like someone hit him…"

The rest of Trevor's words died off as Kegan ripped open the back door. "Charlie!"

The kitchen was empty. "Charlie?" The dining room was set for three but she wasn't anywhere in sight.

"Goddammit, Charlie, where are you?" Kegan needed to get a grip on the anger and fear clouding his thoughts. Maybe she was just sleeping or something. He took the stairs two at a time and continued to scream her name at the top of his lungs.

The uneasy feeling that plagued him all afternoon threatened to destroy him. He fought to keep his shit together until he found her. He entered their bedroom and called out to her again. He searched the bathroom and the closet, but came up empty.

"Kegan!"

Kegan shot from the room. The sound of pure anguish in Trevor's voice as he called his name caused ice to form in Kegan's veins. He knew in that instant that he'd found Charlie. He nearly ran into his friend as he came down the stairs. "Where is she?"

"He took her!" Trevor bellowed. "That sick fuck took her."

Kegan didn't have to ask who Trevor was talking about. He fought to control the bile that rose in his throat. The knowledge of what his old man was capable of and the thought of his hands on Charlie had Kegan seeing red. He grabbed Trevor's arms. "Where the hell did he take her?"

Trevor handed him the note clenched in his fist. Fuck, both their hands shook.

Damn boy, you have some fine taste in women. I came by for a chat about that money and a place to stay but found something so much sweeter. I'll be in touch.

"We have to find her. Do you have any fucking idea what he'll do to her?" Rage and pain twisted him inside and out as it surged through every cell of his being. Sirens blared in the distance and he ran to the back door.

Cade was propped up against the porch rail, eyes shut, but breathing.

Kegan knelt down and grabbed hold of his shirt. "Where the fuck did he take her?"

Cade's eyes fluttered but didn't open.

"Goddammit, Cade, wake the fuck up and tell me where he took her."

Sirens blared, lights flashed and a car screeched to a stop in front of the porch as Trevor pulled him away from Cade. The sheriff and a deputy jumped out.

"Shit, Kegan, knock it off, he's hurt." Trevor cursed as he held tight.

"I don't give a fuck if he's hurt. He was supposed to protect her." Kegan tried to scramble back to Cade. He wanted blood, and if he couldn't spill his old man's at that moment, Cade would be the next best thing since he'd let the son of a bitch take his Charlie. The deputy and Trevor held him in a steel grip, refusing to let him go.

"He's been beat in the head and drugged. He doesn't know where she is. He probably doesn't even know his own damn name or who did this to him. Your old man must've hit him from behind," Trevor pointed out.

"You know who did this?" Sheriff Johnson asked as he bent and checked Cade's wounds.

Trevor tugged Kegan to his feet, the grip tight on his biceps as he pulled him farther away from Cade.

"My old man did this and took Charlie. Trevor, what the fuck are you waiting for? We have to find her." He struggled against the two men holding him. His heart was breaking and he could barely breathe.

Trevor wrapped his arms around him in a bear hug from behind and pressed his cheek against his. "Shh, shh… You beating the shit out of everyone that's here to help us isn't gonna find her." Trevor nuzzled his neck in an attempt to soothe him. "We have to get our heads together. She needs us, and if we can't think past our rage, we won't be able to. C'mon, big man, take some deep breaths. We can do this."

Kegan knew Trevor was right and was having difficulty keeping his own rage under control. He could feel it in Trevor's tense and twitching muscles against his back, heard it in the rasp of his voice.

He had to try for Charlie. He needed to get his shit straight and think. Where the hell could the old man have taken her? *Think, dammit, think!*

He allowed Trevor to lead him to one of the chairs on the porch and push him down into it.

Thoughts and images raced through his mind as the ambulance arrived and started tending to Cade. Kegan buried his head in his hands, tried to block out the images of his father and the women he'd abused. He shook inside, and despair clawed at his heart.

He was aware of Trevor and Sheriff Johnson discussing what had taken place, what Trevor knew, something about tracking dogs and forming a search party, but Kegan couldn't focus on what was going on around him. He couldn't stop the images of Charlie tied to a bed, his old man over her, hurting her.

As the image of Charlie's pleading eyes filled his mind, Kegan jumped to his feet. "We need to check the abandoned homesteads, now!" He headed down the stairs before any of them had a chance to stop him. He had to find her. His old man wouldn't have any money, didn't know anyone in town. The only place he could have taken her to would be one of the abandoned homesteads, barns or sheds scattered out around town. He didn't know where to start, didn't know if it would do any good. But he couldn't sit here with the thought of her out there with that sick fuck while he sat in a damn rocking chair and did nothing.

"Trev, either get in the goddamn truck now or I'm leaving you here." He didn't have to turn around to see if he was being followed, didn't rightly care if Trevor came or not. He couldn't get the images of what Charlie might be going through out of his head and they ripped his soul into pieces.

"Kegan, you need to wait until we get a full statement and the crime lab out here," Sheriff Johnson yelled.

"I don't need to wait for shit," Kegan bit out. "You sit here and wait. I'm going after Charlie."

He was in his truck and had put it into gear before Trevor caught up and jumped in just as he peeled out of the driveway.

* * * *

Charlie tried to open her eyes as her brain flickered and tried to focus, but they refused to obey. A thick haze gripped her mind. *What the hell happened?* She tried to sit up but had no control over her arms and legs. The only thing she saw was darkness.

She wasn't sure how long she had been out, had floated in the blackness unable to think or form a rational thought. Her body hadn't responded and somehow the blackness had pulled her back under. Only after blinking a few times did she realize she was staring at a dirty ceiling with the paint peeling, barely visible in the dark.

Why does the ceiling look like it's falling down?

Her stomach rolled as something nagged at the back of her mind — Kegan, his eyes? Blackness narrowed her vision and she fought to keep it at bay, but it was growing too rapidly.

The dark claimed her once again.

Chapter Twenty

Charlie's eyes snapped open. A faint gray light illuminated the dilapidated ceiling.

A silent sob broke from her throat. Only then was she aware of the warm tears sliding down her temples. Thankfully, she couldn't remember whatever dream she'd had that was powerful enough to bring her tears into reality. She was shivering. She tried to roll over, seeking the body heat and comfort of one of her lovers, but was unable to move.

She tried to move just her hands but couldn't, the same with her feet. As her senses came back online, she became painfully aware of the throbbing in her head. Groaning harshly, she tried to swallow, but her throat was dry and thick. A horrible taste at the back of her tongue reminded her of something unpleasant and familiar.

She fought past the haze that seemed to have taken over her brain. She needed to get up. Every instinct told her to get free and she struggled at the restraints that bound her, but they didn't give. Something forced her head to the ground and she realized a tight binding pressure was across her forehead. She tried to look around as panic washed over her, but could only get glimpses of her surroundings. She seemed to be in a room, the air around her stale with rotting wood and mold.

Where the hell was she?

She tried to call out for Kegan and Trevor, but her throat was too raw and she could only force out a pitiful moan. She had to get it together and no more tears. She just needed a minute to think past the haze and figure out what had happened. She took deep breaths in through her nose as the pain in her throat made it impossible to breathe through her mouth. Her lips felt stripped of their flesh.

Images began to flicker. Soaking in a hot tub... Special night with her cowboys... Dread... Dressing... Tight grip... Kegan's eyes.

Another sob broke from her as the image of Kegan's eyes flashed in her mind. Wait, something was wrong with his eyes. They were still the brilliant sapphire blue she loved, but they were so swollen and red...

So tired...

Old...

Realization hit her like a sucker punch to her gut, the bile threatening, burning.

Oh God! No! Please, this isn't happening!

It hadn't been Kegan's eyes she had stared into before passing out.

Drake. Somehow, Kegan's father had brought her to this place. She tried to free herself from the restraints. She needed out now! She froze at the sound of a deep, evil-sounding laugh.

"Struggle all you want, darlin'. I like my women with fight in them." Drake loomed over her, leering with filthy yellow teeth, the stench causing her stomach to roil. "Kegan's got damn fine taste in women. You and me, we gonna have us a mighty fine time together."

She breathed harshly and sweat broke out across her skin. She squeezed her eyes shut to block out the image of the fiend hovering over her. *Please let me be dreaming! I want to wake up. Please.*

Charlie jerked as a hand touched her cheek, causing her flesh to crawl. She gritted her teeth and clenched her jaw to hold back the scream that tried to erupt from her throat.

She refused to scream. Wouldn't give the bastard the satisfaction. Her insides trembled with the herculean effort it took not to let it escape.

"I remember you when you were just a shy little thing chasing after my boy." His putrid smell grew stronger as he leaned down, lips against her ear. "I jerked myself off more than once thinking about tying you to my bed, that fine ass up high, and ramming my dick so far and deep in you."

She clamped down on her trembling muscles, held her breath. *Oh God, please no*, her mind screamed, but she kept the words from crossing her lips by pressing them together tight. She wouldn't plead, knowing the man got off on hearing women beg for mercy. Kegan and Trevor had to know she was gone by now. They would find her, wouldn't ever stop looking for her. She just needed to hold on until they arrived.

Drake pulled back and grabbed her hair as he sat back on his haunches. "Yeah, well as much as I'm sure you would love to feel me balls-deep in your pretty little ass, I ain't gonna fuck ya just yet. I got a feeling my boy will be more generous with his funds if you're in one piece."

His grip tightened in her hair and she winced, felt it being pulled from its roots, but refused to scream or acknowledge the pain. "You better hope he's feelin' generous, 'cause if not, I'm gonna take out my due deep inside you."

He yanked one last time to punctuate his threat before he walked away. She held her breath as he moved, and only when his footsteps started to fade did she let it out and silently cry.

She prayed Kegan and Trevor found her before he came back.

* * * *

Kegan and Trevor had searched every known abandoned homestead within a ten-mile radius of the ranch, keeping a less-than-jubilant Sheriff Johnson apprised of their progress and checking in regularly. Trevor completely agreed with Kegan's refusal to take Sheriff Johnson's advice and allow him and his deputies to do the searching. They wouldn't stop. If they wanted to throw his and Kegan's ass in jail, they would just have to wait until Charlie was safe. They'd searched through the night and well into morning, but still they refused to give up.

Drake couldn't have taken her far. He had no car or money, couldn't even know the area. *What the fuck am I missing?*

Trevor refused to give into his need for sleep, knew Kegan felt the same. He worried that Kegan was barely holding onto his sanity, the deep lines around his eyes and the hard set of his jaw a testament to how hard he tried to hold on to his emotions.

"Let's swing by the ranch, grab another thermos of coffee and check in with the sheriff before making the rounds again, yeah?"

Kegan laid his head back against the headrest and released an exhausted sigh. "I don't know what to do, Trev. I feel like my heart has been ripped from my chest. Tell me what to do. Please, I need some help here."

The agony in Kegan's plea nearly tore his own heart out. "I already told you what we are going to do. Head back to the ranch, check in and start looking again."

"Look where?" Tears fell from Kegan's eyes, left glistening trails down his cheeks, and wrenched claw marks in Trevor's heart. "Where else is there to look?"

Trevor pulled the truck to the side of the road and put it in Park before he turned in his seat to face the man beside him. "Don't you fucking do this. Goddammit, Kegan, don't you dare!"

Kegan didn't open his eyes. "I'm not doing anything."

"The hell you're not. You're blaming yourself for what your old man's done, and it's not your fault."

In a blink of an eye, Kegan was in his face, rage, guilt and hopelessness swirling in his livid blue eyes. "Yes it is! I should have been there with her, should have refused to leave the damn ranch."

"Then I guess you blame me too, huh? Half that guilt you got weighing on your shoulders is mine."

"No…"

"The hell it's not. I wasn't there either and left the ranch same as you. So, sorry, bud, but you're just gonna have to make room for one more at the fucking pity party you're headed to."

Trevor braced himself for the fury he knew Kegan would unleash on him, but to Trevor's surprise, Kegan's shoulders slumped and he leaned back against the headrest of the truck again. Eyes closed, he heaved in a breath in an obvious attempt to get control of himself.

When he had first met Kegan, he'd never talked much and always turned inward in some silent battle to keep a rein on his emotions, afraid to lash out. It wasn't until Trevor had learned of the horrors in Kegan's life when he was younger that Trevor had understood what a hellish battle it was for him to maintain control.

After they had bought the ranch together, Kegan had eventually begun to open up about his childhood, and as time went on, he said he found it easier to talk to Trevor about shit rather than having to go it alone. He hated to see Kegan revert to his old ways, couldn't stand the anguish and pain on his face. He would do anything to keep his best friend from having to deal with the pain alone.

Trevor ran his fingers through his hair and clasped his hands behind his neck. "Talk to me, Kegan. Please don't shut me out."

Kegan stared out of the window, not really seeing anything, but unwilling to look Trevor in the eye. He tried not to give into the despair that consumed him, that had settled over him like a thick, black, ominous cloud. Something in the back of his mind nagged at him, but he couldn't quite get a grasp on it.

Kegan closed his eyes, poked around the edges of a faint memory, something he had buried deep. Whatever it was that would explain the hopelessness taking him over, only part of which was fear for Charlie's safety.

He continued to poke it again and again. The bubble popped and long-repressed memories came rushing back.

"Daddy, whatcha doin' with yer bed?"

"Boy, get your ass back in bed before I tan your hide." His dad's voice was stern and angry, his breathing labored as he pulled the mattress through the hall.

Kegan stood at the door to his room and watched his daddy fight with the old floppy mattress. He knew he should do as he was told, but he couldn't seem to get his feet moving. He stood staring, watching his daddy struggle. He knew good and well that if he was caught disobeying him, he'd get a whoopin' with the man's thick leather belt and fists, but still he couldn't move.

He waited…waited to hear Daddy move out into the living room so he could run to his parents' room and find his mamma. She couldn't protect him from the old man's anger anymore or stop the brutal blows he was sure gonna get. She'd tried too many times and each time she ended up beat up even worse than he was. Mamma had learned that when she tried to protect him, it was worse for him. His daddy was always meaner and hit him a lot more times after he put Mamma in her place. Kegan was glad when she stopped trying to protect him and would hide in her room and whimper with each blow he took. At least then the beatings didn't seem to be as bad.

He made his way toward the open door to their room. He'd heard her screaming in the night but had been too scared to leave his bed, had only pulled his pillow up over his head and tried to drown out the sounds of slaps, thuds and screams. It wasn't the first time he'd heard his daddy beatin' on his mamma in the night. But just like Mamma, he'd learned fast not to try to stop it because it only made Daddy madder.

Standing in the doorway, he was surprised his mamma wasn't there. The bed was just a frame, both mattresses missing. He silently moved toward the kitchen after hearing the back door slam and clutched the bear Mamma had given him when he was a baby, the same bear that Daddy would whoop him good for if he knew he still had it. Daddy said he was not a pansy baby and had forbidden him from keeping it. Mamma had rescued it from the trash and hidden it under his bed for him, told him to be sure it stayed their secret, and he had. The house was dark and he couldn't hear anyone moving around. Kegan hated the dark, but he mustered all his courage and kept moving, his need to find his mamma stronger than his fear.

"Mamma," he whispered into the kitchen, but the only sounds he heard was the drone of the old Frigidaire and his daddy cursin' in the backyard. He crept to the sink and pulled over the little stepstool Mamma had gotten him so he could help with cooking and dishes, and peered out into the backyard. He watched as his daddy poured something all over the mattresses laid out at the burn pit and set them on fire.

Kegan stared at the leaping orange and red, fascinated and lulled by the dance of flames. He couldn't help but wonder why Daddy was burning his bed. Where were he and Mamma gonna sleep now? A movement at the corner of his eye made him hop down from the stool and run toward his room as he spotted Daddy moving back toward the house.

In his room, he leaped across the floor, landing in the center of his small bed and pulling the covers up over his head. He lay there for what seemed like forever, shaking and silently praying that Daddy wouldn't know he'd been bad. God seemed to be answering his prayers because Daddy didn't even come into his room, and for the first time since he could remember, he didn't get a spanking at all the whole day.

At supper time, he finally worked up enough courage to ask. "Daddy…where's Mamma?" Before the words had even fully left his mouth, blinding pain exploded in his head and he was hurled across the kitchen and slammed into the cupboards. Kegan cowered against the cabinet, using his small hands to cover his face as his daddy stood over him and began raining down blows on his head.

"Don't you ever talk about that bitch in my house again, you hear me, boy?"

He wanted to tell him he wouldn't, that he would be a good boy, but the blows kept coming and Daddy kept screaming.

"The slut done up and left me to take care of your sorry ass."

Kegan wanted to cry and beg God to let him go with his mamma, prayed that she would come back for him and take him to wherever she was. But darkness started creeping up on him, and he embraced it like an old friend. In the dark there was no pain.

He'd given up on God after that day, 'cause no matter how good he'd been and how he'd done all his chores without complaint, Mamma had never come back for him. He'd never asked his daddy again where she had gone and had never made another promise to God.

Kegan blinked away the tears as he returned to the present. He knew he was shutting down, especially from Trevor, but he wasn't sure he could let him in, not with this. If he told him what he suspected his father really was, it would only cause Trevor more worry and pain, which was the last thing he wanted to do.

Trevor was in as bad a shape as Kegan was without knowing the true evil that his old man was. Trevor knew about the sick sex games, the rapes, and of course, the prison sentence, but he didn't know how far the man could go. Not only was he a rapist but a murderer as well.

"Dammit, Kegan, talk to me. I'm going crazy worrying about Charlie and I need you to stay with me

267

here. I need us to stick together and figure out how to find her, and we can't do that if you shut me out."

Kegan opened his eyes, his gaze locked on Trevor's. He winced at the pure torment in his friend's eyes. *Ah hell.*

"I'm just trying to think, but my damn brain is like mush. I know I'm missing something, I just can't wrap my head around it." *Liar.*

"Then let's talk to the sheriff, maybe he knows of some place we haven't looked, something we missed." Trevor laid his hand on Kegan's thigh, gave him a reassuring squeeze. "Don't try to figure this out alone, we need each other. We have to keep our heads together, she needs both of us."

Kegan nodded, hating that he was keeping shit from Trevor, but what good would it do to tell him? Trevor didn't need the extra fear, and Kegan certainly didn't need to put voice to that part of his past right now. He needed to find Charlie.

As they stepped through the back door and into the kitchen, Kegan's jaw dropped at the sight before him. Sheriff Johnson had their kitchen set up like a military strategist. Maps, papers and recording devices had taken up residence on the counters and walls.

"Hey, glad you're back. Come take a look at this." He walked over to the map he had taped to the cabinets. "The red circles are places that we need to check out. We got the support of two other county law agencies willing to help and State sent down a chopper to do an aerial search, so I need an update on where you've searched. We don't want to waste time checking any of the same places twice."

Kegan stepped closer to the map and looked at the size of the area they needed to cover. They'd stayed in contact with the sheriff throughout the night so most of the places were already crossed off. Hell, they hadn't even made a dent in the areas that still needed to be covered. They pointed out the last two places they had searched and Sheriff Johnson ran an X through them.

A feeling of powerlessness and self-doubt began to worm its way through Kegan. "Shit, I didn't realize there were so many abandoned places around here."

"A lot more than there used to be. The economy is for shit and it's hit this area pretty hard. But these areas aren't just homesteads—some are shacks, caves and such. I've had my men scouting in town for any information, but so far no one's seen a stranger fitting Drake's description. I think it's safe to say he didn't go into town. No reports of stolen vehicles or break-ins, so I'm gonna assume that he is still somewhere close. You know how people are around here, if he had been in town, someone would have noticed him."

"Has he tried to call?" Trevor asked.

"Not a word yet. The phone's been ringing off the hook, people calling, offering any help they can give, hundreds helping in the search. You two don't worry. We're gonna find her."

Kegan wished he could feel as confident as the sheriff sounded, but he had a damn hard time clamping down the dread that had taken up residence in his heart and his gut.

He took the coffee Trevor offered him and went back to staring at the map. He found comfort in the feel of Trevor standing next to him, shoulders touching in a gesture of silent support. How in the hell would they make it through this if they lost her?

Kegan had been a goner for her the first time he had laid eyes on her. Back then, she had been such a pain in the ass, always following him around like a lost puppy, going out of her way to irritate him, but the looks she had given him had melted him from day one. She'd always had this look in her eyes when they were young, like he was her hero. No one had ever given a damn about him until her. Funny thing was, he had never felt much like a hero—hell if anything, she had been his. His daddy hadn't let him go into town much—he hadn't even been allowed to stay after school long enough to really make any friends, and joining a sports team had totally been out of the question. Charlie had been his only real friend. He remembered the moment when Charlie had moved from being his only friend to his everything.

It had been his fear of becoming like his daddy that had made him leave her, and his damn pride and self-loathing that had kept him away. Eight long years without her, and now she was with him again. He was finally getting a chance to live his life with the two people he loved the most, and he'd be damned if he'd let that bastard steal one more minute of his happiness away from him.

"Let's go, Trev, time to bring Charlie home where she belongs."

Kegan turned and walked back out of the door with renewed determination. Nothing would keep Charlie from him ever again.

Chapter Twenty-One

The way the sun shone through the exposed areas in the ceiling told Charlie it had to be around noon. How long had she been here—a day, two, more?

Where the hell were Trevor and Kegan? Why hadn't they found her yet? She refused to let panic take over her again. She needed to keep a sharp head if she was going to figure out how to get out of here or at least how to stay alive until someone found her.

Drake had mentioned that he wasn't going to hurt her unless Kegan didn't pay, and knowing Kegan as well as she did, she had no doubt that he would do whatever it took to save her.

Charlie strained to hear any sounds of Drake nearby, but the room was eerily silent. She pulled at her restraints, hoped like hell that one of the bonds would break free, but they held strong.

A prickling sensation at Charlie's wrist made her flinch. The tingle moved from her wrist toward her elbow, and her breath caught. Something was crawling on her, moving up her arm. She shifted her gaze to the side and caught sight of something large and black moving slowly toward her shoulder. Before she could think better of it, a scream from deep in her chest filled the air. The feelings of tiny legs across her flesh made her skin crawl.

A flash of pain in her mouth cut off her scream as shock and agony overwhelmed her. She blinked, focusing on a movement over her as another blow to her face made her eyes water and her vision blur. Charlie bit her tongue and held tight to whimpers as the blows continued to storm down on her.

"You fuckin' bitch, I told you not to make a sound. Why the hell can't you follow one simple command? You're just like her, never could keep her fuckin' mouth shut."

Her? Slaps continued to rain down across Charlie's face, neck and chest in a frenzy as he screamed obscenities.

The coppery tang of blood filled her mouth and warm wetness oozed from her nose and trickled down her cheek but she refused to give into the fear and pain. She kept her mouth clamped shut and her eyes squeezed tight. The pain was excruciating, and just when she thought she couldn't bear another minute and she silently began to beg, the blows stopped as quickly as they had begun.

She didn't dare open her eyes or unclench her jaw for fear that she wouldn't be able to stop the scream lodged in her throat. She held her breath, willed the tears streaming down her face to stop and focused on the pain. It simmered deep inside her.

The hate she felt for Drake consumed her until her tears dried up. She'd be damned if this man would have the satisfaction of seeing her pain or her tears. She heard his footsteps pound across the floor as he left the room, muttering unidentifiable curses, and slammed the door.

Charlie let out the breath she'd been holding and parted her broken and battered lips to spit out the blood that had collected in her mouth and threatened to choke her.

She tried to open her eyes but the swelling made it impossible. She let the hate for Drake consume her mind. She focused on it, pushed back the pain.

How many times had Drake beaten Kegan? He'd always had bruises, a fat lip or a blackened eye. He wouldn't ever admit that Drake had done it, but she had known the truth, known he was lying when he kept repeating that he'd fallen, a horse had kicked him, or that he'd been in a fight with one of the other boys in town. She had seen the shame and anger in his beautiful eyes when she'd forced him to look at her. How the hell had he survived this kind of treatment? How in the hell had he kept his big, soft, loving heart that he always showed her when he'd lived such a nightmare?

She let the sweet images of Kegan and Trevor wash over her. She could survive this—she wouldn't let Drake take Kegan from her again. If…

No!

Not if, but *when* she got home, she would do everything in her power to make sure that the three of them would never have to endure the pain of their pasts ever again.

* * * *

"So you gonna tell me where we're headed?" Trevor asked.

"Did you notice anything weird about that map?"

"Other than the fact there is a shitload of places we still have to check out? Not really, why? What did you see?"

Lord, let me be right about this. "I noticed that all the places we've checked out made big circles, most of the places were at least five to ten miles from our place."

Trevor stared at him, confused. "What are you getting at?"

"Hold on." Kegan swerved off the road onto an old service road rarely used anymore. It was hidden with overgrown weeds. "It hit me as I was staring at that map. I was so out of my head when we realized Charlie was gone that I hadn't even given it any thought until this morning. There were no tracks in our driveway and since it had rained the night before…"

"Shit, he walked away!"

"That's what I'm bettin' on and I doubt anyone picked it up since he was taking Charlie against her will. If he drugged her like he did Cade, then he couldn't very well hitch a ride with an unconscious woman over his shoulder."

Trevor stared out of the window as they bumped along the deeply rutted road. He ran his hands through his hair and his knee started its irritating shaking thing.

"Trev, spit it out, what are you thinking?"

"I'm thinking just because it wasn't on the map, and most don't know about it. I do. I've known about the old Conners' shack for years and not once did I think about checking it out. Hell, it's on our fucking property and Charlie could have been practically outside our front door all night!"

"Hey, stop that shit. I'm the one who flew out of the house half-cocked without a thought of what I was doing and didn't pay attention to the help anyone was offering. I forced you to follow me around without any kind of plan."

If anything had happened to Charlie, he knew that neither he nor Trevor would forgive themselves for running around like chickens with their heads cut off. She needed better than that. She deserved someone who was going to protect her, keep her safe, and he had failed to do that. He hadn't given Trevor time to think before he'd forced the man to follow him. Now, just like when he'd left Charlie that day by the riverbed, he knew he would never be good enough for her.

Trevor reached in the glove box and grabbed the pistol they kept there that they used for coyotes and other vermin. He checked the clip before dropping one in the chamber.

"Stop up here before the next turn in the road. We're almost to the Conners' place, and if your old man is there, I don't want him to hear us coming."

Kegan pulled off the road as far as he could before cutting the engine. He reached behind the seat and grabbed his old shotgun, silent as he loaded it and put extra shells in his pockets. His gut told him this was the place Charlie had been taken to, but he was scared as shit of what he might find. He had seen the aftermath of what his old man could do to women, and his gut clenched when he thought of Charlie subjected to the man's perversions.

He no longer trusted himself to do the right thing, especially not with every instinct within him screaming to storm the place. He wouldn't make the same mistake twice and looked to Trevor for guidance. "So how we gonna do this, Trev?"

"Give me a second to think. If we go in guns blazin', we could end up hurting Charlie. If he sees us coming from too far off, he'll use her as a shield against us."

"Think we should call for backup?"

"Nah, not yet, we don't even know if she's here. If not, then we've pulled a bunch of people from searching for no reason. Those trees there" — he pointed out of the window in the direction of a small grove of pines — "after those, the place is pretty wide open. If we move from the trees, he'll spot us with no problem in the daylight."

"Well I ain't waiting until dark to check out this place, so I suggest you come up with a Plan B."

It took all of his control to sit in the truck when he thought Charlie could be just over the hill from him. He forced himself to sit tight, his body shaking in protest with the surge of adrenaline that ran through him. It made him crazy wild when he thought his actions might have already caused her to suffer more than she should ever have to. Above all, it made him determined not to take any more chances no matter how bad his body fought him. The thought of Charlie suffering filled him with a violent rage that he kept at a simmer just below the surface.

"I ain't suggesting we wait till dark. There's a creek that's south of the place. It runs pretty close to the back of the shack. The banks are fairly steep so it should hide me well enough, and you can cover me from the tree line there."

"Fuck that! Oh hell no. There's no way I'm letting you go in while I sit up here with my thumbs up my ass!"

Trevor turned to Kegan and looked him square in the eyes. "Listen, this makes the best sense. You're a great shot. I can barely hit the broad side of a barn with that damn shotgun. I wouldn't be able to protect you and Charlie if something went wrong, and how in the hell do you think I would be able to live with myself after that?"

Kegan leaned back, mulled over Trevor's proposal. He was right, but dammit, Kegan didn't have to like it. What he did have to do, though, was use his head for once and do the right thing for Charlie.

"All right, let's do this. But I'm telling you right now, if I hear or see one thing that looks off, I'll storm the damned place with or without your signal."

Trevor nodded, and they opened their doors, stepped out, then walked to the front of the truck. They stared off toward the tree line. Trevor was probably thinking the same thing he was right then and more than likely saying a little prayer.

Kegan wasn't much on prayers, but today he prayed that Charlie was okay and that they would get to her in time. His last prayer was for the three of them to finally live together without their pasts trying to destroy what they could have.

"Okay, Trev, let's do this."

Trevor hadn't lied to Kegan about not being able to hit shit with the shotgun, but it hadn't been his only reason for not wanting Kegan to be the one to go in. He could handle sacrificing himself to save Charlie, but he'd be damned if he would ever sacrifice Kegan.

The man had become everything to him since the day they had met, and Trevor owed him his life. For the first time, he felt complete and he owed his happiness to

Kegan. They'd had a great life together, but there had always been something missing and he knew it was Charlie.

If he lost either of them, he would never be complete again and couldn't bear the thought of living a single minute without them. He pushed that thought from his mind. Just the idea of it was enough to make him crumble, and right now, he needed to stay focused on freeing Charlie.

"You hunker down under those trees over there and set yourself up with a good shot at the cabin. Give me fifteen minutes to make my way around the back to get in position. If you hear my whistle or a gunshot, I want your ass down there pronto." Trevor looked over at Kegan who stood rigid, staring off toward the trees.

Though Trevor knew his answer, he still needed to hear it. "Kegan, if I get a clean shot, I'm taking it, and it won't be a warning shot. I won't hesitate to take down your old man. He may be a sick fuck, but he is still your father. You gonna be okay with this?"

Kegan turned to him and the look in his eyes chilled Trevor to the bone. His lips turned up in a snarl. "I just hope I'm the one with the clean shot."

* * * *

Charlie was still trying to get her breathing and heartbeat to slow down after the vicious attack when she heard Drake's footsteps coming close again. She hadn't made even the slightest whimper during the attack or after, so why the hell was he coming back? When the footsteps stopped, she knew he was close but her swollen eyes and the unshed tears blurred her vision. She couldn't see him, only heard his harsh breathing.

"You're damaged goods now," Drake spat from beside her. "You ruined my chances of getting top dollar for you because you couldn't keep your fuckin' mouth shut."

The impatient tap of Drake's shoe against the floor and his harsh breathing were the only sounds in the room.

"How do you suppose I should be compensated for my loss?"

His footsteps moved closer. She felt his breath against her face, and the rancid scent of him made her sick to her stomach.

"Since you couldn't do as you were told, don't you think you owe me a little compensation for the money you just cost me?"

Charlie refused to acknowledge Drake, wouldn't be baited to scream or beg. She held perfectly still, hardly breathing. The cold steel of a blade ran from her chin to her collarbone, but Charlie refused to flinch at the touch.

"Seein' as you like to scream and I'm feelin' in a generous mood today, I think I'll give you what you want."

He continued to move the blade back and forth across her neck. Drake's breathing was harsher, but her nose had swelled and clogged with blood so his stench was more of a taste in the back of her painfully dry throat.

This isn't happening. It's not happening. Nothing more than a bad dream. Charlie chanted over and over in her head, desperate to block out reality. She kept up the mantra, willed it to be true as the straps of her halter dress were cut away and the material pushed down to expose her breasts.

This isn't happening. It's not happening. Nothing more than a bad dream. Cold steel brushed across one of her nipples. *This isn't real.*

When teeth latched hard onto her nipple and a rough hand pinched painfully at the other, Charlie bit into her battered lip and tried to stop the sob that escaped her lips. *This isn't real.*

She forced herself to focus on Kegan and Trevor. They would come for her. She couldn't give into the fear or the pain—she just needed to hold on a bit longer. She refused to let her mind think about what was happening to her body or what would happen to it if they didn't come.

No dammit, they're coming. Kegan was her hero, she knew it in the depths of her soul. He always had been and she wouldn't doubt him now.

"Let's just see what I'm gettin' for my generosity."

The fabric of her dress was cut and her thong violently ripped away. Agony and despair simmering in her gut worked its way up her throat, adrenaline kicking in, demanding she fight, but she gave in to neither. She swallowed it down and continued her mantra, rising above her body. *This isn't happening. It's not happening. Nothing more than a bad dream.*

A stab of pain caught Charlie so off guard, she couldn't stop the scream that rushed past her lips and continued once it was set free.

But her screams couldn't drown out Drake's hideous laughter.

* * * *

Keeping cover at the base of a large low-lying pine tree, eyes glued to the landscape before him, Kegan kept the shotgun aimed at the front door. It had only been a few minutes since he and Trevor had parted, but it felt as if it had been ages.

The waiting was going to kill him, sure as shit. He could see no movement from within the shack, yet somehow he knew Charlie was there, could feel her reaching out to him.

How in the hell could he just sit here and wait for Trevor's signal when his body screamed at him to move. What if Trevor was wrong? What if while he was lying here like a fucking lump of coal, Charlie needed him? Even if his mind could assimilate that she was with his old man right now, he couldn't accept that she was being subjected to his cruel abuse.

Trevor had to be right. Kegan had to hold onto that. It was the only thing that kept him from storming the shack.

Kegan's heart stopped dead in his chest as a blood-curdling scream filled the air.

Charlie.

Without a thought other than getting to her, he was on his feet and sprinting down the hill, legs and arms pumping, his mind begging his body to move faster. The scream continued and wrapped around him as he ran, giving him the strength to push his muscles harder, faster. Without slowing, Kegan crashed through the rotting door and stepped into a hellish nightmare.

In a split second, he took in his surroundings. There on the floor lay Charlie, naked and bound, her face bloody and swollen. Her mouth opened wide as she continued to scream. Drake was hunched over, one hand shoved between Charlie's legs while the other held a knife against her throat.

Instantly, he crashed into Drake and the two of them flew against the wall. Kegan used his body to hold Drake against the floor, then grabbed his long graying hair in both hands and slammed the man's face into the wooden floor beneath them.

Over and over, he banged Drake's head. A red haze had taken over his thoughts and his body. The image of Charlie's broken and bloody face fueled his rage into a burning inferno. The man beneath him went still, muscles relaxed and still Kegan continued to pound Drake against the floor. Seconds or minutes later—he wasn't sure how long he continued to let his rage and pain consume him—Charlie's whisper penetrated the haze.

"Kegan... No..."

He looked down at his hands. Blood covered them and a large pool had gathered beneath the head of his lifeless father. He let the hair fall from his fists and felt no remorse for the man as he turned in Charlie's direction. Her tiny hands were bound and stretched tight over her head, and her legs were spread out painfully far apart and tied toward the far walls. A strap covered her forehead to hold her head in place and prevented her from looking in his direction.

"Charlie." He crawled toward her and knelt beside her, his hands shaking so bad, he was afraid to touch her. Her face was swollen and broken—it contorted her features beneath the blood that ran from her mouth and nose.

"Ah God, Charlie." He couldn't hold back the tears that streamed down his face from the ragged pain that twisted his gut.

"Kegan," she whispered.

"Shh, don't try to talk, baby. I'm here, you're safe now." He reached a trembling hand out, needed to touch her to be sure she was real, but was afraid that even the softest of touches would cause her more pain. He untied her hands and placed them gently by her side before he removed the rest of her restraints.

"I'm so sorry, baby. I... I should have been there... Should have..." Kegan couldn't finish. Anguish consumed him, and in that moment, the guilt of what had happened to Charlie, what he had allowed to happen to her, came crashing down on him.

She didn't move or try to reach out to him, just lay there so still. He watched the slow rise and fall of her chest, the only indication that she was still alive. The damage to her beautiful face was so severe it scared him. She was a tiny thing, how the hell had she endured this? He reached out and brushed his fingers against her skin. She was so cold. Kegan started to unbutton his jacket when a flash of movement beside him caught his attention a millisecond before the noise.

Pop.

Kegan turned to see Drake slumped against the wall, knife in hand, with a perfect dime-sized circle in the middle of his bloodied forehead. Turning, he saw Trevor in the doorway, gun still raised and pointed at Drake.

The sound of a small sob from Charlie had Kegan jerking his head back around and back to his senses. His only thought as he lifted her gently into his arms was to get her the hell out of there and to a hospital.

Trevor moved up beside him and placed his coat over her body. Kegan clasped her tightly against his chest and rushed out of the shack, Trevor at his heels calling the sheriff to meet them at the hospital as they ran toward the truck.

Trevor cut ahead of him and threw the passenger door open before he raced around to the driver's side. Kegan slid in, Charlie snug against him. He stared down at her face buried in their coats, her breathing gentle as if she were sleeping. He hoped she was sleeping, or at the very least passed out from exhaustion, so she didn't have to endure the pain of her injuries.

Looking at her battered face, Kegan was paralyzed by the fear, rage and loss warring through him. He didn't give a fuck about the loss of Drake, the world was a much better place without that wasted excuse for a human, but for Charlie's loss. Would she ever feel safe again?

"How is she? I need to know something here." Trevor's desperate voice broke the silence as he whipped the truck around and headed toward town.

Her breathing grew more shallow, her pulse weaker. "Ah shit! I think she's going into shock, get us there now!" Kegan roared.

He'd waited too long. It was his fault, had driven all over the damn county when Charlie was being tortured. He should be the one broken and battered, not this tiny little thing in his arms. He desperately wanted to alleviate her pain, bear it for her. It should be his burden, not hers.

Kegan brushed the hair back from her pale face. "I've got you, Charlie, just hold on for us. We need you. Please, baby, just hold on." He held her firmly against him as Trevor pushed the gas pedal to the floor.

Chapter Twenty-Two

The small emergency waiting room felt more like a cage and Trevor the animal imprisoned in it as the metaphorical bars pressed heavily in on his mind.

He and Kegan had gone over the story with Sheriff Johnson, the FBI agents, as well as countless doctors, social workers and other hospital staff. The emotional toll had been exhausting, and through it all, the only thing he wanted to do was snatch Charlie up in his arms and take her home where she belonged.

No one had told them anything about her condition except the polite 'She's going to be fine', or the one that made him craziest, 'We're doing everything we can'.

What the fuck did that mean? Did it mean that a bigger hospital could do more? He knew that probably wasn't fair, they would airlift her to a larger hospital if they didn't think they could handle it, but dammit, this wasn't just anyone. Charlie deserved the best. Trevor's pacing became more of a two-year-old temper tantrum stomp as the minutes ticked by. Why in the hell wouldn't they let them see her?

Kegan wasn't faring much better. He sat in an old butt-ugly green plastic waiting-room chair, brooding, and scowled at anyone who came near him. He had successfully pissed off no fewer than a dozen nurses, a few orderlies and various others trying to find out what the hell was going on. They had threatened to send his ass to jail if he didn't calm down and stop disrupting everyone in the place. Now he sat hunched in his chair, tense and growly, but at least he hadn't threatened to kill anyone in the last two minutes. Huge improvement.

Trevor threw himself in the chair next to Kegan. "I say we take the place by force, how about you?"

Kegan's scowl deepened. "If they don't tell us something soon, I swear she won't be the only one lying on a fucking cart."

Well at least he had lasted a whole two minutes.

"She has to be okay," Kegan mumbled more to himself, the hopelessness and sorrow thick in his voice as he scrubbed his hand across his face.

Trevor reached over, pulled Kegan into a tight embrace and forced the man's head against his shoulder. He didn't need to say anything. Nothing he could say would make either of them feel better, he just needed the contact of Kegan against him as an anchor.

Trevor felt as if he would shatter into tiny pieces and needed Kegan's touch to hold him together. Kegan gripped his shirt as he pressed his face against Trevor's shoulder, his breathing harsh. Was he crying? Hyperventilating? Either way they both needed the comfort the other offered.

A nurse stepped into the waiting room and both men bolted to their feet.

"Mr. Kingsington? Mr. Colburn? I just wanted to let you know that Miss McCarty is resting quietly and the doctor will be out shortly to speak with you."

"When can we see her?" Kegan demanded.

"You'll have to ask the doctor that. He'll be with you in just a moment."

Trevor sat back in his chair and dropped his head into his hands, relief washing over him. Charlie was going to be okay. They would be able to take her home and work on putting all this ugliness behind them.

They both sat in silence until the door opened and Dr. Brooks strolled out. They surged to their feet again.

"Please tell us she's okay," Kegan practically begged.

"Yes, she's resting comfortably. We sedated her so she is not in any pain at the moment. She suffered a broken nose and substantial trauma to the rest of her face. I have to warn you, her appearance will be quite a shock now that the swelling has fully set in, and the bandages pronounce the discoloration. Fortunately, the injuries should heal nicely and I don't expect any permanent damage." He looked back and forth between Trevor and Kegan, a sympathetic expression on his face. "Let's have a seat, please." Dr. Brooks gestured to the chairs they had just vacated, and moved to take a seat on the coffee table opposite the chairs.

This couldn't be good. Why the hell did they need to sit down for the rest of the report? Trevor's insides began to clench. He wasn't sure he wanted to hear the rest of it and yet knew he needed to.

Dr. Brooks waited for them to sit before he continued. "Miss McCarty underwent a series of exams, one of which was a rape kit. Before she was given a sedative, she gave me permission to go over those findings with both of you."

Trevor grasped Kegan's hand in his and hung on for dear life. He had known this was a possibility but had tried to block those thoughts out of his head. It would be hard enough for him to deal with it, but it would be sheer agony for Kegan to endure the thought of his own father raping the woman he loved.

"She suffered some slight vaginal tearing from the assault, but the wounds are superficial and confined to the exterior area. There were no interior wounds and the tests came back negative for seminal fluid. Miss McCarty has confirmed the findings and informed us that her attacker did touch her sexually, but only with his fingers and she was rescued before it could go any further."

Kegan slumped forward, brought their joined hands to his face and rested his forehead against them. "Thank you. Please, I want to see Charlie."

Dr. Brooks stood and nodded. "I'll give you a minute to collect yourselves and then the nurse will show you back to her room." He shook each of their hands before he left them alone.

A few moments later, a nurse appeared at the door. "Are you ready to see Miss McCarty?"

Kegan scrambled to his feet, followed by Trevor. "Yes, ma'am."

She motioned for them to follow her. "Right this way."

Kegan worked to control his strides, desperate to run past her to get to Charlie, but knew he needed to keep himself composed. Charlie was going to need him to be strong for her.

They moved down the brightly lit hallway, people scurrying about, moving in and out of rooms. As they passed a large nurses' station, people gave them sympathetic looks. The nurse opened the door at the end of the hall and he brushed past her.

Kegan's breath caught and his chest tightened painfully as he looked at Charlie lying against the stark white sheets of the hospital bed, pale and vulnerable.

Various tubes and wires were attached to her and the white bandage across her broken nose stood out in a stark contrast to her bruised skin. Her eyes were black and swollen but thankfully she didn't appear to be in pain, her breathing a slow, peaceful rhythm. Even with the entire trauma to her face, she was the most beautiful thing he had ever seen. She was alive and that was what mattered. Under all the damage was still his Charlie. He didn't want to wake her, grateful that she wasn't in pain and able to sleep, but he needed to touch her, feel her warm skin against his. He needed the reassurance that she really was alive and safe.

Kegan moved quietly to her side, Trevor close behind on her other side. They each took one of her hands in theirs.

Kegan bent his head and gently kissed her knuckles. "We're here, Charlie," he whispered against her skin, just to let her know that they were with her.

As Kegan stroked her skin and looked at the damage done to her, he nearly collapsed as guilt filled him, and it took everything he had to stay on his feet when he wanted to drop to his knees and howl. How the hell had he let this happen to her? He should have killed that bastard years ago when he'd had the chance, should have kept hitting that goddamn smiling face until it had disappeared forever. This was his fault. He had asked Charlie to trust him and look how he'd repaid her for that trust.

He laid his head next to their entwined hands, tried to set aside the self-loathing and blame he truly deserved. He'd deal with that later. Right now, she needed him to be strong for her, make her feel safe again. He wasn't sure how the hell he was going to do that when his whole world had been ripped apart and turned upside down. He couldn't let the feeling go that he'd failed her, it was lodged so tightly and interwoven into his entire being. He barely remembered a time in his life when he hadn't wanted Charlie, and now that he had finally gotten a chance with her, it had nearly destroyed her.

You've never been good enough for her.

Damn, that hit home. He'd never been good enough for her and never would be. He would do everything in his power to help her through this ordeal, give her everything she wanted and needed.

And when she was strong again, he would give her the gift of walking away. She wouldn't ever have to endure this kind of pain and suffering because of him again. She deserved so much more.

* * * *

A caress against his hair startled him awake. Kegan didn't remember closing his eyes, but he must have dozed off. He raised his head and met Charlie's gaze. Her left eye was swollen shut, but her right eye was open and stared at him with a dazed, unfocused look. He tried to decipher the expression, but couldn't read her emotions. Did she hate him now? It was no less than he deserved.

"Ah Jesus, Charlie. Please forgive me."

A single tear rolled down her face as she tried to raise her head from the pillow.

"Easy, baby." He reached up with his free hand and gently pushed her back down. "You need rest. You're going to be fine, but you need to lie still, sleep and heal."

Trevor leaned up and brushed the hair back from her face, gently pushed it behind her ear. "We're both here, baby, and we're not going anywhere."

Charlie turned her head slightly in Trevor's direction. "I hurt." Her voice was barely audible and hard to discern from her swollen lips, then she turned her head in Kegan's direction.

"I know, baby, just lie still. I'll call the nurse for you." Trevor reached out and pushed the call light.

A bored-sounding voice came over the intercom. "Can I help you?"

"She's in pain," Trevor gritted out.

"I'll send the nurse right down."

Within minutes, a nurse entered the room and moved to the IV lines sticking out of Charlie's arm. "This will make you feel better, honey." She checked Charlie's wristband, compared it to the syringe she held before administering the pain medication.

Seconds later, Charlie's body relaxed but she still continued to stare at Kegan.

"There you go, you just rest and I'll be back later to check on you," the nurse informed Charlie. She double-checked all the monitors and lines before instructing Kegan and Trevor to call if Charlie needed anything else, then slipped out of the room.

Kegan couldn't take his eyes off Charlie. She continued to stare at him with a dazed look, blinking once, twice, then closed her eyes as the medication did its magic and relieved her pain so she could drift back to sleep.

Kegan wondered what she had been thinking as she'd stared at him. The tear that had fallen from her eye had ripped his heart into a million shattered pieces. He had seen the physical pain in her eyes but also the emotional pain.

He couldn't help but think that the look he'd seen in her eyes was an acknowledgment of what he felt, what he knew. This was his fault and what he'd seen in her eyes, the tear that had run down her battered cheek was proof that she knew it too.

Trevor watched Kegan over the next couple of hours while Charlie slept. His muscles hadn't relaxed one bit, continued to flex and tick, though he appeared to be sleeping with his head against Charlie's arm.

He had tried to talk to Kegan a few times, to convince him to get some real sleep, but he refused. He seemed to have withdrawn into himself. In fact, the last time Trevor had tried to talk to him, Kegan hadn't even bothered to respond, though Trevor knew he wasn't asleep. Kegan blamed himself for what had happened.

The guilt didn't only stem from not checking the Conners' shack before they had, but that it had been Kegan's father who had done this to Charlie. How the fuck was he going to prove to Kegan that it wasn't his fault and that he held no responsibility for what his old man had done? Dealing with Kegan when his mind was set was like trying to reason with a rabid dog with his teeth sunk into your arm. Damn near impossible.

Charlie stirred and Trevor tightened his grip on her hand. He glanced at Kegan. He'd lifted his head too and stared at Charlie, pure agony dancing across his eyes.

Dammit, he needed to find a way to block out his own heartbreak and figure out how in the hell to take away the pain from both of them.

Charlie moaned and turned her head in Trevor's direction. Kegan visibly winced when she turned from him.

"Hey, baby, how are you feeling? Do you need anything?" Trevor leaned in closer, knowing how hard it was for his girl to speak. He felt the brush of her breath against his cheek.

"Wa…water."

He picked up the glass from the side table and carefully placed the straw to her lips. When he realized she couldn't form a seal around the straw, he drew water into the straw, his finger over the hole to hold the water in, then moved it to allow the liquid to slowly seep into her mouth when he placed it against her lips. "Better?"

Charlie nodded slightly, then mouthed, "Hurts."

Once again, he called the nurse and she came quickly, checking the lines and monitors before sedating her. Charlie never turned her head in Kegan's direction, which clearly hadn't gone unnoticed by Kegan either. He withdrew further into himself as he slumped back down to rest his head next to the now-sleeping Charlie.

All through the night, the same scene played out over and over. Kegan would get up to relieve himself or take a sip of water, but other than that, he didn't move from his resting place next to Charlie. He never slept and she never turned to look at him.

By eight the next morning, Trevor had finally had enough. He flat-out couldn't stand to see Kegan suffer anymore. He stood and moved around to the other side of the bed and grabbed Kegan. "Let's go."

Silence.

Trevor leaned closer to Kegan's ear, kept his voice down to a low snarl. "Get up, unless you want me to wake Charlie when I start to yell. If not, I suggest you get your ass up out of that chair now."

Kegan raised his head and stared at him, his face defeated. He took one last look at Charlie before he slowly rose and followed Trevor out of the room.

Trevor didn't stop until he reached the small private waiting room that was reserved for doctors to discuss patient conditions with loved ones. He held the door open and ushered Kegan inside. "Have a seat. It's not a request."

Kegan stared at him for a moment but then followed Trevor's demand and took a seat against the back wall. Trevor pulled a chair over so he sat directly in front of him.

"Whatever it is, spit it out. I wanna get back to Charlie," Kegan said impatiently.

"You're not going back in that room until you get your shit together."

"The fuck I'm not—"

Trevor waved at him. "Look at you! You look like shit. When Charlie does wake up, she needs to concentrate on healing. She doesn't need to worry about you falling over from exhaustion or starvation."

Kegan averted his eyes, unwilling to look at him. Shame, regret and guilt were all visible in the man's body language. "She won't even look at me."

"Dammit, Kegan, you're seeing something that isn't there. She barely opens her eyes, she's so drugged up. I'm not even sure if she is aware of her surroundings, much less that we're in the room with her." Trevor ran his hands through his disheveled hair. "She loves you.

I watch her with you and pray like hell that one day she'll love me as much as she does you. How in the hell can you doubt that?"

Kegan continued to stare at the wall behind Trevor. "I don't deserve her, never did, and this just proves it."

Trevor was pissed, trembling with it, close to losing it and wanted nothing more than to lash out. He wished he could kill the bastard that had hurt Kegan and Charlie all over again. He surged to his feet. "I'm sorry your father was such a sick, twisted fuck and caused you and Charlie so much pain. I wish I could change what the two of you have been through because of him, but I can't. The only thing I can do is try like hell to make the rest of our lives better and put this nightmare behind us."

Trevor stabbed a finger toward the door. "Right now, though, I'm going back to Charlie and you're staying the fuck out until you've had something to eat and have slept. I won't let anyone ever hurt her again and that includes you. It would hurt Charlie to look at you right now. Not because she blames you for what happened, but because of her, you worried yourself sick."

He turned and left the room and closed the door firmly behind him.

Before returning to Charlie's room, he arranged for food, a pillow and blankets to be taken to Kegan. He knew Kegan wouldn't return to Charlie's room until he got his shit together. He would never hurt Charlie for anything in the world if he could help it.

Trevor spent the rest of the day at Charlie's side. Shortly after Trevor returned to her room, Dr. Brooks approached him and suggested that Charlie receive a continuous sedative drip around the clock to allow her body time to rest and heal.

Trevor agreed and since it had been administered she had not woken once. After battling with more than one staff member and threatening to tear the place down if they tried to make him leave, they finally caved and brought in two sleeping chairs, placing one on either side of Charlie's bed for him and Kegan. By dark, as Trevor stretched out to get some much-needed sleep of his own, Kegan hadn't returned. The only thing Trevor could hope for was that Kegan had taken his advice and gotten some sleep, though he doubted Kegan would be able to, no matter how hard he tried.

He stared at the even rise and fall of Charlie's chest, letting it lull him. He blocked everything from his mind other than the fact that Charlie was here safe and everything was going to be okay. He held onto that belief, taking it with him into slumber.

* * * *

Someone gently shook his shoulder and Trevor woke with a start. He opened his eyes to find an elderly nurse standing over him.

"Sorry to wake you, sir, but we're getting ready to bathe Miss McCarty before she has to go down to X-ray."

Trevor sat up and looked toward Charlie, who still slept. "Why does she need more X-rays? Is everything okay?"

"She's fine. Dr. Brooks just wants to check and make sure he didn't miss any broken bones. It's difficult to get accurate pictures when there is a lot of swelling. Since the swelling has diminished considerably, he just wants to be sure he didn't miss anything." She patted his arm reassuringly. "Go on and have some breakfast, get yourself cleaned up. Dr. Brooks has ordered that the sedative be reduced so she should start waking up later this morning." She winked at him. "I'm sure you'll want to look your best when she opens her eyes."

Trevor ran a hand over his three-day growth of beard. "Yeah, that's probably a good idea. Have you seen Kegan this morning?"

"Sorry, I just came on duty and haven't seen him. You might want to check with the night nurse on your way out. Perhaps she'll know."

"Thank you. I'll do that." He stopped at the door and looked back at Charlie. "I won't be gone long. You'll call if anything happens, right?"

"Go. Nothing is going to happen, she's fine."

Trevor glared at her.

"I'll call, I promise. Now go so you can get back here before she wakes up." She gestured him toward the door with a stern look.

"Thank you." He snuck one last peek at Charlie before he quietly eased out of the room.

Chapter Twenty-Three

Charlie blinked a couple of times, trying to clear the fog that had enveloped her brain and to get a fix on the unfamiliar surroundings. She tried to lift her head but pain shot through her.

The memory of Drake rushed back and reminded her of why she hurt so badly. She remembered seeing Kegan as he lifted her into his arms and the feeling of being safe.

Was it a dream? Kegan? Drake? All of it?

She turned her head a fraction to the right. White sterile walls and blinking monitor screens... She remembered these scenes with Gram and instantly recognized she was in a hospital room. Her eyes traveled downward and warmth filled her chest. Lying in a chair next her bed, his dark curls tumbling haphazardly around his gorgeous face, was a sleeping Trevor.

Charlie tried to turn to the left and seek out Kegan, but the pain on that side of her face and the useless swollen left eye made it impossible to see. She tried lifting her head, but once again agonizing pain shot up her neck, exploding in her head, and she was forced to lie back. She squeezed her eyes shut with a frustrated moan. She needed to see Kegan, to know he was here and safe with them.

Warm hands caressed her arm. "Hey."

Charlie opened her eyes to a see Trevor's concerned face just inches from hers.

"How are you? Are you in pain? Do you need anything?"

Charlie tried to smile but winced at the effort. Her lips felt huge and uncooperative. Charlie lifted her hand and placed it against Trevor's chest. He instantly wrapped his hands around it.

"What do you need, baby?"

"You," she murmured.

"Ah hell, Charlie, that's an easy one. You got me, babe, all of me." The brilliant smile across his face melted Charlie's heart.

"Ke—" She swallowed hard and licked her dry lips. Kegan's name came out nothing more than a whisper, but Trevor knew what she wanted.

Pain flickered in his eyes for the briefest second, but then disappeared again and made her wonder if she had actually seen it. He kept one hand pressed against hers that covered his heart, and with the other, he pushed back the stray hairs that surrounded her face.

"Kegan is fine. He'll be back soon."

Charlie couldn't help but notice the look of doubt on Trevor's face. The smile didn't reach his eyes, and hard lines around his mouth and eyes betrayed the effort it took. A twinge of pain hit her heart. Something was wrong. Was Kegan hurt? Had she only been dreaming that he had lifted her into his arms and carried her away from Drake? Nausea threatened her stomach at the thought of Drake, but she pushed it down.

"Is he okay?" Her words sounded mumbled and unidentifiable.

"Shh, he's okay, I promise. He just needed to get something to eat and some sleep." Trevor stroked the skin below her ear. "You've been asleep for two days. He's gonna be pissed he missed you waking up."

Two days? The last thing she remembered was Kegan's arms, feeling safe.

"He…he carried me from…"

"Yeah. Shh, don't think about that right now. Concentrate on healing so we can take you home." He laid his head on the pillow next to hers. "You're safe now, that's all that matters."

Home. Damn that word sounded so good.

The only thing she wanted to do was snuggle between her two wonderful men and forget about all the ugliness that was Drake. How he had nearly taken her away from Kegan and Trevor and the pain when she'd thought she was going to die without them knowing how she felt about them. They had both told her how much they loved her, but she had never told them. Charlie wrapped her free arm around Trevor's neck, held him close and whispered, "I love you."

His body stiffened and he wrapped his hand tightly around hers. Hell, maybe this wasn't the right time to tell him. What if Drake was right and she was damaged goods? They might not want her anymore after Drake had touched her. The silence that stretched out was awful. She hadn't wanted to make him feel uncomfortable after everything he had done for her. "You don't have to say anything. It's okay… I…"

It hurt so much to speak, her lips and throat were raw, but nothing compared to the pain in her heart. Trevor pulled away and she wanted to weep at the loss, of what Drake had stolen from her. She expected Trevor to turn away in disgust, but he hovered over her face. His eyes glistened with unshed tears and his gaze burrowed right into her soul.

"You don't know how scared I was that I would never get the chance to hear those words. Christ, Charlie, I love you so much."

Charlie's heart soared. He still wanted her, loved her. The light feeling in her chest and the miraculous joy surging through her made the sting of pain from Trevor peppering her face with kisses almost bearable, but she couldn't quite swallow down the whimper that the sting demanded.

"Fuck! I'm sorry. Crap. Did I hurt you?" He jerked back, but Charlie tightened her grip on his hand, refusing to let him pull away too far.

"It was worth it."

He raised her hand to his mouth, kissed each one of her knuckles. "I promise I will never give you a reason to regret loving me." He pressed a gentle kiss to the delicate skin of her wrist. "Thank you."

Charlie rejoiced in Trevor's admission, her heart so full it was nearly bursting.

She couldn't help but feel the loss of Kegan not being with them. Her heart was only truly full when the three of them were together.

* * * *

Over the next two days, Trevor was obsessed with caring for her. He refused to let her stand without him at her side, plus fed and bathed her, brushed her hair for hours on end and soothed her with soft words and warm caresses until she fell asleep.

Under his gentle care, she grew stronger. The swelling to her face was nearly gone, just the ugly black and yellowish bruises remained. She looked like a circus sideshow freak, yet Trevor looked at her in awe, as if she were the most beautiful thing he'd ever seen. She was amazed at how the normally forceful, commanding man could be so giving and nurturing.

As wonderful as he had been, as beholden as she felt, at this moment she was enraged at him. She stared at him, fire in her eyes and arms crossed firmly across her chest and dared him to avoid her question.

"Where the hell is Kegan? And if you tell me one more time that he's sleeping or eating, I swear to Christ, I'll come up out of this bed and spank your ass."

"Mmm, my baby is feeling better. I think I may enjoy being spanked by you." Trevor smirked and waggled his brows.

She shot him a look that should have fried him where he sat. "Trevor, you're avoiding the question. Stop pacifying me and tell me what the hell is going on. You don't think I haven't noticed that he's been absent for the last two days? I swear on all that is holy, if he's hurt and you didn't tell me, there won't be a place in heaven or hell for you to hide."

He turned his back on her and resumed his task of packing up her belongings. She was being discharged and as excited as she was to be going home, she couldn't ignore the heaviness in her heart at not seeing Kegan.

Rae, Dr. Stone and most of the ranch hands, including Cade, had stopped by to see her. She had been grateful for their company, but it still hadn't been enough. She needed Kegan.

Trevor had told her over and over that Kegan hadn't been hurt, not so much as a scratch anywhere on his body. If that were true, then she could only think of one other reason that he wasn't here with her. The anger she felt at Trevor for being so damn evasive drained away with the notion that she already knew the answer.

Drake had beaten her until she was horribly disfigured, and though Dr. Brooks assured her repeatedly that the damage wasn't permanent, it was still damn awful to look at. Hell, she didn't want to look at herself, so she avoided mirrors like the plague. She supposed she was damaged goods now, wasn't that what Drake had called her? Was that why Kegan wasn't there? Was the thought of her being touched by Drake so repulsive to him that he couldn't stand to look at her without being reminded of what had happened? She really didn't want to hear the answer but she couldn't stop herself from asking.

"He's leaving me again, isn't he? Is that why you won't tell me anything?"

Trevor shrugged, his back still to her. "I don't know, Charlie."

With one small sentence, Charlie was hurled back in time to when she was eighteen and had first realized Kegan wasn't ever coming back for her. The agony, grief and heartbreak were as fierce now as they had been then. How the hell was she going to survive them this time? Now that she knew what it was like to feel his love, his body against hers, inside her.

She didn't have to try to come up with fantasies about what his lips would feel like against hers or the way he'd aim that shy smile at her when she woke up in his arms in the morning. She knew exactly what she was losing this time. As hard as it had been the first time, there was no way it was going to compare to the sheer torture of going back to a life without Kegan.

She scooted off the bed and headed for the bathroom. She avoided looking at her reflection as she splashed water on her face. She had survived Drake and she had survived Kegan leaving her before. She wasn't that same stupid little girl she'd once been. She was now strong and independent.

You might as well crawl away somewhere and say fuck it because you are never going to get over him. You want him, want Trevor, you want it all. What the hell have you ever done to deserve it? Grow up! When have you ever been enough for anyone?

Charlie dropped to her knees on the cold, hard tile floor and squeezed her fists so tight, she could feel her nails cut through her flesh and hoped the pain would drown out the voices in her head.

Everyone always leaves you.

She squeezed harder.

Trevor will be next. He loves Kegan and will follow him.

Her palms burned.

You were born to be alone!

A sob broke from her throat as she felt the blood start to ooze from between her fingers.

Trevor rushed into the bathroom, knelt next to her. "Baby, what is it? Are you in pain?" He tried to wrap her in his arms, but she fought against him.

"It's okay. I got you."

"Let me go," she cried, her nails still buried deep in her flesh, the pain something other than her heart to focus on.

He tightened his arms around her as she continued to struggle. "Baby, listen to me. Please."

Charlie continued to battle helplessly against his strength until her body finally gave out and she slumped against him. "I can't... I can't do this again."

Trevor picked her up into his arms and carried her from the bathroom then sat in the large sleep chair with her cradled against him. Charlie gave up on holding back the tears that had welled up in her eyes and let them flow as Trevor rocked her gently. He didn't try to talk or reason with her, simply allowed her to lie against his warm body and let the tears come until she couldn't cry anymore.

"I'm sorry Kegan's not here. So sorry that it's causing you so much pain." He placed kisses against her hair. "He shows up here every night while you're sleeping and just sits in the chair staring at you."

Charlie sniffed. "What?"

Trevor looked down at her hands, at the blood that had bubbled up between her fingers. "What the hell?" He pried her hands open, looked at the mangled mess of her palms and hissed, "Jesus, Charlie."

She pulled her hands free and bunched up the hem of her gown in each hand to put pressure on the cuts. "They're fine. What do you mean he comes here at night?"

"He just sits there staring at you. Doesn't touch you, won't look or talk to me, just stares at you."

"Why doesn't he want me to know he's here?"

"He's hurting, Charlie. He loves you so fucking much but he's blaming himself for what happened to you."

Trevor's beautiful dark eyes filled with such sorrow it nearly stole her breath. Kegan had told her that he'd stayed away from her before because he didn't think he was good enough. He couldn't possibly still feel that way after what the three of them had become together, could he?

You're starting to hope again, Charlie. What good has hope ever done you?

"But he saved me?"

"Kegan has never thought he deserved you, never thought he was good enough for you. Now with what happened to you because of his own father, he thinks he finally has proof that his beliefs were justified."

Charlie stared at him in shock. "That's the stupidest thing I've ever heard! You're just trying to make me feel better, and to be honest it doesn't, it just pisses me off."

Trevor smiled that lopsided smile she loved so much, but it didn't reach his eyes. "I should paddle you for calling me a liar. I told you I would never lie to you."

Charlie ducked her head. "I'm the one who doesn't deserve him."

Trevor tilted her head up, forced her to look back at him. His eyes burned with intensity. "Now I'm the one pissed off. You two are going to give me gray hairs. I swear, Charlie, if you give me gray hairs before I'm thirty, I'm so gonna spank that little ass of yours — and not in a good way. How in the hell did I fall in love with the two most stubborn people on the planet?"

"Just lucky?"

Trevor growled at her, then nipped her chin. "Let's go home. I think the three of us have some shit to sort out, wouldn't you say?"

Charlie still wasn't convinced. She knew Trevor would do and say anything to keep her from crying, but she did want to go home. She wanted to put the ugliness of Drake behind them if they could, and she knew they couldn't do that sitting in a hospital room.

She placed a soft kiss to Trevor's cheek. "Yeah, take me home."

She wasn't sure anymore if home was with Trevor and Kegan, but prayed it was.

* * * *

As they pulled up to the main house of the Trev-Ke Ranch, Charlie felt giddy with relief when she saw Kegan standing on the large front porch watching their approach.

He really was okay. She could barely wait for the truck to stop before she bolted out of the door and ran to him. He didn't meet her halfway or open his arms to her, just stood there watching her come toward him. A tingle started at the base of her neck and creeped down her spine. Something was wrong.

Charlie slowed, but continued toward him. He looked so tired and drawn. The dark circles under his bloodshot eyes were testament to a man having had no sleep. His usual rosy complexion was ashen and drawn, his hair in disarray around his bearded face. Charlie hadn't ever seen him look so broken, not even after the many fights he'd had with Drake. Her heart ached for him.

She took the stairs slowly. "Kegan?"

As she reached the top step, he finally blinked and reached out to pull her against his broad chest. He shook so badly as he leaned into her, she feared his weight would topple her.

"Welcome home, Charlie." His voice sounded rough and unused.

To Charlie's utter shock, he placed a kiss on the top of her head, then pulled away and walked past her toward the truck. "I'll get your things."

Charlie couldn't do anything but stare at his back as he descended the stairs. His usually powerful, confident stride was tense and erratic.

She met Trevor's concerned gaze and saw the hopelessness he felt. Charlie wanted to weep, but she was too stunned. She couldn't speak, too overcome with grief to move. She watched as Kegan opened the back door, pulled out her suitcase, then headed back toward the house. He kept his eyes down at his feet and never looked up as he moved past her.

She was still trying to get a grasp on what had just happened when Trevor pulled her to his chest. "Give him time."

Time? She wasn't sure time was the only thing Kegan needed. She wasn't really sure what he needed, but had a sickening feeling it wasn't her.

Chapter Twenty-Four

Charlie wore an oversized white T-shirt and comfy fleece pants with pink hearts. As outfits went, it was pretty silly — still, it wasn't as bad as what she looked like without PJs.

She avoided looking at her face in the mirror. The ugly bruises and scabbed skin only served as a reminder of what Drake had done to her, and not just in the physical sense.

Kegan still hadn't come in from fixing fences, though she knew the crew had returned long ago. It could only mean that he was avoiding her, and she couldn't really say she blamed him much. Hell, she couldn't stand the sight of herself and probably looked like the Bride of Frankenstein. Charlie turned from the room and shut off the lights before she could dwell any further on feeling sorry for herself. It wouldn't do her a damn bit of good to let self-pity take root — it wouldn't change a thing.

Trevor was already in bed when she made her way in the dark, guided by his slow, even breathing, hoping she wouldn't wake him. She carefully slid beneath the sheets, stayed close to the edge as she stretched out on her back. Charlie lay silent, eyes toward the ceiling, though it was too dark to see anything in the nearly pitch-black room. She was afraid to close her eyes, scared that the images of Drake would return.

Lying in bed, clothed and feeling alone was at least an improvement from the nightmares. She hadn't even realized how hard she was straining to hear sounds of Kegan entering the house until she jerked when Trevor's arm wrap around her. She hadn't even felt him move toward her on the bed.

"You okay?" Trevor whispered as he pulled her closer against him.

"Yeah, I think I am right now. I'm just not ready to close my eyes yet, ya know?" The weight of his arm across her was a comfort and took away some of the loneliness, yet here in *their* bed also reinforced what was missing.

"It's okay to sleep, Charlie. I'll be right here and won't let anything happen to you."

"I know, but there isn't a whole lot you can do to protect me against the nightmares."

Trevor was silent for a long time, breathing deep and even, but he didn't sleep. His fingers continued to make random patterns against the fabric of her T-shirt and across her back. "Feels weird with you being clothed. Do you realize it's the first time we've allowed you to come to bed like that? I must be getting soft."

Yeah, and it was the first time Kegan hadn't joined them, but she wouldn't say it out loud. No doubt Trevor felt Kegan's loss as strongly as she did. "I figured I'd save you one night of having to look at my uglies," she teased, doing her best to make the statement sound light, but it came out sounding sad.

The instant the sentence was out of her mouth, Trevor rolled them until she was in the center of the bed, then leaned over her. He brushed his lips lightly over hers, then across her cheeks. He pressed his lips to each bruised area of her face, a mere wisp of gentleness that touched her heart like a delicate sigh. Trevor pushed her shirt up, gently made his way down her body with a kiss or a swipe of tongue here and there as he moved, until he placed light, tickling kisses to her belly.

"You're still the most beautiful thing I've ever seen since the moment I first laid eyes on you."

"That's because it's too dark to see my new freaky look."

Charlie instantly missed the heat of Trevor's body when he pulled away. Only then did she realize how close she was to losing it and how his nearness had kept her from falling over the edge of despair. He couldn't totally make up for Kegan's absence but Trevor's touch kept her from being crushed by it. She held her breath when he turned on the soft light of the bedside lamp and leaned back over her as his eyes wandered across her face, down her bruised and battered neck and shoulders.

Trevor gently pushed her T-shirt over her head and arms, looked right into her eyes. "Yep, even in the light, you're still the most beautiful thing in my world." He brushed his lips against her shoulder, and his fingertips lightly feathered against her belly. "If I'm real, real careful can I kiss your uglies?"

Charlie let out the breath she'd been holding, but she couldn't speak, too overcome with emotion. As much as she loved how commanding and dominant Trevor could be, she loved him even more in this moment for knowing exactly what she needed. She nodded, unable to trust her voice.

Trevor gave her one of his brilliant smiles, dipped his head, then gave her body the same delicate attention he'd given her face. Charlie lifted her hips off the bed as he pushed down her pajama bottoms, the warmth of his hands followed by his lips and tongue. By the time he reached her feet and her pants were gone, her arousal had begun to push aside her need for his gentleness, replaced by a hunger much more primal and immediate. Trevor moved back up her body, mumbling endearments against her skin, and her desire for a deeper contact made her squirm with impatience.

"Please," Charlie moaned as he reached her thighs, his touch amazing, but not where she wanted it the most.

"Tell me what you need."

"You," she begged, reaching down to tug at his dark curls and encouraging him upward.

Trevor placed a light kiss to her hip, his gaze on hers. "Are you sure? I don't want to hurt you."

"You won't. Please, Trevor, I need you so bad I ache." She needed to know that she was still desirable to him. Needed to feel his powerful body against hers, inside her, to remind her she wasn't alone, that she was alive. She wanted the reassurance Drake hadn't destroyed everything in her life.

Trevor brought her to climax over and over again with hands, mouth and body until she lay with him wrapped tightly around her, protective and possessive.

It hadn't only been she who needed to reconnect, needed reassurances. Trevor had nearly sobbed as he'd come deep inside her, had yelled out her name repeatedly until he'd collapsed onto her, his tear-streaked cheeks brushed against hers.

For the first time since she'd been kidnapped, they had taken a step toward healing. It was a relief but they both knew it wasn't enough.

Charlie had reached out unconsciously during their lovemaking, automatically searching for Kegan, only to encounter Trevor's hand that had been seeking the same thing.

A moment shared, an unspoken acknowledgment that even as wonderful as their passion was, they still yearned for the touch of the one person needed to complete them.

* * * *

At dawn, Trevor left a sleeping Charlie to search for Kegan. He knew she'd be scared and a little confused if she woke up alone, so he'd left the light on and a note telling her to wait in bed for him so he could give her a proper wakeup when he returned.

The last thing he wanted was for her to doubt herself any more than she already was. For fuck's sake, had he actually cried as he'd come last night? Jesus, he was turning into such a fucking sap, but he couldn't help it. He'd never been so scared in his life as when Drake had taken Charlie, and with the helplessness he felt about Kegan, he just couldn't seem to get his emotions under control.

Well, the stuff with Kegan had messed with his head for a while but he was beginning to accept what was growing, or more honestly, what had already grown between them over the years. It was more of an unspoken acceptance at the moment and not something that seemed right to act on when Charlie had been missing. Now that she was back where she belonged, he'd give anything for the three of them to truly be a threesome, but first he had to figure out a way to reach Kegan through his grief and help him work through it.

He wouldn't give up. Trevor knew what he needed, knew what Charlie and Kegan needed, he just didn't know how he was going to make them realize it was standing right in front of them.

After searching the house, unable to find Kegan, Trevor headed out to the barn and spotted Cade.

"Hey, Cade, you seen Kegan this morning?"

"Mornin', boss. Nope, haven't seen him since I saw him head out last night."

"Head out?"

"Yeah, he packed Taz down with a saddlebag and roll, said he needed some thinking time. Everything all right? How's Miss Charlie?"

Trevor rubbed the tension at the back of his neck that seemed to have taken up permanent residence lately. "Yeah, everything's fine. Charlie's settling back in and seemed to have a good sleep last night. I just want to set the schedule quick and get back before she wakes up. You need anything?"

Cade handed him the clipboard with the daily schedule. "I already have it set for you. Figured you didn't need the extra worry right now. If you want me to make any changes, just let me know."

Trevor looked down at the clipboard, then back up at Cade without reaching for it. "Thanks. I trust you got it right." Cade was a damn fine hand to have around. Solid and he took care of shit that needed to get done, went about his day without bitching no matter what they asked him to do. Cade had followed him and Kegan when they'd left the old man's ranch to set up their own and had been a big reason they'd been so successful. Shit, he was a dolt. He hadn't thanked the man for all the shit he'd put up with recently. Christ, how the fuck had he forgotten that Cade had been attacked by Drake too, and he hadn't even asked the man how he was? *Fuck!*

"Shit, Cade, I forgot to ask you how the hell you're doing. Piss-poor excuse goin' on about my own shit, I didn't even ask how your head was healing."

Cade pushed back his hat and knocked his knuckles against his forehead. "Can't hurt this hard-ass thing, don't even give it another thought." He looked down at his boots and shuffled. "I'm sorry I didn't stop him." Regret was evident in his voice.

"Don't even go there. I know you did all you could. I'm just…" Damn, he felt like he'd lose it again. What the hell was wrong with him? He cleared his throat. "Yeah, we're good. I'm gonna head back up to the house. When you see Kegan, let him know I'm looking for him, all right?"

Cade pulled his hat down back over his eyes and nodded. "Yeah, I'll tell him. Now get the hell out of here and let me get to work." He started to turn, then stopped. "Tell Charlie I'm…uh… Just tell her I'm glad she's okay."

"Yeah, I'll tell her, and Cade?"

He looked back over his shoulder and met Trevor's gaze. "Yeah?"

"Thanks."

Cade nodded once then walked off toward the schedule board.

Trevor headed back up to the house and wished he could set things to rights with Kegan as easily as he had with Cade.

Chapter Twenty-Five

The warm May morning was perfect, well as far as the weather was concerned. Not a single cloud in the sky, the temperature was already warm enough to go without a jacket, and it wasn't even ten a.m. yet.

For once, the weatherman had been right and it should be up in the high seventies by afternoon and nothing but perfectly blue skies. Too bad Charlie didn't feel as great in her skin as the sun felt against it.

The last couple of nights she'd slept with Trevor snuggled close, but Kegan hadn't joined them. She could hear him come in late at night and try to be quiet when he snuck into his old room, but Charlie knew.

She would wait for the sounds of the back door then his footsteps on the stairs. It wasn't until she heard him settle into his room that she allowed herself to drift off to a fretful sleep. It wasn't exactly the security she needed, but at least she felt somewhat better knowing he was at least in for the night.

Charlie did her best to return the comfort Trevor offered. She knew she wasn't the only one missing

Kegan. Trevor had tried to get Kegan to talk to him more than once but would ultimately throw his hands up in frustration and walk off in a huff. It wasn't new for the two of them to have a rough go telling each other how they felt, but she thought this time might be a little different and sympathized with Trevor's growing uneasiness.

It was getting so bad she was afraid to poke at anything too deeply, scared shitless that if she did, heartache and pain would drown them all. Yet at the same time, she wished something would happen. Anything. Living in limbo was hell in its own right, unable to go back and change wrongs, but none of them seemed to know how to move forward.

Charlie leaned against the door of the barn waiting for Cade to finish with his chores. He'd promised her he'd help get her up to speed on all she had missed when she felt better. Trevor wasn't happy she was in the barn this morning but if she had to spend one more minute sitting on her ass moping, or worse yet, watch Trevor do the same, she'd pull her hair out.

"Jesus, Charlie, not only have you got two hot and sexy cowboys in the house, now you're keeping some in the barn too. No wonder I can't find one, you greedy bitch."

Charlie couldn't help but laugh at Rae's mock glare as she walked up, put her arm around her shoulder and bumped their hips together.

"Hey, Rae. Did you come all this way to visit me or just to ogle the eye candy? Wait, never mind, stupid question."

"The eye candy," they said in unison and laughed easily.

Rae hoisted up the large pink-and-brown striped bag she carried. "I got manicure and pedicure supplies, and fat-ass snacks that are so decadent they'll wipe out any depressing thought you've ever had." She winked with a slight smile. "And if that don't work, I got us enough fuzzy navel fixings to have us singing old show tunes and wiggling our asses until the Fourth of July."

"I'm *so* about that. But since I'm already wiggling to the pain med dance, I'll have to settle for drowning in decadents and virgin fuzzy navels. How about I introduce you to the eye candy and then we can head up and hide in my room with your little bag—uh, big bag of wicked goodies."

"Oh yeah, lead the way, oh queen of hot man flesh."

Charlie laughed and led her best friend toward Cade, Rae's tongue wagging all the way. "Hey, Cade, got someone who wants to meet you."

Cade tipped his hat back and wiped his hands on an old rag as he headed over to them.

"Rachel, this is Cade Jamison. Cade, meet my sometimes sane friend, Rachel Lang."

Cade reached out and took Rae's outstretched hand, but instead of shaking it, he brought her hand to his lips and tipped his hat at her with the other. "Pleasure to meet you, Miss Rachel."

Charlie nearly busted a gut at the look on Rae's face. The way she swayed a little and flushed at his greeting, one would think she'd never had anyone kiss her hand before. Charlie gave her a nudge to get her to focus before she started sputtering.

"Oh. Ah. Hi… Jesus, don't do that and then expect me to use my brain for anything intelligent like talk."

Too late.

"Well, I'll just have to make sure I try it again sometime if that's the reaction I can expect." Cade chuckled. The deep tone of it told Charlie that Rae wasn't the only one affected.

Rae blushed nice and pink and stared at the man as if he'd just told her the secret to the universe and he was it.

No way. Rae blushing? That has to be a first.

Charlie looked back and forth between them, tickled as all hell. "Rae, shut your mouth before you attract the flies. And you, Mr. Cade, stop trying to distract Rae. We have a date with fuzzy navels. Can I take a rain check on getting back up to speed on things?"

Rae clamped her mouth shut but the silly expression on her face remained, along with an awed sparkle in her eyes. Cade recovered a wee bit better but he still didn't take his eyes off Rae.

"Uh, yeah sure, Charlie. I'd hate to keep two beautiful ladies from their date with peaches. I can get you caught up in no time. You haven't missed a lot."

"Thanks, Cade." She pulled a reluctant Rae back toward the door.

Cade tipped his hat again and drawled real nice and sweet, "Truly was nice meeting you, Miss Rachel. Sure hope I get the pleasure again real soon."

Rae stared back at him and nodded her head like a fool as Charlie forced her out of the barn. Charlie reached over and wiped Rae's chin. "You're drooling."

Rae blinked at her a couple of times with a dazed expression on her face then visibly shuddered. "Shut up," she grumbled and swatted at Charlie.

They both cracked up. For Charlie it was like a balm to her soul and she slung her arm over Rae's shoulder and led her to the house, feeling better than she had in days.

Charlie and Rae spent the next two hours painting toe and fingernails as she filled Rae in on every detail she knew about Cade. She had a good feeling that it wouldn't be the last time the two of them would cross paths. They were both great people and she could so totally see them together. Why in the hell hadn't she thought of hooking them up before?

It wasn't until Charlie had blue toenails with little pink polka dots and matching fingers in a reverse pattern before the conversation turned to her relationship with Kegan and Trevor.

"The bruising has started to fade. How are you really feeling?" Rae asked as they sat together against the headboard, legs stretched out to let the ugly nail polish dry. "And I don't want the *I'm fine* version you try to lay on everyone else."

"I'm not sure if the yellow coloring is much of an improvement over the black. I think it might clash with the color of my eyes," Charlie responded, ignoring Rae's order.

"Nah, you still have enough dark color under your eyes that it sets them off nicely." Rae stared at her expectantly, no doubt waiting for Charlie to tell her how she really was. When Charlie remained silent and only smiled, Rae rolled her eyes. "Okay whatever. So when you gonna resume horsey duties?"

"Hell, I'm more than ready now. You know how I hate just sitting around. I'm going stir-crazy, but if it were up to Trevor, he'd have me stuck in bed twenty-four-seven and not in a good way. I swear, Rae, the man would carry me from room to room if I'd let him."

"I say enjoy it while you can. You'll be up to your elbows in mares soon enough." Rae gave her a sidelong glance. "I wouldn't have pegged Trevor for the nurturing type. Figured he was more like the commander and Kegan would be more the one making a big domestic fuss over you."

The mention of Kegan pushed aside some of the good mood Rae had created in Charlie and slapped her nice and hard in the chest like a sucker punch. The reminder of his absence was enough to take her from giggling and happy to sad and misty-eyed in seconds flat.

God, she missed him so much. Missed waking up to his silly, eager grin each morning, the way he looked for her during the day to sneak a kiss or a hug. She loved the way he and Trevor used to wrap around her each night and stroke her gently until she drifted off to sleep.

"Charlie?"

"Yeah?"

"I asked how Kegan was taking all this, seeing as it was his dad. He's got to be devastated, poor guy."

Charlie wished like hell she could get back to the happy buzz, but that wasn't likely to happen now. "I heard Trevor say that Kegan insisted on paying to have Drake buried. Nothing fancy, but he paid the cost of what the county would have had to. Trevor didn't sound like he was too happy about it, but then again, I'm sure Kegan wasn't either. Guess he wouldn't have felt right about others having to pay for the bastard."

"Did you ask him about it?"

Charlie scooted from the bed, swaying a little. She suddenly couldn't stand the thought of being in the bed she shared with Kegan and Trevor. The walls began to close in on her, the air heavy and thick, making it difficult to take a deep breath.

Suddenly the room started shaking, and she thought maybe she'd gotten up too quickly until she realized that it wasn't the room that shook but her own shoulders. She found herself wrapped in Rae's hug, head resting on her shoulder as she gave into the sobs that wracked her body. She let every last tear slide down her face and cleanse her of the pain, anguish and the hellish nightmare of Drake.

Rae stayed wrapped around her while she revealed how Kegan hadn't been there when she'd woken up in the hospital and had avoided her at all costs since. Every bad feeling and fear she had kept bottled up tumbled out, and Rae took it all until there was nothing but an uneasy kind of peace and a hint of exhaustion that might just promise a serene rest.

She let Rae support her until she was finally able to make some clear choices and understood that as bad as she wanted things to be like they had been before Drake had come back into their lives, it wasn't going to happen.

With that realization came the decision that she couldn't stay there any longer with the way things were. As much as her leaving would hurt Trevor, she would never ask him to choose between her and Kegan, and that was exactly what she was doing by staying.

Running away wasn't a great decision, would devastate her physically and emotionally, but what other choice did she have?

Staying in Kegan's home and forcing him to work from morning to night to avoid her just didn't seem fair to either of them. Everything at the ranch was a reminder of him and all she had lost.

Charlie didn't want to leave, but it was time.

Chapter Twenty-Six

The herd made its way along, slow and easy, as Kegan and Cade moved them from the back pasture. For once, they behaved and only needed occasional reminders to keep moving.

Kegan hated having time to think. It was so much easier to keep busy and not have to feel. He didn't want to think about Drake and what he had done to Charlie. No, what *he* had allowed Drake to do to Charlie. He had come to the realization that he and Trevor had kind of forced themselves on Charlie, forced her to give into their demands. He was no better than Drake. He might not have used physical strength, but he had still coerced her into something she hadn't wanted and it had damn near killed her.

You should have stayed away from her.

Too late for should haves now. Being a selfish bastard, he had nearly destroyed one of the people in his life that meant the most to him. Well, that wasn't entirely true either. Trevor meant the world to him too, and the selfish side of Kegan wanted to keep him, to continue their lives the way it had been before he'd found Charlie again, but the rational part of his brain knew Trevor loved Charlie and deserved her.

"She's gonna leave." Trevor spoke in a deep whisper. Kegan had been so wrapped up in his thoughts he hadn't realized Trevor had ridden up until he was right behind him.

Kegan didn't have to ask who. He knew Charlie would leave. How could she not? It was just a matter of when, not if. There really wasn't anything he could say that would change it. He nodded as he continued to watch the herd make its way toward the south field and tried not to feel.

"Did you fucking hear me? I said she's gonna leave us." Trevor's words were more of a menacing growl.

"Yeah, I heard you."

Trevor pulled his horse up alongside Kegan. "What the fuck are you going to do about it? It's your goddamn fault, fix it."

Fix it? How am I supposed to fix it? He couldn't take away what Drake had done or protect Charlie when she'd needed him the most. She'd be a hell of a lot better off if he just left her alone like he should have in the first place. Kegan continued to look straight ahead, not really seeing anything.

"Answer me, dammit!"

Kegan pulled his Stetson down farther over his eyes, avoiding the rage humming from the man next to him. "Trev, go on back up to the house. There's nothin' for me to fix."

"Bullshit. You're gonna fucking fix this or… I swear to God, Kegan, you're going to regret it."

I already do. I regret letting that sick excuse for a man touch her. I regret the pain I caused both of you. Ah, fuck it, what can I say? "Go home, Trevor. It's better this way."

"You selfish prick," Trevor roared.

The statement had no sooner left Trevor's mouth when the breath was knocked out of Kegan as he hit the ground. He turned at the last second, trying to figure out what the hell had just happened. He barely avoided the fist that barreled toward his head. "What the fuck?"

Kegan tried to scramble out from under the weight of Trevor's body, but the man rolled at the last instant, grabbed onto Kegan's coat and spun him until he was flat on his stomach. Before Trevor could get a solid hold on him, though, Kegan pressed his knee into the ground, pushed upward and threw Trevor backward.

The rage Kegan had tried so hard to keep suppressed boiled over and spilled rapidly out of him. He lunged for Trevor just as he kicked out and Kegan went flying backward and landed on his ass in a blink of an eye with Trevor straddling him. He pulled his fist back, ready to let it fly into Kegan's face.

"Go ahead. Fucking hit me." Kegan surrendered and relaxed his body. Hell, he wanted Trevor to hit him, maybe then the pain in his face would be greater than what ripped through his heart. Hopefully, Trevor would beat him until he didn't have to think or feel anymore.

Trevor lowered his fist to his side slowly, keeping his hand clenched tight, but whatever he saw as he stared at Kegan had his anger fading from his dark eyes.

For long moments, Trevor just continued to stare at him as if he were a complicated math problem to work out. He gave up, pulled himself to his feet and held out his hand toward Kegan. Trevor helped him up, then abruptly turned to mount his horse again.

Before he turned his horse back toward the ranch, Trevor looked him square in the eye. "She's not the only one you'll lose."

God, how had his life gotten so fucked up so fast? Kegan swung up onto his own mount and avoided the curious looks Cade gave him as he reined the horse toward him.

"Don't even ask." He spurred his horse in the direction of the herd and went back to work. The hardest part, the part that was impossible, was trying not to feel.

It was going to be a long day and even longer night.

* * * *

Trevor wasn't sure what the hell had gotten into him. He certainly hadn't planned on kicking the shit out of Kegan, but the man's refusal to meet his gaze or even talk to him had pushed him over the edge.

He'd tried being patient, to give Kegan time to get shit worked through in his own head, but he was tired of being patient.

He'd spent so much time trying to keep Charlie together, rarely allowed her any time alone with her thoughts and worked to keep her spirits up while her body healed that maybe he'd neglected Kegan in doing so. He had hoped that once Kegan buried his old man, knew once and for all that the man wouldn't be around to ever hurt any of them again, he'd come around. He hadn't and continued to withdraw further and further into himself, and no amount of patience or fists seemed to be able to stop the descent.

As Trevor rode closer to the barn, he thought about everything he and Kegan had been through since they'd first bought their spread. They had been able to overcome a lot of shit and it wasn't like this was the first time they'd gotten physical with each other.

The small outbuilding where they kept the fertile mares away from the stallions was a testament to that. They hadn't had the money to hire anyone to build it at the time so they'd figured what the hell, how hard could it be? Three fucking days in the scorching summer sun and they'd barely had the framework done. An argument over how to set the doorframe had ensued and suddenly they'd been rolling around in the dirt trying to force one another to cave to their idea. It had taken Cade and a big tub of ice water to cool the situation down, but it had worked out and they'd finished the building with damn fine results. However, a tub of cold water wasn't going to help them with their current situation.

The self-doubt and certainty it was his fault for Charlie being hurt had set Kegan on this downward spiral. He was scared. Trevor totally got it. He knew Kegan loved her more than life and wouldn't hurt her on purpose.

If only Kegan would realize he was hurting her a lot worse than Drake Colburn ever could. She needed reassurances and to feel safe again. As much as Trevor tried to be everything she needed right now, he couldn't be Kegan.

"What the fuck am I going to do?" he asked the empty field around him. He couldn't just let Charlie leave. But if it was what she needed, should he follow her?

He didn't believe she wanted to leave, but more than likely felt it was her only option at this point. On the other hand, he didn't believe that Kegan was pushing her away on purpose and if he ever needed anyone in his life, it was now. So how in the hell could Trevor just leave him too and follow Charlie?

Trevor balled his fist up tightly and screamed at the sky. "Somebody want to tell me what the fuck I'm supposed to do?"

His whole world was falling apart and he had no clue how to hold it together. He'd been with Kegan for years—amazing years of work, laughter, fights and living right. Now when they finally had everything they could ever possibly want, it was being ripped from their grasp and there was fucking little he could do to hold onto it.

Trevor hung his head and let the horse make his way back to the barn. He wasn't a praying man, never really had much use for God and religion, but at this moment he wished he could find a little faith.

Please, someone just tell me what to do, how to make this right.

He left Gallie with one of the hands to brush down and made his way back to the house without a word to anyone.

He needed to find Charlie, to keep her close until he could figure out how to make her stay.

Chapter Twenty-Seven

Staring down at the biscuits and gravy Mrs. Miller had set in front of her made Charlie's gut churn.

"Eat up, honey."

"Thank you." Charlie knew before even picking up her fork that she wouldn't be able to eat it. It had been ten days since her discharge from the hospital, and in that time, Kegan had spoken only a few words to her about mundane things. He had avoided her as if she carried the plague. The one time she had finally mustered the courage to confront him, he had literally run in the opposite direction. Her appetite wasn't the only thing that was missing these days.

She missed Kegan.

She'd given up on approaching him since it seemed to cause him near physical pain to be anywhere near her. It had been sheer torture to lie in Trevor's arms each night and listen to the silent house, knowing Kegan was lying alone in the room next to theirs. She couldn't take it anymore. As much as she appreciated everything Trevor was doing for her, how he had gone out of his way to make her feel comfortable, it wasn't enough. He and Kegan were a package deal. They belonged together. One without the other was like having a cup with a hole in the bottom. It was just impossible to fill. Kinda like her heart was feeling.

"You're leavin', ain't ya, girl?"

Charlie looked up into Mrs. Miller's eyes, where she had taken the seat directly across from Charlie.

"What makes you think that?" She averted her gaze quickly, looking down at her biscuit as if she were about to eat it and her world wasn't falling apart.

"Lot of years of watching people makes recognizing someone about to flee fairly easy. I wish I could tell you it'd be a bad idea to leave, that you should stay, but I ain't so mean that I would even ask you to stay on my count. I'd miss you. It's been nice having another woman around the house."

Charlie looked up, stunned by her admission.

"I know one thing for sure, Charlie. That boy loves you and he's just feeling sorry for himself and acting ten shades of stupid by living in the past. He's just forgotten what's right in front of him." She winked at her. "He'll figure it out when he realizes you've up and left. Then he'll have to figure out what he wants the most. He'll either continue to beat himself up over what he can't change or move forward."

Mrs. Miller stood, wiped her hands on her apron, before she removed it and placed it over the chair. "I'll see ya real soon, baby girl." She turned and headed out the door, but turned back to toss over her shoulder, "I'll keep them lockets safe for ya until you come back home." Then she was gone.

Shit! She had forgotten all about the lockets she had purchased for Trevor and Kegan. The ones she'd planned to give them the night... *Nope, not going there.*

Charlie stood and shook her head to dispel the images. She refused to let them control her and keep her in fear when he was dead and gone. She had work to do. She either had to figure out how to get her life back with Trevor and Kegan or move on. Living in limbo was pure-ass torture and being she was so not into S&M, it was time to force their hand one way or another.

She walked to her purse sitting on the counter by the back door and retrieved her cell phone. After dialing the familiar number, she waited until it picked up on the second ring.

"Hey, Rae! I'm ready."

"You sure about this?"

"Hell no. See ya in an hour." Charlie ended the call and returned the phone to her purse before Rae tried to talk her out of what she was about to do.

* * * *

After his shower, Kegan slipped on his jeans and searched for a smaller belt.

He'd lost so much weight over the last few weeks he needed to find something that fit unless he wanted to hold his damn pants up all day. The loss of weight didn't bother him as much as the fact that he still had no desire to eat. Shit just came back up anyway. For a while, he'd made it almost a game to see how long he could hold down his meal. Now he rarely even tried to eat.

When he couldn't find a new belt, he gathered up the extra fabric of his jeans in one hand, his old belt in the other, and headed toward the kitchen in search of something to make a new hole. With any luck, he could sneak in, grab a knife, then get out before he ran into Trevor. They'd had their fights in the past; it was hard for two men living and working together every day not to have the occasional disagreement, even some that had gotten a little physical.

He knew it was frustration on Trevor's part that had made him lash out, but as much as Kegan understood it, there wasn't a damn thing he could do to fix it. For now, he just hoped like hell that he could avoid the man until he could figure out how to make things better for all of them.

Charlie leaving was another thing he couldn't fix. It had been damn near impossible not to beg her to stay after Trevor had informed him she was going to leave. As much as he wanted her to stay, he knew it was better this way. She shouldn't have to deal with him.

Going back to her own place would be a good thing for her. He was sure that with time to think about what she wanted, without him and Trevor pushing her into things, she'd realize she was better off without him.

Neither he nor Trevor had given her more than a moment to think about what it was they'd asked — demanded — from her. What woman in their right mind would want to put up with two arrogant bastards like him and Trevor? It was just a fantasy to think they could actually find one woman to make their lives complete. Kinda like the fantasy of thinking he was actually good enough for Charlie and could have a future with her.

Charlie had accepted them and look what that had gotten her…a whole lot of hurt and a man who couldn't protect her when she needed him the most.

Charlie was it for him, always had been, and he would never love anyone as he loved her. But, now that he knew she was okay, was strong enough to stand on her own, and his father could no longer hurt her, he had to let her go.

He couldn't ever imagine himself with anyone else. But even he wasn't selfish enough to destroy her just to make himself happy. He wouldn't even do it to make Trevor happy either.

As Kegan entered the kitchen, he said a silent thank you that Mrs. M and Trevor were elsewhere. He quickly headed for the butcher block and stiffened as familiar footsteps walked in behind him. *Shit!*

"We need to talk," Trevor drawled quietly.

Without turning, Kegan grabbed a knife from the block. "Yeah, I suppose we do."

"No need for that knife, I just plan on talking."

Kegan couldn't help but snicker as he turned. "Yeah, like I'd need a knife to take you."

Trevor waved him off and leaned against the counter opposite Kegan, watching as he dug a new hole into his belt. "What the hell are you doing?"

"What does it look like?" Kegan had to widen his stance to keep his pants from falling down as he worked on the belt. Once he'd made the hole, he threaded it through the loops on his jeans and fastened it. Still wasn't quite tight enough, but at least they weren't falling off.

"Jesus! How much weight have you lost?"

Kegan shrugged in response. "So talk."

"I need to know where your head is."

Kegan shrugged again. "Meaning?"

"You're hurting her."

He knew he was, and it ripped his fucking heart out every time he thought about it. "What do you want me to say?"

"I want you to say what happened to Charlie wasn't your fault and mean it so we can all move past it."

Kegan slumped against the counter and stared down at his feet, unable to meet Trevor's gaze. "I can't do that."

"Yes you can," Trevor demanded.

Christ, he was tired. In his head, in his heart, in his soul, just so fucking tired. He shuffled to the liquor cabinet and pulled down a bottle of whiskey, then two glasses. Setting them on the table, he motioned for Trevor to join him. He might as well get comfortable. The hard set of Trevor's jaw told Kegan he wouldn't be able to walk away and ignore him this time. Undoubtedly, the man would follow him around until he gave in anyway. He poured them each a drink then threw back nearly half of his before he met Trevor's gaze.

"Go ahead and say your piece."

Trevor sighed. "I'm not gonna try and convince you that what your old man did wasn't your fault. I know you well enough to know when you get something in your fool head, it's nearly impossible to change it, but I do want to ask you one question."

Kegan eyed him with suspicion, drained the rest of his glass, then poured a second before answering. "This should be interesting."

"When I first met you, we were both like two truly fucked-up people trying to figure out where they stood in the world." He grabbed his glass, stared at it for a moment, then continued without taking a drink. Instead he ran his hands through his hair. "It took us a bit, but we finally figured out it wasn't so much us that were messed up, but the shitty families we were born into."

If that isn't the understatement of the year.

He didn't say anything, knew Trevor would eventually make his point, so he nodded, urged the man to continue. The sooner Trevor got whatever it was off his chest, the sooner he could take the bottle of whiskey, go back to his room and drink until he was numb.

"You and I, we worked hard to prove something to ourselves. Made a good life and earned the respect of lots of people in this county. Refused to let what happened when we were young to define us as men."

Kegan drained his glass, savoring the warm feeling as the liquid moved down, knew that soon enough, it would bring him the sweet oblivion he needed. "Trev? You want to hurry up and get to that question." He pointed toward Trevor's legs. "And could you do it without that damn knee-shaking thing?"

Trevor looked down at his legs and instantly the shaking stopped, as if he hadn't realized he was doing it, but the hands were back in his hair. "The point I was trying to make was that you and I, we've come a long way, right?"

"Yep." Kegan started to rise, but Trevor reached out, grabbed his forearm and stopped him.

"Where the hell you going?"

"You said you only wanted to ask me one question and you just did, which, I may add, I answered, so I'm going back to my room."

"Sit your ass down and stop being a prick. You know that wasn't the question."

Kegan reclaimed his seat. "Yeah, but I could hope. Ask your question already, will ya?"

"Fine. I want to know why, after all this time, you now think Drake is so all damn important that you're going to let him have complete control over your life?"

Kegan's mouth fell open. He couldn't have been more stunned if Trevor had sat in front of him and grown a second head. "You're not serious? I won't even dignify that with an answer."

Trevor stood, placed his hands on the table and looked down at Kegan. "I'm not really looking for an answer. I just want you to think on it. You're letting Drake hurt me, you and Charlie. Is he really so important that he's worth all three of us suffering?"

Trevor didn't wait for his response. He turned and walked out of the kitchen without giving him a second look.

Damn the man anyway. Kegan snatched up his glass and the bottle of whiskey from the table and made his way back to his room.

An hour and another two shots later and Trevor's question still festered inside him.

'Is he really so important that he's worth all three of us suffering?'

Hell no, the man wasn't important. He'd been a sorry excuse for a human his whole life and didn't deserve even a second's thought with his passing. Trevor had done mankind a favor in taking him out and the only thing Kegan hoped now was that the bastard was suffering in hell the same way he had made so many others suffer while he was alive.

'Complete control over your life.'

The hell he did. Did he? Wanting Charlie to have a good life, one she deserved, didn't have a damn thing to do with Drake, did it? Sure, he could admit that some of his insecurities stemmed from growing up under Drake, but they didn't define him. He hadn't been able to protect Charlie against Drake, hadn't been enough for her. That was why he had to let her go. It had nothing to do with Drake, just his own shortcomings. He wasn't allowing Drake to still hurt her.

Was he?

Chapter Twenty-Eight

Charlie sat staring out of the window. The landscape took on a dreamlike quality as it swirled and blurred into an array of bright colors. She'd finally made the decision to leave the ranch and though she knew it was the right decision, the only one she could make, it didn't make her feel the least bit better.

She was a complete mess. Hell, she'd always been a mess, but now it was for a different reason than when she'd first come to the ranch. She'd been unsure of her future and had been clueless as to how to manage the pain and anger from the past, but eventually she had thanks to Kegan's and Trevor's love and patience.

Her dreams had nearly come true when she had finally let go and accepted the fact that she was completely and irrevocably in love with two men.

It had felt so right, scribbling the notes to her men, planning and fussing over the preparations of their dinner together when she would finally tell them both how she felt.

Now in the wake of Drake Colburn, her dreams were crushed and her body, mind and soul completely devastated. It wasn't what Drake had done to her that had destroyed her new, fragile dream of being with Kegan and Trevor, but what Drake had done to Kegan. Drake had taken her fairy tale and turned it into nothing but a heartbreaking nightmare.

Trevor would undoubtedly rush to find her as soon as he realized she was gone and that was why she had no intention of returning to her apartment. Charlie felt guilty for the pain she was going to cause Trevor. It wasn't his fault things hadn't worked out. He had worked so hard at making her feel comfortable, had made sure that she didn't have time to sit and think about her heartache for too long.

Hell, she doubted she would have had the will to get out of bed each morning to face the onslaught of emotional pain if it hadn't been for Trevor's refusal to allow her to wallow in self-pity or question herself and every choice she had made. As much as she hated what she was doing to Trevor, there was no way she could ever stay at the ranch and watch him make a choice each day between her and Kegan.

No matter his good intentions, he couldn't fix what was happening between her and Kegan. Eventually it would drive a wedge between them. It was unfair to force him to choose. No one should ever have to make a decision like that. With that in mind, she had done what she thought would be easiest for both him and Kegan, and walked away.

Dr. Stone had been more than happy to give her a little extra time off, telling her to take all the time she needed and they'd resume her training when she was ready. She had thanked him for his understanding, assured him she wouldn't be gone long, yet she had no intention of resuming her studies or training in Redfield. No way she could remain that close to Kegan and Trevor and not be reminded every minute of what she'd almost had.

Tears threatened to spill from her eyes but she blinked them back. She was tired of the tears, the pain in her chest and the way her thoughts kept running in a loop of one depressing scene of her life after another.

The stereo being turned off and Rae's soft voice brought her out of her mangled thoughts.

"Why Florida? You hate the heat and sand and you've never been big on tourist traps. St. Petersburg is like so touristy."

Charlie drew her gaze away from the passing scenery and laid her head back against the headrest of Rae's car. "I'm not going for the sights."

"Yeah, but you're more the mountain cabin recluse kinda girl. I just can't picture you sitting on the beach alone. If you'd just give me a couple of days, I could get the time off and go with you."

Charlie sat up straighter as Rae took the exit for the airport. God, she hated flying. It was the only thing she'd ever experienced that caused her to go into a full-blown panic attack. The first time she had flown when she was seventeen, she had been up and out of her seat, headed for the exit door as the plane had taken off. It wasn't until a flight attendant had forced her back to her seat and held her down that she'd realized she had even made an attempt to open the door. She had been sitting one moment in the cramped little seat trying to figure out how to get her seat belt tightened and the next she hadn't been able to breathe. It had felt like her heart would jump out of her chest.

To this day, she usually avoided flying at all costs. The irrational panic still crept up on her each time she flew but she had learned to deal with it, though at the end of every flight she was completely exhausted, her muscles tight and cramped. Yet this time she welcomed it. Hopefully, she would finally be able to take advantage of her flying ordeal and get some very much-needed sleep once she got to her hotel room.

"I wish you could go with me, Rae, if nothing else, to just get me through the flight, but I need some time alone, ya know? I need to get my head on right and make some big decisions about my life and my future. I need to do that without influence one way or the other."

"Pfft, like I'd try to influence you," Rae sniffed.

Rae pulled up to the departing flight drop-off area and parked the car before Charlie commented further. "I really appreciate that you'd even offer to go with me. I know you have a lot going on right now and it means the world to me you would drop everything and come with, but I really do need some time alone."

Rae reached over and squeezed her hand. "Yeah, I know you do, but it doesn't stop me from wanting to be there for you."

Charlie pulled on Rae's hand to bring her closer for a hug. "I promise I'll call when I get settled at the hotel and every night as long as you keep your promise."

"Yeah, yeah, I know. No telling the cowboys where you are. I don't agree with it, but a promise is a promise."

Charlie squeezed Rae one last time before she let her go and opened her door. As Charlie stepped out onto the pavement, Rae leaned down so she could look up at her. "You want me to wait with you until you board?"

"Nah, I'll be okay. Besides, you need to get back to work. Thanks again for everything, Rae. Talk to you tonight."

She closed the door, pulled her bag up on her shoulder, then headed toward the airport with a wave back at Rae. She had a couple of hours before she had to board the plane. Since she was no longer taking pain meds, she had just enough time to find an airport lounge and work on getting enough liquid courage in her to help her endure the flight.

If she was lucky, in her exhausted state she could drink enough and be passed out before the plane even made its taxi down the runway.

* * * *

Kegan had no more than gotten to his room with the intent on spending another day with Mr. Jack Daniel until he couldn't think straight when a rap at the door had him tensing and he yelled out angrily, "Go away."

"Don't you yell at me, young man."

Crap. Kegan jumped to his feet and opened the door. "I'm sorry, Mrs. M, I thought you were Trevor."

She brushed past and waved him off, then crossed the small room to take a seat on the bed.

"Won't you come in?" Damn but the woman was even pushier than Trevor.

She patted the mattress next to her. "C'mere, boy, and sit down."

Why the fuck couldn't they just leave him alone for one afternoon? When did everyone in this house get their fucking degrees in psychology and think it was okay to analyze him like a goddamn guinea pig? With a frustrated sigh, he sat next to her.

"What the hell is wrong with you?" Mrs. M asked.

"Excuse me?"

"You're acting like a damn spoiled brat, treating people the way you have the last couple weeks."

"Mrs. M—"

"Shut it," Mrs. M demanded and pointed a warning finger at him. "You're gonna sit right here and listen, boy. That girl has been through hell, but it's nothing like the hell she's been suffering from what you're doing to her."

"I don't—"

She cut him off with a glare. "You don't think I get it? I've been around a damn long time and I get it just fine. You think you're not good enough for her and somewhere in that messed-up thought process you've decided it gives you the right to make the choice of whether she wants to be with you or not. You think you get to decide what is best for her without a care for what she wants. Pretty arrogant on your part, wouldn't you say?"

Kegan didn't know what to say to that. She just didn't understand the whole situation with Charlie, and he wasn't about to explain it to her. He doubted she would understand what he was sacrificing for Charlie.

Mrs. Miller patted the back of his hand. "You're sacrificing your happiness thinking you're doing what's best for her."

Kegan stared at her in stunned surprise. Could the woman read his mind?

She held his gaze with a spitfire gleam in her eyes. She rose from the bed and turned toward him. "Not only are you sacrificing your happiness for nothing, you're sacrificing Charlie's and Trevor's as well. Think on that. Are your insecurities worth hurting the two people you love?" She reached into her apron, pulled out three small black boxes, then placed them on the bed next to him.

Leaning forward, she placed a soft kiss to his forehead and whispered, "You are deserving." She turned and left, before closing the door softly behind her.

Kegan sat and stared at the closed door for long moments. What the hell had just happened? Mrs. M had never bit her tongue or held back her thoughts, so it shouldn't have surprised him that she would give him her opinion now.

He simply didn't want to have to think or feel, but obviously Trevor and Mrs. M weren't inclined to allow that. Kegan reached down and picked up the small boxes she had left for him, let his fingers brush across the soft velvet fabric.

He took a deep breath. Inside the first box, he recognized Charlie's locket. He carefully disengaged the delicate clasp, expecting to see the same picture of him when he was a boy.

Instead, there were two tiny pictures, recent ones of him and Trevor. He closed the box, setting it back on the nightstand before he opened the next. Inside was a small masculine, cross-shaped locket and a small piece of paper pushed into the lid. He lost his breath when he discovered inside the locket were pictures of himself and Charlie on each side. This one was meant for Trevor, so he didn't read what was obviously a note.

He closed the box and placed it next to Charlie's. Kegan held the last box, his big hands trembling. He knew what he would find inside and still couldn't make his fingers. He stared at it, let the shaking in his hands settle and his heart restart before opening it.

Inside was another masculine cross, but this one contained pictures of Trevor and Charlie. He gently closed the locket and removed the note from the lid.

Kegan,

You and Trevor have made me feel complete. For the first time in my life, I feel whole. I spent most of my life dreaming of a future with you and now my dreams have come true, but my dreams were never as perfect as my reality. I never thought I would ever love anyone as much as I've always loved you, but I'm so glad I was wrong. You and Trevor are my future and I promise to love you both with every beat of my heart forever.

Thank you for completing me.

Love always,

Charlie

Kegan sat and stared at the letter. He read it over and over until he knew every line by heart, and still he stared at it, thinking. He wasn't sure how long he sat there when he finally ran a hand over his damp face and pulled himself together enough to replace the note in the box and set it next to the other two.

He'd finally made a decision and wasn't sure if he had waited too long. He wasn't even sure he'd made the right decision, but he knew what he had to do.

Kegan stood and walked out of his room in search of his best friend. It was time they talked about their future, which included all three of them.

Chapter Twenty-Nine

Charlie sighed in relief when she walked into her room at the Howard Johnson. Not that the room was anything special, but the air conditioning was on full blast and instantly cooled her sweat-dampened skin.

Now she remembered why she hated Florida. The thermometer might have read in the mid-eighties, but the humidity had her feeling as if she'd been dropped into the bowels of hell.

"Geez, how in the hell do these people breathe with the air so heavy and wet?" She dropped her bag next to the door and stripped off her damp clothes. A shower sounded damn fine right about now.

The room looked like most big hotel chains, the only difference was the colors were all in pale blues, tans and creams and the pictures on the walls were of seascapes instead of landscapes. The bedspread on the large king-size bed was the same gaudy pattern as most hotel rooms except done in the colors of the beach and ocean rather than the normal dark greens and burgundies.

She set her cell phone on the small table next to the only chair in the room. She'd turned it off after about the third time it had vibrated with a new message from Trevor. It wasn't that she didn't want to talk to him, just not tonight. She was bone-weary and in her current state wasn't so sure she wouldn't give into his demands that she tell him where she was.

She had a hard enough time winning battles with him when she was fully awake and happy, being tired and miserable just asked for failure. She'd call Rae, let her know that she'd made it and everything was good. But first, she wanted a cool shower and a cup of coffee. By then, maybe the effects of the airport lounge indulgence would be out of her system.

After a quick shower, Charlie pulled on a pair of old sweats and a T-shirt then took her cup of coffee out onto the balcony to let her hair dry naturally. It only took ten minutes to realize what a really bad idea it was. She was sweating like a stuffed pig and retreated back into the cool air of her room with damp, frizzy hair. She pulled the big chair over to the closed sliding window and sipped her coffee as she took in the sights. The humidity might have totally sucked but the view was amazing. Just below her balcony was a small crystal-clear pool set between the hotel and a small cabana bar, and beyond the bar was a beautiful beach and ocean. Maybe she could take a walk along the beach later when the sun went down or first thing in the morning. Surely, it couldn't be this hot all day and night.

She set down her mug, grabbed her cell and dialed Rae's number.

"Hey, Charlie, I take it you made it okay?"

"Hi, yeah, it was a good flight. I didn't puke or panic or anything, but holy hell, it's hot here. Why didn't you talk me out of this?"

Rae chuckled into the phone. "Like I could have. You're a woman on a mission and nothing short of me hog-tying you would have kept you from going."

Charlie had put a lot of thought into leaving, but not a lot into the impulsive flight to Florida. Still, even with the heat, she didn't regret coming. She really needed the time alone and a change of scenery. Florida had seemed like the best way to get it at the time. "Thanks for dropping everything and giving me a ride, I owe you one."

"You don't owe me anything," Rae insisted. "In fact, I owe you big-time."

"Huh?"

"Well from what I can gather, Trevor stormed off the ranch looking for anyone who may have seen you. He called my cell phone a couple of times as well, but I didn't answer. I wanted to talk to you before I talked to him. Anyhoo, I guess Cade figured he'd call and give me a heads-up that your cocky cowboy was looking for me. I may have mentioned that I might need someone big and strong to protect me and keep me out of the house for a while."

Charlie couldn't help but laugh. Leave it to Rae to use someone else's drama to get herself a cowboy. "I take it Cade volunteered to be your bodyguard?"

"Nope, not yet, but I'm hoping after he takes me out to dinner later tonight, he'll be guarding my body."

"You have no shame."

"Well, what could I do? I mean, the man is a living god, and you have a lot of room to talk, Miss 'I need two cowboys to satisfy me'."

Charlie winced at the comment about her two cowboys. She didn't have two anymore and each time she was reminded of what she'd lost made her want to crawl into bed, pull the covers over her head and wish the world away.

There was never going to be one man who could satisfy her like Kegan and Trevor did, and not just sexually.

Trevor had proven to be a rock, had kept her strong and made her want to get out of bed each morning, even when half of her had been dying as Kegan had withdrawn further from them. He was demanding and cocky, but he was also so loving and carefree that he had been the bridge that had allowed her and Kegan to find each other again.

Kegan, on the other hand, was quiet and gentle. He was the one who liked picnics, riding and spending quiet time together. But he was fierce and aggressive when he needed to be.

The two of them together made for the perfect man.

"You still there?"

"Yeah, just thinking. I guess I have a lot on my mind right now, kinda zone in and out at times."

"Well, just don't be thinking on all the negative crap and none of the good. If I know anything for sure, it's that those two men love you and you love them. It will work out. I have to believe that, because if you don't deserve your happily ever after, what chance do the rest of us have?"

"Thanks, Rae. I'm just not so sure this was the happily ever after I was meant to have. I know Kegan's hurting, but he promised me he wouldn't leave me or let me go again, and he's already broken it." She blinked back the tears. They weren't helping. "Not sure I can give him a third chance."

"Hey, I know you'll do what's right for you in this. You're strong and however this plays out, you'll make it through."

"Thanks, I'm gonna go see if I can get room service to bring me some more coffee and a bite to eat. I'll call you later in the week, okay?"

"Yeah, sounds good. I'll talk to Trevor before Cade gets here, let him know you're okay and to give you some time. Want me to give him a message for you?"

Charlie thought about that for a second, and then realized there was nothing she could say to make him feel any better. "No, I don't think so. I'll talk to you soon."

"Bye, Charlie, love you."

"Love you too." She turned off the phone and set it back on the table. Maybe tomorrow she'd think about turning it back on to check the messages, but right now she just wanted to stop thinking.

She hoped her brain would take the hint and give her what she needed tonight.

Peace.

* * * *

"Goddammit," Trevor roared before he threw the phone across the room, watching it shatter as it hit the wall.

He was pissed and just fucking shaking. If he didn't find Charlie soon, he was going to lose his goddamned mind. What the hell was she thinking, going off all alone and leaving him worried as hell?

Oh, he was so going to spank that stubborn, pigheaded, sexy ass but good when he got his hands on her. At least had Kegan come to his senses and was ready to talk.

Trevor just wasn't sure if he wanted to kiss him for finally waking up or kick his ass from one end of the ranch to the other for getting his head straight one day too late.

He rubbed his eyes with the palms of his hands and rested his elbows on the desk. How was he supposed to find someone who didn't want to be found but desperately needed to be?

"Thought you might need this."

He looked up and cocked an eyebrow at Kegan just as he set a cordless down in front of him. "What the hell for? I don't know who else to call."

Kegan took the chair across from his desk. He looked so tired and drawn, with big dark circles under his eyes, as if he hadn't slept in weeks. Trevor wanted to be pissed at him, to yell and scream that it was his fucking fault Charlie had left.

Dammit, he just wanted to fight with someone. To fight and scream and smash shit sounded a whole lot better than the pain and emptiness he was experiencing at the moment. Yet as much as he wanted to blame someone, he took one look at Kegan and knew that whatever he said wouldn't punish Kegan any more than he had already done to himself.

Kegan shrugged. "Figured you'd want it in case it rang. I take it Rae wouldn't tell you where she's gone to?"

"That little shit knows where Charlie is and I even threatened to beat her within an inch of her life, then apologized, begged and pleaded. She still wouldn't cave."

He had half a mind to hunt Rae down and spank her stubborn ass too. Get some practice in before he had to give Charlie a matching red ass for not answering the phone. Maybe he'd give her an extra swat for turning the damn thing off and make all calls go straight to voicemail. He'd already left about ten messages.

Kegan stared at his hands as he fidgeted with his fingers. The man needed some sleep and if he didn't get it soon, he was going to fall flat on his face. At least a few winks before they found Charlie. Trevor needed him to be coherent if they were going to talk Charlie into coming home where she belonged.

Trevor stood and picked up the phone from the desk before he moved around to stand in front of Kegan and held out his hand. "C'mon, I'm taking you to bed and you're gonna get some sleep, then we'll go find her and bring her home."

"Not sure I *can* sleep," Kegan responded but took Trevor's hand and stood up, allowing himself to be led out of the room and up the stairs to the room they'd shared with Charlie.

Kegan hesitated upon entering their room, but Trevor gave him a push and helped him take off his boots and clothes, then pushed him onto his stomach on the big bed and under the covers.

Kegan folded his arms and rested his head on them. "I don't know if I can sleep."

"Sure you can, 'cause I'm going to help you," Trevor assured him. He set the phone on the bedside table, stripped down to his boxers and climbed onto the bed.

"I don't know if I can get it up," Kegan remarked and yawned.

"Oh trust me, I could get it up for you if I was so inclined," he commented, then straddled Kegan and sat on his ass.

"You sound pretty sure of yourself."

"I am. I'll prove it later."

Kegan lifted his head and looked at him with a strange expression, but Trevor simply smiled and let Kegan chew on the suggestive implication. Trevor pressed his palms against Kegan's lower back and, keeping firm pressure, ran them up along Kegan's spine.

"Damn that feels good," Kegan groaned and closed his eyes.

Trevor didn't comment, just let the silence fall over them. He massaged Kegan's shoulders and up and down his back, working out all the little knots he found until Kegan's breathing became deep and even. Once Kegan was lightly snoring, Trevor carefully slid off Kegan and lay next to him.

Trevor wasn't sure he'd be able to sleep, but he was glad he was able to help the big guy get a little. They had talked most of the day about what had been going on in Kegan's head and how they needed to keep the lines of communication open if this was going to work.

Kegan didn't promise he could overcome his insecurities, instead had said, "My promises don't mean much." But at least he had agreed he would try his damnedest. Trevor inched closer to Kegan and gently rubbed along the small of Kegan's back, keeping him relaxed and loose. He had no doubt they could work this out and be what each other needed them to be. They had enough love to go around, but didn't do so well at showing it all the time.

It was something he planned on working on. Kegan and Charlie were damn stubborn, but he had his own difficult streak in him and when he wanted something as badly as he did Kegan and Charlie, he could be downright pit bullish in getting what he wanted.

He had half his family where they belonged and tomorrow he'd work at getting his other half home, happy and safe.

Chapter Thirty

A cold front had moved into Florida, or at least that was what the weatherman called it.

It was a gorgeous, seventy-something day and no humidity. In Charlie's world, it was perfection. The cooler temperatures and it being midweek during a time of year when tourism wasn't real big left the beach practically deserted. Which was fine with her. She needed the peace and quiet seeing as she was going to stop being a coward and listen to her voicemail. When that was done, she would call her men and tell them she was coming home.

She'd spent the last couple of days trying to do the same thing that had always worked for her in the past—avoid painful thoughts and feelings by hiding them behind a confident, untouchable façade. This time it wasn't working. Truth be told, it really hadn't worked that well in the past either and it worked not at all now that she didn't want it to.

She was totally in love with two stubborn cowboys and instead of hiding and pretending the world couldn't hurt her this time, she was going back to Redfield and take what she wanted. She'd show Kegan how much of a *bichito* she could be.

Right after she listened to her voicemails she would grovel on her hands and knees, beg Trevor's forgiveness — for worrying him, that was.

Charlie sighed and pushed the voicemail button on her cell phone.

"You have fifteen new messages. First new message."

"Hey, Charlie, gonna be a little late getting back to snuggle, couple of the hands are out sick. Should be home by lunch. Love you."

"Next new message."

"Where are you? Mrs. M said she saw you heading out with Rae. You know, it wouldn't hurt to leave me a note. I'd hoped to have lunch with you, maybe a mid-afternoon snuggle. Call me when you get this. Bye."

"Next new message."

"Dammit, Charlie, where are you? It's after six and I can't get hold of you or Rae. You're starting to worry me. Please, baby, just call me and let me know you're okay."

"Next new message."

"Hey, Charlie, it's Rae, just got off the phone with Trevor. I know you wanted some time alone to think and shit, but the man is going out of his head. I think I have him calmed down some, at least he's not threatening to call out the FBI after you, now he's just threatening to spank me. What do ya think, should I let him?"

"Next new message."

"What the hell were you thinking taking off like this? Goddamn, Charlie, how the fuck are we going to work this all out if you're off God knows where alone? I know this shit with Kegan ain't right, but if we work together, we can bring him back. I know we can, but I need you here to help me. Fuck, Charlie, don't do this."

"Next new message."

"Threatening Rae within an inch of her life didn't work. Shit, didn't think I would ever meet anyone as stubborn as you, but she may be right up there with you. Anyway, not sure if you're listening to your voicemail but wanted to say goodnight and sweet dreams. I miss you. Please stay safe for us. I love you."

Charlie's chest tightened and she rubbed at the ache. She'd screwed up leaving the way she had. Trevor hadn't deserved the worry she had put him through, but it had seemed like the right thing to do at the time, the only thing she could think of. She couldn't stop the tears that slid down her cheeks as she continued to listen to the messages.

"Next new message."

"Morning, babe. Man I miss waking up next to you, but you'll be pleased to know that I got Kegan back in our bed last night. He finally slept more than a few minutes, though I had to threaten to beat him. Yeah, well, he and I had a good long talk and while he still has a ways to go to get back to himself, I think that if… I mean *when* you get home, he'll be right as rain. We love you, babe, take care and be safe for us."

"Next new message."

"Hey, Charlie…um…Trevor wanted, well we wanted to let you know that… Ah hell, baby, please just come home. I miss you something fierce and Trevor misses you too. I know I'm the one that made you run off. I understand if you don't want to talk to me and all, but if you could just call Trevor and let him know you're okay, we sure would feel a lot better. Love you, bichito, please be safe."

"*Next new message.*"

"Hey, babe! I just wanted to wish you sweet dreams. I finally got Kegan to eat a decent meal tonight, and I think it's the first time since…well in a long time that it didn't come back up on him. He's sleeping for the second night in a row, which is a huge improvement. He doesn't stay asleep, though. I think he's like me and needs something soft to wrap around in order to truly let go and sleep. He reached out for you in his sleep earlier and he's currently snuggled up to me, but has one hell of a frown on his face. I think he knows it's not you. Just remember we love you. Good night, babe. God, Charlie, please be safe for us."

Charlie hit the End button on her phone. She couldn't listen to what she had done to them anymore. What a selfish bitch she could be at times. Hiding and hurting people because she was too much of a damn coward to open her mouth and talk shit out. If she had been smart, she would have wrapped herself around Kegan, grabbed on tight and held him while he was hurting instead of wounding everyone even more and leaving Trevor to take care of Kegan on his own. With guilt nearly choking her, Charlie grabbed up her things and headed back to the hotel. She had a call to make that was way past overdue.

After room service had brought her a coffee with Baileys and a side shot of whiskey, Charlie got her nerves under control enough and picked up her cell phone. She threw back the whiskey in one big gulp then hit the Call button. As soon as Trevor picked up after the first ring, Charlie burst into tears. So much for liquid courage.

"Charlie, baby, is that you? Are you okay?"

She sniffed and swallowed down the lump in her throat. "Yeah it's me. Trevor, I'm so sorry I made you worry. I just wasn't thinking right and ran." It was all she could say before the sobs overtook her again.

"Shh, baby, don't cry. I can't stand it when you cry and I can't hold you. It's going to be okay."

Charlie couldn't stop the sobs that escaped, the tears just fell freely like a warm waterfall down her cheeks.

"Baby, it's okay. Tell me what you need and I'll make it happen."

"You," she cried. "I need you and Kegan and I want to come home."

Charlie let everything go with each tear. The pain, fear, self-doubt, she let the tears wash them all away. She didn't want to live without her cowboys and she couldn't pretend that losing them wouldn't affect her. It would destroy her. A life without them would never be a life. Her true happiness could only be found in the strong arms of the men who owned her heart.

"Baby, get up and answer the door."

His statement made her pause for a moment. What was he talking about? "What?"

"I need you to get up and answer the door."

Charlie stood, grabbed a tissue, then wiped her eyes and running nose, sniffling. She heard a light knocking and started toward the door. How had he heard that over her bawling? "Hold on, Trevor, someone's at the door."

"I know. Just open it."

She reached out and turned the knob, confused at the shift in the conversation. No sooner had she started to open the door than it burst wide open and big arms wrapped around her and pulled her into a tight embrace.

Trevor's voice and scent filled her senses, followed by Kegan's seconds later as two sets of arms wrapped around her. Charlie nearly collapsed with relief.

Hands touched, soothed and caressed as two sets of warm lips kissed her tears away. They had come for her? Even though she had run and caused them pain and worry, they had still come for her.

God, did she deserve them? She wasn't sure if she did but she knew one thing—she was going to work like hell to make sure she did in the future. There were no words that could express how sorry she was that she'd left or how thankful she was that they had come for her and how much she loved them.

She let her body, hands and mouth speak for her as she did everything she could to crawl up inside them, to touch and kiss every inch of skin she could reach. It felt right standing there tangled together.

Kegan pushed his way between her and Trevor, forcing Trevor to wrap himself around her back. He took her face in both of his hands, and she instinctively leaned into his touch. They both stood and stared at one another. It was as if they were trying to convince themselves that the other was truly there. That they weren't dreaming.

Kegan broke the silence first. "Saying I'm sorry will never be enough. I'm always going to question how I could possibly ever deserve you. But I want to try." He stroked her cheeks with trembling fingers. His sincere blue eyes bore into hers. "No promises, Charlie. But I know if you and Trevor are next to me, I can overcome anything. I know you've given me more chances than I really deserve, but if you can find it in your heart to forgive me for leaving you again, you'll never regret it."

He released her face, took one of her hands, placed it over his heart and covered it with his own. "Please, make this heart complete."

With her free hand, Charlie placed Trevor's hand over hers and Kegan's. She leaned in, kissed his lips softly and spoke against them, "Now, all our half hearts are complete."

Epilogue

The birthing season had finally wound down to a slower, more manageable pace. It had been an extremely successful season with an explosion of new foals. Only one mare hadn't made it through the birth of her foal, and although Charlie had been able to save the baby, she still felt a pang of guilt and regret that she hadn't been able to save its mama.

She had named the colt Roddy, which meant Strong One, and had taken a personal interest in raising him. He'd shown such strength adapting to life without his mother and a curious wonder of everything around him, yet had a stubborn streak a mile wide and had proven to be quite the little jokester.

Charlie opened the gate to Roddy's stall. She stepped in and was instantly pulled forward by the harness she held in her hand. And so the daily game of tug of war began. Laughing, Charlie pulled and twisted but made little ground with the spirited whelp.

"Oh, you want to make this tough, do you?"

Roddy responded with tugs and shook the harness until she was forced to let go and watch as he bounded away, head high with a little prance in his step as he showed off the prize he'd won.

"You are totally incorrigible, young man. Getting your own way and then flaunting and strutting around like a peacock." Charlie couldn't help but laugh at the unrepentant pride in Roddy, which reminded her of two other incorrigible men she knew. "You, young man" — she put her hands on her hips and gave the colt a mock scowl — "are as bad as your owners."

"Hey, I take offense to that. I don't believe I have ever pranced around with that much cockiness a day in my life."

Charlie turned and gave Kegan the same mock scowl. "You, Mr. Too Damn Cute, with your dimpled smile, are the king of getting your way. What have you been teaching my precious little Roddy?"

Kegan stalked toward her, a sly grin on his full lips and a mischievous glint in his eyes. "Mr. Too Damn Cute, is it?" He continued his way toward her like a predator stalking his prey. "I thought it was Mr. Tall, Cute and Completely in Love?" He moved into the stall, stopped inches from her, then lowered his head until his lips were just a hairsbreadth away from her ear. "But right now, I want to be naughty."

Warm, moist lips caressed the sensitive skin below her ear and moved downward. Charlie nearly melted from the sensation and a moan moved past her lips as her body responded instantly to the need Kegan always brought out in her with just the simplest of touches. "How naughty?" she whispered as she surrendered to him.

Strong arms wrapped around her and lifted her off her feet as she was pulled into a tight embrace and Kegan's lips descended over hers—nipping and demanding entrance.

Charlie opened wide and he dove in, exploring her mouth with a hunger that left her reeling. He sought her tongue with his, kissing her hard, with one hand on the back of her neck to control the kiss as he massaged her backside with the other.

He broke the kiss and pulled back. He dropped his hand from her neck then moved it to her waist and pressed her tighter against the hard length of his erection. "Gonna show you just how naughty I can be." He kissed her again as he began walking out of the stall. Oh, she was looking forward to finding out how naughty Kegan could be.

In the last month since she'd returned from her little adventure, she'd given up her apartment, moved to Trev-Ke Ranch and given herself completely to her cowboys.

They in turn had given themselves completely to her. They still had some work to do on Kegan's doubts and Charlie's own insecurities, but once again, Trevor had become the bridge between them. They were all learning to keep open and honest communication, the most important tool they had.

Charlie was still a little uncomfortable about how they were perceived in the community, especially since her men had insisted upon renaming the ranch Trev-Char-Ke, letting everyone know she was permanently sandwiched right between them. She wasn't bothered enough by it to change a single aspect of their relationship, though. What they believed and brought to her life was more important than any sneer or rejection she might receive from anyone in 'society'.

Charlie was jolted out of her musings and laid across a blanket-covered bale of hay, her wrists wrapped in soft leather reins.

"I'll show you Trevor's not the only one who can be naughty. I'm going to bind you so you're not allowed to touch, only feel." Kegan flipped her over onto her stomach and his warm hands caressed her hips as he pulled her up onto her knees. "This pretty little ass is just at the right height so I can take my time. Torture you nice and slow."

Charlie looked back over her shoulder as she heard a zipper being pulled down and the clank of a buckle being pulled free. She watched through lust-filled eyes as Kegan took the cell phone from his hip, laid it next to her on the bale, then began to slowly remove his clothes. He told her in a deep and husky voice exactly what he was going to do to her until she was hoarse from screaming in pleasure.

Rough, callused hands caressed her trembling thighs as he bent to lick his way up her spine from base to nape. "I love doing all kinds of naughty things to this luscious body of yours." Firm fingers massaged her ass as his wicked tongue continued its assault on her flushed skin, the steady sound of her unrestrained need loud in the quiet of the barn.

"Now, if I just had something to keep these legs spread wide for me," Kegan whispered.

"Will this work?" Trevor asked as he walked into the barn naked, a predatory grin on his face, a long red rope in one hand.

Kegan chuckled. "Oh, yeah. Let's get naughty."

About the Author

SJD Peterson, better known as Jo, hails from Michigan. Not the best place to live for someone who hates the cold and snow. When not reading or writing, Jo can be found close to the heater, checking out NHL stats and watching the Red Wings kick a little butt. Can't cook, misses the clothes hamper nine out of ten tries, but is handy with power tools.

SJD loves to hear from readers. You can find her contact information, website and author biography at http://www.totallybound.com.

TOTALLY
BOUND

Home of Erotic Romance